GROUND

Jadelin Gangbo

JACARANDA

This edition first published in Great Britain 2024
Jacaranda Books Art Music Ltd
27 Old Gloucester Street,
London WC1N 3AX
www.jacarandabooksartmusic.co.uk

Copyright © Jadelin Gangbo 2024

The right of Jadelin Gangbo to be identified as the author of this work has been asserted in accordance with the Copyright, Designs and Patents Act 1988.

All rights reserved. No part of this publication may be reproduced, stored in a retrieval system, distributed, or transmitted in any form or by any means, including photocopying, recording, or other electronic or mechanical methods, without the prior written permission of the copyright owners and the publisher.

A CIP catalogue record for this book is available from the British Library

ISBN: 9781914344688
eISBN: 9781914344701

Cover Design: Rodney Dive
Typeset by: Kamillah Brandes

This is a work of fiction. Unless otherwise indicated, all the names, characters, businesses, places, events and incidents in this book are either the product of the author's imagination or used in a fictitious manner. Any resemblance to actual persons, living or dead, or actual events is purely coincidental.

to Boris Gangbo

*You sleep, buried in a wheat field,
not the rose nor the tulip
watch over you in the shade of a ditch
but one thousand red poppies.*

—Fabrizio De André

PART 1

Seven

I was six years old the night I was born. I woke up, eyes wide open, a black kid uncannily alert to something coming. My twin brother was with me. He was always with me. I was always with him. We slept in the same bed. Perhaps he was born then too into the same pool of fear I was sitting in. I don't know what it was exactly that forced us up. Perhaps it was our sister calling, or maybe it was that sixth sense, our survival instinct, which kicked us out of a deep sleep. Or maybe it was the heat, the smoke, the fire brigades and police sirens howling from outside as they approached our house. Whatever it was, we were staring up at a long dark cloud of smoke that covered the ceiling above our heads. It seeped in from the cracks around the door and ran along the ceiling to find its way out through the windows. A thick continuous flow of smoke that resembled a black dragon, skirting on my bedroom's ceiling which I stayed staring at. It was something new, something that I never imagined I would see, something that shouldn't be inside a house, and although I could not work out why was it there, why my bedroom was suddenly filling up with smoke, I was perfectly aware of what I was meant to do. With no words, no hesitation, my brother and I got off the bed, put our shoes on. We opened the door and lashes of fire slammed into our room. In the corridor, crackling flames were licking the walls. Everything was catching alight. Our house was on fire. The furniture, the carpet, everything was burning. Our eyes stinging from the smoke. Without looking back we ran off along the corridor, my twin brother and I and our sister, a tall, skinny,

14-year-old girl who shared the bedroom with us. She was the one who had taken care of my brothers and me since our parents left. She was Debra-Jo. Our Blessing. Our sorrow. Our loss. She made sure that both my brother and I were following her. I felt her hand grasping my arm and she drew us near her as we left the room. We ran into the rest of my siblings halfway down the corridor by their bedroom. There were only three of them, all in the same dream-like state of shock, still wearing pyjamas like us, their eyes full of apprehension and panic, yes, panic, because something was not quite right; one of us had not left the room yet, and leaning halfway in and out their bedroom, my older brothers were calling out his name. 'Klaus! Klaus!' No one dared to adventure inside the room for there was more fire inside that room than out in the corridor. The ceiling had caught fire. Flames were rapidly growing and spreading all over the carpeted floor. The window curtains were ablaze. So was my siblings' bunk bed. And on one side of the room, engulfed by the smoke, I could see my brother Klaus, eight years old back then, high forehead, lying on his bed, and I didn't know whether he was dead or sleeping. But then I saw him moving, but he would not get up still, no matter the fire and how loudly my brothers called him. Klaus, the second youngest, seemed nowhere near waking. At best, he whimpered, tossing and turning because of the heat as if he was just having a bad dream. Meanwhile, the fire had circled his bed. One of the corridor walls behind us had gone entirely lit and the smoke was growing thicker and thicker to the point I started feeling it entering inside me, and I started coughing, and now I was getting scared. Scared that something new and dreadful was pending on us. It was one of those moments where you see with clarity what the world looks like, the mechanics of it, you see what it is all about, all of a sudden you understand there is a thin line that separates life and death, and that line is always there. Always with you. Possibly your most intimate possession. You understand that people can die. They can die on the spot, they can burn alive, they can suffocate. It was impossible to foresee whether my brother Klaus asleep inside a burning room would awake at the sound of our frantic calls or stay asleep; it was beyond our power. Aside from calling his name out loud there was not much more we could do. We were not heroes, none of us had enough guts to rescue him from inside a burning room.

However, my brother Klaus did wake up. His eyes wide open. He sprang up over his bed as soon as he realised the threat he was facing, withdrawing from the fire. Painfully lost in his own world as usual, he gazed at us calling him from outside the room through the curtain of smoke as though we never met before, as though we weren't even there. It was the gaze of an alien. Then, with a big leap, he jumped over the fire and reached us. We all ran to the end of the corridor through the mix of darkness and luminosity, then down the stairs in our pyjamas—Klaus, Lorenzo, Sigmund, Ocean, Debra-Jo, my twin brother and me. The smoke dissipated and the presence of the fire lessened as we left the top floor. Still, we kept running as fast as we could until we reached the ground floor. Only there, we met our servant and several firemen who had just stormed into the house to rescue us.

A crowd of people from our neighbourhood had gathered outside the house, that winter night of 1982. That was even stranger than the blaze itself—the sight of all these white people standing in our courtyard as if the whole thing, the fire, our life up to that point, had been nothing more than a drive-in screening of a set-up reality show. Like a Truman show or something, featuring a dysfunctional Congolese family whose saga had been followed by an audience that had been standing there all the time at our expense. People who had never put foot on our soil before, wearing coats on top of their pyjamas, some on their bikes, whole families, newcomers walking in through the gate, car lights slowing down and pulling off the road, it felt like the whole neighbourhood had suddenly gained the right to access our acreage. All of them bound in a surreal silence, charmed by the fire's authority as it burned the house, unfazed, with a thick black column of smoke rising up to the dark night sky. In the middle of the scene was a fire engine. The team of firefighters, some on land, some on the engine's ladder, at work to subdue the fire with water hoses. The blue light of a few police cars still glowing intermittently as the officers did their part in keeping the residents safe. One was assigned to stay with us, a towering guy in blue uniform who handed us some covers that we wrapped around ourselves as we rested on his car, watching the fire with him. Of all the things that were happening that night, the oddest was the speed with which my siblings and I switched from being victims of this misfortune to just some people in the crowd—common voyeurs, watching someone else's house burning down as if it had never belonged to us, with as much interest as any of the other onlookers. There was now an inconceivable distance sitting between us and that place, our home, that door we had just come out from, the windows to where most of the firefighter's effort was directed to. The world was now a quiet place. Of a quality I have never experienced before and I would never experience thereafter. Despite all the noise in the background, I could hear nothing, not a sound, neither voices nor birds, nothing at all. Sound had been eclipsed by solely visual experience. And I remember this clear feeling I had, as I stood watching at it all, I sensed that I was a simple witness to something extremely rare and of devastating beauty.

Our house was a three-floor villa set on a generous piece of land at the edge of a small town in Italy called Imola. It was a grand stone house, encompassed by a ring of vegetation, mainly pine trees and bushes. A gravelled driveway stretched some yards up to a large iron gate that overlooked the town's main artery. In the middle of the front yard was a white, stone fountain. Behind the house, a large meadow. It nearly looked ideal, but now, now no more, after half of our house—the second floor and the attic—had gone burnt. The first floor, where our bedrooms were situated, had sustained minor damage, but still, we were forbidden by the authorities to reach them, nor to use the stairs, once we were allowed to move back into the house. They told us we could use only the ground floor. Blackening of walls and stairs and the burnt handrail that once led to our rooms were clearly visible as we looked up from the bottom of the staircase. On the ground floor everything was unusually still and quiet, yet appeared to be normal, under the familiar warm light of the pendant lamps. My siblings and I wandered hazily around our restricted area, around the hall, the living room and the kitchen. While firemen went on working around the house, double checking, testing for safety, the policemen and social workers dealt with us. They took us through an investigation that went on until morning and took place largely in the living room where all seven of us crammed together on the couch. I guess we went all for the sofa because we felt safer sticking together in the aftermath of the accident. It was an accident indeed, caused by Sigmund—one of my brothers.

At the origin of the accident was the fact that Sigmund, my second oldest sibling after Debra-Jo, had the habit of studying late into the night by candlelight since the only bed-table lamp in their room had long been broken, he told the authority—a policeman and a social worker, both conducting a separate investigation. The boy, my brother Sigmund, looking smaller than usual, went on with his deposition from one end of the sofa, clearing his throat now and then. He said he could not recall whether he fell asleep over his book while leaving the candle on, or if he blew on it, but too faintly. It was the policeman who came up with a plausible reconstruction of the incident. He believed the flame was still burning when Sigmund accidentally knocked the candle over with some jerky movement of his arms while sleeping. What followed was deducible, he said; the flame ignited the carpet and spread all over the house. 'Ovvio,' he said. I wondered how it was for Sigmund. A 13-year-old boy, responsible for an accident of this scale. Police, municipal police, carabinieri, firemen, social workers, the whole Italian forces worked jointly on the case just because a kid had failed to blow out a candle. Added to this pressure were all the possible scenarios playing over in his mind. What would Dad's reaction be in all this? What would become of us now that we were told we could not live at the house anymore? In fact, the house had been condemned, we were forced to leave. But where? Would our parents be able to sort out all this mess overnight? Where were they? Sigmund had no answers on this. We had no more than he. But the authorities obviously wanted to know. 'Where are your parents? How long have they been away? Do they often leave you home alone for that long?'

'Not often but it has happened on a few occasions,' our servant said, standing barefoot and pyjamaed on one margin of the conversation, arms hanging down along the body. 'They usually leave the kids in my custody.'

'Are they going to school?'

'Yes, all of us,' my sister said. 'We walk to school all together, first thing we drop the twins, Klaus and Lorenzo to the primary. Sigmund, Ocean and I go to secondary school.'

'Do your teachers know you've been living by yourselves all this time?'

'They're not at home alone, as I said, madam,' clarified the servant. 'They're with me.'

'Right. So, I guess you're the one in charge?'

'Theoretically, yes, but at the end of the day it's me who is in charge of my brothers,' my sister affirmed proudly.

'I see.'

'He helps out. That's all. Like a servant does.'

'I see. How old are you?' she asked the servant.

'Eighteen,' he answered.

'Ok. How long have you been working for them?'

'It has been six years.'

'Alright, and you were saying,' she went back to my sister, 'that your parents are businesspeople and they went on a business trip, am I right?'

'Yes madam. My father travels all around the world for his job. Sometimes my mother goes with him, sometimes she stays home. She's his wife, she has to go with him.'

'Can you confirm?' she asked the servant.

'Yes, it's true.'

'Did they let you know when they would be back?'

'No.'

'Do you know where they are, where they went?'

'To Africa,' my other brother, Ocean, the third oldest, stepped in.

'Whereabouts in Africa?'

'The Congo.'

'Democratic Congo?'

'No. Congo-Brazzaville,' my sister answered back, 'or maybe they went to Benin.'

As they questioned us endlessly, we were all coming down the slope of the fire-induced adrenalin rush. Our bodies began to sink heavier into the couch and we made small rearrangements to get as comfortable as we could without having to give away our spot on the sofa. My mind was roaming somewhere far I could not recognise. I felt exhausted, I looked at my sister and thought how much I loved her. She stood for us no matter the circumstances. In those days, during my parents' long absences, while everything around the house was falling apart, and even the servant was neglecting his job, it was my sister who made the effort to keep it all together. She got us up in the morning, prepared breakfast and made sure we were all sound and clean, that we had our homework done, that we went to school and came back home not too late. She cleaned our rooms. She washed our clothes. It was she who sat proudly in the middle of her six brothers in the evening watching TV on that same couch we were sitting on now.

By the time the social service workers and the police and firemen had left, I fell asleep on that same couch tangled up with my siblings. It was nearly morning. I guess we all had a deep sleep, aside from

Sigmund. He was old enough to realise the degree of disruption he had caused to his family and how bad it could have been if one of us had been injured by the fire. However, sometimes I wish I could travel back in time with my new understanding of things as an adult and tell the young Sigmund that he should not feel guilty for the accident. Rather the opposite. He should feel proud for having been chosen by the hands of fate to perform a key role in the development of our family history. In fact, I do believe he played the part of the whistle-blower. It took a fire to alert the authorities that seven kids were being left by their parents and had been living unguarded for too long. Moreover, I believe Sigmund's fire worked as a fracture sign between two worlds, the past and the future. Since we left Africa, and our parents were gone, what had been destroyed was the last bond with our roots. From there on, we were about to walk only in no-man's-land.

LONDON, PRESENT DAY
I

Days are growing longer; there is still light at four in the afternoon when I decide to go for a quick walk outside before my next patient arrives. I hang my white medical coat back on the hanger, put my winter coat on, go out. And I run into you in our alley. You have just left your house, two doors from mine down our little alleyway, pulling a trolley full of what appears to be props, I guess, for your new show. You also carry a backpack, and wear brown desert boots, black jeans, a long dark flannel coat and a floral scarf. There is some clownish pride in the way you walk that drives me insane, and I already find myself working myself up with thoughts like, I'm just going to do it, today I'm doing it, I'll grab her and kiss her. But I know that I won't do it. I can't. You can't. We can't do such a thing. You have a partner and a daughter you want to protect. We can't do it. Therefore, I'm forced to settle for that thin smile that forms on your face once you notice me. It grows wider and shyer, the smile, and you charge on with your proud walk as you get nearer. We walk together to the entrance of the alleyway.

'What you're up to?' you ask me.

'Taking a little walk. And you? Going to perform somewhere?' I say, pointing at the trolly full of props trailing behind you.

'Yes, I'm performing in Bristol tonight.'

I meet your gaze when I raise my eyes from your props, deep dark eyes on a white, pale face that hadn't seen a ray of Portuguese sun in a long time. Eyes that possibly never stop dreaming of home. Wavy, long dark hair parted on one side, and those eyes still staring at me, full of hidden ideas, some of which amuse you somehow.

'Why don't you come with me?' you then say.

'Now?' I say.

'Yes, now. I have a double room booked anyway. And it's inside a boat. We go to London Bridge by Uber and take a train from there. Have you ever slept inside a boat?'

Something about your presence, your look, whatever force emanates from your body, tells me that either the decision to come with or stay will be bad. The idea of sleeping inside a boat with you sends me into orbit already. But, yes, it's mad, I say to you. What about your man? What tells you that we'll behave if we get drunk and sleep together in the same bed? You know, two like us will never be able to hold back. You say maybe we can hold it. Then you say maybe we can't, we are not mature enough. Then I say I don't even know you, I have been your neighbour for so little time, and that it's crazy, and that I have work commitments, and the kids, but they are all excuses because my kids are with their mother until the end of the week, and I have no work today and I could clear my schedule tomorrow, or come back in time for work and come to Bristol with you.

As we wait outside the entrance of our alley, your cab arrives. I help you load your bag and trolly inside the car boot, and the picture of a night out with you outside London with all possible scenarios playing in my mind seems so close and ridiculously good. Too good. In fact, we both grit our teeth in doubt about the idea when you are about to climb inside the car, and you say, 'Let's just leave it. I like you too much to go on a trip with you.'

'Yes,' I agree, 'let's just leave it.'

'The pauses you do while speaking,' you say with a smile. 'I like them.'

'Ok,' I say hesitantly.

'Alright then. I see you soon, Red. Maybe we could do something with the kids this Sunday.'

'Deal. Good luck with your show, Telma.'

'Thank you.'

You enter the car, wave goodbye the last time, and I watch the car drive you off until it disappears at the first turn.

I resume my walk, forcing you out of my mind. I walk down Lower Clapton Road in the direction of Hackney Central. I walk past Clapton Square, the local Sainsbury's, St John Church's large front yard, and head down to Narrow Way. The streets are busy, prevalently of the affluent gentrified demographic which has been growing steadily in the last years. New signs of their instalment in Hackney catch the eye each day—the new white wealthy couple looking at property listings at the window display of the new up-market estate agent. The new family of young professionals with two blond toddlers moving in the redeveloped warehouse across the street that was once a squat. Another convenience store closing down because the rent has become unaffordable. Another bearded white kid on a bike pulling up the shutters of his new café. I walk. I walk down Narrow Way. Even here things have changed, although this part of the borough seems to resist somehow to the wave of renovation that is pushing the old population out of the area, as if it was the last bastion left of the old Hackney. Or more like a reserve of the indigenous of Hackney. Turkish, Asians, Black Caribbeans, Nigerians, White Working Class, all contained in between McDonald's and the Wetherspoon. A growing number of the destitute have settled outside the betting shops and around the little wall by the end of the Pembury council estate. A limping girl tramps up and down the street dreaming of her next round of crack. Among the growing numbers of beggars, rough sleepers and drug addicts there are a few guys who seem to have given up any hope, and succumb to their final stages of sanity, so deeply lost that they no longer care whether they are sitting in a puddle or walking with their dicks hanging out. They can't see themselves from the outside. I doubt what they see matches in any way with the world most people live in. They look around with the resigned expression of someone who sees more than most of us. Maybe they see the irony of it all, our ridiculous struggle to keep up, make it through, achieve, show off, take care, fight against, persevere, preserve, reject and believe, demand and feel passion. They have already found out that at the end of the day it all comes down to ten quid per day to make sure they go to bed with something in their bellies. Or a little thrill in their bloodstream. I like their expressions. The one that sits down on the floor all day and repeats the same mantra, 'Good morning, love,' in the same tone of voice, maybe with a dog at their side, a cover over the legs, a cup, a card describing their issue. Their poses, their expressions, to me, don't look that much different from the poses and facial expressions of Buddhist monks sitting on some cliff somewhere in Tibet. My son told me one day when we were walking that he noticed that most of the beggars sitting quietly were white, while the ones going about somehow struggling were black. Are the majority of the ones ranting down the street, the ones who wake you up in the middle of the night shouting down the road, 'Fuck you man fuck you man,' black? Maybe in this area, I guess. Depends on where you live, son, I wanted to say to him. The point is not that the number of underprivileged black people have suddenly risen in this area. Unhappy black people have always been around. The only real big change is that they are more visible now, they have taken to the street since all local pubs and bars and community hubs where black people used to congregate have been shut down by the police in the last years or sold to developers. The same troubled black men you see all the time outside the betting shops, or haplessly hanging around the middle of the street, were mostly inside an Afro Caribbean pub once, and therefore, you could not see them. But they have always been here. Most, for their entire lives. The shit is that there is a very clear message in this rapidly changing area and that is, you are no longer welcome unless you understand the meaning of a four-pound latte.

GROUND

I remember the wonder of setting foot in Hackney the first time I moved here from Italy. Hackney's diversity made me feel at home from the very beginning, more than anywhere else I've been. Even more than in Italy. Here, in Hackney, I was simply one foreigner among many others. As penniless as the bunch of white lads having a pint with me at our local pub. As *coloured* as my fellow neighbours from the nearby council estate. I loved the fact that nobody ever noticed me when I entered some of the crap cafés which were in the area. I was just anybody. A random guy coming in and out a shop. A random guy walking in the street, where I could breathe a strong sense of community among people, and see representatives of different ethnic groups talking to each other, they helped each other out in time of need, their kids played together. Then the gentrification kicked in. With the new upper-class demographic moving in, that sense of cohesion that characterized Hackney died off, simply because the rich have nothing to say to the poor, they have not shared cultural references, they entertain themselves in separate circuits, feed and buy in separate shops, have a separate existence, a deep social economical divide between the old Hackney and the new Hackney have ensued and is growing by the day. Hackney's renovation meant for me that I turned out not to be that anonymous anymore. That feeling I tried to escape from when I was in Italy of being noticed, of being looked at with suspicion before any crime, of being met with surprise as if I was always in the wrong place wherever I went, whatever shop I entered, this had all come back once again, now through the eyes of a new entitled population taking over Hackney. I know it partially has to do with race, and partially depends on how much money you have. It can't be said that the hipster who looked at me with suspicion when I entered his café was racist. I have no proof he held any prejudice towards me just because he looked at me. But I know that something crossed his mind as soon as he saw me. I knew he felt less safe with me in his café. It's rather a quick visual phenomenon. Visual discrimination, I would call it, evaluated by people who quickly associate your hoodie, and the colour of your skin and the recent episode of stabbing that occurred around the corner they heard about on the news, no matter if they have friends who look like you, or play in bands with people like you, or share the same passions and ideals as you. It seems that in times where everything is processed visually with images and photos on the internet and apps, dating shit, Facebook and Instagram, we have trained our eyes to perform visual association at a rate never met before, a rate that even runs past the time you need to perceive you have just been subjected to a degree of structural racism as soon as you have stepped into one of these silent, only-white, young professional cafés. And this exercise of speed-looking might have changed the speed of our judgment too, making it seem more and more accurate. We are now able to make our mind up with a single glimpse and get it 100 percent right all the time, with increasingly less room for doubts and second thoughts. Not a chance. In or out. Cool or not cool. This guy is just another crackhead coming to spoil my breakfast. Eyes rise from lattes and Macs and hands draw their iPhones on the table a bit closer, feet pull the backpack on the floor in between legs. People swipe you away with a finger. Left or right. In the fraction of a second they have decided whether to buy you or not. Nothing suggests to them that you are man like them at the first sight. There is not a great deal of intuitive emotion working in there, or maybe I'm wrong, perhaps it's just a visual type of intuitive emotion. They know me. They know who I am. In their own way. Whereas myself, standing before their eyes, I'm growing less convinced that I know myself. Less and less with every passing year. You don't know me either, dear Telma, and something tells me you never will the way I would like. But I want you to know me. I want you to know my story. I wasn't always this 40-year-old bearded black man walking the streets of Hackney in his hoody. I wasn't always this lone individual. I was somebody. I too had a past, in another place and time, with parents and siblings. I was once a child.

GROUND

Walking Over Dirty Clothes

How would I describe my family? We were immigrants. Economic immigrants I suppose. We had moved from Africa—Congo and Benin—to Italy in 1980, two years prior to the fire, following my dad's ambition to establish his African enterprise in the peninsula. Sometimes it's hard to believe how brief our time together as a family was, and yet, our family life in Imola, before the defining flames, seemed like any other normal, I'd even say, typical family, if it wasn't for a few things. How do you say it in English? A few variations? Few factors? We were many. We were black—as I already mentioned, probably for many Italians the first negroes they would encounter in our small town. And we were wealthy. Quite wealthy, indeed. To the extent that local people encountered us with incredulity most of the time and, of course, they had questions about us. Directly, indirectly, with a look, people questioned about the newcomers. Such as who was that man—my father—who they had seen recently being interviewed on the regional news as he introduced his new plan of opening a new local TV channel to the public? Who were those well-dressed black kids who caused the parents, children and teachers to stare as they were being dropped at school by a white chauffer driving a Mercedes-Benz, or a Jaguar, a Land Rover, a BMW, depending on which was available? Neighbours knew we had a bunch of people working for us, including a chef, a servant, a personal tutor, Dad's personal assistants. Our classmates who came for playdates would inevitably get the word out about our showy glass lamps, our high-ceilinged rooms, the spiral marble staircase, the vivid African paintings in the living room. That living room. My memory's happy place. That's where I still virtually go to when I feel in need to look back at the close-up big pictures of my parents hanging on the wall. My mother is in her twenties and beautiful, long braided hair, smiling, an ivory necklace. He's shirtless, in his thirties, with a moustache and sideburns and a cowboy hat, his gaze pointing in the direction of my mother's photo, while she looks out at him. There was a clear sense of an African '70s aesthetic we had just left behind from those photos—the globe-bar that opened up in two halves, displaying bottles of spirits, the stereo incorporated in the sofa of brown-orange-yellow patterns. Masks and statues carved from ivory and wood, djembes and tapes. A brown radio with knobs, the TV with a long array of buttons and, of course, us. All seven of us. Always together. My siblings and me. We banged at the djembes, chased each other all over the house. We pretended to be seven Bruce Lees, slashing things in half with a hand stroke. We held off the menacing karate guards as we posed for Uncle's photo shoot—the twins in front, the bigger ones behind, with Debra-Jo, the tallest and the oldest, in the middle, her too holding her killer Bruce Lee stance.

Despite the fun we had, and all the trappings, a melancholy mood vented across the many empty rooms of the house, which were occupied only in part, and only partly furnished, with just the bare essentials. Unopened boxes were scattered across the place. Interiors with potential had gradually turned into oppressive storage rooms, filled with pieces of merchandise that our parents would trade around Europe and Africa. On top of the African bazaar-like ambience, was a wild assortment of people who passed through our place all year round, loud family and friends, visitors from Africa wearing large, colourful *boubou*; my old man's new Italian friends; his committee of African, European and Asian business colleagues, traders coming to negotiate with him, in suits, holding briefcases, in their mirrored Ray-Ban's and golden watches as was the fashion of the day, slick and forward-looking. He received them in the conference room on the ground floor, where they often sat around a long table, each one provided with a microphone, and they discussed for hours, exactly what, I never knew, but they acted as if they were about to take over the world, or like they were some congress like the United Nations, when, at the end of the day, it was all merely about getting choked up with money. Besides, they could hear each other well enough without microphones, but that was the thing, that was him, that was my father's singular way of operating: for prestige and pure enjoyment. My father came across as an unusual man. He was an eccentric, gifted businessman. Just to give you an idea of the sway he held over people, take a group, a group of potential buyers or partnerships gathered around my father who's there telling them a story, no one would leave without a contract being signed. People didn't trade with him out of convenience only, they wanted to do business with him because they'd fallen in love with him. I remember hearing one day when I was hanging around the house, amplified laughter of several people bursting out of the conference room. Then my father came out of the room and stopped me. 'Hey you! Where's Mbila? Tell him to go and buy me and my pals some ice cream before we die down here, would you?! Go on. Quick, quick!'

Mbila, our servant, had been working for us for as long as I remember. My mother made him come over from the Congo to Italy soon after we moved into the villa. His full name was Masambila. Medium build, in his late teens, a quiet type who seemed to always wear the same shabby trousers and cotton shirt and to walk around the house nearly unnoticed. One of his tasks in the villa was to look after my twin and me when we hadn't started nursery yet and everybody else was busy at school or work. My brother and I grew fond of him despite the fact that he hardly displayed any sign of affection. We would eventually reach a point during the day where we moved whatever we were playing with into the room where he was at work, and played near him. If we were lucky we could get him singing us a song, a Congolese nursery rhyme he murmured with his quiet and unemotional voice.

Based on the account he gave the police, he was at home the day my parents left and told him they were going abroad for a work trip but were not specific about where and how long they would stay out of the country. Even when my siblings asked him, 'Where are they?' he just shrugged his shoulders, 'I don't know.' The fact that nobody could say with certainty where our parents were, or contact them in the face of the major incident we had just suffered, led me to believe one thing: that they left us on purpose. They have abandoned us. The world had plenty of cases of children being abandoned by their parents, so why could this not happen to us? At some point, I could even swear that I witnessed their escape. I saw them leaving from my bedroom window. One night, when I woke up to go to the toilet, I heard unusual noises coming from outside in the courtyard, and I went peering to the window and saw my mother and my father furtively loading their luggage inside the car, helped by Mbila. They clambered inside and drove off along the driveway and out the gate. This image got engraved in my mind, but at the same time, it was not as clear as it might have been. I'd say it was a vague image to which I would not pay much attention to throughout my days for I could not have cared less whether they abandoned us, left for a work trip abroad, or whether someone knew or not where they were because nothing really changed for me. It made no difference when I came back from school and found out they were missing. I had grown used to their absence for one reason or another. It was only as weeks turned into months and my parents were still away that I began to notice that there was something different about this last trip. I was too young to grasp what it was exactly, but it was as if the spirit of the house had begun to die. There was no more governing force, no anchor, everything was unravelling, the walls had begun to melt. We had no more visitors; the now unpaid Italian tutor, the driver and everybody else we used to see around the house stopped coming. Things began falling apart. The mood of the family went downhill and motivation to do even the smallest chores had seeped out of us. No one, not even Mbila, bothered any more with the house maintenance. Broken windows were left broken. If your bed had collapsed, you just learned how to sleep in an awkward position. For any broken light bulb there was a candle. Food dwindled, the budget too. Even more disconcerting was the sudden access to anywhere in the house, even rooms you were not allowed to go in, such as my parents' bedroom and the conference room. All the mystery and charm had gone. I would look at Dad and Mum's stuff getting covered with dust, left exactly as it was the day the two departed from Italy. I would finger patterns through the dust over the conference table, worked out how to turn on the microphones and the speakers and had a go. I would hang out on the stairs, walk up the stairs to the attic and then I would be plunged downstairs again by boredom, even if I was in the company of six other people. Something new and strange was occurring. There, I can say, I made my first acquaintance with solitude, which at the time I could not possibly name or explain, but there it was indeed, settling deep inside my system as I walked around the sinking house. It felt as if I had been fooled, even if I couldn't figure out how or by whom and why I should have felt this. I had lived across different countries and cities in Congo, Benin, Cote d'Ivoire and now Italy, but it was only there, in the villa, that I started to detach from the ground. That familiar African dust that had risen up in the air so many times after my pals and I had run around neighbourhoods, had settled down for good. I walked over dirty clothes and messes left wherever, and ate mainly eggs, those eggs we were getting free, fried eggs, boiled eggs, every day for breakfast, lunch and dinner they were giving me nausea. Then, there was no way we could use the cars with no money to buy the petrol. Mbila could not drive to buy a thing, neither to take us to school, so we had to walk now. Like everybody else. We were normal, average people, suddenly. Gold had stopped falling. Whether it was raining or not, in the early light of the quiet morning, we set out on the road to school earlier than usual, cutting through the grass field at the back of the house that had been left to grow wild. When we arrived at school, we cleaned off our muddy shoes before entering the classrooms. The same bunch of black kids that not so long ago, people had seen arriving in a Jaguar. The same kids. Now closer to the typical imaginary of immigrants in need. It was soon after this that that fire set the house ablaze.

Pino

A large man called Pino came to check on us as soon he was given news of the fire. He was one of my dad's best Italian friends and a business associate, the same person who found the house for us in Italy. This white-haired fellow with a face as crimson as a red pepper, and piercing dark eyes, who was often chuckling about something or the other, now wandered around the ruins of our house in disbelief. I cannot recall the number of times he cried, 'My god!' as he ran his hands through his white, lank hair hardly stopping to ask us if we were ok, clearly in apprehension for us, and of course for our parents, once they were to be informed about the incident. He tried to console us, pledged he would find them immediately, hunt them, call them and do whatever was in his power to sort out this issue as soon as possible. I believed him. Pino was the closest person to a relative that we had in Italy at that time. Since he met my father back in Africa in 1977, our lives had run intertwined, and we had all grown affectionate of him. He was the man who walked all the steps we needed to take to settle in Italy. He paved the road for my father's businesses in Italy by finding him the right connections, deals, merchandise, even the TV channel opportunities; in fact, all the people working for us were recruited by him. I remembered him as my father's white shadow, this big white man in his clear grey-bluish, common-looking suit and a brown leather jacket, always coming in and out of our house with Dad. Both talking vehemently about some urgent matter or laughing about something. When he was not busy driving my father around doing business, he would come to us with some jokes or magic tricks, like the pulling-off finger, the nose disappearing and reappearing in between his knuckles, the egg pretending to break and pour on top of the head, until Dad would show up, putting on his coat and saying, 'Let's go, let's go!' He'd harry him to come out with him and Pino would grab his coat and follow Dad outside. He was the man who first exposed us to elements of the Italian culture. The first songs of Vasco Rossi, Adriano Celentano and Gianni Morandi we listened to and learned to sing came from his cassettes. His comments at the TV shows we watched together had become our comments. I remember the days out on the seaside at Riccione on the Adriatic coast or when he took us to have barbecues at his house in the countryside with his wife and teenage daughter. He was a generous, friendly, happy chap, the gregarious Uncle Pino, yes, he was like a family member.

That evening, the night after the fire, the good man took us out for a pizza in a nearby restaurant. By the way people looked at us as we arrived and sat at a table and had our meal, it seemed obvious they knew all about the incident. Imola was a small town after all. Murmurs spread as fast as the ashes. We ate our pizza with barely any conversation. Then, when we finished, the restaurant owner, a small guy with a moustache, came over and shyly said he wanted to offer us all a dessert, I guess, out of empathy or even solidarity for our new misfortune. We had our profiteroles and tiramisus. Then left the table and stood waiting behind Pino while he paid for our meal at the cashier and then walked out with everyone inside the restaurant looking at us. We climbed inside his car. Then drove back home. He came inside with us and stood at the entrance in the penumbra, looking around himself, still in disbelief at how the house's appearance and our life had dramatically changed. He then called Mbila, gave him money to keep us going for a few days more. He vowed again that our situation would be dealt with and not to worry, then he left, hands in his coat pockets, something always dangling inside—keys, coins. Meanwhile for us, a sense of melancholy took possession of us as we walked into the ruined house at night after our nice restaurant meal, complete with dessert, people, good lighting, in a healthy environment. We felt the general mood plunging right away. We turned on the electric heaters and dragged some extra mattresses, given to us by some compassionate neighbours, into the living room and tried to kill time by watching TV even though we knew it wouldn't work since we had already tried the night before. The electricity was still working, but the fire had damaged the antenna wiring. So, there we were, sitting on the mattresses on the floor, watching Lorenzo, the middle brother, pushing the TV channel buttons up and down, hoping that something would appear beyond the white noise, but nothing happened. We played a few games. We talked. We imagined how our younger siblings were doing in the Congo, for, yes, we were not seven in total, but ten. Ten siblings. Soon to become eleven. Seven living in Italy, the three youngest in the Congo.

Pino returned a few days later to take us to a temporary accommodation assigned to us by the social services. His mood was cheery and loud, resonating with the cold, clear, winter light of that morning as he gave us some chocolate bars, and helped us to pack up our few belongings to leave. He had managed to reach our parents at last, he said, and told them about the incident and the state in which we were living, but, unfortunately, our parents, regardless of how worried they were for us, could do very little. They were having problems themselves somewhere down in Africa and were unable to return at the moment. Pino remained vague over the nature of the problems our parents were facing, and seemed to be omitting something when he said, 'What matters is that you guys are fine. As long as nobody gets hurt everything else will be sorted. We'll get over it. You just need to hold on a bit more, can you do that?'

'Where are they?' asked Ocean.
'They are in the Congo.'
'In Brazzaville?'

'No, in Point-Noir.'

We fell in silence for a little while, relieved somehow for being able to locate them, at least geographically. We had a house down in Point-Noir where we had spent some time when we still lived in the Congo. Being able to visualise them in that place gave us the impression we were slightly more in control, and that not all was lost in the end. This conversation occurred outside the villa's courtyard on a cold winter day. The seven of us and Pino, wearing coats and woollen hats, were gathered by Pino's car—a Fiat Uno—waiting for Mbila to come out of the house. Klaus was running his finger along the contours of the car's rear window, giving us his back. Standing among us with crossed arms, leaning against the car, Sigmund was still unusually quiet; he had not yet recovered from the incident. Mbila finally came out of the decrepit house carrying a backpack on his shoulders. He locked the front door with his keys and, as I looked at him walking towards us, the courtyard's gravel crackling under his shoes, Lorenzo asked Pino, 'Can we talk to them?'

'To Mum and Dad?' asked Pino.

'Yes.'

'We won't have time today, I'm afraid; we have a long journey ahead of us.'

'Tomorrow?' asked the kid again.

'I promise, I'll arrange a phone call with them as early as the end of this week.'

'Did they tell you when they are coming back here?' returned Ocean with his typical dry voice and serious stance.

'Look, to be honest with you guys, I don't really know what happened, I don't know why, but they seem stuck there in Congo. Just give them some time. The only thing we need to worry about now is getting you away from this dump. Do we all agree that this place is crap now?'

I knew Pino meant to be light-hearted with that remark, but I could see that something sinister crossed his eyes as he pointed his big hand over the house. There was something eerie to it now as we all stared at the house for the last time. The black stains rimming the broken windows. The black and collapsing roof. Half of the wall surfaces burned and darkened. Only deep silence steamed from within. Silence from the vegetation around, from the fountain we had circled around many times with our bikes. From the gate we'd seen Dad's car driving in. That melancholic silence, typical of objects, which, you sense, will stay there, in that environment, enduring time, and being restored one day, or put down, while we humans move on.

We got into Pino's Uno with few belongings left from the fire. Just a few suitcases with clothes and bits and bobs recovered from around the house. Seven kids plus the servant and Pino, all packed in a car that had seats for only five passengers. I sat on Debra-Jo's lap in the front while my twin brother and the others and Mbila were crammed in the back seat. Chances that police would stop people for overcrowding in cars at that time in Italy were very low. We travelled all day, only stopping whenever my twin and I suffered carsickness. The landscape hardly changed after hours on the motorways. Car after car. Always straight ahead. Some people from other cars pointed at us. You could read their lips saying things like, 'Look at how many niggers are in that car.' There was not much talking, even Pino kept silent, only the radio was on, with some random songs from Celine Dion or Whitney Houston, or the commentary of a football match or the news. Whenever we felt numb and achy from holding the same position, we stopped at one side of the road and shook ourselves. We stopped also a few times to eat and to refresh at the service stations. Then we carried on travelling until it was dark. We slept in a car park more or less sitting in the same position we held during the journey. I don't know how my sister managed to sleep with me sitting on her lap. I guess we were all very tired. Nonetheless, we woke up very early in the morning, stretched in the parking lot, had breakfast in the station, washed our faces and then headed back on the road again.

We arrived at our destination early in the morning in a small town in the north of Italy, at the border with Austria. The most immediate solution the social services had to offer was not a house, but a small clinic, a two-storey GP's practice that apparently had been in disuse for a while. A middle-aged stocky woman, who seemed to be waiting for us, made her way out of the main door as we parked the car. She handed a pair of the building's keys to Pino and showed us around the house—just the areas we were allowed to live in temporarily, which accounted just for a small portion of the building, whereas all the remaining areas were kept locked. The clinic waiting room, with a TV and the reception desk, she explained, was to be our living room, the empty cafeteria, our dining room. We had a clinic kitchen with all facilities perfectly working and two bedrooms at our disposal with solid metal hospital beds, and other hospital equipment such as IV holders and wheelchairs parked around the place. And an intense smell of bleach. Then she took Pino aside to talk to him privately on the corridor by the exit door while we sat in the waiting room, our coats still on, blowing condensed air into our fists, trying to visually acclimatise with our new home. Once the woman had gone, Pino returned and sat next to us on one of the waiting room chairs. All of us faced in silence a white wall and a shutoff TV mounted in a corner as if we were waiting for a film to start playing, or for a doctor to enter the room and ask who was next. Then it felt like Pino was about to say something, presumably a joke, but thought against saying it. He gave Mbila some money and the building's keys instead, got up, said he would put all his effort to find us a more suitable accommodation, possibly a proper house, and be back soon to bring us there. He kissed each of us goodbye, and was then off, back in his car to undertake another day journey back to his home.

René

My father was born in Benin in 1942. He was 24 years old in 1966. He worked as the Principal of a primary school in Enugu State, in south-east Nigeria. It is strange to imagine him in that guise; I would not have said he was the kind of man who would devote his time to providing kids with knowledge and taking care of them. I can hardly imagine him taking care of anyone. But based on the information I received from various sources, that was his job at that time. Managing a school. My father was a very imaginative person, his mind stirring with ideas. He'd wake up in the middle of the night if something urgent arose in his mind, and he'd sit down at a desk and write it down. It is possible that his writing included issues beyond school-related matters, what that was exactly, nobody can say with certainty, but the spectrum of his writing might have been extensive, ranging from work-related ideas, dreams, visions and even some creative work. Poems perhaps? What type of visions though? Spiritual? Humanitarian? Prophetic? Or purely hedonistic and selfish? What was it that pervaded the mind of a principal such as my father back then in a primary school in Nigeria? How to reduce the school's 50 percent dropout rate? How to purge the school from unnecessary revolutionary rhetoric? Plans to sever the relationship with the Catholic missionaries once and for all? These facts remain mysterious to me. And for instance, did he qualify for the job? And why was he in Nigeria? Did he move there just because it bordered Benin? The list of questions can only increase.

In Nigeria, 1966 was a year of dramatic decline. Long-standing ethnic tensions between Nigeria's main ethnic groups were at the origin of the Biafran War. The Muslim Hausa-Fulani joined forces with the Yoruba to persecute the Igbo population in the aftermath of a political assassination that saw the death of the leaders of the country's dominant party. The raid was imputed to the Igbo because mostly Hausa-Fulani and Yoruba politicians were killed. These events unfolded within a context where Igbo living in the north were historically resented by their poorer neighbours and scapegoated as invaders for originally being immigrants from the eastern region, and for having hands on better jobs and occupied most of the national executive posts. Hell was unleashed following the political killings. The streets were filled with protest and throughout the north and the west regions, attacks against Igbo residents exploded into wide-scale genocide. The anti-Igbo pogroms drove an exodus of Igbos into the east, their traditional homeland. Millions of refugees escaping from massacres were received in makeshift public service structures set up for the crisis. One of those places was the school my father ran. He had reacted swiftly to the crisis by interrupting the school lessons, turning the school into one of the many refugee settlements springing up all over Enugu. Yet the humanitarian crisis which had hit East Nigeria had just begun. East Nigeria's leader led a secessionist movement for an independent Republic of Biafra where Igbos could have their own homeland. The federal government opposed it and went to war against the newly formed republic of Biafra, with the support of both the United Kingdom and Soviet Union, all in the grip of fear of losing access to Nigeria's major oil fields located in the Eastern region. Meanwhile, the government of the Republic of Biafra formed a civil service and an army for his newly formed country. It nationalized private businesses to draw funding, expelled foreigners from the country, seizing their assets. My father happened to be one of these expats. However, the government of the new Republic offered my father the chance to remain in the country as a concession for giving services to the community in managing the school and assisting the Igbo refugees and war casualties. My father declined the offer, feeling that he was no different from those who were being deported daily. 'If West Africans were all supposed to leave,' he said, 'then naturally I would leave too.' He was thus put on a train with many other non-nationals to be transported across a vast country wrecked by a civil war which would leave over a million dead.

After his departure from Nigeria, my father settled in his parental house in Cotonou, the economic capital of Benin. I know nothing of the father of my father. I don't even know his name and it occurs to me that this is actually the first time in my life that I consider the possibility that my father had a father himself. As for my grandmother, her name pops up frequently. I have little memory of her as she died when I was still a toddler. She was called Debra. My sister was named after her—Debra-Jo. My grandma was one of the few educated Beninese people during the French administration where she served as a secretary in a government office. I don't know what took her from there to become one of the influential figures in Cotonou, maybe it was her connection with the French occupiers and inherited wealth from her family. She was the local philanthropist who would distribute money and food to a long line of beggars that gathered at her front door every Sunday. She was still there when my father returned to Benin in the aftermath of the Biafran War. However, my father didn't stay there for long; he was impatient and on the move. Only a couple of weeks passed after returning to Benin before one day, he woke up with a clear vision of what he wanted to do. He wanted to become a plumber. The idea had come from sayings he overheard about Gabonese people who apparently disliked working as plumbers, making it a good market for plumbers in Gabon. That was how in 1968, young René left his home again and set off for a new adventure in Gabon. As he set foot in Libreville, my old man asked people where he might find the best plumber in town. He was directed to Didier, a Congolese man who, like my dad, was driven to Gabon by the dream of a lucrative profession. Didier hired my father as his assistant. A corner of his office, a mattress on the floor and two meals a day accounted for his salary.

René helped Didier by handing him tools and tossing away parts of rusty pipes and observed how it worked. Soon he was able to complete a full job by himself and had begun to receive a salary. He left Didier's corner as soon as he was able to pay rent. Then he opened his own plumbing enterprise and within a few months, the former Principal, now turned plumber, had so much work that he had to hire an assistant himself.

Yet again, something obstructed René's professional growth. This time it was not a war or a humanitarian crisis. It was just plain boredom: he had had enough of being a plumber. The fun part was over once he had mastered the profession and acquired essential business management skills. He quit the job. He handed the whole business over to his assistant for free, took with him a share of the earnings and set off for a new quest in a new country. His country of choice this time was the People's Republic of the Congo, also known as Congo-Brazzaville. The Congo where I was born. Congo-Brazzaville neighbours Gabon and Didier, his plumbing colleague, talked about the place a great deal. Yet my father was not significantly impressed by Brazzaville during his first days. He strolled around the capital, observing things, people, customs, recording the cultural differences between there, Benin and the other countries he had seen, partially because it was in his nature to examine and observe, partially because he was looking for ways to make a living. All said, my father noticed some differences between the Congolese traditional clothing and the Beninese. The Congolese fabric was duller, flat and boring, not as flashy and graphic as the ones he used to see back home. Congolese traditional clothing fell short of that outspoken narrative underpinning West Africa's fabric. There were none of those colourful and picturesque printing patterns picturing fruit, newspaper headings, musical notes or presidents' heads he used to see back home. They were not as communicative as the West

African fabric. My father had learnt from his mother that West Africa's modern and ancestral stories were encoded into the powerful visual symbolism of their garments. Those patterns concealed the story of the fine and intellectual Islamic tradition that groups of nomads had brought from Mali down to *Allada* across the Sahara desert and the Songhai empire. Sometimes they were proverbs, local folklore or simply records of day-to-day domestic life or of the history of Benin when it was still called Dahomey. One could read in them the lucrative trade that the Kingdom of Dahomey established with the earliest Portuguese traders. The legendary city of *Agoingioto-Zongoudo* built ten metres underground by the King *Dakodonu*. The Kingdom of Dahomey' southward expansion during the *Agadja*'s rule. The irreverence and hedonistic lifestyle of the Regent of Dahomey—*Hangbe*. The first victory of the *Mino* warriors against the *Oueme* people. But above all, the themes, the quality, the visual impact of the Beninese fabric made for a stunning product which my father believed the Congolese people would not resist. So my father took the train back to Benin, filled up a bag with Beninese fabric and brought it to Brazzaville. The plan was to trade West African traditional fabric in Poto-Poto—Brazzaville's main market—to a Congolese clientele, but he would soon find that it was not as easy as he imagined. He was refused a place in the market. In fact, he was sent away because he didn't have a trader's licence. He knew no one and he was a foreigner. Even worse, the garments he showed to the sellers and the market managers garnered little interest. This Beninese fabric, they said, was too rigid at the touch, and waxy, and too colourful, too exuberant. Besides, the waiting list for a market stall was long and there were plenty of local people who had been waiting for years, so why on earth should they give a place to a newcomer? To a Beninese, no less?

But my father, the Principal, refused to give up. He improvised his own market spot at the far edge of Poto-Poto market by laying a few of his West African cloths over the floor on top of a mat. He kept it up for a few days. However, aside from few glances and enquiries and a couple of sales, my father's products had little impact. He knew that the problem was not the nature of his product but the way it was presented. His post was in fact marginal and too small, forcing him to keep the clothes on display folded and piled up. He concluded he had to change strategy if he wanted to succeed in his new business and finding the right location—a larger spot right in the centre of the market—was absolutely crucial in this respect. So he inspected the centre of the market figuring out how to get his place there with the same care of a robber planning his next job, watching over the bank for the best way to get in, until something caught his attention: the heavy smoking sandal seller's stall in the market's centre, the ideal location. He observed that the man often left his stall unguarded for a destination that was not yet clear to my father. So he followed him and found out the man simply left his stall to go hunting for cigarette butts left on the street. He picked them up, smoked them on the spot and returned to his stall. So the Principal went to buy a packet of cigarettes himself, lit one as he passed by the sandal seller's stall, taking a couple of drags before throwing the entire cigarette on the floor and carried on walking, noticing out of the corners of his eyes how the sandal seller dashed to get the cigarette from the street. The Principal repeated the same operation several times, obtaining the same result—the man walked behind him, picked up the leftovers and smoked them until he reached a point where he could not hold himself back anymore and addressed my father directly, asking why on earth was he wasting all those cigarettes. My father explained to him that despite the fact that he loved smoking, he had to follow the advice of his doctor to only smoke the tip of the cigarettes due to a nasty thing he had in his lungs. Baffled, and feeling sorry for him, the sandal seller asked him about his occupation.

'I work here in the market,' my father said. 'But I have to leave because I'm at a loss. You see, I don't have a proper stall.'

'No way! There is no need for you to leave!' said the sandal seller who obviously didn't want to lose a once in a lifetime opportunity to tap into such a generous provision of cigarettes. Instead, he made sure to keep the free cigarette supplier as close as he could by inviting my father to share his stall with him.

So that was how my father had finally found his stall in the middle of the market, and he and the sandal seller became good friends. Both gained something from the deal, an ongoing provision of free cigarettes for the sandal seller, and the perfect spot for my father's fabric. Soon, however, my father saw no reason to sustain the role of the half-smoker any longer and eventually he triumphantly announced to his benefactor that he had succeeded in quitting. The sandal seller, only partially pleased by his friend's liberation from nicotine, returned to his old habit of collecting butts. But he was about to gain something greater. His sandal sales began to grow at an extraordinary rate. René's flashy West African product had become a major attraction now that the Beninese fabric was openly displayed revealing all its grandeur, and it seemed that his sandals and those clothes paired perfectly. Western African fashion soon boomed in Brazzaville and spread across the whole country. Everyone wanted their clothes to be made from that waxy and vibrant new fabric. The demand grew to a level that René had to travel back and forth from Benin to Congo to bring more stock. This is how traditional Western African suits became Congolese, and that of many other sub-Saharan countries too.

By the time my father was 26, he and the sandal seller had become two rich men. When he reached his first million, my father left the boubou business entirely in the hands of the sandal seller. He was not interested any longer, and besides, many more entrepreneurs had taken a share. The Principal aimed at something different; he went to Paris this time and came back to Congo with a stock of prêt-a-porter clothes. It was a hit again. Even more so than the Beninese traditional clothes business. His name soon reached every corner of sub-Saharan

Africa. Via radio, TV, cinema adverts and word of mouth, his shops drew in crowds. It was at that time he was given the nickname the *Man of the Shoes,* because shoes from Paris were what he sold most. He also introduced his own brand at some point, his name marking the shoes of half of Brazzaville's upper classes. He had shops in Benin, in Congo-Brazzaville, Congo-Kinshasa, Nigeria, and Central African Republic. All his family got involved to some degree in managing René's franchising. In part due to his large family taking over, in part for loss of interest, once again René left the business he created to embark upon some other project. At this point, it was clear that this work-based nomadism was intrinsic to my father's nature. He was not the kind of man who'd get all overheated from amassing wealth. It was not like him to hammer the same nail over and over; true satisfaction hit him only during the process of building wealth, especially if he had to build it from thin air. It was the creative process itself that had power over him, that propelled him out of bed at night right to the desk and got him into action the day after. The challenge, the blurred space in between the birth of an idea and its realisation, that journey into the unknown, the tabernacle of ideas, was maybe the space where my father dwelled the most. Once he had succeeded with whatever he had set himself to, the fun was over and it was time to move on to a new project.

Although I know very little about my father, and among my siblings and our mothers we have all experienced very different aspects of him, we all agree on the fact that he was endowed with great generosity. He gave things away easily. The downside, however, was that his easy ways of giving made him a target for opportunists, among which were members of his family. René loved them very much and sadly was unable to tell them *no*. In consequence, he gave them everything, his boutiques, a bakery, flats, even the hotel he had built himself, which is still working nowadays. It was the first big hotel in Cotonou and he gave it for nothing to his sister Tantine Marielle Tawema.

The clothing business started collapsing soon after René left due to maladministration, corruption, internal diatribes and other accidents, including a fire. One by one all the shops closed down until there was no more trace of the formerly prosperous business. After him, many others followed his steps down the prêt-a-porter industry, but it was his name—the *Man of the Shoes*—that stood out in those days when people talked about fashion in sub-Saharan Africa.

But René's projects were destined to succeed and after the clothing business he set up what would become a well-known furniture factory. He recruited local artisans and sent them to be trained in Europe to specialize in European-style furniture engineering and building. Once they were back, René's Furniture company became a major supplier for government infrastructures, schools, council facilities and local authorities. Also, in the private sector, housing agents and businessmen all came to him to order provisions of furniture and stationery products. René had the connections to provide everything from Europe. He wasn't satisfied, he kept investing in land, properties and new businesses—laundrettes, a cinema, a service that provided petrol to small businesses from the main subsidiaries. By then he had already met his first wife, Natalie, with whom he had four kids—Debra-Jo, Ocean, Lorenzo and Klaus. Sigmund was the result of an extramarital affair with his previous partner, Maman Chantal. Then he met my mother.

GROUND

LONDON, PRESENT DAY
II

I look at you from my terrace, my dearest Telma. I can see you nearly every day from here. You smoking over the wall of your terrace, which sits just two houses away from mine, amid a chord of several adjacent flats that overlook Lower Clapton Road. Sometimes you sit on the floor playing with your daughter. Sometimes your boyfriend is with you although I see him less frequently, mainly in the evening smoking a cigarette. We just wave ciao between him and me while you and I stay talking because we have become friends. Today you are there by yourself. You unfurl your legs until they hang over the ledge of the balcony, so close and miles away. Your long dark hair held together in a single braid, dark eyes gazing at the traffic jam below as you tap your cigarette into an empty can. 'Hey Red!' you say when you notice me. 'You cut your hair?'

'Yeah, yesterday,' I shout over the traffic noise.

'You look younger,' you shout back.

'Thank you. Are you well?'

'Yes, you, how you're doing?'

'I'm very well.'

The truth is that my anxiety is peaking these days. Even dogs seem to be doing better than me, and the thing is, I don't know if it's doing me any good to delve into the past in this state of mind, but I reached a point where I need to get to the bottom of it. I'm tired of having to deal day after day with this feeling of being suspended in a limbo, not here in London, nor anchored in my body. Where then? Where is this place I'm living in? I spend most of the time awake from insomnia, and by the time I manage to get to sleep I'm disturbed by long exhausting vivid dreams. When I'm awake I find myself clenching my teeth so as not to be carried away by daydreaming. I have already grasped the point that my blueprint is just hopelessly black. My tongue is black. My liver is black. I am hoping that if I tell this story, I might understand the meaning behind it myself. I might be able to meet myself and understand my brother Klaus, my sister Debra-Jo, my mother and my father at the end of this tale. Am I using the right words? Am I? Perhaps I don't know how to speak English. Fuck this language, English, I mean. Fuck me the day I got into writing in a foreign language. But to write in English is my only option. It represents me in this specific time of my life, it's the most immediate me, an Afro-European, an Afro-Italian, living in London. French, my mother tongue, is not that strong anymore. It deteriorated long ago, during my childhood; Italian soon became my dominant tongue; eventually I turned it into a profession, becoming a writer in my early 20s. I published short stories and novels, gave lectures and readings and taught creative writing. I was so comfortable with it that I never suspected one day it would fail me. That is exactly what happened. It hurts when you lose the ability to tap into the subtleties of your own language. All the more if you are a writer. Like hands for a pianist, the voice for a singer, language is the fundamental medium for a storyteller. There is no way I could feel that I am a writer with poor use of my language. Writing in a foreign language is for me like being drilled in the head. It's standing on the wrong side of the world. It shapes me in a way I'm not sure I like. Being an outsider, failing to speak my own language, speaking both new and old languages poorly, forcing me to look at things from different angles, it affects my identity. Even my own beliefs have changed, the perception I have of myself, my confidence, my taste, many things that I once found compelling, like writing and reading, have ceased to be so. I started living in ways I thought would have been impossible, gradually spending more time, days, months, years, without writing or reading at all. A new language is ultimately a new mind growing inside you, while the other one, the old one that had brought you to this point, atrophies and, at some point, you gain two or more distinctive views over life depending on which mind-language you're wearing. I don't know what is going to happen next, where else I will flee to, if ever I will emigrate again, but for the time being, what I know is that the mind I wear now is this one, a broken English mind. It is through this broken English mind that I'm experiencing the world I'm living in, therefore I might have to get to the end of this work with my broken English.

One thing I am sure of is that as a practitioner of Chinese medicine, I am supposed to act as a decent man. This is what I've being saying to myself lately when I look at myself in the mirror. I am a decent man. There are not many black men operating in the field of complementary medicine around here. Of course, I like the idea of helping the general public with its many aches, but in so doing, I also like the idea of representing my people in this otherwise poorly diverse sector. I got my degree from the University of Westminster a few years ago and now I've set up my own clinic in my house, with a massage table, acupuncture maps on the wall, moxibustion kit, and cupping cups and boxes of needles and all the medical tools I need well sorted in the storage shelves.

My last patient today was a guy called Harry. I'm giving him support as he tries to come off nearly ten years of heroin addiction. He's doing very well. He's been clean for three weeks now. I like him, he's one of the kindest people I've met since I've been living in London. With him I'm working along the redrawing program he was given by the NHS with methadone. I choose points that have a soothing effect on the liver-system and calm the heart-systems mainly just to suppress his cravings while treating the symptomatic issues which seem to be more of a priority for him. Since Harry is more broke than me, we arranged to do some bartering as a payment method. So every time he comes for treatment he brings some random stuff—candles, incense, a pack of sushi rice, some Turkish baklava. Last week he came by with a bag of pears. Plus he offered to help me sort out the alleyway I share with other residents that has not been maintained for quite some time. His girlfriend was a gardener after all, so they come one day with some gardening tools after they arranged to deliver a ton of white gravel which was left at the alleyway gate early one morning. We spent some time cleaning the alley from all the garbage and weeds, then we laid down and spread the new gravel on the ground. It was a nice experience, the sound of the gravel being worked with the rakes, the manual outdoor labour itself. As the work progressed, and the alleyway floor became neat and beautifully covered with white gravel, memories of a distant past surfaced in my mind. That rattling sound made by raking the gravel, walking on it, felt similar to the walking we did on the snow back at the clinic, during a winter many years ago.

Snow

A month had passed since we were dropped at the clinic. The temperature had fallen nearly to zero degrees. It was cold, colder than it was in Imola up there on the northern border of Italy, cold enough to kill any drive to go out for a stroll, or even to play around in the courtyard. In addition, I think, we were all going through a sort of collective depression. We had received no news from Pino yet, not a sign from our parents. We were left to our own devices, and with neither routine nor schooling, we had nothing better to do than watch TV all day. The sound of the hanging TV droned on all day whether there was someone sitting watching it or not in the waiting room. The sheer amount of Japanese cartoons we got addicted to. All those American series, *Tom Sawyer*, *Little House on the Prairie* or *Little Women*, playing in front of us a positive cinematographic version of what could have been a more functional version of our life. Not short of twists and turns, of course, but joyful at least, coherent, predictable. Those kids' lives stirred with adventures and were punctuated by achievements, love and bright days. They ran vigorously across wide expanses of countryside with a sense of entitlement, feeling like they were one with their land. While we, sitting on the other side of the screen, on the sharp, rigid stage of the real world, we barely knew who we were, where or what we were standing on. We knew we were somewhere in northern Italy, but the name of the town we didn't know. We never felt the desire to go out for a walk and to meet the inhabitants of the little town. The yard outside the clinic accounted for our exercise.

The TV replaced our souls. The wheelchairs with IV holders, and rolling beds, became the structures of our playground. I reached my bedroom driving one of those things one day, the bedroom I shared with Debra-Jo and my twin brother, Redeso, the cluttering of their voices coming from inside. I descended from the wheelchair and found them inside the room, she, laying across her bed, doing most of the talking. Him, sitting cross-legged on the floor. I sat on the floor as well listening to them. Then Debra-Jo stretched her arm on the floor to reach a suitcase she kept under the bed and dragged it out. She then pulled out a small African wooden toy from one of the suitcase side pockets—a long, tiny man pulling a cart.

'I found it this morning,' she said. 'Smell it! It still smells of Poto-Poto market!'

'Must have been there for long,' Redeso said, stretching out his hand to receive the toy from Debra-Jo.

'Not that long,' she said, the winter's dusk light falling across one side of her fawn-like face, her hair kept short but messy by negligence. So were her clothes, a random woollen jumper, skiing trousers and monk shoes, the clothes of someone who had ceased caring about herself. She rested her chin on her arm, staring at us with curiosity. 'It was just two years when I left Africa.'

'Seems like a long time,' said my twin brother, his hair cut newly short by our sister, the same as she had done with me. While most people treated us as the same person, Debra-Jo did not; she treated us as separate individuals. With Redeso she was chattier, I think because he was more present than me. More interested in what was happening around him. More curious.

'What do you think they are doing, Happiness and our sisters?' he asked her.

'I don't know,' she answered. 'What do you think?'

'I don't know either.' He shrugged his shoulders while remaining focused on the new toy Debra-Jo had given him. 'They play. Go to school.'

'Things change, you know?' she said. 'One day is this, then puff, and it's like you've never been here.'

'You're saying we're going to leave this place?' he asked her.

'Yes, we won't stay here forever. We'll leave very soon. Say, do you miss them, your siblings in Africa?'

'Yes, I do.'

'What about you?' she asked to draw me into the conversation.

'Yes,' I said.

'You know what,' she said. 'You two should ask Dad to get Happiness, Mavie and Moon to come live in Italy with us. He'll listen to you!'

'Dad?' my brother said. 'Or maybe we can ask him to take us back to Congo. It wasn't bad there. Wouldn't you go?'

'Who, me?' Debra-Jo said. 'I'd fly there tomorrow!'

'Because you don't like it here much, right? Everyone stares at us,' he said.

'I was happier back home. What about you?' she asked.

'I don't remember.'

'And you?'

'What if everyone doesn't really like us here?'

'We tell them we don't care! Do you like yourself?'

'Yeah, I think so.'

'Do you like me?'

'Yeah.'

'So, that's all we need!'

'What if Mum and Dad don't come back?' I asked her.

'Nonsense!' she said. 'Of course they will come back. They always come back. As soon as they close the big business deal they're doing in there, they will come back with lots of money and fix our house so we can move back there, or they will buy a new one. Granted!'

Debra-Jo always looked fine, whatever the situation was. Like our father, she was optimistic by nature. Although she looked shabby in those days and didn't comb her hair as often as she used to, you wouldn't say she was having a tough time. But she was, indeed, going through a tough time. She attended to us on one front, doing all she could to keep us clean and our morale up. On the other front, she was forced to battle our servant Mbila nearly every day for every detail emerging on our daily arrangements. The two of them had fallen into a feud over who should be in charge. Mbila believed he deserved to be the leader for various, legitimate reasons: he was appointed by our father to look after us. He was the eldest, wisest, the only one truly of age. Not surprisingly, money, instruction and the clinic's key were given to him directly by Pino. At least you could say he was the man, while Debra-Jo, we knew, was just a kid. However, her point was also valid. First of all, she declared while pointing a finger to him one day during dinner, she was our sister. Secondly, she noted, the ultimate and fundamental duty of a servant was to serve, regardless of his age, and the changes in circumstance. The tension eventually escalated. At each clash, Mbila gained power until we lost authority over our servant. Everything became strange and soon, Mbila began ruling over us. He told us when to stop watching TV, to eat and sit properly, and of course, proud, reactionary Debra-Jo was not the type to sit back and be controlled by a servant. On the contrary, Mbila's illegitimate takeover encouraged her to fight him with even more grit. Over issues such as letting us watch TV half an hour more, or allowing Klaus to waste as much shampoo as he wanted in his bubble bath, she scored points against him quite comfortably in the beginning, then started losing ground more regularly, until, one day, things took a dramatic turn.

On a day it was snowing, Klaus stormed into our room excited. 'Come and see, it's snowing! It's snowing!' We jumped out of our beds and ran with him to look out the window, mesmerized by the sight of the snowflakes dancing down from the sky. All the ground and the trees were covered in white. The rooftops in town and the church's bell tower were covered with a thick layer of snow. For us, who were still relatively new to it, it was like living a fairy tale. Watching it from the window was not enough, we wanted to get our hands on it, make all the things we did the previous year at the villa and saw people doing on television—fighting with snowballs, building snowmen, digging tunnels, jumping on snowdrifts. That morning, our appetite for life had been switched on again. We dressed quickly, put our shoes and coats on and dashed downstairs aiming for the door. Then our servant came out of the kitchen asking, 'Where you going?'

'We're going out, can't you see?' my sister snapped.

'Not now. Go and have your breakfast,' he said.

It wouldn't have been a big deal for us to get our coats off and eat that breakfast and postpone the fun to later, just to make him happy, but for Debra-Jo it was a matter of principle.

'Mind your business,' she said.

Masambila stepped in front of the door barring the way.

'All of you, go and have breakfast!' he repeated.

'Are you serious?'

'Yes.'

The creepy thing about Masambila was the amount of time he could spend on his own. He was one of those people whose hard life had equipped him with an impressive level of tolerance. I never saw him losing his temper. Never. Even that day he controlled himself effortlessly. 'It's time for breakfast,' he said coolly.

'Move away from the door,' Debra-Jo insisted.

And there Masambila made it clear. 'I'll punch you in the face, Debra-Jo, if you carry on acting like this,' he said.

'What? Is that what you said? You'll do what? Did you guys hear?! What he said he is going to do?'

'Now, take your brothers upstairs and tell them to take their coats off or I punch you in the face.'

At this point Debra-Jo laughed. She laughed nervously. It was unheard of, a servant threatening his master's daughter. Besides, it was with total lack of irony that Masambila had made his threat, which wasn't even really a threat after all, rather him simply following the thread of his own logic, a rather basic and brutish one. *If necessary, I will use physical force to accomplish my duty.* She laughed. We stood watching in silence. There was something unsettling about his detachment. His eyes held memories of a miserable life as a servant back in Congo, memories we overlooked. Who was this person? What was his history like? I'm sure it was a history without much juice, not much of anything. Maybe he was one of those poor villagers who was given away by his starving parents at a young age to rich people in exchange for nothing, just to ensure he survived the famine. Everybody has a different life experience. You could read such truth written in capital letters from Masambila's quiet stance as he faced Debra-Jo, waiting for her to obey him. There was not much my older brothers could do to help Debra-Jo since they were as scared of Masambila as we, the youngest, were. Our only hope was Debra-Jo. She seemed to be the only one genuinely able to defeat Masambila. Maybe she was bluffing. Maybe she counted on the gentlemen's gender code, or trusted that the servant would never dare put his hands on his master's daughter, his master's favourite. Or maybe she was acting out of a bravery to not let us down.

Debra-Jo and Mbila went outside. Their feet sunk into the snow. The typical silence after fallen snow was deafening. The sounds of their steps were clean. Their movements too. From the door, we all watched Debra-Jo acting so confidently we started growing positive she had a chance to win the fight. After all she was a tall girl, taller than us all, as tall as Masambila. Who knew, with all the Bruce Lee movies we had seen, Debra-Jo might just have learned enough kung fu to actually do something remarkable. Masambila looked sorry for what was happening. He waited for her to take a position. As she came towards him holding up her fists like a boxer, he simply fully hit her on the face and with that, the match was over. She fell backwards and crashed onto the ground and sat there for a while with the stupid expression of surprise you have when you experience for the first time how painful a punch can possibly be. Shocked by the sight of her own blood dripping down her nose, Debra-Jo stood up holding her nose with both hands. The blood dripping down through her fingers stained the snow red. Masambila asked her if she had enough. 'Yes,' she said and remained standing there with her hands over her bleeding nose, our paladin of justice whom I admired and respected for having shown so much courage. Mbila came inside calm as usual and went into the kitchen. We all went upstairs to take off our coats without him having to say a word. From there on no one ever opposed him again.

It snowed several times more after that first dramatic day. Layers covered my sister's blood stains. New snow, new footprints. No news from Pino yet. The days dragged, wheelchairs and IV holders were left all over the place. The television droned on, playing the same programmes day after day. We waited it seemed endlessly for Pino to come and take us to the new house as he'd promised. We didn't care if it was a small flat and that we had to do without a chauffeur and personal tutor or even if our parents were involved or not, we just wanted to go back to some form of normality. It didn't matter, our parents were not the priority anymore, we just needed a house. It was obvious that by watching TV all day in a clinic's waiting room, and having our meals in its anonymous cafeteria, we were becoming truly ill. What was even worse was that things between Debra-Jo and Mbila didn't stop with that fatal fight. Things grew worse. It was no longer about logistics, about who should be in charge. Masambila crossed the line and invaded my sister's most intimate territory. He went down a dark route, revealing a part of himself you'd never guess, a Dr Jekyll and Mr Hyde. The upright guy who worked for us during the day would turn into an obscure being in the night, who crept into our bedroom. The one we shared with Debra-Jo. He crawled up to the foot of my sister's bed where he sat hidden in ambush like a beast waiting to stalk. I soon grew able to figure out when Masambila was in our room. Even if I couldn't see him, I felt his presence, I knew he was there. All I had to do was to get down from the bed and go to the toilet and I would see him as I walked across the room: a man hiding in the dark, his shadow thrown across the floor by the moonlight that lit him up as he put his finger on his lips to silence me. The same story went on every night. She knew he was there too. She was frightened. She couldn't get back to sleep. She would stay lying on the bed in total tension waiting to see him rising from behind the bed and come over her. He covered her mouth with his hand. We twins turned over, as he ordered, facing the wall, and listened to the sound of Debra-Jo defending herself as far as she could from being assaulted. The thing went on every night. She was alone in a recurrent nightmare. No one came to help her. My brother and I were too scared, too young. Even if we were to be brave enough to rescue our sister, we still had no notion of the degree of violence which was being carried out, not enough to push us to react. Neither her, probably. Nor him. Nobody in there. Every night she was cut off from the ordinary world, abandoned to her solitude. Every night as the lights went off, she sank into desolation and waited to experience man in his most demeaning form. No police came, no neighbours, no God nor gods, no Pino, no parents, no nurses, not firemen or social workers. In that clinic, we stood outside of civilisation. Every night, Masambila would open the door, sneak inside the room and stand there waiting like a predator. Then he would get on top of her. She fought back, trying to wriggle away from underneath him. She kicked and punched but from under the servant's hands came only muffled screams.

Every night I prayed to God that the silent fighting would come to an end, but every time it seemed it lasted longer than the previous night. I was never sure whether Masambila succeeded in getting what he wanted, or if Debra-Jo was resilient enough to make him abandon his plan. I never knew what he was trying to achieve back then. Perhaps he'd never gone as far as raping her. Perhaps that was not his intention. Maybe that was his understanding of love, and all he was doing was trying to persuade her to let him sleep next to her. I don't know. I would just fall asleep after whatever it was was over and he had left the room. I would supress the whole thing the next morning. Nobody ever mentioned it, life just carried on as usual, the only difference being this weight of silence compressing all the other silences that accumulated as the days passed. It was just one more of those cruelties that never took place. We all just sat down at the table to eat fried eggs and café latte which Masambila had prepared for us as usual. Debra-Jo ate them too. The only true trace of what happened the night before was the hint of shame shown in Masambila's face. The man hiding in ambush at the feet of my sister's bed was the same man who would then sing the African nursery rhyme to my brother and me while ironing our clothes.

***

I remember an anecdote I read about King Solomon's use of a device that helped him go through tedious times in life. He used to wear a ring on which it was inscribed, *Even this will pass*. I don't remember now where I read it, but it's true, the king was right. It might not look so when you are in the middle of a crisis, it may seem painful, excruciating, endless, but it's just a matter of time before the end comes, and until that day, you just have to keep reminding yourself that it will indeed pass. It passed. About a month after we arrived, we heard the sound of Pino's car driving into the parking area. We dashed outside like a bunch of people who had been lost on an island for a decade and gave a big hug to the big man. His big hands whitening as he held and pressed us against him. The white man from the civilised world. Our uncle. 'My kids.' He told us that he thought about us every day, and that it was time we returned to Imola. The atmosphere in the clinic immediately brightened and lifted. We got all loud like Pino, bigger and taller and funnier, once again the kings of the palace. Mbila moved aside against a wall in the corridor to let the big group pass by.

'Good morning, Monsieur Pino,' he said.

'Hello fellow, how is it all going?'

'All good, Monsieur Pino.'

'Did you manage with the money I gave you?'

'Yes. I have actually some left. Do you want me to…'

'Nonsense. Keep it. You never know, young man. Well, listen up, all! What if we put this place back in shape and leave! We have a long journey ahead. Better if we get straight to it.'

We joined forces to clean the clinic. We packed and loaded our luggage into the car, had lunch with the sandwiches Mbila had prepared us, while listening to Pino and Sigmund exchanging jokes. I remember putting on my blue and green windbreaker and zipped it up to the chin with pride and finally we walked out and got into the car. All except Masambila who apparently had some misgivings. He stood outside the car, quiet, calm, impassive as usual.

'I'm not coming,' he said, arms hanging down as usual, with fingers completely relaxed.

'Come on fella, get in!' encouraged Pino. 'We managed to all fit in once and we'll manage again.'

'Thank you, I think it's time I go my way. It was an honour to work for you, guys.'

None of us engaged with him in any way but Pino.

'Oh come on, man, don't be silly, get in!'

'I've made my mind up.'

'What are you going to do?'

'I'll work something out! Please, do not insist, Monsieur Pino.'

'Are you sure? It seems silly to me.'

'I'm sure of my decision, thank you very much, Monsieur Pino.'

'Good luck then, Masambila.'

And that was it. That was the end of another chapter. Masambila was gone, and the strange thing was that, despite all the talking we had during the car journey, no one ever mentioned him and his nocturnal activities. It wasn't that important any more in this new order of things. The gates of the clinic's yard were the last place I saw him as we moved towards our next destination. I can't state confidently enough why Masambila chose to end things that way, whether he had had enough working as a servant, or whether he planned to start a new life as a free man in Italy or fly back to Africa. Perhaps he was acting out of remorse for what he did to us. I don't know. I watched him getting smaller and smaller through the rear window as I looked back. Despite what he did to my sister I felt sad that things had to turn out in such a way that we had to leave him behind. He was part of us after all. Like him, like us, like anybody else on this planet, all the billions of people trapped under the pressure of gravity made witness to the relentless cycle of birth and death. Looking at Masambila fading away it suddenly occurred to me that the *victim* was the only true kind of person to ever exist on this planet. It simply was more convenient for us to never talk about Masambila. Mentioning him would be an admission that we had gone through something too heavy to bear. Talking about him would have been like rubbing a sinister lamp holding a diabolic genie who had no intentions to please us. Indeed, it would have reminded us of what happened in the clinic, something we could have fought. We were seven against one after all. It was easier to pretend that we had never met him. And we keep pretending it, even now that we are all adults. I know that avoiding talking about him will not keep him away, but it keeps him dormant. He remains there, at the edges of our perception, and whispers to us from time to time, in a cyclical way, like the seasons that remind us that the past will never let go, regardless how hard we try. The past is still here. The actions of that man are still occurring today with the same degree of violence, causing the same level of pain and still shaping the life of my sister, my brothers and mine.

JADELIN GANGBO

My Mother

My mother was born in Point-Noir, People's Republic of the Congo, in 1956, in times where all around the world nationalist struggles were bringing about independence from colonial rule. The Revolutionary Movement of Indian Independence, the Mau-Mau in Kenya, the anti-British Arab Liberation Party in Palestine, all these groups, fighting for decades, proved that victory was possible. Longstanding struggles in Vietnam, Algeria, Cyprus, Aden, had weakened the French and British administrations with countless casualties and social disruptions. General De Gaulle was resurrected from the dead to save the Fourth Republic and keep together colonies of the French Afrique which were slipping out of hand into costly, collapsing, belligerent territories. He sat at the negotiating table in his tour in Algiers with the leaders of the Algerian Front de Liberation National, whose fierce battle for the cause of Algerian independence was ravaging across the nation. Bombs thrown into cafés by guerrilla groups. FLN mobs going from house to house slashing and killing indiscriminately the white settlers. The French reprisal against the Arab community backlashed new attacks from the nationalists and plenty of *pied noir* fled back to metropolitan France with just their suitcases as the only thing that was left of nearly a century of occupation. Domestic and international pressure mounted in a way that the imperial powers had to surrender to the inevitable, and between 1957 and 1975, one after the other, they conceded independence to their former colonies. The

GROUND

People's Republic of the Congo, also known as Congo-Brazzaville, gained independence on 15 August 1960. Fulbert Youlou became our first president. People gathered on the streets to celebrate. Little Sofie, my mother, four years old then, was strolling in the middle of it all with her family, among the crowd, dancing in street parades and parties that went on for days. She learned new songs of freedom and a new national anthem. She watched as the old flag was lowered and a new red, gold and green flag hoisted, by now familiar shared colours of new nations.

As qualified nurses, both my mother's parents had the means to provide their kids with a good education. Her mother, Aminata, left work when she first became pregnant. Consequently, her father had to provide for the entire family. This man had a clear vision for his children, paying particular attention to my mother, Daddy's favourite, the one he considered the brightest, and would make sure she became a big shot, like some European women he had heard about. Named Alongi, baptized as Olivier, better known as Olié, he was well seen in his community, a simple man, a hard worker, who had good manners and the interest of his nation and Africa as a whole at heart. Although he was raised a Catholic in a time when missionaries crusaded against polygamy, he ended up sharing his household with two wives. He married the second one when Sofie was three, and had ten children in total from both wives with Sofie coming somewhere in the middle. The good man also had an extra child from an extramarital affair who died at a very young age. As a state nurse, subject to constant real-location, Olié and his family had to migrate frequently. My mother spent her first years at Kinkala, a small town in the region of Pool, on the south-eastern side of the country. She moved with her family to the capital, Brazzaville, when she was seven. At 12 she was parted from her mother, when the woman, disgruntled with her marriage, divorced and returned to her native village at Sibiti. The change did not bring much disruption in Olivier's household. It was common for people of her generation in Congo to change mothers and to not be so attached to their parents. Yet her father took good care of her, he cultivated her with conversations she barely understood in matters of philosophy, literature, politics.

Before meeting my father, my mother was enjoying a normal happy life. She would have completed high school, enrolled in a university course on oil management, got a place at Elf Congo, or the Italian Agip-Congo, and hopefully fulfil her father's dream of becoming one of the first African women CEOs in the country. And only then, after she had secured herself a spot among the best, only then, would she have married. Like many of her peers, Sofie used to study in the open air in the parks with her friends, usually at the park by the Congo River, the one next to the French Embassy, one of the nicest parks in Brazzaville, very well kept, with paved pathways, neat wooden benches, well-trimmed grass, and lush gardens. There, she and her friends would study until it got dark, and when they went home, helped with the housework if there was a job which needed doing, and then waited for Saturday nights to go to the disco to dance to James Brown, Diana Ross, Tina Turner, Bob Marley, Jimmy Cliff, wearing their belly bottoms and miniskirts they secretly carried in their bag and put on in the toilet. Discos were considered the places nearest to a modern lifestyle, with air conditioning and all, nearly the neatest and best functioning infrastructure you could possibly find in the country. They were also highly valued by my mother's entourage because African music was rarely played in them, only American or European hits. It was the bars, populated by old men, which were more likely to play African tunes and therefore considered places for people who were not going anywhere fast. In fact, African music was called bar music, while middle- and upper-class girls such as Sofie and her friends liked to identify themselves as Europeans or Americans, not Africans.

GROUND

It was 1973, the day of her seventeenth birthday, when my mother, walking home from school with her friend, met my father for the first time.

'Hi,' said a man at the wheel of a blue Toyota pick-up that pulled up by the side of the road to take a chance with the girls. 'How would you two like posing for an advert?' he asked them. He was approaching his thirties, wearing a 70s-style moustache, a golden watch glistening in the sunlight around the wrist he had hanging out the window. Something about his face and his confident approach led the girls to guess who he was. They knew him from his adverts at the cinema as the *Man of the Shoes*. Naturally, my mother—shy and unpretentious, with not the least interest in starting a career as a model—never posed for René's adverts. She just started dating him. He'd wait for her outside her school nearly every day and drove her around the city. There were dinners outside, cinemas, dancing, parties, kisses, lots of I-love-yous, and walks, with some exceptional twists. Often, they were seen hanging about with some of the big shots of the Congolese financial and political scene who were my dad's acquaintances, the likes of Bokilo, Congo's national director of the Banque De l'Afrique Centrale; members of the Parti Congolais du Travail, Bikouta-Menga Gaston, the director of Tele-Congo. The minister of public works and infrastructure, Idrissa Kamusi. High ranking army officers, deputies, chiefs from different ethnic groups, all had some connection with René. Those were some of the most absurd times of her life. An ordinary girl from Kinkala village was all of a sudden seen hanging around in the company of Brazzaville's most influential figures, wearing fine jewellery and clothing, and being driven around the city by the *Man of the Shoes* himself.

From the beginning, my mother had doubts about René. She knew he was married and had five kids—Debra-Jo, Ocean, Lorenzo, Klaus and Sigmund. Besides, he had little time to spare for her since he was often abroad for work, and when he was home in Brazzaville, he had to share his time between her and his family. Sofie's father despised him. Words such as stupid, selfish, libertine and greedy pig filled his mouth when he talked about René. As a result, father and favourite daughter polarized over the subject of her controversial affair with a married rich man, and their once close relationship cracked. The climate at home changed, Olié's inspiring talks about politics and philosophy were replaced by silences and argumentative attempts to persuade Sofie to slow down. Yet Sofie saw in René something that Olié could not see, and went for it, embracing any risk, including the prospect of turning into his concubine.

In René's household the climate was not much different. Things were souring between him and his wife Natalie who was aware of René's affair with my mother and had no intention of sharing her husband with another woman. She took any opportunity to argue about it, which eventually escalated into fights with detrimental effects to their marriage. By the time Sofie was nineteen, she was pregnant with me and my twin brother. At last, my father was introduced to my mother's parents. Reluctantly, Olié had to allow him in. He couldn't digest the fact that his favourite daughter, the one he cultivated as a model of emancipation, was pregnant so young. Before starting university, even before finishing high school. With a man who was nothing more than an unscrupulous money-maker in his eyes. But what could he say? He knew himself that emancipation starts from anyone's freedom to pursue one's own path. There could not be room in his house for any woman to become a CEO if she was not first free to become whatever she decided to be. Besides, his daughter was pregnant and in love. He just had to let go of his plans, let go of her, but with some conditions—he said to the businessman who, during the encounter had never stopped looking attentively in his eyes. He asked him two things: for Sofie to have her own house, and to be allowed to go to university. René consented.

St Theresa of the Child Jesus

It was 1982. A day in January, about a month from the night our house went up in flames. We were on the road again. Driving away from the clinic of the nameless town, back to Imola after the social services had found a place for us. Strange memories from the most recent time hunting us. Our minds in a haze like we were living in a never-ending dream. It was still cold. The cabin was saturated with smoke from Pino's cigarettes. My forehead resting on the car window on the back seat, I listened to him humming along to Lucio Dalla's *Caro Amico Ti Scrivo* that was being played on the car stereo, while I followed the familiar landmarks of Imola rolling into sight. A dozen church bells stuck up over the skyline. The green window shutters of yellow and orange houses were outwardly opened and secured. Lots of old people in flat hats hung around bars in sunglasses, even in winter. Some young adults wore wide-shouldered coats. The cinema billboard advertising *E.T.* told me that things had moved on since we left. We drove across the historical centre of the town, along the Via Emilia, until we reached a yellow old building that had all the look of a convent. Pino pulled off next to it, got out of the car in his brown vison coat, and pressed at the intercom panel. We heard the voice of an old woman answering at the intercom over the rumbling of the engine Pino had left on. 'INSTITUTION OF ST THERESA OF THE CHILD JESUS' read a plate on the front wall of the building. Then a pair of intimidating, sturdy automatic wooden doors opened slowly as Pino walked back to the car. We drove forward into the building and waited a few seconds more for a second gate to open, this time an iron gate. Then was the turn of a colourful stained-glass gate bearing a religious theme. This last door drew apart like a stage curtain might, and closed behind us, as if to announce the end of an act and the beginning of the next for the seven homeless children.

We parked the car in the interior courtyard of the convent, in front of what looked like the main building, and got out, noting how extraordinarily quiet it was. The whole structure rose around a square courtyard with a portico running around its borders. Several closed doors rimmed the portico. On the front wall there was a painting of a tranquil natural landscape of a lake under a sky covered with soft, white clouds. A statue of a religious figure stood in the middle of the yard. The Virgin Mary, or someone else, possibly this St Theresa of the Child Jesus of whom I had never heard a thing before. I looked around very much impressed by the silence, as though we had entered a soundproof place. There were no more openings to the outside world as soon as all those gates had closed behind us, except the sky above that was bright blue and deep and square-shaped, mirroring the courtyard.

A short nun dressed in her traditional black robes rushed out from a door of a wing of the building and walked towards us. Her tiny moccasins shining like black pebbles. She introduced herself as Sister Domenica. She had a few words in private with Pino, then addressed us directly, mainly Klaus and us twins, the three youngest. 'Who is Redeso and who is Redesof?' she asked, leaning down, looking at both of us as hundreds of people had done since we were born. Her eyes, bouncing from one to the other trying to spot differences. Then she sought clues from Pino, but he was no better than her at distinguishing us and threw up his arms as if to say, 'It's a mystery, you need to ask their brothers.' She kept on being confused though our brothers helped her in telling us apart. The fact we had quasi the same names made things more difficult. He was Redeso. I was Redesof.

'I've seen twins in my life, but never seen anything like this!' she said. 'I'm sure we'll find a way! Well, I guess it's time we move inside, shall we?'

We nodded our heads in response, more out of a sense of social obligation rather than a real intention, in the sense that we were not expected to say no. We had no say in the matter, and personally, I was not aware of what was happening. I was counting on moving to a normal house, but instead I was following a nun into a religious institution with Redeso and Klaus. We followed her reluctantly, and with a sense of disorientation, as we realised we were the only ones walking in with her. Lorenzo, Ocean, Sigmund and Debra-Jo were waiting outside, around Pino's car, glancing at us in a new strange way. A look that was hard to interpret. It was both a look which people give when they hold back their emotions and when they are concerned. They seemed as if they were posing for a grim photoshoot. Debra-Jo smiled and said, 'I'll see you soon.'

I gave her a hesitant smile, a nod in return. Amidst all the changes we were going through, this one felt different, somehow more challenging, mainly because it happened without warning; nobody told me that we were about to split apart. And how did my older siblings know? Was it arranged behind our back? I wasn't sure of what I was meant to do, if I should carry on following the nun or walk back outside, if whatever was happening to us was ok, if all families were supposed to break apart at some point. These guys were some of the most important people to me; I felt like they were letting go of me.

'Hey,' Debra-Jo called us again. 'Remember what you promised. You need to do your beds, ok?' Ocean, with a long austere blue coat over the green Adidas tracksuit, gave us a thumbs-up. Sigmund, the kindest smile. Lorenzo, he wasn't sure what to do. He then nodded as if to say, *it's all cool.*

I nodded back at him, reaching the zip of my coat to pull it up again, just to find out it was already up to the top.

***

Three ghosts. Klaus, Redeso and I followed Sister Domenica in a tour around St Theresa of the Child Jesus. We walked nearly hovering over the floor, like three uncertain ghosts indeed, through the recesses of a new haunted house. Haunted because we arrived at a time of day when the place was mostly empty but you could sense the presence of people living there. All the dwellers were at school and at work. Not even the nuns, who lived in a separate, private wing of the institution, were in sight. The immensity of the facilities, the big empty rooms and quiet corridors, the number of chairs, tables and beds, which clearly served many people, the novelty of it all made it seem unlikely you could ever become familiar with it. If the clinic we just left was alien, this place looked even more so. Sister Domenica showed us the playroom, tables stacked against the wall, the piles of toys sorted in plastic boxes like in a nursery, the refectory with a line of tables arranged in a U-shape along the walls, the toilets downstairs, the toilets upstairs, the study room, the stationery storage, the bedrooms for the little ones, the bedrooms for those who were a little bit older, the bedrooms for teenage girls. There were even more bedrooms on the floors upstairs and in another wing set up for single mothers and their kids.

The last place was the laundry. Inside there were two more nuns at work, busily sorting out all dwellers' clothing, mending, ironing, folding and shovelling through piles of clothes. 'Do come in, please, don't be shy,' they said to us, aware that we were newcomers. We went in while Sister Domenica waited at the door.

'What a beautiful trio we have here. What are your names, kids?'

'My name is Klaus. These are-are-are my brothers,' stuttered Klaus. He has suffered from a stutter ever since.

'My name is Redeso.'

'I'm Redesof.'

'Oh, I won't even try repeating them. I never remember foreigner's names. They're so strange. But why did your parents give you the same name?'

'Because they are twins,' intervehed Sister Domenica from the door, as if she knew everything about African twins.

'The three of them?'

'No, just the two youngest.'

'*Oh mamma mia*, I didn't even notice. They all look the same to me. Did you just move to Italy?'

'No, no. We c-c-came two ye-ye-years ago,' said Klaus.

'From which beautiful country?'

'Co-co-co…'

'Congo?'

'Yes.'

'Ah, must be horrible in there! There are always wars!'

'Yes, there are!' popped up again Sister Domenica all proud as if she was the one who saved us from war.

'It's not th-th-that Congo. It's another Co-co-Congo,' corrected Klaus.

'How many Congos are there?'

'Two. We are fr-from Congo B-b-b Brazzaville. Not K-k-Kinshasha.'

'Thank goodness!'

We spent the rest of the morning settling down in our bedrooms. Klaus was roomed in a relatively small one, which he shared with three other people—a Somali guy of his age named Yusuf and a single mother with her son from Chile. Redeso and I, being younger, were placed with the youngest residents in a twenty-bed dormitory. The same type of metal beds that we had in the small clinic. The same smell of bleach. Sister Domenica led us to the toilets; she handed us each a towel. We took a bath inside in the main bathroom of our dormitory floor. A new, well-folded set of clothes awaited us on top of our beds inclusive of pants, socks and new shoes. The nuns tried to match us twins with clothes that looked as similar as possible. Light blue corduroy trousers, white long-sleeve shirts with high neck, orange woollen jumpers with knitted theme and desert boot-like shoes. Once we got dressed, we sat in silence on our beds, waiting for the nun to return to give us the next instruction. Redeso and I were placed near each other. With our beds' long edges resting against one wall, we could view the entire room while sitting on our beds. The many beds, bearing the gold and black colours and logo of the institution, were all neatly done. A big wooden wardrobe lay at the end of the room, taking up an entire wall. Redeso and I looked around ourselves with not much to say. Memories of life in the villa and in the clinic we recently left, still vivid in our minds but weakening. Debra-Jo was right when she said a few days earlier that things change quickly. Who would have ever said we would have found ourselves in this place, separated from our siblings? We stayed there immersed in our thoughts and impressions for a while; sounds of foreigners' lives reached us from the floors upstairs and downstairs, more faintly from the street below our window. Then, Sister Domenica came back into our room. She checked our teeth. She checked our nails. Clipped them off. Told us to come downstairs with her to help her set the table for lunch. She also called Klaus from his bedroom. But the boy was asleep, alone, in his new room. So she pulled down the blinders a little and let him sleep, whereas Redeso and I followed her downstairs to the refectory. She handed each of us a small pile of plastic plates, which we distributed around the tables, along with plastic cups, cutlery and towels which were rolled inside personalised towel rings. Soon the atmosphere changed; we could hear a multitude of footsteps and voices coming from outside. Gradually, two lines of kids, led by another nun, flooded into the hall, all talking over each other, rattling and scrambling as they took off their coats and placed them on the hangers on the wall. They rushed upstairs to put their backpacks in the studio room and came back down again, in groups or individually, all appearing to feel at home. They stormed into the refectory, and amidst the mayhem of their chats, laughs, screams and runs, they noticed us, standing there baffled and shyly in the middle of the room, but, like kids who got somehow accustomed to changes and to the different ethnic groups coexisting in the institution, they didn't pay us much attention, except one kid. A blond kid, around our age. He emerged from the group and pointed directly at us. 'What's your name?' he said with a northern Italian accent.

'Redeso.'

'Redesof.'

'Are you new?' he asked.

'Yes,' Redeso said, guessing what the kid meant by being new. 'And you?'

'Been here a while.'

He then gave us the brightest smile. 'My name is Marco,' he said and ran off to take a seat at his table.

***

While we were settling into St Theresa, my other brothers, Sigmund, Lorenzo and Ocean, were at St Catherina, a boys-only institution in a different area of Imola. They were given a starter kit, which included a toilet paper roll, a toothbrush, a toothpaste tube, soap, a towel, and a key for the green metal army-like lockers lined against the wall at one end of their bedroom.

The man who handed them their new accessories was a big tough guy from Eritrea called Mr P, the institution's vice director. Mr P gave them a quick summary of the general rules, then assigned Ocean and Sigmund each a bed in a twenty-bed dormitory, Lorenzo in a separate twenty-bed dormitory, and left. First thing Lorenzo did once he was alone in the big desolate dormitory was open the window. I suppose as a way to reconnect with the world outside, that world that had already a strong pull on him. He stayed peering distractedly at the lane below outside the institution's walls. He could only see a small portion of it, and just a small number of people passing by because the window had a safety grid that prevented him from leaning further out. He stayed there staring outside melancholically like a prisoner. Until Sigmund and Ocean entered the room, holding a package for him. It was a brand-new tracksuit, which Sigmund handed him.

'Mr P said to have a shower and wear this. We're going to have a snack downstairs if you want to come with us,' said Sigmund.

'Yeah, I'll meet you downstairs.'

***

Only Debra-Jo remained. Like Charon—the ferryman who carried the souls of the dead to the underworld across the river Acheron—Pino dropped us off in blocks. There was only one left to be carried across the river. The two of them sitting inside the car driving across Imola. The big man with his red face at the wheel, white hair pulled back, and the skinny young black girl seated next to him. Nobody behind her, nobody on her lap as had been the case so often, only empty seats and, perhaps, the true, empty essence of things. Pino drove in silence; he was clearly upset by how things had turned out for us kids in such a short space of time. He seemed sadder than Debra-Jo, or simply more in touch with his emotions. He was the father of a teenage girl himself, after all, and as such was able to fathom Debra-Jo's emotional landscape, especially after all she had been through. The girl kept quiet, mainly to hold back her tears, and looked out at the landscape crawling by. 'Look,' said Pino, tormented by the lingering silence. 'I really can't come to terms with the way things have turned out. I wish I knew how it works, why it is that for some people life is so easy, and why for others it is so… I mean… It's been a mess from the very beginning for all of you. What is it! Look, I'm so sorry. I need to be straight with you. It's not going to be easy for you, guys. Not at all.'

'Is it far, the place I'm going?' Debra-Jo asked distantly.

'We're nearly there.'

'Is it a nice place?'

'Between me and you?' the big man turned light-hearted again. 'I'd say it's the best. Lots of outdoor space and plus, let me tell you, it's very, very girly!'

Pino was right. Debra-Jo's institution, called Oasis, was the best among the three. In that it had less of the oppressive prison-like feeling of St Catherina, and more open to the outside world and friendlier than St Theresa of the Child Jesus.

It was an institution which could have been mistaken for a geriatric home, set on a quiet, wealthy residential edge of town. There were no walls, just green hand-painted metal railings which enclosed the building. Even the size of it all was more humane. There was a cosy garden outside with a white-pink patterned swing. Next to it was a basketball and volleyball patch enclosed by a high railing. A nun came outside the building adjusting her veil. She was surprisingly young, in her early twenties, Debra-Jo observed.

'Hi Pino' the nun said to the big man. 'And you must be Debra-Jo, right? My name is Sister Gaudenzia.'

She said this while stretching her hand out to the young girl. But Debra-Jo didn't respond. She didn't even try taking her hands out of her coat pockets, and just threw a glance at the nun as she withdrew her hand. It took a little time, perhaps a few seconds as the two gazed at each other, to sense that their encounter held something that would turn out to be crucial for both of them.

'You look very sad,' Debra-Jo said to the nun.

'Both of us, darling,' the sister answered. 'Come, let's go inside.'

Prayers

Debra-Jo went through a mild form of depression during the first few months in her new home, the Oasis. That same enthusiastic and optimistic girl, our fighter, had now lost faith and interest in the world around her and dissociated from things and situations. Her response dimmed when anyone approached her, as if something ephemeral had hijacked her senses, and like an automaton, dull and hazy, she lived her life in those days, it seemed to us, like it was a slow train passing across the distant horizon. What was the point of reaching out to people if they had to go away at some point, as people always did, and what would she have done with it, with those people, with whatever life had to offer, at this stage of her life once she had grabbed hold of them? She felt best when left alone, even when among people, while talking to them, smiling, playing their game, responding to the social obligations, she felt glad that nobody possessed enough strength to break into her personal space. All the people from her class were new. Her high school was new. Young, white students stared at the only black girl in the whole school, the new girl standing up in front of the class while she was being introduced by the head teacher halfway through the school term. The black girl wearing a funny backpack and a generic second-hand shabby dress that had all the look of coming straight from the storage room of the Oasis's laundry.

'This is Debra-Jo, please welcome her!'

'Welcome Debra-Jo!'

She sat at a desk next to a girl whose characteristics said nothing to her, in a classroom filled with insisting stares and murmurs that provoked no feeling in her, no embarrassment nor annoyance, these were just faces, empty faces, floating at half-mast, no different to those others that had been staring at her since she had first set foot in this country. She went home at the end of the day, had lunch with Sister Gaudenzia and the small group of girls who lived with her in the institution. They were ten girls in all, including Sister Gaudenzia. Two sisters—Marilena and Francesca. A diva—Sabrina—then Paola, Federica, Milena, Laila and Debra-Jo's roommate, a punk-rock girl with black lipstick named Gabriella. The small number of dwellers made for a cosy and lively climate, more like a family unit than an institution, a family with its up and downs, joys, struggles, frustrations, headed by Sister Gaudenzia, both the head and supervisor of the place and one of the family. In the sense that being that young and easy-going, she operated on the same level as her girls, as she'd called them. She took part in gossiping with as much enthusiasm, shared her opinions about music, American films, magazines, and boys, clothes, makeup, and could easily get caught into bitching and rows as much as her girls.

***

That winter, the stage of so many changes for our family, was finally dying out. The air had become warmer. No more need to blow warm air onto the hands nor shake them alive; no condensation from the mouth when you exhaled. Inside the plant pots, where she'd found only dew when she first moved in, now vegetation was germinating. The same thing was happening to the trees and a variety of plants in the garden.

My sister sat on the swing. It had already been a couple of months since she moved to Oasis. There were noises of kids in a nursery in the distance, she could hear them screaming and rushing about the playground as she gently rocked by herself on the swing, the creaking of the chain with rust. She thought about her brothers, who she had seen on and off when they came to visit her or when she went visiting them. About a dog she had found once in Brazzaville and brought home. About her mother, her biological mother, Maman Natalie, and the last time they were together. Her mother's bedroom, the bed covered by an old, yellowing mosquito net, ripped and mended here and there. Her mother helping her prepare her suitcase, then walking her down the stairs, to Dad's car, where Lorenzo, Klaus and Ocean were about to clamber in. A life of displacement, she remembered. The worst part, the worst instrument seemed to be the memory, regardless of the direction it took. Those nights in the clinic, the heavy, dense darkness lying in and outside the clinic, unravelling inside her, the weight of his body over hers, the grip of his hands on her, she shuddered at the images of Masambila lying over her. It was not the first time it happened, to re-experience the abuse. But she knew how to cope. She knew how to manage her pain, by waiting for it to subside.

Sister Gaudenzia came out of the building, walked forward, and sat next to her on the swing. Things were strange between the two from the very beginning. They had been living two months together and never had a proper conversation yet, and it seemed they were not to have one today. Debra-Jo was closed towards the nun. Monosyllabic and ready-made answers were the best the nun could get out of a conversation with her. Then, if the nun had no more questions, Debra-Jo would let the conversation die, and silence would rest there in between them, until Sister Gaudenzia gave up and had to leave empty-handed. The same was about to happen this time, except Debra-Jo opened up.

'Why did you choose this life at your age?' she asked.
'Pardon?'
'Why did you become a nun?'
'Well, this is a question!' The sister relaxed backward on the swing. 'I didn't really *choose* to. It just happened. You know we all have a purpose in life? It's just a matter of finding it at some point.'

'What if I don't have a purpose?'

'We all have it, darling!'

'We are all different though.'

'I see what you're getting at, we are all different, for sure, but yet we are all still in the same boat.'

'Just because God said it you believe it.'

'There is no record that God ever said that!'

'Who said it then?'

'It's just a saying: *We are all in the same boat.*'

'A saying,' she repeated vaguely within herself, as though the phrase conveyed something new or reawakened something she had forgotten. Maybe some of the sayings she heard from her Grandmother Debra, back in the big house in Benin. Then she added after a brief pause, 'Do you think you could have *chosen* not to become a nun?'

'Let me tell you how it happened,' answered Sister Gaudenzia, rubbing her hands together with zeal at the prospect of sharing an episode of her past with Debra-Jo, happy of finally connecting with her.

'Not many people know it in here. I was nineteen. I was living in South Tirol, which is where I'm from, in a small village up in the mountains called Schenna. I was not much of a religious type, I mean, I went to church and all like many others on Sunday. I was raised in a Catholic family. But nothing about me would have suggested I'd take my vows one day. I went to school, hung about with my friends, not more nor less than any other girls, continued my life and followed my ambitions. Then something happened. I had a night of somnambulism. The only night of somnambulism I ever had. I sleepwalked in the middle of the night across the countryside, from my village to another town ten miles away. I'm sure cars went by but no one stopped me and I walked and walked and walked, for ten miles, along the main road, across the fields, on the road again, and reached this village, and when I woke up I was on my knees, inside a church, right in front of the altar. I woke up and I was praying, I woke up right in the middle of an Ave Maria. Holy Mary, Mother of God… I woke up saying, and do you know what I did? I just carried on praying. What could I do?'

A faint smile appeared on the face of Debra-Jo, in the manner of the same buds she had seen sprouting on the plants and trees around her. And the sister was moved by it.

'You darling, have an amazing smile.'

'Thank you.' Then she asked, 'Sister Gaudenzia, you said before that you had ambitions. What would you have been if you hadn't become a nun?'

'Oh wow, such a long time ago. I wanted to organize events. Cultural events in my little town.'

'Cultural events. That's an odd job, do people do that?'

'Yes! There was not much going on in my town aside from wine and the communist party festival. I had a friend who was a good photographer, but he was really shy, too shy to do anything with his photos. I also had an old, abandoned family sheepfold. It came to my mind that I could put the two things together, clean the place, paint it, refurbish it, make it nice, you know. It was an amazing big space, then I'd get my friend to take photos of all the people in town and then hang them up in there. How I would have loved doing it!'

We Were Growing

While the nun and my sister were talking, we were growing. Indeed, we were growing. A few millimetres taller every day. Our steps down the stairs sounding heavier. Our bones craving for more calcium. We were growing sharper, thicker, more aware of the surroundings. Our minds were collecting pieces of information wherever they found the opportunity for building the self's beliefs and scripts. The original idea was to give life to people who would function in time. Healthy creatures on their own rights. Agile, chirpy, strong even in the face of their own flaws, spreading outwards like trees, blessed and facing the sunlight with pride like sunflowers. We were meant to respond efficiently to any calamity, with a sense of having been nourished by the experience, having gained something at the end of it, no matter the type of end, which could be death. The essential was to understand that you had lost nothing. We were meant to be confident, have self-esteem, to pursue our life purpose by reading and understanding life signs and the messages the dreams conveyed, to interact with people and their surroundings in a healthy, peaceful way. And whenever the mess went beyond our coping capacity, we were meant to be able to survive anyway, by stretching the hand asking for help. We were growing.

Redeso and I swapped classrooms sometimes. I listened to his teacher's lectures, played with his classmates, he'd take the conversation from where I left off when we swapped back again to our real classes. Whenever people in institutions called him my name, he didn't mind. When they called me his name, I didn't mind either. But generally, they called us Twins. Or Twin when addressed individually. We were rising in crescendo like the trumpets of Jericho. A few millimetres per day taller. Klaus was learning breakdancing. He played electro music on a small stereo he was given by one of his classmates' parents and practised every day in the playroom. While we were all playing toys and games from our imagination, he was trying out new moves, refining his moon walk, feeling what joints were involved on performing the electric. When he wasn't training he was bouncing his tennis ball against a wall, playing kick-ups with it and keeping count, hanging around with his friend Yusuf. We were growing. Each day we woke up at sunrise. Like any other kid. Like our classmates, and the kids in Africa, in Europe, the Arctic, fishermen's and bus drivers' kids, the children of executives and miners. Although we had little or no contact with our parents and younger brothers and sisters, we were growing upright just as any other kid. The point is that it doesn't really matter whereabouts you live and who raises you at the end of the day. Whether in an institution, on the street, or in a more conventional setting, as long as you are guaranteed regular meals and a bunch of pals to hang out with, or even in the absence of all these factors, you just grow. We followed a strict schedule in St Theresa of the Child Jesus. In spring we woke at sunrise, got dressed, waited in two lines for everybody to be ready before heading downstairs in the refectory to have breakfast with some thick biscuits and caffe latte. Then, back upstairs to brush our teeth, then we went to school. All sound and clean, the nun leading us in two straight lines. When it was not her leading us, it was one of the single mothers. Once back from school, we had lunch, had a couple of hours playing in the playroom or outside in the courtyard if the weather was good. A bell rang at half past two calling for homework. A couple of hours after classroom we were in the line again heading downstairs for tea break. We played until suppertime, and ended the day watching an episode

GROUND

of a series, often a Latin soap opera on TV or *MacGyver*, *The A-Team*, *Dukes of Hazzard*. We were being shaped from all angles by American junk, by school demands, by Catholic narrative. Shit was infiltrating our synaptic transmissions faster than any neurotransmitter. Christian iconography hung on every wall including our bedrooms. I saw Jesus dying at any point of my day, from morning to night, in every room, even at school, in my classroom, in the loo, and in the corridors, and on our resting day of Sunday a huge Jesus would be dying on a huge cross in front of an assembly of believers that moaned in front of him too early on Sunday morning. Jesus died every Saturday afternoon in the little private chapel on one wing of the institution, in the semi-dark candlelight projecting on the walls, flickering shadows of kneeling nuns. We said together ten *Ave Marias* as we rolled the small beads. A *Padre Nostro* as we got to the big bead. Then ten *Ave Marias* once more. Catholic symbols and language were conveyed through our supervisors, nuns and teachers on a daily basis, and even among us, intentionally or not, we were bouncing its rhetoric back and forth. Pope John Paul II was our Mick Jagger. We had to attend mass twice a week and catechism lessons once a week. We topped up with collective and individual prayers before meals and bedtime. Older ones, kneeling at the confessor for their sins, and queuing to receive the Holy Host, were a source of fascination. The list of potentially sinful behaviours grew exponentially inside our heads without us being aware. New sins blossomed mysteriously from thin air. Italian had become my dominant language by the time I was eight, and it improved and gained in subtleties anytime I resized my voice up to the chapel's frescos to confidently sing the Christian religious lyrics as part of the church choir. We had assemblies with bright, young fellows of the Catholic Action group who came to entertain us armed with guitars and good intentions on some boring winter afternoon where we sang again. We were growing. Few millimetres a day. And we sang again.

Everyone had a story to tell in the institution. As I experienced such a variety of lives, I started getting my head around the fact that nothing was straightforward in the strange world we lived, inside as much as outside the institution. My new family was made up of dysfunctional kids and disabled people, young gipsies caught robbing flats and brought in the institution by the police, children whose low-income parents struggled to sustain them, or were forced away from home by social services for some unfortunate circumstances. I grew up playing marbles with kids whose parents had life sentences, listened to rock music with single mums coming from an history of addictions and abuse. I witnessed a whole family of refugees from the Balkans coming to stay carrying a backpack full of what was left of their life from a country torn apart by war, who taught us how to put gel on our frizzy afro hair. And for this reason, precisely because we all came from problematic histories and had met in that little bubble, whether for the long or short term, we were all caring towards each other to some extent. I can confidently say I met in there the kindest people one could possibly find in life. For every lone child there was another child adopting him or her as brother or sister. Then there were the single mothers. The simple fact of them being stable in our life, their presence, a cuddle, a hug, a few nice words, a treat, worked as a buffer to soothe many of us from the effects of the daily lack of parental affection. The care from those women were our sole means of orientation. Their reactions, what they said, how they looked at us, helped us to ponder whether we were growing fine or not. For the rest of the time we were left working things out by ourselves. You take the risks of your life experiments on your shoulders. You have a go and see where it takes you. It might hurt if you were to take the wrong step, but you still carry on.

Among our circle of young friends, Marco, the kid we met on our first day in the refectory, the kid with a bright smile, became our best friend. He was the kindest boy one could possibly come across. He was from

Livorno, and very generous. Always ready to help and comfort the other, a passionate kid. However, he bore a dark history: he was habitually beaten up by his parents back home, so harshly that one could see the mark of fear permanently sitting deep down in his glowing eyes. Everything about him—his hunched bearing as he energetically ran all over the place, the melancholic held-back rattling sound of his laughter—all pointed to the indelible history of being brought up in fear. He was mine and Redeso's best friend, but not consistently in the sense that we acknowledged him on and off, sometimes we played with him, other times we ignored him, or we dismissed him in the middle of a play when we had grown bored of him and wanted to play with somebody else. Whereas for him, things were straightforward, he simply looked at us as his best friends. It was so since the very first day we set foot in the institution, when he approached us, introduced himself, and escorted us into St Theresa's life, explaining about people and roles and rules and games. Being among those kids who went back home during holidays, Marco would stay at his uncle's house in Livorno as established by the social services and would see his parents only rarely. He looked always very happy to see Redeso and I whenever he was back from Livorno, his eyes trembling with commotion, he'd hugged us tightly and shared facts about his holiday effusively and, above all, he'd never come back empty-handed, but always with a huge bag of eye-catching chocolate bars and candies. Redeso and I would grab the treasure and store it inside our bedside tables every time he came from home, a ritual.

It so happened, one Sunday night, right after dinner, on the last day of the Easter holiday, that Redeso and I were playing alone with toys in our bedroom, when, at some point, we realised someone was hiding behind the door. We were ten years old now. We had moved from the dormitory to a more contained room we shared with Marco and two other kids. We also had a stereo, which was playing a cassette of Duran Duran. We carried on playing with our Transformers, kneeling from the opposite sides of Redeso's bed, as though there was a mirror in between us in the middle of the bed. A pair of Oxford shoes, brown trousers with the fold line running down the legs, a woollen sweater vest over a white shirt made up for our Sunday's outfit. Two minutes from when I first heard the mild shuffling sound of someone from behind the door, the presence was still there. I could see him out of the corner of my eyes, reflecting on the window, Marco, who had just come back from an Easter week in Livorno and was obviously trying to surprise us in the hope we'd engage in the game and say something like, 'Who's there!' so that he could triumphantly leap out and claim: 'It's me, I'm back!' But not. Not with Redeso and me. The climax he was expecting was far from coming. We went on animating our robots over the bed, ignoring him, up to when, after a little while, tired of waiting, he pushed his head out of his hiding place and kept it unequivocally in sight for us to see it was him. But again, we ignored him. He gave up in the end. Short and with a stocky build, the boy brushed some blond hair from his forehead as he came out of his hiding place with disappointment and a feeble, 'Hello.'

'Hello,' we answered back, already annoyed by his presence.

'You got new Transformers?' he asked, sitting aside, on his bed, watching us play.

'Yes.'

The vocals we did for the sound effect of our game and the music of Duran Duran were all you could hear for a length, until the boy started unpacking his bag, saying, 'Why don't you hug me anymore when I'm back? You used to.'

'It's not compulsory,' my brother said.

'Yes,' I added. 'I don't feel like hugging my friends all the time when they come back.'

'At least you could look at me.'

'Look, if you have to put us under pressure just because you are back, you could stay there a little longer.'

Along with his clothes, he pulled out a present for Redeso and me, the usual bag of treats. He gave it to us and went on unpacking, gazing now and then at us storing our goods inside our bed table drawer and returning to our game.

We were not aware that it was pain driving us to be cruel with Marco. It was a way to protect ourselves from the love we felt for him, from the void he left in us every time he went away, as if he abandoned us. We had learnt a fundamental lesson during our earliest years, a really simple one: there was no space available for unconditional love. So we naturally developed a self-regulating love mechanism that opened and shut down to people according to how close they came to us. The closer they'd get, the less likely they were to get into our exclusive twin world. It was just another way of surviving through the silenced grief that the dismantling of our family was causing inside us. Yes, we were a tight community in the institution, everyone was ready to give a lot to each other, to share, but not everything, not the most wounded part of yourself. I can speak for sure for Redeso and me. We were growing up in a way where life experiences impeded us from becoming those functional love-giving people we were meant to be. We were not spreading outwards like trees, nor facing the sunlight with pride like sunflowers. We felt we lost something important.

Her Visits

Meanwhile, time passed. News from our younger siblings in Africa, Mum and Dad, was rarely passed down to us, and anyway, this news carried no meaningful developments. We rarely saw Pino. My mother was the only one who came up to Italy to visit us. Never Dad, neither our other two mothers, Maman Chantal and Maman Natalie—Sigmund's mother. My mother came to visit us randomly, every one or two years. I remember those visits as being particularly strange, nearly mystical events, as if it was an alien coming down to earth and calling me by my name with a French accent, *Redesóf.* I generally learnt she was coming out of the blue, sometimes with just a day's notice. The source of the news could have been one of my older siblings, a nun, or even one of the single mothers, like, 'Are you happy your mum is coming tomorrow?' My reaction was more or less the same every time—brought back to reality with a snap of the fingers, and suddenly I had to draw a quick line from that word 'mum' and all the packet of emotions and memories that came with it, that had been parked somewhere in the back of my mind some years ago. I looked into the distance like a kid with Alzheimer's, trying to remember something that got lost on the way, while dealing with the conflict of emotions such as excitement and apathy and obligations towards somebody I barely knew; obligation towards a sudden change in circumstances that now wanted me to switch into a son and stop playing the orphan. I never managed to fully figure out what my mother's visits truly meant to me, she was a stranger, but of course, I ran and hugged her anytime I saw her passing through the institution's glass door.

Maman Sofie stayed in the same hotel during her visits, a modest guesthouse in the historical centre of Imola. She had to ask room service to bring some extra chairs to accommodate all seven of us in her double bedroom the days we went to visit her, which was soon after school, or at the weekend. We sat around her, she sat drawn back against the wall, legs lying along the bed, wrapped in her African pagne, thin braids tied back in a loose ponytail, red nail polish on her toes. It often struck me how young she looked compared to my classmates' mothers. As though time ran the other way for her. She looked younger at every visit. With a warm bright smile one day, the frail, sombre expression of disempowerment of yet another day of failing us. A young woman. A young woman. Quiet in manners, slightly nervous as she attempted her best to fulfil the role of the mother she never was, the mother of seven Italian kids who were growing estranged from her. Two biological and five adopted. She tried at least. The only person from the African lot coming to check on us. However, I don't carry any special memories of her visits, nothing particularly exciting happened, aside from enduring those long days. We just sat in that room for hours caught between silences and chats. Mainly the eldest children dealt with her, while my twin and I played on the floor with some toys she had brought, overhearing now and then bits of conversations about general matters—school, health, mischiefs, gossip, girlfriends, boyfriends. Mum gave us news about the people we left in Africa, our younger siblings, Dad and friends, updated us on how negotiations to buy our new house were proceeding. Our house, our way out of the institutions, the house Dad was perpetually in the process of buying which for one reason or another was never happening. She talked about it as if the time we were about to move into it was right around the corner. Then there was the new cars affair, another of Dad's stunts; he was arranging to buy the older ones a brand new car each and motorbikes for the youngest. All news came with verifiable data, cost estimations and time schedules. There would be lots of emphasis on the details such as the size, colours, brands, the speed, the opulence, the prestige, and we all cheered, daydreaming, optimistic for all that lay ahead, and holding onto this deep sense of pride of being the sons of such resourceful parents.

We hardly went for a walk with Maman Sofie. There was no going to the fun fair or for a tour on the lake, anything like that. At best we walked downstairs to have lunch at the restaurant hall with grilled rare beef steaks, fries and coke. I was happy when she came to collect Redeso and me from school. I still remember the urge I had to show off my mother to my classmates and their parents and to all those people who throughout the years had grown used to only seeing me being picked up by nuns, to prove to them that somewhere along the timeline, when things were running accordingly, I too was like them: a kid who got picked up by his parents. Then, of course, it would eventually come to the time that she had to fly back to Brazzaville. A hug, a kiss. No fuss at all, I simply shed off the skin of being somebody's son and got back into my orphan's one, back with full strength and zeal into my daily life. I have to say I felt more comfortable in that skin after all. That one, that boy running on the loose with other underprivileged kids, was the closest I could ever get to myself.

Sister Gaudenzia

Things went back to normal for my siblings too when Maman Sofie left. Sigmund, Ocean and Lorenzo carried away with them to St Catherina the juicy taste of grilled meat they had eaten at the hotel restaurant and the dreams of brand-new cars and private bedrooms in a new house. Klaus went on buying motorbike magazines for a while, seeking the right scrambler to show to Dad when he was ready to grant his purchases. Debra-Jo shut herself in her room to catch up with her studies in preparation for high school final year exams, glad to be able to graduate in time before moving into the hypothetical new house. By this time, three years from when she first moved to the Oasis, Debra-Jo had grown into a beautiful 17-year-old girl. She was of a beauty that drew men's and women's eyes alike anywhere she went. And yet, there was no trace of her flaunting her grace, it looked more like that she was hardly aware of it. She earned her pocket money by doing some modelling work for local commercials, with no intention of turning it into a profession whatsoever, she fell into modelling as a mere consequence of her beauty. A pair of jeans, a plain jumper, Debra-Jo's needs and aspirations were down to earth—a position as an accountant, a faithful husband and a bunch of well-behaved kids. Debra-Jo did well at school. Excellent marks in all the subjects. Teachers had only good words about her. From the quiet, lone wolf she was in the beginning, she grew into a popular and influential girl among her friends at school as well as at the Oasis and in the local community. She had sway on people not so much because she was particularly cleverer than others, or charismatic, or sociable, or controlling, it was rather a thing she had, a solid centre that drew people into her orbit. There was only one person with whom she had some sort of friction. This was Sister Gaudenzia.

Sister Gaudenzia, who remarkably managed the Oasis by herself, felt sad most of the time. Sad for reasons that yet eluded her. Depletion from running the institution maybe, the girls, their many little pains that affected her, loneliness, the inherent sadness of living, she couldn't really say if any of these were the culprit of her grief or if it were something else, something she had not grasped yet. Too often she'd catch herself with a lump in her throat right in the middle of a conversation, or she would burst out crying while brushing her teeth alone in the toilet. The girls, who were unaware of this side of their nun, and never imagined that she could be sobbing alone in the toilet at night, simply saw in Sister Gaudenzia a strong and capable woman. At times stubborn and annoying, even vengeful, but overall, well-intentioned, good-hearted and friendly. Some people could also see a sensual women hidden behind the veil, but not without reasons. One of her girls, Gabriella, Debra Jo's roommate, would not abstain herself from calling her Hottie, or making remarks to her such as, 'You'd raise the dead!' The girls loved her because they felt she was like one of them. They laughed at the same jokes, listened more or less to the same music. She was to them more like a sister than a superior. But with Debra-Jo, Sister Gaudenzia was different. There was always some distance between the two. They could be cold with each other, in such a way that people could doubt they even were acquaintances. There was none of that chit-chat the nun had with the other girls, she had no words about music and films and boys with Debra-Jo. The same was for Debra-Jo, she interacted with the nun only when necessary, and in a formal way, a ceremonial encounter, and only when with others, they loosened. Their relationship led people to think that it was poisoned by reciprocal hatred, but no, that was not the case, the two women never had arguments, never talked behind each other's backs, virtually nobody ever heard Sister Gaudenzia complaining about Debra-Jo and the same went for Debra-Jo; she never spoke of the nun in degrading terms. It was more that, at some point, one would cease to exist in the eyes of the other.

Some girls in the Oasis liked to think Sister Gaudenzia was in awe of Debra-Jo, or that she was driven by jealousy of the grip Debra-Jo had on people, particularly on the girls from the institution. If the sister said, 'Debra-Jo, come here I need your help!' Debra-Jo would come down and examine the problem and, if she could sort it, well, she would do it and then leave without sparing a single word. 'I need your opinion in this matter, Debra-Jo.' The same. Debra-Jo would give her fair opinion, and again leave with detachment. They could also be found sitting in the same room for hours without talking to each other once. Coming back from the supermarket, carrying bags of food, walking side by side but in silence. But the truth was, Debra-Jo and Sister Gaudenzia were not indifferent to each other at all, nor did they hate one another. Both women were just treating one another with utmost respect. As if deep in their hearts they knew one another very well indeed, the wise cold distance set between two old acquaintances, aware they had made a pact somewhere in time. In fact, I don't think Debra-Jo would have ever had that first episode of somnambulism if she hadn't met Sister Gaudenzia.

That night Debra-Jo took her covers away and slid out of bed, her eyes still shut. Coincidence had it that Sister Gaudenzia was just coming out of the toilet when she came across Debra-Jo walking through the corridor, visibly sleeping, and decided to follow her. Debra-Jo went down the hall, grabbed a set of keys from the board on a cabinet by the main door, opened the door, and went out. Sister Gaudenzia, with no time to collect her veil from her room upstairs, left without it. She just had time to grab her coat from the hanger and put it on, and snatched Debra-Jo's too, given another winter had arrived. She carefully rested it on Debra-Jo's shoulders as they stepped out the institution's gate, out into the street, and kept on walking, side by side. They may have appeared as two friends having a very early walk to the eyes of a lazy observer. The nun, her short, dark brown hair showing, a pyjama vest under the winter coat, could not remember the last time she went outside without wearing her robe. She derived a sense of relief and satisfaction as she allowed herself to feel she was just a woman walking in the night. Both women in sandals, feet getting cold, they walked the streets of the quiet residential area. Across the hilly landscape where wealthy villas sat behind dark bushes and trees at the edge of the road. They walked up a hillside road, the sky brightening with stars the further they moved away from the city. A cat leaped down off a wall, a car pierced the quietness as it passed them. The two stopped at a crossroads, one lane leading to a field, one carrying on to a high street. The nun allowed Debra-Jo the time she needed to choose which way to go, and carried on next to her, along a dirt lane that ran across the fields. They climbed up a hill, up to the top, reached a point that Debra-Jo found suitable and sat on the ground. Sister Gaudenzia sat next to the girl, trying to figure out what in this place was of interest to her. Why this place? A hill overlooking nothing else but the void. What was she contemplating, if anything?

What happened that night carried something significant for the nun. She had never met anyone else suffering from somnambulism, and now she was experiencing it from one of her girls, the one with whom she had shared her own experience of somnambulism which had led her to become a nun. Aside from basic notions of theology and catechism, Sister Gaudenzia had received a relatively poor education in the matter of spiritualism, just a tiny glimpse of what accounted for the wide spectrum of the experience of her soul. However, there were things she gave for granted that did not necessarily have a logical correspondence to her belief system—that everything is fundamentally good and that all is part of a universal design. And life talks to us. Talks equally to all its creatures, though not always unequivocally. She believed in dreams as the language of life. She believed that there is a connection between beings, their environment, as well as within the inside and the outside realms. There are things lying underneath the layer of what we can perceive with our five senses that are even more real and rooted, more lasting than the so-called truth, maybe endless, unyielding, where a variety of planes of existence coexist and merge into each other, but she knew for sure, whatever that was, in spite of its complexity, it was reliable. She had found herself sometimes, in a completely spontaneous manner, close to calling that experience of being, God. But only close. Never dared to go any further. Ashamed, and appalled by her own blasphemy, she would indeed take back and discard any of those speculations and carry on living amidst two contradictory worlds: a world of separation in which she was made to take her vows, where God ruled as a separate entity, versus one of unity that she'd sensed now and then spontaneously, where all was one with God. All the symbolisms were stated clearly for her. The tabernacle on the altar. Jesus on the cross right in front of her. The church. She had opened her eyes right then. She had woken up right in the middle of her saying a Hail Mary. And the Walk. The long blind walk to another town's church which could be interpreted as a pilgrimage, a mission she had to undertake. The message was clear for her. But for this girl, this girl whose life had been put under her care, what was the meaning of this journey to this side of the city over a hill overlooking the void? Was she looking at the void or at everything? Was that a request for nothing, something, or freedom?

Finally, the girl stood up from the ground, the nun did the same. They walked all the way back home. Sister Gaudenzia pulled Debra-Jo's coat away from her shoulders as soon as they stepped inside, and let the girl walk up to her bedroom where she slid into her bed and kept on sleeping soundly for the rest of the night.

LONDON, PRESENT DAY
III

Pain tolerance is entirely random. What is painless for some is unbearable for others. I still don't understand whether acupuncture should be pain-free or not. Views on the subject are disparate, some, like the Japanese, stick the needle just under the skin. Chinese and Koreans penetrate the muscles. Some schools of Asian thought suggest patients should feel nothing. Most support the theory that an achy sensation, called *Daqi*, should be felt by the patient to ensure the treatment is effective. There are so many variables. Even among patients there are so many types. There are some tough-looking patients who are overwhelmed by the pain of the slightest puncture. Some others cannot bear the sight of needles sticking out their body. Some find that singing in a loud voice helps them overcome their fear of needles. Some feel the pain even before the needle insertion.

After the treatment I wait for the patient to get dressed. She books for another appointment. She pays. Then leaves. My next patient is Harry. I open the door for him, he says hi and has brought me a book about a Chinese medicine diet he found in a charity shop. 'Oh cool, thanks,' I say. We sit at the table for something between a chat and a follow-up. The guy is doing well. His sinusitis is nearly gone, nose unblocked, no more episodes of diarrhoea. No falling back into heroin. After he lies on the couch, bare chested, I stick needles on his legs, one on the chest, two in each arm. Yes, I saw some bad-ass-looking people sweating with fear during needle insertion. Then there are the wimpy looking ones, like Harry, who lie down quietly the whole way through. He doesn't make any fuss even while I manipulate the needle, which is generally where people might feel pain, since I play around with it, pulling it in and out of the body, twirling and twisting it. Harry lies there unfazed, eyes shut. I dim the light and leave him alone in the room after I finish the needling. I go back inside only once to do some more light manipulation. For the rest of the time, I sit at the desk and write down my findings on him in my notes. Then I take out the needles and prepare the treatment room for the next patient as soon as Harry leaves.

Two days later it's Sunday. Sunday afternoon. I hear knocking at my terrace window as I'm there sipping my tea in the living room. It is you. I wonder if we have the power to keep it as it is, just a friendship, if we can prevent it from slipping into a catastrophic mess, I find myself thinking. You and your five-year-old daughter. You have jumped across two terraces from your house to mine to spend the afternoon with my kids and me. Your daughter carries a box of Lego. You carry two cans of beer and you wear shorts, sandals, grey polished toenails. I open the terrace door, yelling at my kids that you guys are here and the two rumbled down the stairs with fervour to meet and play with your daughter. You and I sit on the sofa, our conversations punctuated by gaps of silence and sips of beer and interactions with the kids playing with toys in front of us on the floor. We talk about art, performing, scripts, writing, Chinese medicine, skin problems, beer size around Europe, difference between T and B cells, Brexit and gentrification. I have to say that physical space between us has shrunk during the course of our friendship, that too often we found ourselves sitting too close. But never as close as today. Your thighs pressed against mine. Our shoulders touch. Then you lean over me and eclipse your head behind my head and for a while I have no idea what you are doing, if you are looking for something on my shoulder, reading the label sticking out from my top, or are about to say something. You just stay there a bit in silence, your face hidden behind my head, this incredible being, I guess feeling, listening, smelling me, while your breasts are lightly touching my shoulder. Then your voice from behind my head whispers, 'I don't know what it is, but I feel as if I'm on MDMA when I'm with you.' I say nothing in return although I know what you mean, I feel exactly the same way. High, when you are with me. I crash under a sensory overload to the extent that I have to hold myself back from grabbing you and kissing you, there, right in front of the kids, and I guess, if we were alone, that would have been the most likely outcome. And that is the reason we are mindful to stay in the same room in which the kids are playing—our last hope to anchor us from drowning our families in some massive crisis, and to prevent a man, your man, further suffering upon witnessing our obsessive friendship. It would help if one of us moves out of the area, if he took you out of London. Myself, I'm way too weak to cut you out of my life, you are a far too difficult challenge. Suddenly, I have the intention to get up from the sofa and move around the room just to stay away from you, but I cannot get up. Otherwise, you would notice I have an erection, an erection that cannot ease and persists even after you break physical contact and are now simply talking to me from a distance. Your voice, your presence, the idea of you—even when I close my eyes picturing gruesome scenes, some scissors stuck in my eye, worms feeding on a corpses underground—still, you are driving me insane. Whatever you do, whatever you say, whether I listen to you or not, I am hard and there is nothing I can do to ease it out. I just sit leaning forward with my arms crossed over my dick. There is something about your restless legs that are giving me a headache. You can hardly find a comfortable position for them, and keep rearranging them. You are obviously as nervous as me and express it through restlessness. I through immobility. After a little while you fall into silence watching over the kids playing and, I guess, thinking of ways to solve this problem, our problem, our friendship, that has grown to a point to cause us physical discomfort. Then you do this most unusual thing, probably one of the most sensual gestures I've ever received. From where you are, sitting next to me, you lift one of your legs obliquely and stroke my forehead with your bare foot, coiling your toes with those shiny grey polished nails just over my eyebrows and ask me, 'Are you ok?' It happens so slowly and is so surreal that I question if it truly happened or I am just being fooled by my drunken, groggy imagination.

'I think I'll go,' you say.

'Yeah, it's a good idea, I think.'

But then you wait for longer, staring in front of you, I don't know if at the kids playing or something beyond them. Then you call your daughter. 'It's time we go.'

'Can we play a little more, Mum?' she tries.

'Oh, my love, I have a few things to do. We can come and play another time.'

'Ok.'

You both say bye to my kids. You raise your hand to me in a sign of greeting. I raise mine and you leave while I sit here, left to witness the atrocity of perfection. Would I ever be here and met you if it wasn't for the night Sigmund had that little accident with the candle when we were kids? Indeed, pain tolerance is entirely random.

GROUND

Walking With My Brothers

Sigmund came to collect Klaus, Redeso and me from school one day in the autumn of 1986. He had grown into a robust sixteen-year-old boy. Always ready to cheer us up with jokes and frequent acts of generosity. He was akin to our father in this aspect, even his squinted gaze was reminiscent of the *Man of the Shoes*. That day he wore a bomber jacket as was the fashion among Italian teenagers of that time, a pair of jeans and caterpillar boots. As we were walking with him to St Catherina for our fortnightly visit where we were to have lunch with our other two siblings, Lorenzo and Ocean, we updated him on our lives. Then we all set off to meet Debra-Jo at the Oasis where we were to spend the rest of the day. We walked away from the town centre to the outskirts, along Via Emilia. Brown and yellow leaves freckled the pavement along a tree-lined road. The six of us, Sigmund, Ocean, Lorenzo, Klaus and us twins, like a gang, made me feel special. Walking around the road, hands in my pockets, the sound of Ocean whistling a tune disappearing behind the roar of the cars whizzing beside us. Ocean had reached sixteen, too. He and Sigmund were sort of heterozygote twins, just born from different mothers. As opposed to Sigmund, Ocean was lean and tall; he had grown even taller than Debra-Jo, and was already wearing that Grace Jones-like haircut and plain austere clothes that would characterize him thereafter. Lorenzo was about to turn 14. He had developed a passion for music, was into fashion and fashionable clothing, and was growing up handsome; I'd say the prettiest in our family. As for Klaus, Redeso and I, we were still just kids. Four years had passed since we left home, six from when we left Africa. I think we were doing well overall. I don't remember having had a particularly difficult time, nor do I remember missing my parents, my siblings in Africa, or my old life in the house in the area of Zolino. When I think back at that day, the day I was walking with my brothers on the streets of Imola, as to many other days I spent with them and Debra-Jo, a sense of contentedness sweeps through me as I feel like we had created something special back then, a self-sufficient family which was happy in its own way and needed not much more than what we had.

Debra-Jo popped her head out of a window after we arrived and buzzed us up. She came to meet us midway down the stairs and led us through the house, to the living room while saying things in her usual soft manner. She got us to take our coats off and brought them to her bedroom. Over time, Redeso and my relationship with Debra-Jo had been rendered more superficial compared to the time we lived together. But anyhow, it still felt warming and reassuring to be around her. We spent the afternoon chatting with her, the other girls from the institution and Sister Gaudenzia while having tea in the living room, some of them sitting on the sofa, some on the floor in a relaxed climate of familiarity. Then, when the climate turned quieter, and the girls had left us alone, the seven of us would drift back into our usual family matters—our youngest siblings, the house, the cars and motorbikes, often with little critical opinion; in fact, we were rather optimistic, if not naive, over the whole subject. Our speculations were based on bits of information we had gathered from Mum's last visit, or from closely related people such as Pino. Whatever bit of news crossed the Mediterranean from Africa we looked at as a serious matter that needed urgent evaluation from all seven of us. Something that we truly believed was imminent. Not only did we put full trust in those promises, we also believed that whatever implementation they needed to be fulfilled was on its way too. Whatever it was we were waiting on needed to be big and sensational, blowing people's minds to bits and putting it all to rights, in line with Dad's megalomaniacal ways. There was no point in him committing to a project if it was not going to be monumental. We were not waiting for a flat, but a villa twice as big as the old one, with double beds for each of us, and a swimming pool, tons of toys, bikes and cars. Dad's pompous narrative was more contagious than the miasma of the beggar's life we were living, so vicious and contagious that we were oblivious to the discrepancy between our fantasy and our real life—the actual state of being orphaned kids. After all, why doubt Dad's intentions? Buying us a house and a bunch of vehicles didn't seem to be a big deal compared to the fortune the *Man of the Shoes* had managed to build up over and over throughout his life. We were the sons of a magician, a great man. You took a flight to any backwater in sub-Saharan Africa and you mentioned René and people would immediately know who you were talking about. We never stopped trusting deep in our hearts that we'd get out of institutional life the very *next* month. Even if the facts pointed to something else: four years had passed since we moved to the three institutions; the millionaire, the same person who, as a young ambitious man, had managed to get a place in the centre of the Poto-Poto market in Brazzaville with the use of a cigarette trick, this man would have sorted us out long ago if that was in his power, if ever we were meant to get back to our old life. But there we were, falling for whatever we were told. All of us except Klaus. Klaus knew very well how delusional we were being, and he didn't mind telling us. 'You ta-ta-talk shit just be-be-because you don't want to see that he-he-he forgot us.' But we didn't want to listen, we'd rather dismiss him with the usual remarks.

'What you're talking about, you rotten apple!'

'Always such stupid ideas!'

That night we were dropped at St Theresa by our brothers sometime past dinner time. Klaus rang the bell. 'It-it-it's us,' he said to the nun who answered at the intercom, and a small door cut out from one of the two big sturdy ones opened. Klaus ran up the stairs to his bedroom as soon as we entered our area, and Redeso and I continued to the playing room where our friends, the youngest kids, were having the last round of leisure time before bedtime. 'Hey twins!' called out Marco, hopping out of a small group of boys whom he was hanging with. It was evident even before he reached us that something troubled him, he was nervous, his voice crackled, and that fearful stare he had sometimes was now full, nearly erupting out of his eyes. He was gripped by fear.

'I think Yusuf is angry with me.' He panted in between a grin of disappointment and a look of confusion.

'What happened?'

'I'm not sure, twins. He's like, I don't know, he said he's going to beat me up!'

'Maybe he was joking! Why should he beat you up?' I asked him.

'He really said that, though.'

The boy scratched his neck, exaggerating his hunched posture as he threw fleeting glances out to the corridor, fearing for Yusuf to show up anytime.

'"I'm fed up with your bullshit," he told me, "I swear to God that this time I'll crush you like a fucking cockerel," He really said that. But I don't know what I did to him. I'm very confused. Why does he want to beat me?'

'What if you go talk to him?' Redeso asked.

'I don't have that confidence,' said the poor kid.

I did not know what to make of his account. I just randomly scanned the room with my eyes looking for any clue in the scenery, but it was in vain, nothing helped to bring context to what Marco was saying, not certainly the other kids who seemed to be going about their lives oblivious to the conundrum troubling the boy. We never really understood what Marco did wrong, if he ever did anything wrong, or if it was just due to his inherent goodness pissing off the wrong people. Maybe he ran in defence of the wrong party, or said something annoying, got somebody in trouble by trying to help them, something that made Yusuf—Klaus's best friend—furious. Whatever the reason, that night when we were all in bed sleeping—everyone but Marco I suppose—Klaus and Yusuf broke into our room and ruffled around with Marco, trying to pull him out of bed.

'Now we're going to cut your tongue off, idiot!' they said.

He desperately grabbed and hung to the feet of the bed while he was being pulled away by the two.

'Twins, please help me!' he cried in fear, a fear that, I assume, had doubled in intensity when it merged with all the episodes of physical abuse he had experienced in the past. Nevertheless, my twin brother and I didn't move a single finger to his aid. Nor did we spare a single word to condemn the two. Not for lack of guts or for any specific ethical reason as far as I know. Neither were we too young to stand up for a friend, as was the case with Debra-Jo and Masambila, we were already eleven. We simply didn't help Marco because it felt normal to us that something like this could happen in the middle of the night. We just watched him being dragged away out of the bedroom, my brother Klaus silencing him by pressing his hand over his mouth. It felt normal, except seeing my brother Klaus in that robe. As it turned out, the poor kid was dragged all the way through the corridor and locked inside a toilet with the two. They stuffed a sock inside his mouth and beat him up.

The nuns' reaction to such a singular episode of violence in the history of St Theresa of the Child Jesus was swift and merciless. Yusuf and Klaus were transferred to live in St Caterina right after the incident, since it was clear that they had grown into teenagers and no longer fit into the caring and loving norms of St Theresa of the Child Jesus. As for Marco, he was taken to hospital that same night after he was found by one of the single mums, all alone in the toilet, all coiled up on the floor, crying in despair. They kept him in the hospital for a day. He came back with an arm in a plaster and his face as swollen as a balloon, and none of that shining glee he used to emanate whenever he crossed the gate of the institution on his way back from Livorno. He was not the same person anymore. He looked at us from far in the distance with resentment, his eyes red with tears, his movements slowed like he had grown into an old man in the space of a night. The meaning of solitude was synthesised into that boy that day. He never came close to us anymore. We never tried to approach him. Never spoke again.

Days went on. We got up every morning with the nun turning the lights on and raising the shutters. We went to school. Little girls played pretend family in the playroom in the afternoon and skipped rope. Little boys dealt with cars, balls and played gangs. Some stopped pissing in bed. Some found a coin under the pillow from the tooth fairy. Sometimes we went for a play date at a classmate's house. Sometimes we fell sick. Sometimes we got erections in the morning. Some could say the alphabet backwards. Some got a new coat. Some learnt for the first time that death was real. On Saturday evenings and Sunday mornings we went to church. We stayed for a few kicks of the ball in our Sunday outfits in the parish church backyard at the end of mass. Those who were entitled to would go back home for weekends and school holidays. The remaining kids could be found outside in the courtyard, at dusk, at some point gathered around one of the single mothers who told stories. Sometimes it was the Eritrean mother, or the other one, the one from northern Italy, or the one from southern Italy. Or the Chilean mother with a gold filling showing on one of her front teeth and shiny long dark hair. Then summer made its way, enveloping us all in boiling hot weather. And the school year ended. A week after we all got into the institution's blue minibus and a big truck-driver-looking nun drove us to a house owned by the institution on the Adriatic coast, leading our jubilee choirs to God—'*Stay here with us, the sun is already waning. If you stay among us, night will never come*!' We stayed in there with God, in the seaside house, at Pinarella near Rimini, the whole month of July, in see-through plastic sandals and swimming trunks, transiting from playing on the pine grove, a post-lunch nap in semi-darkened bedrooms, and a swim, building castles and racing tracks on the sand for our colourful little plastic balls that bore pictures of Italian racing cyclists. In white, sunscreen maritime dress code, the nuns read something or kept the youngest in check under the shade of a huge umbrella. They spoke some words with the usual chatty neighbouring old women standing outside the fence that enclosed the institution's portion of the beach. There was no concept of free beach on the Adriatic coast, just owned, overcrowded fenced plots of beach punctuated by dense lines of umbrellas, deck chairs, and ashtrays marked with colours and logos of the lido bar's name. And St Theresa of the Child Jesus had its own, a piece of beach that probably had a whole different feeling during winter.

We were back on the minibus in August, with the same truck-driver nun, now in white, all singing '*You are my life, nothing else I have! You are my way, my truth!*' and we rode away from the Po Valley, and wound our way up steep serpentine mountain roads to the institution's other house in a little town in the Apennines in Tuscany called Piancaldoli. Strangely, we had more ice creams there than at the beach. We got back in touch with the small-town residents we left the previous year—the post office owner down the road, the guy with the motorbike, the guy with the dog, the four old men still sitting in the same spot outside the butcher shop, the gadget shop owner's kid pulling a cart, and everybody else we'd met at the parish church last year. Bells sounding every half hour, clear, distinctive into the dead quietness and more convincing than anywhere else. It always felt we were the only tourists there.

One day, once we were back from a day trip in the forest, a nun who had just driven from Imola for a stay handed Redeso and me a letter. It was from our mother. We found a corner away from the group to read it. She was announcing the birth of our baby sister whom she'd called Monique. She wrote she was glad that Dad had finally let her choose a name. The letter went on giving an account of how everybody was doing and finally stated that Dad was organizing a trip to Africa for all of us to celebrate Debra-Jo's eighteenth birthday the following year.

The following year came eventually and the trip actually happened. I was twelve. Dad sent Mum to Italy with seven tickets to the old continent. Sister Domenica helped us pack our suitcases and drove us to St Catherina with the blue Fiat 500 from where our mother arranged to collect us all. My brothers had their luggage ready in the courtyard, all excited and nervous for the waiting. Then Debra-Jo came, wearing sunglasses and dragging her suitcase. Then a taxi drove into the courtyard. Maman Sofie got out looking more stunning than usual. We all hugged her. She was also much happier than usual. We were too. We talked and acted frantic as if we were constantly on the verge of getting sucked into a black hole and missing our flight. Another taxi was called to accommodate all of us. We loaded our luggage in both cabs and finally set off to the airport still in disbelief of what was happening. We were flying back to Africa after having missed it for years. We were about to see our younger siblings, Dad and all the friends, the past we'd left behind. And of course, our old African house. Seven shining, smiling siblings and a mother, their ears plugged up by the drop in cabin pressure as the flight ascended. We were going home.

Brazzaville

Memory is deceiving. Even when you are ready to swear to God that what you experienced was true, it could turn out that it was not. It could be that a large part of your remembrances is indeed nothing more than the result of some editing the memory undergoes according to some obscure self-serving mechanism. Some events might not have taken place, for instance, at least not in the way we remember them. Others could be purely byproducts of somebody else's experience that infiltrated your memory during a symbiotic conversation and were recrafted into a product that fits your purposes. Sometimes we mix up real experiences with events we drew from a film we saw, a dream we had, or we tap directly into the cultural chest of the place in which we are growing to fetch new, more suitable elements to add, adjust—or even replace—specific past incidents of our life. That was my case, that's what happened to me a summer evening many years ago as the Air France flight I was aboard with my siblings was landing at Maya-Maya in Brazzaville. I realised that my memory had me fooled for years. The white Italian day-to-day landscape I'd been used to for so long, the entirely white TV content, my subjective visual corridor crowded with masses of white people coming and going, eating, talking, working, at school, on the street, on public transport, in public areas, a white-people-based reality that had dominated my life in the last years had tricked me into believing that the world was entirely white. And all the characters populating the memory of my past in Africa had been white too, so I had no doubts that in the

Congo, the vast majority of people would be white as well. This belief was so deeply rooted in me that I was amazed by the scene that opened before my eyes from the airplane window as we landed. There were only black people working across the airfield. The complete reverse scenario we flew away from several hours earlier in Italy. What I'm trying to say is that I had forgotten that Africa was black. I was stunned as I threw puzzled gazes around the scene like any white tourist visiting Africa for the first time. Skins darker than the darkest I had ever seen, a flood of frizzled hair, these workers driving carts, sweat trickling down similar-looking faces, flagging, pulling ladder trucks, everybody operating in a way that was alien to my former way of processing, that made it seem like they never questioned their own identity and place in the scheme of things. There was nothing odd, nothing out of the ordinary for any of them to be holding so comfortable a bearing and being part of so striking a multitude of African people. The whole thing became even more absurd once we walked out the gate into the airport hall. The number grew out of proportion, and didn't seem about to subside at any time, but kept on swelling instead until all available space was filled up with black people. Once I had got past the shock, I was left with only excitement and a sense of relief in rediscovering there was a place in the world where black people were the norm. Where I was the norm. Where I wouldn't have to put up with kids calling their friends over to look at the negro. I was spared from adults giving me that commiserating look they inherited from news of the Biafran War. I was sane, fit, ok, here. Just a boy. I'm sure my siblings felt the same. We walked with a mixed sense of entitlement and unfamiliarity, peering around with wonder as we carried our luggage through the airport, discovering old and new features of our homeland—hand-printed bill posts, market stalls selling street food, the slow pace, the heat, the *lingala*, les *mamans, les papas, les ton-tons, la musique noir* played everywhere, and people trying to sell you anything, services, food, gadgets. Then there were the three robbers. The decorative touch of the airport. Three men standing up on their feet beyond the check-in desk, right behind the flight attendants, clearly serving a civil punishment. They had their backs facing the public, hand-cuffed, dark red strips of recent lash wounds showing on their bare backs, heads covered with cardboard boxes over which was written, *Je suis un voleur*—I'm a thief. The three were undoubtedly displayed as a measure of robbery prevention. I tried to picture the execution and the executioner, a man with the mandate to whip another man, not necessarily someone from the security force; the honour to execute the physical punishment could have been offered directly to the robbed man as a refund for the damage suffered, maybe one of the food sellers, or a traveller like us coming back home whose bag was robbed. Whatever the case, bystanders carried out their activities without paying much attention to the three thieves, except sporadic looks of condemnation.

Waiting outside the arrival area was Dad, the Principal. He wore plain trousers, a white shirt opened at the chest, flip-flops, a cowboy hat and he sported a moustache. It was hard to access the spectrum of his feelings amidst our own emotional turmoil. It was charged with colliding emotions, I guessed for all of us, to see Dad in the flesh, amidst the oddities of our childhood landscape, this man who had been lingering in our imagination for many years. A mystery to all of us, though in different ways, depending on our age. He was clearly touched, too. He looked nervous standing there, suddenly faced by his seven progeny whom he hadn't seen in years. Maybe he was not as prepared as he thought he would be, not entirely aware of what was about to happen until it did happen. Perhaps he had imagined this very moment for days right down to the smallest detail, the old man might even have struggled to sleep the night before, readying himself to receive us, but then only once he was faced with us at the airport, could he acknowledge what this contingency was truly about. He kept himself together, though, greeting us briskly, and getting straight to practical matters. He led us outside the airport to the car park, grabbed our suitcases, and helped by our chauffer, loaded them in the trunks of two black Mercedes-Benzes that had come to collect us, now avoiding eye contact, now sustaining it for a second at the seven stares casting over him, his mouth full of small talk. Things were not that different for us, as I told you, we too were nervous. All was too absurd. Too sudden. Too far from the usual. All too unexpected. Mom, the flight, Africa, and now Dad, the Principal, in the middle of all his carrying, lifting and putting suitcases in the trunks as if his children had just returned from a short holiday rather than six years in Italy, in the villa, in institutions. There was something about the way we looked at him that said we shared the same thoughts: 'This is Dad. Our living myth.' And all it took was a flight. All our talks over the years, our fantasies, our admiration, our frustration, anger, sense of abandonment and longing, all converged now into a physical presence of a man in a cowboy hat pulling his head out of a car boot on a sultry African night. Then it sprung forth, the clear night sounds free from the electromagnetic load we were used to back in Italy. Whatever I looked at seemed to be talking with no secretiveness. The air was warm and dry. A short guy in a colourful shirt and a toothpick in his mouth came forward asking Dad if we needed a taxi.

'Do we look like we don't have a car to you?' he answered.

Yet the guy persisted, this time offering to help load our luggage, our chauffer growing unnerved too by the man's obstinacy. Soon other sellers came by, pushing forward their products in spite of Dad's brusque responses. There was something in the way they glanced at us—more guarded than they were with our parents—that suggested they knew we were outsiders. They spotted right away we were from Europe, from our clothes perhaps, from the fact we were coming out of an airport looking lost at sea, or simply people are endowed with the innate ability to differentiate outsiders from insiders at first glance from times where the presence of the other could determine life or death.

GROUND

***

We clambered inside the two black cars and set off home. Dad at the steering wheel of one car, Mom on the passenger seat next to him. Debra-Jo, Redeso and I on the back seats. Klaus, Lorenzo, Ocean, Sigmund riding in the chauffer-driven car behind us. Warm air fanned through the windows. Dad talked over the car's grumble for most of the journey. I caught something about *le imbécil la que ne sait pas conduire, acheté assez de Fanta, mais le poulet…* but I was not quite sure when he was talking to us, to Mum, to himself.

Poor street lighting forced parts of the world outside the window into pitch darkness. There was not much traffic on the highway from the airport, mainly motorcycles and moto-taxis carrying one to four passengers plus luggage and goods. The streets narrowed, became bumpy, damaged with cracks and holes, then unpaved as we left the major roads and entered deep into the city. We drove past garage-like shops and around groups of people in outdoor bars conversing against the backdrop of loud televisions, mamans washing their pots after dinner in their front yard under the light of gas lamps, kids playing outside. And those looks. People's stares again. Even when they could hardly see who was inside the car, no one missed anything. Especially if it was an expensive-looking car. I recognised our street as we drove into it and approached the high walls encompassing our house. Green and white jagged glass topping the walls. A servant pushed opened the brown metal gate letting the car into the front yard. My younger siblings came out and stood on the veranda, Happiness, Mavie and Moon, holding the newborn Monique, lit by the outdoor light that gave the scene a sense of stillness that defied time. It was clear they had been waiting for us, six years older than the last time we met, their best clothes on for the occurrence, all clean and neat, like three well behaved kids that looked as if they were about to go to church. A strange glow in their eyes of awe, mixed expectations and contained joy.

Meeting up once again after all these years apart was indeed an incredible event for all of us. A very strange one. We had grown so distant from each other that we needed time to break the ice. We needed to acquaint once more with a boy whose feet had grown longer than mine. A girl I had only met a few days before moving to Italy. A six-year-old girl and a one-year-old baby we were meeting for the first time. No wonder we were all edgy. Something else also played a part in widening the gap between us. It was the deference Happiness, Moon and Mavie yielded to us, by keeping a degree of physical distance and talking only when necessary and submissively, due to a cultural convention that expects one to pay due respects to a person in a superior position, whether an employer, the parents, or the older siblings. I have to admit it pleased me, and I indulged a little in that rare, forgotten sense of being ranked higher to another being and not always taking the lowest place. Another thing emerging was that it was clear to us all from the very beginning that we had grown into two distinct sets of people, two groups within the same family, culturally, in the way we looked, in our behaviour. However, it seemed we were all equally high on something. Particularly Dad, who was getting more and more nervous. He opened beer cans one after the other, walked in and out of rooms assuring that all the plans he had made for the night were running as scheduled. Presentation was at the top of his list, although the guests were only his offspring. Everything was nicely set up, nothing left out of place; the house scrupulously neat, the large colour TV on, a brand-new looking hi-fi playing some Kassav music. A long L-shaped sofa lay against the wall. Photos of him, Mum, us at different stages of our childhoods in Congo and Benin hung on the walls. Wooden and ivory oblong statues. The scent of forgotten food perfumed the house all the way from the kitchen. We were led by our younger siblings into the kitchen and politely instructed we could get as many beverages as we wished from a fridge that was packed with all sorts of coloured fizzy drinks of patterns and brands I had never seen before. A second fridge was filled with food. And a whole bench-freezer too, packed with meat and fish and things wrapped in banana leaves. We got hold of our cans and strolled around the living room, killing the heat with our cold drinks with great satisfaction, entreating ourselves with the variety of people who had come to celebrate us. People I barely knew—families and our parents' close friends—everyone talking loud, with smiles, glimmering eyes that jumped from one of the European visitors to the other, abounding in commentaries and observations about how we had grown, how ridiculous it was that we looked the way we looked. There was stamping of feet on the floor, slapping of hands on thighs, teeth sucking, remarks of disbelief and perplexity towards everything that was being said. People I thought I was meeting for the first time but who remembered us all very well dove into memories that flooded into the room with waves of bright magnificent colours. Debra-Jo, Sigmund and Ocean, still familiar with Lingala, our mother's tongue, were able to engage in more adult conversations with the variety of members of our family. Chats switched from French, Lingala and poor Italian. Here and there, the booming of baritone chuckles. Barefoot servants in worn out T-shirts and traditional wraps served out the dinner, topped up our drinks, brought bowls of water to the table for us to wash our hands, and were sent out for an emergency run to the shop to buy some more baguettes. They would succeed in bringing that baguette even if the shops were closed at that hour of the night. The oldest servant was less than twenty. The youngest, a ten-year old boy from the block called Slim, was Happiness's friend. You'd catch sight of their heads popping out from a corner just to peek at the Italian guests and naughtily disappearing as soon as they were seen. You could only guess at the gossip taking place in the kitchen. Surely, the whole block had been informed about what was going on in the big walled house by now. *Les fils de René sont arrivés*!

After dinner, the party moved outside to the veranda. The thin column of smoke exhaling from the green mosquito repellent coils mingled with Dad's Marlboros. Whether he was being silent or amusing, he dominated the conversation somehow. Mum sat next to him, a far more passive participant. Relatives and friends challenged my older brothers and Debra-Jo by comparing Congolese pop culture with the Italian one. Football players. The Vatican. Lamborghini. Gianni Agnelli. Giorgio Armani. There was a lot of nostalgia among the crowd, lots of talks about accomplished tasks and those still waiting to be ticked off.

Meanwhile, things had evened out nicely between us twins and our younger siblings. The interplay between our sense of superiority and their deference that had kept us distant at the beginning of the night had faltered, giving way to a more genuine interaction. We were the same old bunch again. Stronger than the pull of time. Thirsty for each other. Redeso and I played with our new baby sister Monique, who was already crawling. Six-year-old Mavie had turned into a feminine little version of Dad. Moon was eight, laid-back and soft in manners. And Happiness, our brother, nine then, big round head like a watermelon, and wide, bright eyes, the same caring kid we had built wire cars with six years ago. It was all coming back, the time we used to spend together, chasing each other and shouting all over the house. The fights. The wild rides around our block. People used to call us the three twins.

'*Venez*,' he said at some point, his eyes motioning to the front gate as though there was a secret present waiting for us right behind that metal door. The three of us left the veranda, our family chatting, and walked outside the gate to the street. There were no presents behind the gate. I'm not sure if it was his intention to show us something or if we just misheard, but there was indeed something equally valuable waiting for us outside. As soon as I stepped out into the street, I felt for the first time since our arrival that I was really in Africa. There were no more barriers between me and my homeland. Not the floor of a vehicle underneath my feet and the boundaries of a cabin, nor the paved flooring of Dad's house, nor the collective mass of family mediating between me and Brazzaville. My feet stepped down right on the ground, the land where I was born, where the quality of the night felt different from the evening taking place within my house walls, where the sound of laughter reached us as if from far away. Here a more eloquent and terse narrative was at play within the silence and stillness offered by the world waiting right in front of me. Veiled in darkness was local life. I could make out faint presences in the middle of their evening chores. There were people socializing or simply quietly existing in the late night. They sat in front of their houses, on the other side of the street, and more people in both directions. The more I looked, the more I saw. A woman sweeping her front yard, her kids in pants playing at the edge of the lane, one of them naked, toddling by the foot of a mango tree. A group of girls chatting, one braiding the hair of a little one. They looked back at us as they carried out tasks. Some waved hello. Some said something to us in Lingala, a language Redeso and I had long forgotten or never learnt. Happiness answered on our behalf. An old man came forward, then a woman carrying a sleeping baby wrapped against her back and a man walking a rusty motorbike with some bags filled with goods secured with a few rounds of elastic rope. They questioned Happiness while they stared straight at us twins with no qualms, twilight of old memories showing in their eyes while nodding at Happiness's answers. They nodded in our direction as if to say, 'They have grown up... the twins... I see, well, all the family is there now.' Then someone said something in French directly to us and walked away. Things I forgot began to return in response to elements of the landscape and details about people that caught my attention. Fragments of memories surrendered to my needs and re-aligned before me as out of a breath of universal justice. My connection with it all. My deeds. My debts. I was able to remember, now, quite a lot of things. The woman who had just talked to Happiness and caressed my face and walked away, it turned out I knew who she was. I remembered walking with her when I was a child before we set sail to Italy. I remembered her bathing me and Redeso in a basin on the street, perhaps on the same spot where we stood now. I remembered the colour of the plastic basin. It was blue. I remembered those little details of my past in Congo only after she walked away. More memories were beginning to unfold from the oblivious growing and branching out, gaining in firmness and visual force. My granny, my maternal Maman Aminata, sitting on a stool chatting with a neighbour, with the same woman who was now sweeping her front yard. The woman was pregnant at the time and was smashing some food with a wood rod on a big wooden crusher. It was as if the ground beneath my feet had started to feed me. The things that were once mine had initiated the process of flowing back to their embryonic owner, rising up from underneath my feet through my vessels, as though, right on the spot where I stood, I was plugged into my primal source of power.

Everyone else was still asleep when Happiness and us twins woke the next morning. Judging from the quiet and the faint bluish morning light streaming inside, it was very early. It was Happiness who woke us up. He did so with no words, just tapping on our shoulders. We found him already halfway dressed. We got dressed too. Under that early morning light, our room looked more spartan than how it appeared the night before. It was minimally equipped with no other furniture than three foam mattresses placed on the floor, one beside the other to form a single bedding. A ceiling fan spun slowly above us. A jalousie window overlooked a part of the cemented backyard. A pair of geckos rested in complete stillness over the wall next to the window, then scuttled up to the ceiling to freeze again. A big stripy spider harmlessly hung on its web up on a corner. Happiness carried out his operation in complete silence as he got himself ready. We followed him across the quiet, sleepy house, through the living room and went outside to the front yard. We went down a small flight of stairs and reached the well at the other end of the courtyard. Happiness lifted the rusty metal lid away, let down a bucket to fetch some water and pulled it up by recoiling the rope. The sound of the rusty wheel squeaking and the rope pulling contrasted against the early morning silence. Birds and us, the only beings awake. When Happiness dipped his hands in the water and washed his face, I understood what we were there for. We washed our faces too, the water cold and invigorating. We washed our heads, necks, arms and arm pits, we brushed our teeth with a single toothbrush and a toothpaste that Happiness had got from a ledge next to the well and put it back there once we had finished. Once we had bathed, we were ready to start our day, so we went back inside to have breakfast in the kitchen with bread and butter and milk made out of condensed milk and water.

Happiness's autonomy on getting up at his own time, getting himself ready, and preparing his own breakfast without having to ask for any permission, showed how restrictive our lives really were in the institutions. We went outside again, this time into the street. Brazzaville was getting up. Residents, outside their houses, were washing their faces in basins, preparing their breakfasts on stoves under laminate roofs. Some had spent the night sleeping in hammocks outside their homes. People called out questions to Happiness as we passed. I remember a girl washing her hair in a basin, water poured on her head from a pot she held herself, face tilted to the side. She called Happiness to come across the street to her, more an order than a request, just because she wanted to see us close up. Others joined in from their homes or just stood afar participating in the discussion. Some smiling, some inexpressive, arms crossed, a leg tilted sideways, some shouted back and forth from different parts of the street. Here and there, Happiness translated between Lingala speakers and us. Some stranger would answer on our behalf. An old man invited us to come inside his house with an insistent gesture of his hand as we were walking past. We went in. A trail of kids poured in even though the invitation was restricted to us. They entered the humble house and sat on the floor with a surprising sense of entitlement, without having to justify themselves, or to ask for permission to be there, as if any house, or private happening, such as the return home from Europe of old neighbours, was an open and shared matter for the whole community. These kids were doing nothing more than carrying out their task as natural witnesses to local life. As they sat on the floor around us, they quietly recorded us being offered our second breakfast of the morning by the elderly man's wife. Again, condensed milk, bread and butter, and a slice of ham. A sleeping dog that had been previously pushed outdoors to make room for us had lazily crawled back in to reclaim his spot. An extra stool was recovered from behind a curtain. One of the witness-kids got sent on a mission by the old man to buy a bottle of orange juice and off he ran; he seriously ran to fulfil his task despite knowing that he would not get anything in return. He was neither annoyed nor did he challenge the request, but ran off committed as an athlete competing for a relay race at the Olympics. Who for? For the old man, for himself, for us? Who for?

Redeso and I met most of the neighbourhood in just one day. Principally, Happiness's circle of friends, the group of kids with whom we would spend the whole summer holiday. We hung out with them from morning to bedtime, playing football, marbles, building things out of waste material, cars made of wire with man-sized wheels set on a stick that was hooked as the front axle. You'd find us spending hours manufacturing full body armours made of cardboard boxes pieced together with disposed electrical wires and metal bullets for our slingshots, shaping them with pliers and hammer. And then we shot at cans and birds, and rolled down the street inside truck's tyres found around waste pits. We played a marbles game with bottle lids we collected from the road. Sprawled on the ground, watching some of our friends competing against each other with outstanding acrobatic stunts under the boiling sun that darkened our skins. Some of these kids were exceptional athletes, even some of the youngest were capable of competing in backflip contests with something like twenty to thirty backflips in a row like it was nothing. Seeing a perfectly executed somersault was commonplace. So was handstand walking for long distances. Some, like a kid nicknamed Péle, played football and juggled the ball as skilfully as a top football player. Every day was an adventure. Hard to forget all the exploration we did in our area by cruising across old ruins, wild bushes, sugar cane fields, markets, swamps, and slums, and merging with other local gangs. Some gangs made of fearless girls could send you on the run with a look after you witnessed them fighting. I remember one of these girls biting a nipple off a boy in a fight. We also hunted mice with traps made of tins and some elastic bands, and celebrated with ritual dances whenever we caught one and killed it, and skinned it and roasted it and shared the meat between us. One of those days, as we were out exploring the remains of an old church, its collapsed roof exposing the sky, we came across a small assembly of young girls and boys playing drums in the tall wild grass that had taken over the nave. There were about a dozen of these kids playing. It struck me, that day, to see this well-co-ordinated orchestra conducted by a boy who was barely sixteen. The kids drummed on empty oil barrels. Dusk had turned the sky orange. Our gang—with Slim, Péle and the other kids—sticks and slingshots in hands, bare feet, soiled up to our knees in dirt, some just in pants, stood in silence, watching the concert before us.

Gerard

It came more natural for my older siblings, Debra-Jo, Ocean and Sigmund, whose French had remained intact and were relatively fluent in Lingala, to adapt to our new reality. Dressed in tailored traditional suits our parents had purchased them, they blended with the locals. They were always out and about with friends and the adults of the family when not out visiting their mothers, their real mothers, Maman Chantal and Maman Natalie. Maman Chantal was Sigmund's and Moon's real mother, while the biological mother of Ocean, Debra-Jo, Lorenzo and Klaus was Maman Natalie. Both Mamans lived nearby, one managing a skin cream stall in Poto-Poto market, the other ran her own successful import-export business. Both mothers hadn't remarried since they broke up with Dad. They carried on living as single women, seemingly accepting another woman raising their children as a fact established by local traditions. Kids were seen as part of the indisputable assets of their father in many African cultures, they were expected to stay with him and be raised by his new partner, in this case my mother Maman Sofie, in the event of a separation. I noticed during those days that it was a difficult process for my siblings to acclimatise again with the mothers they never lived with or who never visited when we were in Italy. Certain things can't just be mended in a few shallow days out. No matter the good intentions, things had moved way too far for them to establish what could be termed a proper mother-child relationship. Whatever they tried to give to each other would bounce back as if from another planet, like dealing with malfunctioning devices. Or something in a tepid, disappointing, irreconcilable friendship. No surprise that Klaus would need convincing that Maman Natalie's concerns and recommendations about his tragic school performance were genuine, or that Lorenzo felt he was talking to the void when he shared his passion for music with his mother. I often heard my siblings say they felt closer to Maman Sofie than to their mothers. She was the person they called mum.

Tonton Martin was my uncle, my mother's younger brother, a generous and introspective student of law, with light reddish skin, lean and tall, often wearing a jumper or a shirt tucked inside a pair of plain cigarette jeans. Tonton Martin owned a red Suzuki Jimny Cabrio, in which he drove my older siblings around town for chores, tours, shopping, nights out and leisure trips to the seaside. He was central to my older siblings' social lives; whatever was up, Tonton Martin would bring it to them. It was at one of Tonton Martin's friends' parties that my siblings met Gerard, an old friend of Ocean's from primary school. Galvanised by such an unexpected reunion, the two old friends warmly hugged. Ocean then introduced Gerard to Sigmund and Debra-Jo. Gerard introduced them to his circle of friends saying, 'This is an old classmate of mine. They are the children of the *Man of the Shoes*. Les Europeans!' At these words people's attitudes changed immediately. Scenes of Parisian glamour sent signals down their optic nerves, along with stirring underground scenes and ever taller skyscrapers of London and Berlin. A dream for many of those young adults. They looked at my siblings as though they were the luckiest people in the world, imagining the life they enjoyed was extraordinary and rich, while downplaying the chances that you could have a miserable life even in Europe. You could be poorer than the average Congolese, be living under a bridge, or in institutions, get your clothes given by charity organisations, and have leftovers from army stock for meals. Of course, this would not have entered their minds. Just beauty and glitter. So much so that girls fell in love instantly with my brothers and were left intimidated by Debra-Jo. Men too were in awe of her. That was one of the effects of Debra-Jo. Gerard lowered his gaze down to the floor when he shook Debra-Jo's hand. He liked her straightaway, but discarded his own feelings from the start believing they were inappropriate. However, from that day, Gerard became a regular in my brother's circle and at our home. He was an interesting person, originally from Congo-Zaire, a football fanatic with an intellectual edge, often seen killing time with a book he carried with him everywhere in the back pocket of his jeans, an old, overused, B science fiction, *The Galactic* something. A very friendly guy, one of those guys who always had something in store for everybody. But aside from Debra-Jo, his favourite of us all was Klaus. He was fond of Klaus and seemed to be genuinely fascinated by his mind, by his curiosity. He was less restrained with Klaus and sitting with him at our front door, he could let himself go in political conversations, such as the fate of his country, conspiracy theories and mysterious local cultural beliefs such as voodoo. Klaus's thirst for knowledge indulged him perfectly, feeding his lecturer-like ego with plenty of naive questions. I remember overhearing at some point Gerard telling Klaus the unfortunate story of President Lumumba. While the story had no significant impact on me, it was compelling for Klaus, who was just two years older than me. There was always something not quite right that Klaus needed to shed light on.

'Why w-w-w-would the American and B-B-B-Belgian governments do s-s-s-something like that? Why Mo-mo-Mobuto turned against him?'

He couldn't make sense of the cruelty people were capable of committing, and listened with a mix of fascination and disdain to the details of Lumumba's killing. Lumumba was savagely beaten while in custody, beaten up when he was arrested, then while being transferred on the flight, and again soon after the flight landed. He was tortured and beaten again in a toilet, his blood on the fists and clothes of the militia and the civil servants who had him in custody. He was then driven to a clearing in the bush and shot in the head. Buried. Then unburied. Hacked into pieces. Thrown into an acid barrel. Klaus, absorbed by Gerard's account, tried to make sense, to reconcile life as he knew it where only criminals kill other people and psychotics do it with pleasure, to one where high-ranking officers in government acted upon Patrice Lumumba with the same degree of macabre insanity.

'Is there a-a-a-any difference be-be-between them and serial ki-ki-ki-killers?' I heard him asking. Were there people who were entitled to kill?—this is what Klaus actually meant. Was there a type of psychotic behaviour that was socially approved? How many deaths were these individuals accountable for?

With other people Gerard was different. He talked about more mundane things with nearly as much passion such as football, food, friends, girls. Yet when it came to Debra-Jo, Gerard's conversation with Ocean and Sigmund rose to a mystical level and was charged with religious metaphors. 'She's the word of God manifested into a woman,' or, 'Jesus's blood has fallen in abundance on her.' He would use passages of a gospel he knew by heart to stress his point. Nevertheless, he would never venture so far as to consider the remote possibility of dating her. I don't know why, if timidity, decency, or a complex of social inferiority prevented him, but the fact was that an affair with Debra-Jo was out of the question.

But Gerard had no idea that his love was reciprocal. Debra-Jo fancied him. Very much so indeed. A day trip to the seaside with Tonton Martin, a stroll in the market, a visit to one of Dad's acquaintances in some remote village, these were far more enjoyable for her when Gerard was part of the group. She would spend days daydreaming of a romantic life with Gerard in Brazzaville and in Italy, breathing him everywhere she went.

The day the two met alone eventually came. Debra-Jo, who was sent out to do chores at the market by Maman Sofie, bumped into Gerard on her way there. They talked for a little while on the street, then she invited him to come with her to the market. So they made their way to Poto-Poto market together, walked among stalls of smoked fish, dry beans, jars of colourful candy balls and bars of edible earth. Past stalls of cackling chickens hanging head down from high up rods and piles of yam, bags of gari and fu-fu and stalls of clothes, wraps, and cosmetics. Gerard negotiated the price of the skin cream Maman Sofie had sent Debra-Jo for, and once they were done, as they came out of the market, they found themselves walking further away from home rather than going back, until they reached another area and a small house he introduced as his own, inviting her in for he wanted to show her some posters of Italian football players he cherished. She accepted the invitation.

The single-storey house Gerard shared with an older brother was surprisingly big for just two people. And the space inside intrigued her furthermore. It was empty, missing all those common characteristics that to Debra-Jo, made a house a home. There was no furniture, nor doors nor windows but just crude openings in the walls, presumably left unfinished during construction for shortage of funding. The two dwellers didn't even bother putting up curtains to compensate; they just left it as it was, with no barriers separating them from the outside world. The flooring was an extension of the dirt soil that lay outside. A few stools were placed in some key locations and a small camp gas stove on a corner of what was meant to serve as a kitchen, next to a few pots aligned on the floor. The boy led her to his room that was as poorly equipped as the rest of the house, just a mattress on the floor and a stool over which some clothes lay carefully folded. He showed her several posters of his favourite football players hanging on the walls of a room. But rather than paying attention to the posters, which were scant as well, Debra-Jo got lost in the sensorial experience of how the course of time changed from culture to culture. She imagined him sitting on the bed reading some of the overused books and magazines he had piled in a corner, and wondered if there were any other ways to kill time in such an empty house. And to think that this had been her reality once—Brazzaville—visiting friends in houses like this one. Gerard's African reality she had never questioned when she lived there, but now it was so alien.

As she focused on the images stuck on the walls surrounding her, she realised Gerard had a serious passion for Italy. Among the posters of Italian football players were posters of the Coliseum, the Leaning Tower of Pisa, and one of Pope John II.

'I saw this guy once,' she said, pointing a loose finger at the Pope. 'He came to my town a couple of years ago.'

'You're kidding, you saw the Pope?'

'Yes, I told you!'

'Debra-Jo!' he called her still in doubt. 'Did you really see him?'

'Yes, I did.'

'*Mon dieu, c'est incroyable*, you saw the Pope in the flesh. Tell me, how far were you?'

'Wow, you sure get heated up with things. We just saw a man!'

'A man? Did you just call the Pope just a man? You're a strange person, Debra-Jo, how can you say such things! Are saints just men? Was Jesus just a man?'

Still in disbelief, Gerard led her back to the main room where he prepared two cups of condensed milk and cocoa powder with water he poured out from a five-litre jerrycan. They then went outside to sit, the neighbouring house was a few feet away. There was a mango tree in the courtyard to which was attached one end of a hammock, the other clung to a hook on the house wall. A guy lay on it, swinging lightly. It was still very hot in the late afternoon. Not even a slight breeze. Her thoughts shifted to Sister Gaudenzia in Italy. She imagined her walking across the front yard of the institution, right by the swing. Her long fingers brushing locks of rebellious black hair back into the veil as usual. Who knew how the Oasis girls were doing. She found herself feeling uncomfortable with herself, somewhat guilty about thinking of the girls and the Oasis as home. A month had nearly passed since she arrived here in Brazzaville, but she couldn't really distinguish anymore where was home. When she was there, she missed Africa. And now that she was in Africa, she missed Italy. How strange. She should have been home by now with the shopping for Maman Sofie. She had no time restrictions though. And it was nice here, under the shade, with Gerard. She really liked him, although she found him a bit too cloying.

'You need to be careful about what you say, Debra-Jo,' he said. 'If people hear you talking about the Pope in these terms they'll form a bad opinion of you.'

She chuckled out loud. 'What can he do that we can't do? Does he have any superpowers! I'm sure I run faster than him!'

'I see, Debra-Jo! Now you're just being provocative.'

The tones were light now. He too had softened under Debra Jo's influence. He smiled perfectly shaped white teeth as he shook his head, incredulous at Debra-Jo's irreverence. He brought the cup to his lips.

'How do you like Italy?' he asked.

'I like it, but you know, sometimes I don't even know what it truly means to like something. I feel I have some problems telling the difference between what's nice from what isn't. Do I make any sense? Differences between things. There are days where I don't see any difference between people. People and animal, animal and plants. No difference between my little sister and… and you.'

Gerard looked at her puzzled. 'What do you mean? You shock me, today, Debra-Jo! How can you compare me with your little sister? Do you really feel the same for me and your little sister?'

'I don't know.'

'Don't you feel anything for me?'

'For you… Yes… I do feel something.'

'You don't know?'

'Of course I know.'

'No, you don't.' At this point something shifted in the soul of the boy. A nagging fear had settled in as he waited for confirmations.

'I mean, I do, I do love you,' she said.

'Then prove it.'

Without giving it a second thought, Debra-Jo came close to him, held his hand, and gave him a kiss on the mouth, a kiss that enraptured him as though God had just opened the gates of Heaven before him. Then she waited for him to lean over to kiss her lips in return. Gerard was the first person Debra-Jo ever kissed. He kissed her again. He worked his lips on hers until he realised something was not quite right, she was not responding as he expected. Therefore, timidly, worried, ashamed, he pulled his face away from hers. Debra-Jo also felt disappointed and surprised by her own reaction. She hated it, to be kissed by Gerard, with absolute certainty. In fact, she felt like she had just kissed the lips of a dead man and was now holding a cold piece of meat instead of the hand of the boy she had been dreaming about. She stood still, looking at him in the eyes with an impassive stare as he tried a last desperate attempt. Then Gerard hopped up, the cup of milk chocolate in his hand.

'You don't like me, right?' he said. 'Why didn't you say so?'

'I didn't know,' she said. 'I'm sorry.'

Gerard kept on visiting us in the days that followed. He also continued to be part of Tonton Martin's Suzuki expeditions. Yet Debra-Jo stopped coming on the trips when she knew Gerard would be there. Gradually, the presence of broken-hearted Gerard in our house diminished. Life carried on. Long warm days flew by, each of us absorbed in our own experiences and perceptions of Africa, whether alone, or with others. My sister Mavie scuttled around the house to call everybody out to the veranda to witness to the occurrence of baby Monique taking her first steps on a scorching afternoon. The little girl toddled up to Debra-Jo who grabbed her before she could fall and lifted her up in the air and prized her with a twirl. Dad too came to witness briefly. Prominent beer belly pushing out of the open shirt, he observed the scene with dimmed enthusiasm before he eclipsed back to his room soon after the show was over. The *Man of the Shoes* was rarely seen around. When he wasn't out for work, he stayed locked all day in his room keeping up with his administrative job and writing down business plans under the silent spin of the ceiling fan. I'd catch sight of him only when he briskly left his room and walked across the house and went out to the veranda to just throw a vacuous glance around to whoever was there, to whatever was on, always with an eye on his own business ideas, then he grabbed a mango from one of our fruit trees and shuffled along in flip-flops back into his room.

Things were not going as smoothly as they used to for my father. He had fallen into a hefty number of debts as a result of a series of failed business deals he had incurred over the past years. We were technically bankrupt that summer. But my siblings and I had no idea that we were living beyond our means; everything looked fine from the outside. We had plenty of food, cold and hot water flowed through the pipes, the drains worked. We had a bathtub that was as big as a pool which we filled occasionally. We had the gas cylinders replaced in the kitchen every couple of weeks. We had cars, servants, domestic appliances, plus Dad's optimism, his humorous disposition, his megalomaniac complex.

One day he called us all inside the house for a family meeting. We ran around the house and out on the street calling out for each other, 'Hey, Dad wants you in!' We gathered in the living room, around a dining table, around Dad, encircling him. He was the only one sitting. More than a meeting, which would imply a group of people discussing a communal matter, René's meeting consisted of him demanding absolute attention to something he wanted to show us. And that was our house plan. He pulled a big roll of paper sheets out of a tube, unrolled them over the table, pinned them down with both hands, and kept them flat over the edges like a ship captain over a treasure map about to announce an important discovery. He glared at each of us before turning the pages, explaining the meaning behind those intricate geometrical figures in detail. He made a brief interruption to solemnly stare at each of us to ascertain whether we were all following. It was not every day you got to see Dad so zealous about something, especially something involving us, but we all could see the reason. With that monumental house plan, that might have represented the work of several professionals and months of planning, Dad wanted to demonstrate we had not waited in vain all those years of institutional life. That he had put an awful amount of work into the one project that was to culminate into a physical residence for us all. He had shed six years of sweat just for us. 'This is going to be Debra-Jo's bedroom,' he pointed at. 'Ocean will sleep here. This is the third toilet. The swimming pool is going to be built here. We're going to have a servant lodge just beside the kitchen.' It was no doubt an impressive piece of work. Beautiful to look at, rich in detail, and it may also have been the case that those well delivered geometrical figures revealed something wider and more complex than just a house, something that only Dad was able see, probably the ultimate solution for all our problems, a cure for the insecurity, the anxiety, the insomnia, the low self-esteem that were silently germinating within each of us during all those years of institutional life. Perhaps Dad was able to see the consequences of their sudden departure from Italy: life in the clinic, Masambila's abuse, the sleeping in crowded dormitories, the cars and the motorbikes he had promised, the house in Italy that was always underway according to Mum's visits. Apparently, the solution to all these problems, the consequences of their departure from Europe, was hidden somewhere in this architectural draft.

However hard we tried to decipher the lines and shapes, nodding in acquiescence, it did not assuage a growing feeling that there was something even worse than being abandoned, and it was this: the idea that we were abandoned for things like these pieces of paper, for Dad's dreams. It was a hard task to understand how Dad's brain worked during that meeting. Were we all thinking the same thing? Was Dad missing a crucial detail? Where was the house he was showing us meant to be built? In Italy, in Congo, in Benin or in a legendary place? And why did he leave us in the first place? Why did he never lift his ass from that chair and come to visit us in Italy in all these years? This ongoing condition of being kept on hold, picked up and dropped off again fed us with illusions. Abandonment should be clear cut. You should know that you are alone and what is in store for you. You should gain an emotional freedom that allows you to picture your future in the way you want. You're not waiting for any miracles. You had already long chewed and swallowed the fact that some incidents at some point in your past, that you don't necessarily need to know about, had severed your relationship with your parents and amen, you put a cross on it, you were bestowed of an amazing, meteoric, once-in-a-lifetime opportunity: to give up hope. You can take the fact itself as axiomatic, knowing that shit is shit is to set yourself in a state of liberation. It's universally true of the opposite: that not knowing why we were left living that way, and how far we could rely on our parents, were indeed keeping us emotionally chained to a pile of fantasies. A perfect recipe to wear us out in the long term.

I'm sure my siblings felt the same, but nobody dared to question our father. We didn't dare bring up all the other unresolved issues we had been complaining about back in Italy. Not just because whatever was coming out of René's mouth ought to be right, but also, I suppose, because there was no point trying get things straight with him. I mean, it was right on the table, the proof, while he was proudly leading us through his plans, that whatever answer we'd receive would be disappointing. Besides, the truth here, at the end of the day, was that we didn't want to spoil that precious picture of an African family unity that Dad's house planning implied by spitting out a load of bitter and boring, unnecessary complaints. In fact, we all wanted to go

GROUND

back to Italy with a good memory of that summer over anything else. So, after the meeting was over, we didn't bother to comment about it, we just went back to our own businesses.

At the end of August, in view of Debra-Jo's eighteenth birthday, Dad had a cow delivered to our house. A living cow. The poor thing was delivered by a man dressed only in shorts and sandals. On seeing him leading the cow on a rope from far down the road, I paused in confusion while playing with friends at our front door. Until he reached us, walked through the main gate, tightened the rope around a mango tree in our yard like Clint Eastwood would have done with his horse, and went off again leaving the cow there for a few hours. We named the cow Daisy and played on and off with it throughout the morning, until the man made his way back carrying some butcher's tools attached to his belt. He took his sandals off, washed his face and his hands over a plastic washbowl my mother had provided him and got on with the work. He placed an empty bucket under the beast's neck, slit its throat with a knife. In a few hours, Daisy's head was the only thing left on the ground by the mango tree. The blood she left on the ground was partially absorbed by the soil and washed away by the butcher and the servants with buckets of water and the work of brushes. By evening, the beast had been butchered into a large amount of meat cuts. Several trays were piled high with chunks of meat soaked in fresh blood that took up all the space in the kitchen. The butcher and the servants, including our friend Slim, made a fire in the backyard as the night approached. They all worked in synergy to grill the meat and serve us supper.

Many people came to Debra-Jo's celebration, most of the people we spent the summer with: the kids from our gang, Tonton Martin and his friends, including Gerard, uncles, nieces, cousins, Maman Chantal, Maman Natalie, Maman Sofie and Dad's friends. It was a beautiful, melancholic and sublimely meat-tasty night. The firelight glowed on us. Fizzy drinks and beers were opened and drunk, and our meat-chewing brought about more sound than any conversation. It felt as if we had come full circle. From starting the holiday as a broken family, we were now ending it bathed by a deep, reassuring and warm sense of communion which seemed to set up the foundation for stronger bonds ahead. Everything suggested we were more motivated to keep in touch from now on, with more regular visits to Congo, to Italy, more phone calls, and we pledged to start writing letters to each other, to be more receptive. With that night we closed our summer in Africa.

A few days later we would pack our belongings to return to Italy. I remember my little brother Happiness. I remember him emulating us during the preparation for the trip. Firmly convinced he was to fly to Italy with us, the boy filled up his own suitcase with clothes he hastily pulled out from his drawer. There was such determination to his actions that I did believe Dad had booked him a place in St Theresa for the poor guy.

Finely dressed from tip to toe for the trip, he carried his own suitcase out on the street and loaded it in the car along with ours. He kissed his younger sisters and friends goodbye no less than we did, and took his place in the car with us. He jumped out of the car and grabbed his suitcase once we reached the airport. It was only when he tried to pass security with us that Dad realised what the boy had in mind. Perhaps he thought Happiness was just helping us with our luggage all along.

'Hey, where you think you're going?' he asked him as he grabbed the back of his shirt and prevented him from entering the security line. 'Your place is here, don't be silly!'

I felt sorry for him. Sorry for us in general upon realising there was always a barrier of one sort or another in our lives. Whether it was a tangible border or distance. It felt too sudden to say goodbye in that way after a whole long summer spent together. To get to the point of standing on one side of security while they stood on the other, waving, this was a poor way to say goodbye, especially to the boy who had put so much effort into preparing his own suitcase and who had carefully selected his best outfit for the purpose of a voyage in Italy.

PART II

LONDON, PRESENT DAY
IV

This troubled East Londoner starts talking to me while we're both in the queue at the counter of Lower Clapton General Practice.

'I wonder how Cameron feels, having unleashed this hell in this fucking country. As if we didn't already have enough shit going on. Just because he was scared of his own party and the power UKIP was gaining. Fuck him, man. Now look where we are? Nobody took to the streets asking for his fucking referendum. I didn't give a shit about this fucking referendum! Do you ever remember people on the streets protesting to get out of the EU? No. But still this fucking referendum was set. Now that ordinary people are actually taking to the streets asking for a second referendum, the politicians don't want to listen. Fucking idiots! Why? Because the machine has a life of its own? Is it the wire vomiting out population trends? Is it the exploitation of fear, the market, geological developments within an economic cycle, fucking climate change, Facebook, fake news, populist leaders' mastery at channelling people's rage against the establishment? Is it because British people struggle with their national pride, the flip side to politeness and political correctness shit, the huge European bills and its technocratic authority, the wobbly NHS, the wage gap, fucked up social mobility, Cambridge Analytica's algorithm, Trumpism, Islamophobia, the sex drive of Syrian refugees... I don't know, the fear of having Italian and Polish taught in primary school instead of French and Spanish?'

What the hell to say to this guy. I don't give a shit either way about the referendum. I'm not British. And today I'm not even particularly keen to be a European boy either. Deal with it yourself, man. Deal with your divorce yourselves, guys, I woke up on the African side of the bed this morning. I feel Congolese throughout the morning, Beninese in the afternoon. Let me fucking be, man. I just want to read my book. English queues are known for being excellent places to read books because everyone minds their fucking business and right behind me, I find a guy who's the exception to the rule. Of course I don't tell him any of this. I just answer, 'Yeah, it sucks, let's hope for Jeremy Corbyn.'

We move one step forward and the guy rebukes, 'Who the fuck is Boris Johnson! Who the fuck is this guy. Politicians should get five years in jail each time they support their campaign with fake claims shit. The problem wasn't Cameron, mate, he was just some poor bloke who tried his luck and fucked up. But fucking Johnson and Gove, mate, those two are the fucking cause of this mess. If they had put true information out there, you'd see how many less votes they'd get! I wouldn't mind getting them hanged if there were laws that made sense in this fucking country, those fucking bustards! And now there is this lady, oh my!'

Then he got heated up with one of the women at the counter who was putting skin cream on her face instead of calling for the next person in queue. 'Hey, this is not a duty fucking free shop!' and a quarrel started with the woman, and then with the manager, about watch your language, rudeness, staff abuse and so on until, fed up, the guy decided to give up on 'the fucking NHS.'

Whether it was this person or another medium, you just can't avoid the ubiquity of the Brexit saga. It's on your phone, laptop, on supermarket shelves, on the Tube and the buses, in people's conversations in pubs and dinner parties. All you hear is that the country fell in deep shit soon after the referendum. The pound has gone down. Lot of businesses are shitting themselves at the prospect of losing their frictionless borders with the largest market in the world. There are plans for stockpiling medicines and food in case of a no deal departure. The Ministry of Defence warn that they are getting ready to dispatch food with jets and to use the army to carry out various civil functions in case of an emergency and that everyone will be poorer and terrorism will flare back up in Ireland. I read about civil arrest predictions, days-long traffic jams with thousands of lorries at the borders as if we were nearing the Armageddon. I haven't made my mind up yet whether it is better for these guys to leave the bloc or stay. I see nothing wrong in the fact that a country wants to reclaim its own sovereignty and to resist the coercive hold of a punitive secretive supra-national state, but European commission authoritarianism wasn't at the centre of the referendum campaign. The focus of the debate was on immigration. I remember awakening in a brand new place in the aftermath of the referendum. The country was unusually quiet. The quietness of a nation in shock. Everyone was stunned. TV presenters went through the news routine with a sense of foreboding. Politicians, even the winners of the Brexit saga and major leave campaigners like Boris Johnson, took pride in the referendum results while discoursing with croaky voices, looking into the camera, dazed and gripped by fear and a sense of shame for what just happened. Did we just do this? an entire country seemed to be asking. Is this us? Is this the UK? I remember the number of leave voters immediately regretting their vote; some interviewed on the news burst out in tears saying, 'I had no idea something like this could happen in my country! I voted Leave because I was certain we would never leave. This is awful!' Everyone seemed unsettled at seeing how far off an anti-immigration campaign had taken them. At witnessing how fear can persuade a nation into making choices they didn't want to. Fear of the presence of people like you and I in their country.

They say they are fed up with us—immigrants, refugees, asylum seekers from Europe, India, Africa, whatever. We steal their jobs, we drain their coffers with our benefit claims. We bring and force customs and religions that are noxious to them. Us who had once feared for Hackney's gentrification, it turns out, we are the invaders on a bigger scale, the hidden force behind this Brexit crisis. Although we like to think of ourselves as people from Hackney, we have no territorial right on it whatsoever. Brexit was epiphanic for me, it opened my eyes to the fact that we have never been part of the old, or transitional, or new Hackney. We are foreigners full stop. You from Porto, me from Brazzaville.

Two days after the GP in Lower Clapton, I find myself at Gatwick Airport. It's night, nicely warm. I get a luggage trolley for the kids to kill time with while we wait for my mother to come out of the arrival exit. The screen shows that her flight from Bordeaux has just landed at 10 p.m. I roll up an *Evening Standard* that for some obscure reason I'm still holding from the train journey here and scratch my head with it. The kids, tired and bored from the hour and a half journey from Clapton to Gatwick, are long past their usual bedtime, and waiting here, they play in a mood verging on hysteria, although little April looks quite sleepy still, and Bernardo always manages to act responsibly with her even when he plays rough. You know him—always thoughtful. Since Ella and I broke up, he has been taking care of April outstandingly; they never argue, never fight, she trusts him. Now that he is giving her a ride on the trolley, she stares unsure of why she's here at this time of night, being pushed around on a trolley in this unfamiliar place, despite the fact that both my son and I have explained it to her more than a few times. 'We're here to collet your granny, do you remember her?' She can't. She was just a baby when my mother held her last. She has grown up believing that she only has her maternal granny. The idea of another granny, probably black, who'll emerge at any time from a gate in this unusual place, may still represent a cryptic concept to her little mind. Whereas the boy is fully aware. He has met Maman Sofie four times in the space of ten years, establishing with her something close to a familial relationship. When I told him she was coming, he got surprisingly excited, that shallow excitement you can read in kids who have a propensity to be kind.

There is not much of a crowd in the airport tonight. I am about to go and grab some snacks at the nearby Costa Café when my mother emerges with the first round of passengers pouring out of the arrival exit. Wearing a pair of jeans, espadrilles and a light jersey, pulling a cabin case, the 60-year-old woman looks nearly my age. She greets us with one of her bright smiles as she walks towards us. I walk in her direction. This brief walk is the epitome of our relationship. Walking towards each other from the opposite sides of a border. It's our lifelong ritual. Every family has its traditions, like having dinner at the same table, or watching TV together. But our tradition, Mum and I, is this encounter in a *zona di confine*. It has occurred countless times, for four decades. In Congo, in Benin, in Italy, in Bordeaux, in England, at the gate of the villa in Italy, at the gate of the institutions, and the foster home, at Bologna's Marconi Airport, Maya-Maya in Brazzaville, Cadjehoun in Benin, and Heathrow, Stansted and Gatwick airports, outside her many houses and my many houses, this is what my mother and I do from time to time, we meet somewhere and hug. And we're aware of being travelling mates, more than being related, both now standing on the ground of a foreign country, miles away from home. Aware of the time lag and all the things that have gone on between our meetings, of the joy and the pain, the old and the new, the quests and the challenges that life has set up for us during this time of separation. We hug and stare at each other as if to say, *Long time no see!* We give each other a pat on the shoulder. Her eyes get wet. I smile like a 40-year-old son does. I always realise, whenever we meet, that I am expecting someone else, someone similar to her but not exactly the same person who I hold in my arms. I never manage to anticipate what it will be like, until I feel that I'm actually happy, very happy to see her. The kids wait next to us. 'Bernardo!' she remarks with a French accent, hugging my son, '*Come stai?*'

'*Bene!*' he answers in Italian with the English accent and his benevolent smile. I'm surprised to see that kids that age and size are actually able to perform a comprehensive hug in a grown-up manner.

'And this is April!'

'Yes, this is April,' the boy confirms. 'April, say hello to granny, *dai*!'

Unlike her brother, April has to be pushed towards her granny, looks at her at a loss and stands in silence.

'Little April-April! *Tu sei* so beautiful!' she says with in an Italo-American that seemed inspired by a Scorsese film 'Do you remember me? Maman Sofie! *Sono la tua nonna*! Your grandmother!'

'She doesn't, she was too small,' I say in French. Three generations and three different languages. The mother tongue languages of my direct kinship—my kids' English and my mother's French—are foreign languages to me, as much as my main language, Italian, is foreign to these three. We don't have a common language between us and I get lost in translation with my kids and my mother and they get lost in translation together. I reassure April that all is fine with one of our secret expressions as we head away from the arrival gates, me pulling my mother's suitcase, she carrying April on her hip like a trophy. The living proof that her lineage has conquered the UK with another outstanding mixed-race picket stuck into the island soil. She has them spread all over Europe. In Italy, France, Germany, England. The whole lot of grandchildren who make her walk through airports with dignity and pride for some of the incredible things she has managed to achieve in life. For the dimension her family has taken since the time she was a young student in Brazzaville to the present, where she has made ends meet by working as a nanny in Bordeaux for the last ten years, where she enjoys the benefits of being a relatively new French citizen and her devotion to God.

We get a Gatwick express for the journey back home. At this point, April has found her seat as far away as possible from my mother on the farthest end of the row of three seats in front of us, finding shelter next to her brother. Both have lost interest in the African granny. Bernardo, tired of standing in between translations and jerky dialogues, has stopped playing the happy, polite kid with her. Both have chosen to overtly ignore their granny and rather close down into their own worlds of sleepiness and comfortable conversations. My mother seems hurt, judging from how vehemently she insists they become more engaged with her in one way or another. I weigh up whether to intervene in her favour, then choose to stay out of it. At some point she gives up, and the peace which emerges as she lies back, focussing instead on the landscape outside the window, comes as a relief.

I feel faintly anxious. Even with my mother. What's happening to me, suffering from anxiety at forty?

'Redesof,' she says. 'How are things with their mother?'

'We're good. We manage the kids as a shared enterprise. We try to help each other out when we need time off, but apart from that we have grown apart. We are like strangers to each other.'

'I see,' she says looking back away, slightly concerned. 'God is going to open all doors in your life! And the job, is your business going well?'

'Yeah, not bad. How are Mavie and Monique?' I ask her, aiming to divert the focus of the conversation away from me. My two little sisters, now two married women each with a pair of kids. Both live in Bordeaux, too. They have spent all their lives together with Mum, in Africa, then in the north of France, and now in Bordeaux.

'They are well. Monique had her contract renewed with the cell-phone company. Mavie is taking an IT course; I told you she needed to get it done if she wants to get a job anywhere nowadays. Your brother Happiness has offered to help her through, but I don't know how much he can do from Berlin. He has to manage a big IT company himself now, did he tell you?'

'Yeah, you and him told me he just got this place.'

'Let's hope they keep him. I don't want any of my kids to regress. You will all have great positions in life. God will do it! Have you heard from Redeso?'

'It's been a while, actually.'

'Oh well, we'll call him when we arrive.'

My mother's line of inquiry didn't include the other part of the family, my other brothers and sisters. This is because things have changed over the years, the relationship has soured between them all, beginning fifteen years ago when my mother emerged from nearly ten years of silence, after enduring some dramatic changes, including a divorce, a struggle to survive two civil wars in Congo-Brazzaville and the country's downfall into poverty and famine. The questions I'm intending to ask her for my book grow in my mind as the train rolls past fields and approaches the crowded landscape of London, with rows of Victorian brick-work houses, council estates, warehouses and tower blocks. I know I need to be cautious. She is very susceptible to feeling down when she thinks about her past. She has said several times she gets depressed about it. I look at my kids who have fallen asleep over each other and think about Redeso.

Mr P

Redeso and I were baptised when we were twelve in San Cassiano, Imola's cathedral in Piazza del Duomo, in 1988. A large number of people attended the ceremony; the church was packed. Not because Redeso and I were popular, but rather because the ceremony fell on Easter Sunday and was incorporated into the Easter mass, a very popular celebration led by Imola's bishop. And also because it was not every day in Imola you could witness someone having a late baptism, and that those someones were twins and were black, and quite possibly a conversion from Islam, Animism or whatever other pagan religion these kids belonged to. The event struck the local faithful deeply and proved to them these African twins, who God had personally entrusted to the hands of the magnanimous Congregations of St Theresa, were now entering their Catholic family. The hall was crammed. The first rows were taken by people from St Theresa, St Catherina and Oasis, including our siblings. There were also people from our parish, nuns from the Congregation of St Theresa of the Child Jesus and people that we had met along the way, such as several of our classmates and their parents. Two pairs of our classmates' parents were our godmothers and godfathers; one pair stood on my side of the altar, the other at Redeso's. Two nuns stood by our side, playing the role of our parents.

'Redeso and Redesof,' the Bishop said. 'It is with great joy that our Christian community welcomes you. In its name I bless you with the sign of the cross. And after me, you too, parents, godmothers and godfathers, you will do the sign of the Saviour over your child.'

So they did. Then one of the altar boys, a kid from St Catherina, held a basin of holy water underneath our heads one at a time. The Bishop collected the water with a special silver spoon and poured it three times over our heads tilted sideway over the basins. 'I baptize you in the name of the Father, the Son and the Holy Spirit.' The other helper held a pair of white vests for us to wear now that we were immaculate souls and stripped of sin. He handed one to me and one to Redeso. The entire hall fell to a silence of pathos as we put them on. The white tunic. Our faces demure like two black angels, in the full belief that something celestial had descended upon us. A sense of lightness replaced the heaviness and washed away the dirt we had carried from the past.

'You have become new beings,' the bishop explained. 'And you have been dressed in Christ. This white dress will be the sign of your newly acquired dignity. With the support of the world and example of your loved ones, wear it without stain for eternal life.'

***

We tried. Yes, we tried hard to wear it without stain soon after the ceremony and in the following days, holding inside us that sense of purity and holiness we had just gained. We were Christians now. So we acted differently. We talked gently. Walked at a slower pace than usual. Didn't gesticulate as much as before when we talked. Didn't play games that would involve us getting dirty, like football, or playing marbles on the floor. Even at the table, we ate with manners, aware that God was sitting in between us. I felt that everything had aligned in my life as if I had gained a purpose. I felt protected, well rooted in firm ground.

Then, a week from that day, we were given the news. Sister Domenica told us that we had outgrown St Theresa and it was time that we moved to St Catherina. The cold way our departure from

St Theresa was announced was indicative of our ad hoc collocation in life, with Sister Domenica notifying Redeso and me right under the bright white neon light of the main bathroom where we had just washed our hands before lunch, the same bathroom that at night and in morning was full of adults and kids washing side by side, but now was empty except for us three, and I felt all the holiness I had just recently gained pouring out of me all at once and forming a pool of light on the toilet's floor. I remember looking at the long series of sinks set at different heights lined against the walls. Three toilet rooms with bathtubs and latrines on one side. On the other, a large wooden shelving unit filled with all the residents' shoes, each cell labelled with a resident's name, and then looking at Sister Domenica's tiny black moccasins, her small hands clasped at pelvis level.

'You can come and visit us whenever you want, you know?' she said.

'Yes,' we said.

'I'm sorry, twins,' she added.

'We had a good ride though!' said Redeso.

A corner of her mouth twitched as though she had to restrain herself from smiling, but she also had misgivings about our departure. After all, we had been six years under her care. I had no troubles believing that she had developed some feelings towards us along the way as we did for her. But she had to keep a straight face, which came easy to her, considering the number of times she had repeated this ceremony, in different spots around the institution, in a bedroom, in the hall, in the playroom, nearly every week there was someone who needed to be relocated and a new face to be welcomed. She was both a mother of a multitude and a mother to none. She wore the edge of her veil tight against her head so you could see it moving faintly with the pulse of the artery in her temple, a woman who had ultimately no voice over the true course of our lives. She had given us all she could, now the onus lay in somebody else's lap.

***

Sister Domenica gave us a ride to St Catherina the following day in a navy blue Fiat Cinquecento that belonged to the institution. She parked outside the main gates, opened the trunk to unload our bags. The morning sun cast three long shadows over the street as we headed to the main entrance carrying our luggage on that autumn day. The front door opened to a silent reception hall. A boy sat behind a sturdy old desk, bent over a puzzle book, while working a receptionist shift handling phone calls and visitors. We knew him already as he was Sigmund's roommate, also the goalkeeper of the football team at St Catherina called Fulvio. Knowing why we were there, he rose from the chair and walked across the tiled floor and disappeared behind a door. He returned five minutes later followed by Mr P, the assistant manager, a towering man from Eritrea. Mr P had a few words with the nun. Then she gave him a paper docket about us that I had never seen before. I now believe it carried documents about us—identification, legal papers from school, from the registry office, the police station, social services and health care, documenting our lives in Italy and giving an account of our lives since the night of the fire.

'Right, twins,' the nun said, the same straight face she carried in the main bathroom in St Theresa. 'I must go now. I leave you under the care of this gentlemen.'

'Ok,' we said.

'Remember to say the prayers.'

'We will.'

'Good luck.'

She pushed opened the front door with two hands, letting in a beam of sunlight that ran across the pavement and up over the wall behind her. And the tiny black shoes disappeared out of sight.

GROUND

***

Mr P led us to our room as he had done with my older brothers some years ago when they first moved in. The only difference was that this time he had little to show us since we knew the place as well as our pockets after all our visits. We were also very familiar with all the residents, including Mr P himself. The only difference was an intangible one. The confident and outgoing attitude we had when visiting was replaced by shyness now that we were to become a part of the community. I put my bag on my bed to start undoing it, with Mr P's voice in the background going over relevant information mixed in with random talking. I had a blue gym bag for luggage. Sister Domenica had sorted it and packed it up for me. Inside was little more than the essentials for a short-term holiday, a set of four shirts, three or four pairs of trousers, a couple of jumpers and some underwear and some extra junk I chose myself, such as a small radio I was given by a benefactor for Christmas, a pack of batteries, a walkie-talkie, my plastic Velcro wallet, and the golden necklace with my name on it my mother gave me last time we went to Africa. That was all I needed. No matter the number of times I moved house, I knew I should have been used to it, but when I undid my bag for the first time in my new bedroom, that action, opening the zip of the bag, pulling out the first line of clothes, triggered a mild sense of defeat in me. I looked at my brother standing in one corner of the room, gazing outside the window. The window was secured by a metal grid. The view, over the wall of another building, overlooked a quiet road, two storeys below. Redeso looked just as lost but also resigned.

Mr P assigned two free beds to us and also assigned us a wardrobe each, a thin metal storage space unit like the ones you see in some army dormitory. We were given a pair of new padlocks to lock our wardrobes, and a set of keys each, a toiletry case with personal toothpaste, a toothbrush, soap, a towel and a personal toilet roll.

'Ask the supervisor on shift for another roll when you've done with this,' Mr P said. 'No cartons in the loo but in the bin. For a refill, anything you need, just ask the supervisor. Dirty clothes and towels, you chuck them in the hole. But try to keep them clean for at least a week.'

The hole he referred to was a big hole, the radius of an arm, set on the wall of the bathrooms of each floor that tunnelled down to the institution's laundry. As for keeping clothes clean for a week, this was an easy task in that St Catherina had a strict clothing policy that made it mandatory for all residents under school age to get changed into tracksuits as soon as they were back from school.

'Well, if you have no questions, I'm happy to leave you to it. Enjoy your stay!' said Mr P before walking out. I was glad he left. I opened my locker and peered inside at the newly emptied space and began filling it up with my things. Redeso sat on the bed, shifting his attention between details of the room and me, his bag still closed.

'This bed is quite good,' he said.

'Is it?'

'Yes, better than the ones in St Theresa.'

'Is it?'

'We're big now, we need stronger beds. Did it never occur to you we should have our own alarm?'

'What for? It's not different from St Theresa here, you know. They wake you up.'

'Yeah, I know, but it would help us become more independent if we start setting up our own alarm every night, know what I mean?'

'Yeah.'

He then drew courage from within, pulled himself up, went to open his bag, and got on with sorting out his locker too.

'But are you happy we left St Theresa?' I asked.

'No. But we are ok,' he said.

The passage from the comforting, childish, estrogenic world of St Theresa to the rough, masculine world of St Catherina was quite steep to some extent, like the passage from nursery to an army camp. These dormitories were crammed with hair, balls and dicks swinging around whenever dwellers undressed or washed at bedtime. Fights escalated over nothing and were fairly intended to cause harm with noisy punches and bones banging against each other. There were no good guys like Marco to stop fights, so a brawl could go on until a supervisor bothered coming around to stop it. He would end up harassing the group of spectators that had encircled the two disputants, those calling for more blood, cheering their chosen contender. The presumption here was that no one should intervene to save your ass. If for some reason God had dropped you at St Catherina, you had become a man. And as such, it was assumed you were capable of fighting your own fights without whining or backup.

My grief for leaving St Theresa faltered soon after I arranged my locker. I just swallowed it. Whatever it was, it was gone, dumped and soon to be forgotten. Sadness, uncertainty, fear, missing those old friends from St Theresa, I just swallowed the whole lot and made room for the new. I made sure my face showed I was happy. I held my chin up to show that I was tough and proud to be initiated into my teenagerhood, into this new life and strolled down the stairs, jogged through to the courtyard alongside my twin brother, one of us wearing a blue tracksuit, the other a green one. We cut through groups of young men scattered across the yard, and waved at those we were more familiar with, school friends from St Theresa more or less our own age, and friends we had made from visiting our brothers here. I felt cool jogging through the courtyard, saying hi back to people who greeted us. The older guys sat on benches, played basketball, football, hung around, a guy fixing a motorbike. None of them spared a comment on seeing us newcomers and shouted mostly in the derogatory. 'All we needed was just two more dickheads!' One raised the middle finger to us. An older guy grabbed Redeso by the neck with a wrestling grip and rubbed his head with his knuckles. 'So, I heard you two suckers had enough of shagging nuns, right?' A group of them taunted us with a rude rendition of a song about the Virgin Mary and had a good laugh. Then, as usual, we were forced to stand in front of people having a go at trying to tell us apart. 'Who the fuck is Redeso and who the fuck is Redesof?'

The greeting from my brothers was swift. They welcomed us with as much warmth as any other resident, a smile, a few nice words, then off you go, to find your place within the wider family. There was no need for a formal introduction to the head of the institution as the priest, Don Ettore, was familiar with us already. At dinner he stared at us with approval for having come to live in the right place. He sat at the head of the high table with other prominent figures of the institution's hierarchy—the second in command, Mr P, the small group of ladies who worked at the laundry, in the kitchen and as cleaners, a social service worker, Ursola Del Rio, the conscientious objectors and volunteers on shift, a guest as usual, and the oldest resident ever, a man in his fifties named Paride, the only true orphan left from the time the institution served as a proper orphanage during the Second World War. Next to table number one were the workers and graduate residents' tables, which included Ocean and Sigmund. Klaus and Lorenzo had their places among the largest subgroup—boys under the compulsory education age, those who were obliged to wear tracksuits. We grabbed our plastic plates from the table, queued in front of the cooks serving the meal out of a food cart placed in the middle of the room. We carried our meal back to our table, said the Lord's Prayer and ate with moderate room for chatting. After half an hour or so, a handclap from the priest marked the end of the meal, and no matter how much spaghetti you had left on your plate, we dropped our cutlery, stood up, and waited at the table for the priest to make an announcement if there was one to be made. After a second clap of his hands we were dismissed. We left the room in a large group.

My twin brother and I settled in Santa Catherina with no problems. We made friends with the group of kids our age, more closely with Gino, the typical mischievous redhaired boy who kept breaking his left arm; Edoardo, the funny one, the centre of our group, and the youngest of a trio of brothers who all resided at St Catherina, the Paroli brothers. The one with thick glasses was Riccardo Rullo. He was relatively new too, the youngest brother of one of Klaus's friends, born and raised in Berlin by Napolitan immigrants. Kidane, baby faced, like a porcelain Eritrean doll, was both the youngest amongst us and the strongest. He was incredibly accurate when throwing rocks from afar at things and people. We used to spend long ordinary days together doing nothing memorable but killing time as can happen in an institution. We hung out, sat on the wall near the football pitch whether there was a game or not, played random football matches, threw a few balls on the basketball court, assisted someone repairing his motorbike, responded to the call of another who was going to the tobacco shop to play his lottery numbers and would offer to get yours done too. You'd give him your numbers list and money to bet, and he'd bring you back a receipt and change. Sometimes if we sought some privacy we hung out behind the parking lot, hidden by cars, or inside the institution's old bus, the one with the italic inscription *St Catherina* printed on the sides, the bus left rotting in the parking lot for a decade inside which we'd read comics and porno magazines and masturbate. Then there were daily and weekly domestic duties to meet, a wash-up shift, folding bedsheets, cleaning the toilets, sweeping the courtyard. You were called to join the human chain unloading items from vans to carry upstairs or downstairs or in the warehouse, depending on the nature of the cargo. We served as altar boys at the evening mass in the parish church, on Sunday morning, and during the processions around the city for Easter Sunday, for Corpus Domini, Feast of Presentation of the Lord, and Feast of the Patron of Imola Saint Cassiano. Yet I'd say that our biggest commitment was school. In the morning we attended a public school until 1 p.m. Then we were forced to spend the entire afternoon from 2:30 p.m. to 7:00 p.m. in a classroom on the second floor of the institution. That was where we spent most of our time. Apart from a one-hour break, the whole afternoon was gone.

I saw entire days passing by through the classroom window; rainy, sunny, snowy days, leaves falling from the trees of the small garden below. I grew familiar with the people who walked their dogs across the garden I saw from my desk, the bunch of kids hanging out on the benches, the crowd of commuters returning home during rush hour late in the afternoon when the streetlamps turned on. I saw fights escalating over nothing among my peers in the classroom, people being taken to the infirmary and people getting punished by the same invigilators to whom we raised our hand when we needed help with our work and to ask permission to go take a piss. These invigilators were a mix of people—a conscientious objector, a dedicated volunteer from the Catholic Action Association, sometimes a friar from the Caritas group, the institution's social worker, and always a couple of insiders such as Mr P, or some of the older residents, sometimes even poorly qualified people such as my brothers Sigmund and Ocean, representatives from their age group recruited when we were short of invigilators.

At least once a day there were surprise visits form Don Ettore. We realised the priest had quietly entered the classroom by the change of expression on the invigilator's face, before turning our faces back towards the door to see him there, towering and firm, a hand on the door handle. The room fell dead silent, everyone became busy, whether or not you were done with your assignments, because the last thing you wanted was to get caught by the priest idling. Blue eyes behind his grey framed spectacles, white hair over the black suit, he toured desk to desk to inspect your work, head tilted down. He'd then nod some sort of approval to the supervisors if he was pleased with the class environmment and walked out the room with the same discretion and silence with which he had entered.

A few opportunities came forth every day to leave the classroom early. One of those was to respond to Mr P's request for two volunteers to go deliver dinners to the priests that lived in the parish home. That was a nice walk. You'd leave the classroom with another person and go downstairs to the kitchen where two ladies in blue and white uniforms would hand us two covered trays of food for the priests. Out of the institution up to the parish home was a short walk, no more than five minutes, just along a straight lane, with a few opportunities for diversions if you really wanted, but we were content with that quiet and serene little stroll, of that lap of independence and a gasp of air away from the others. We rang the bell once we reached the parish home and waited for one of the fathers to open the door and lead us into the dinner room where a handful of priests, including our religious studies teacher, were waiting for their dinners. We then went back home with a tip, the equivalent of one pound or so.

***

One day I was sitting with Sigmund on an extended bench against the main building in the top half of the courtyard, when I noticed Klaus leaving a football match in the bottom half of the courtyard. He walked in our direction. The visor of his blue basketball cap lowered down to shadow his melancholic stare. He sat down, but instead of acknowledging Sigmund or me, looked back over the courtyard and the game he had just left, possibly out of boredom, where the loud noises of distant voices, frantic steps, and the thud of a ball rose to meet us.

'Why is d-d-d-oing that?' he asked.

Sigmund glanced at me wondering what Klaus was talking about.

'I mean our d-d-d-ad. Why is he is he leaving us here?' I know what he meant, but at the same time I found something absolutely naive in the way he put the question, as naive as a child asking, *Why is there the sun? Why are the clouds, clouds?* A naivete that was his distinctive trait, his way of asking, *Why are we living this way?* The reason was obvious for us. *Because this is the way we are living.* And therefore we had grown past resentment and held no expectations for our parents. We were just living day by day, while Klaus was not. He was hurt. He had been so for many years. The boy felt that there was something fundamentally wrong with the way we were living, that we shouldn't be eating, sleeping, getting up every morning in overcrowded places, split apart from each other, without a family core, without a proper reason. In the sense that we were not orphans, our parents were alive and well, they were regularly in touch with us, and with plenty of resources. *So why?* It seemed that the boy carried on fighting his own intimate fight against our family condition, refusing to put down his sense of entitlement for a dignified life. Neither I nor Sigmund knew what to say to him that day. We could only sense anger stirring inside him although he didn't show it and talked calmly. Sigmund tried to give him a logical explanation to justify our father's actions, but truth was, he didn't know what to say.

'Sigmund, do you a-a-a-accept all this?' Klaus challenged him, looking in front of him rather than at him.

'Of course not. But this is just a temporary solution. Dad is buying us a new house! And what can I do? What do you want me to do?'

'I don't know. You can sit there and watch the show or te-tell him something. Did it never occur to you? T-t-t-tell him what we think. Tell him we ha-ha-have had enough of this. He can't carry on do-do-doing that. He has forgotten us.'

That day I felt more surely than ever that the boy was starving to death for a hug. He was right; why were we here?

***

Klaus was right, but again, his comment about Dad neglecting us didn't sink in as it should have. I had grown too detached from my parents to feel they should have done something for me, while for Sigmund, it was a different story. Maybe because he was older than us and somehow felt responsible for us, he endorsed Klaus's pain and offered him some comfort in the way he could but did not entirely agree with him. Sigmund had the opposite reaction to Klaus's words about Dad's negligence. While Klaus blamed Dad for all the evil, Sigmund defended him, and justified all his actions; he would grasp at straws to never admit any fault of Dad's. The point was, we were all in one way or another infatuated with our father, his stories, achievements and personality, like he was some kind of legendary character. Way too infatuated to look at him objectively and see him for the real person he was with all his strengths and weaknesses. Sigmund would instead encourage Klaus to trust Dad, to be patient, because change was on its way, because Dad was working hard to make that change possible, and he should not insult him and say bad things about him because he was our father. He would then shift the conversation to something else, something more urgent in his view, like Klaus's poor school performance, for example, since there was always something to say about it.

Klaus was a mess at school. Debra-Jo, Ocean and Sigmund were relatively good, Redeso and I less so, Lorenzo pretty bad, while Klaus, Klaus was something else; he was completely incompatible with school education. A day at school was for Klaus a day on another planet. He'd submit his tests untouched despite trying to read the assignment questions several times. He'd stuttered a long, draining *hermmmm* for the whole length of an oral assessment just to be sent back to his desk with the lowest mark possible. It all went on like this for a while until he ended up being labelled 'donkey', and with it, the Klaus case was closed and archived. There was not a great deal of conversation about dyslexia, ADHD, communication difficulties or inclusive education going on at that time in Italian schools, nor was there much attention on students' family circumstances and emotional well-being. You were either a good or a bad student in the spectrum of school learning. Or, finally, a lost cause. Klaus was marked a lost cause. He was parked on the sidelines, and nobody bothered raising him from purgatory after that. Teachers no longer stopped him from leaving the class to go for his strolls in the corridors whenever he wanted. They seemed more at ease on seeing his desk vacant than being occupied by an idiot. I wonder when Klaus started stuttering. Was he stuttering back in Benin? Had he been stuttering since his first words? Was Klaus's speech impairment, his ineptitude at school, his temper and his relentless longing for his parents all due to the type of life he had? Or was this simply Klaus's nature?

Debra-Jo's Second Night of Somnambulism

Debra-Jo's roommate, Gabriella, woke up startled one night at the Oasis. She felt something was wrong, looked at Debra-Jo's bed and saw that it was empty. She thought her friend went to the toilet or something, then heard the gate creaking outside, opening and closing, and knew by then what was happening. She dashed to the window and saw her. She saw them. The nun and my sister going out as if it were a Saturday night. The nun had a jumper on, Debra-Jo her jacket. She was about to shout what the hell are you doing when the nun took sight of her and shushed her with her finger to her lips and an angry look. But far from submit to her carer's intimidations, Gabriella hastily put her shoes and jacket on, grabbed her keys and went out.

Gabriella joined the nun and Debra-Jo's night walk. Sister Gaudenzia was reluctant to allow her to come with them but at the end she gave up just to prevent Gabriella from waking up Debra-Jo. Three years had passed since Debra-Jo's first episode of sleepwalking and Sister Gaudenzia couldn't understand how she had managed to catch it the second time, whether it was a work of coincidence, or something stronger and more mystical. Like fate? The hand of God? What if actually this was just the second time she witnessed it when in truth Debra-Jo had had yet many unsupervised walks? Who could tell? In the eyes of the nun, Debra-Jo was a special girl. It took a long time before Debra-Jo felt safe enough to reveal herself, and yet the nun felt like she had known her since always. The sister had taken care of

Debra-Jo from the first day she had set foot in the institution with her bag and those skinny legs, hands in her pockets and an impervious expression. And now that same girl had turned into a woman, no longer under her legal authority at eighteen. In fact, Debra-Jo was free to leave the institution whenever she wanted, and the nun was aware that that day would come at any point. It was just a matter of time. And yet, just as she sensed the time approaching, the nun could not help feeling anxious about her child's future, whether she was ready to start a life on her own. A lot went through the sister's head during that night walk. She thought about her girls, and Debra-Jo in particular. And she thought about herself. She questioned her own mission in life, the mission God assigned her and which she had fully embraced, ultimately to impart Jesus Christ's message of love. But how was she doing with that? Was she living up to what was expected from such a role? Had she taught her girls how to love and what love was? Had she prepared them to give and receive love before they made their debut into the world alone? How much would it take to teach them about love? Years? A life? More? To lay the foundation of that strange unifying force of love in someone else's life might have made a huge difference. It would have given someone the foundation on which to build their own church outside of any religion, away from exploitation, control or fear. Her care couldn't work on the same standard that you could hope for from others, let's say a mother, a father, or any other carer not spiritually bound. Those people hadn't made any official vow to love. But if life had led you to become someone who works for the message of Jesus Christ, you would profoundly want to make sure that the young person under your charge leaves you with a solid notion of love. After all, that was her function in life when she chose to leave everything behind and follow Christ's teachings; after the night she woke up inside a church; after her long sleepwalk all those years ago. The nun was sure, could put her hand in fire, that all she had done during those years, raising the girls and participating in an ecclesiastic life for the sake of humanity, was driven by love. It was solely to follow the way of love that she had chosen a life of chastity and sacrifice. Still, she had been lately hunted by doubts: Can there be love, any kind of love, if there is no freedom? If there is no fulfilment, happiness or a sense of personal growth or individuation? If she finds herself crying in the bathroom all the time? Debra-Jo's presence had somehow an absent quality and, sensing that, Sister Gaudenzia had also sensed that something strong lay in the meaning of that someone standing next to her. That a body next you, the space that another person occupies with her presence and remains empty when she leaves was something, but what exactly? One thing for sure, she knew people could not do it without one another and Debra-Jo couldn't do it alone. She needed to open up to love. But which kind of love did this girl need? Was she, Sister Gaudenzia, with her chaste and reserved life, the right person to guide this girl? She knew something thorny blocked Debra-Jo from truly connecting with other people, to trust, men in particular, to have faith, to ultimately believe. To believe ultimately in God. So many times, she had felt uncomfortable during mass witnessing the way Debra-Jo seemed mistrusting of whatever was happening in that place; although she didn't act out of scepticism, it simply didn't work for her. What could Sister Gaudenzia expect from her once she went outside into the world without love? Would she be completely alone? How was the nun supposed to feel? Would she blame herself one day? Was she failing her mission as a nun, a carer and as Christ's trainee, if she let this girl step out into the world in that absent state?

That night was darker than the first night they walked that path for the first time years before. The moon was smaller, a waning crescent, but in contrast, the stars were brighter. Brighter and more numerous than the first time. The three women climbed their way up the quiet hillside, the same path Debra-Jo and Sister Gaudenzia walked before.

The soil was parched and cracked after a dry end to summer. Lines of vineyards, recently pruned, came into sight. The three women kept on walking until Debra-Jo stopped and sat down on the exact spot which she had sat on her first night of somnambulism. Sister Gaudenzia and Gabriella sat next to her. Gabriella entertained herself working out the position of the stars: first she found the Little Dipper from the alignment of the Big Dipper, she just needed to extend a line between Dubhe and Merak northward, as her mother had taught her when she was a child. Along the same axis, she would meet the Polaris at the end of the Little Dipper's handle; it was an easy task to assemble the rest of the constellation, especially on such a dark night. Just below them, the band of the Milky Way.

Debra-Jo had chosen again to face the void. Believing the final destination of a sleepwalk should be symbolic, as it was for her when she was led to her fate, Sister Gaudenzia expected that there should be something in store for Debra-Jo here, on this hill. But she couldn't get what that could be and voiced aloud her concern, 'Why is she coming to this place?' But it was Gabriella who answered. 'I don't know. Maybe it means nothing. It's just a place like any other.'

'For me it meant a lot when I ended up at that church.'

'I know, you told me that story, but maybe you overcharged it with meaning. Maybe it meant nothing to you too. Do you know what I mean, you see things the way you want to see them at the end of the day.'

And now, how did the nun take Gabriella's opinion? She said nothing, and sat silent for a while. Although she tended to dismiss Gabriella and found her irritating, something about the girl's opinion struck a nerve and reawakened a wave of doubt that had lingered inside her and had kept returning throughout her life. What if she had really overread her sleepwalking experience? How could she know whether she had interpreted it in the right way? What if the symbolism of that incident was less dramatic than she thought and pointed at something much less important, like 'remember to say your prayers'? What if she was actually living in a completely meaningless world instead? Because if that was not the case, if she really trusted life on earth was ultimately governed by an interplay of powerful symbolisms, even the present one, Gabriella's stupid talking, should work according to the same law, and as a result, should be taken as much into account. She was mulling upon all this in silence giving room for Gabriella to push her opinion a bit further.

'I mean,' Gabriella continued, 'who cares if you are a nun or not. It's the same, right? You're just a really good person for me. And I love you. I mean, the real point here is if you are really happy or not, right?'

Here Gabriella's presence became strong, strong in a way the nun had never felt before, maybe as a result of the unusual circumstances she found herself in, sitting with the two girls outside in the open countryside, under the bright mantle of starlight; probably the first, authentic, intimate night she had ever shared with her girls. On the verge of shutting Gabriella up, she decided to let her talk freely, following her intuition that led her to believe that Gabriella had just taken up a role, perhaps the messenger, like she was talking someone else's words. She grasped that there was something important to hear, and that Debra-Jo had driven them there exactly for that reason, and finally understood the meaning of that void, the void surrounding them, understood why Debra-Jo was facing the void. She was doing it for her. She was showing her friend that from the void, any form of life, every aspect of it, substantial or insubstantial, originates. So too possibilities, solutions, changes—and healing.

'The best time of my life was when my parents broke up,' Gabriella said. 'They used to turn into animals when they fell into arguments. From nothing and boom, hell. It was horrible. My mother would break things, and then you take it on yourself. I felt guilt and so much hatred at the same time, it was like they couldn't see me. It was horrible, and you ask, ok, so what's even the point for me to be here? Just to stand in the middle of their game because that's all it was about: a game between them, all the fucking days, a game. You're like wait a second, these two are only concerned with each other, right? They have no interest in you. They just long for a fight. Anything else is boring. It is boring to notice that I'm fucking there. Hello, can anyone see me? But then it all finished. You wait a bit and play alone in a corner until your mum realises that you're actually there and of course she feels sorry that she forgot all about you and gave you this shit, like she did yesterday, the day before and on and on. You see that she would love to give you more but all that hatred held a strong hand over her, like a magnet, and was pulling everything away from me. Do you get what I mean? Then they broke up. Boom! Another world! She was another person! She was beautiful! All was beautiful! Freedom is this, pure beauty! You could see she was just herself now. She loved herself, she went back doing all the things she had left behind because of him. She started to sing again and took lessons. She went out with friends again. She took me to parties. And in all this, I was central in her life because she was happy and she could see me. I never felt loved by my mother as in those years. I tell you, it was beautiful. When I think about it, I really wish things stayed that way. I really wish I kept cool.'

The time they spent on top of the hill lasted no longer than the previous time. The three women walked back home, my sister still sleepwalking. The nun and Gabriella followed her all the way across the countryside back to the institution. They went inside, let Debra-Jo take her jacket off, put her keys on the key hook, and walk up the stairs to her room. Gabriella followed after wishing good night to the sister. The nun took a pen and a sheet of paper and sat at the desk in her bedroom where she wrote to Debra-Jo.

Imola, 15 April 1990

Dearest Debra-Jo,
 I can imagine you are feeling puzzled at this very moment, wondering why your bed is full of dirt and grass. Well, my

lovely child, you are a sleepwalker. You had an episode of sleepwalking last night and had a previous one some years ago. Sorry if I did not tell you anything before, but I thought it was a one-off and it would scare you more than anything. I tell you now, I must tell you now. We walked together; Gabriella came with us. Nothing really happened to tell you the truth, we just sat on the grass on a hill close by, which explains the dirt. The same hill you chose last time, when it was just you and me staring at the void in silence. While there with you my lovely, my eyes were opened by something I cannot explain. I know I have my responsibilities here, but there are other things in my life and it is also my responsibility to commit to these things. Can you understand me? Oh my darling, it's been so nice to be a nun and to take care of you and the girls, very rewarding indeed, but I strongly feel that it is now time I experience something different and resolve all the things I left behind. I am thinking of leaving the institution. Yes, I am leaving the institution! I am doing it now. I have been thinking about my dream to convert the barn in Schenna into an art gallery. I need to dig deeper into myself to a point where I feel well with myself, where I like what I see when I see myself in the mirror, when I interact with others. I want to meet me again in the most unscrupulous and selfish way, whether through light or darkness, I do not care, they are not to divide but to be converged as part of the indispensable life force. After all, most of the things we have learned and see in the light arise from the dark. And I feel I have to deal with the dark side of my life. My dear child, please do not be mad at me. I know you will understand that it is because I love you all, oh my dear girls! So very much, that I have decided to leave. This is our pact, a witch pact between you and me: I promise you will heal now my child, now that I take my own path, you will heal, you will sense life running through your veins once again and you will love and trust in the goodness of people. I give you back all the good you deserve. What was taken away from you by the worst side of humanity. There is this beautiful Asian saying: Two tigers cannot sit on the same mountain—and it's so true my dearest Debra-Jo! Me and you cannot stay in the same place. We are both too unhappy to be of any help to each other. You need plenty of space to awaken from a long sleep my darling, and I am giving you all the space you need, I leave you my kingdom with my departure. And I hope we will never see each other again. If that should ever happen, hopefully not, well, that would be a very bad sign.

I wish you all the very best, my dear Debra-Jo.

Yours truly,
Anna Cosser

LONDON, PRESENT DAY
V

I receive a call from a new patient who keeps me on the phone for about an hour. He's clearly in a state of severe distress. He needs to talk. And I listen. There is something wrong with his leg, a mysterious rash that is getting worse and is now spreading down to his feet. A second course of cortisone via his GP has produced no significant change. Besides, he smokes a lot, he says, several joints a day, and is desperate to stop because it's not helping and he feels lost and he starts weeping.

'On which leg is the rash?' I ask him.

'On the right.'

'Are you left-handed?' I ask.

'Yes.'

I employ some basic theories of German New Medicine to work out that the guy is having some serious issues with his mother or a figure that takes up that role in his life. Accordingly, such mother-son conflicts generally affect the non-dominant side of the body, the right side for the left-handed, and left for a right-hander.

'How are things with your mother?' I ask him.

That question throws him into a long desperate rant about a turbulent relationship with the apparently nasty old woman who is currently ill and who, I assume, may be a controlling type, judging from the rash located on the outer aspect of the patient's leg, on the yang-defensive side, rather than the inner-yin nurturing side. He's clearly fighting his mother. Or rather, he's defending himself from her aggressions and holds back from kicking her in the butt. He shouts, 'Fuck, fuck, fuck!'—this 30-year-old East Londoner, as he confesses that he took on a huge burden taking full-time care of his partially paralysed mother after her stroke a year ago. Since then she lives in his flat, a two-bedroom council flat which has since turned exceedingly small and oppressive with a controlling mother around. 'It doesn't feel like my home anymore, since she moved in. I feel her presence everywhere!' He takes it out on his two brothers for not helping, yet also excuses them since both live abroad. He's exhausted. And it's damaging his social life and career. It turns out he's a professional judo player who stopped competing when his mother had her stroke.

'Is there anybody else who can also help? Does she not have any other relatives?'

'Everybody wants her dead. She's a nasty woman, a pure concentration of poison, bro! Look, not even her closest sister has come to see her. Do you know, bro, she used to beat us up in a way you can't believe. She fucking ruined my life, that fucking whore! Can you believe she slapped me the other day! Fucking paralysed cunt slapped me in the face! I'm taking care of her and she slapped me in the face!'

I understood that this guy was severely blocked from evolving somehow. This guy was clearly subliminally imploring me to give him the consent to do something that went against his morals something which perhaps none of his relatives and friends had so far dared raise in front of him.

'You need to take her to hospice,' I say to him. 'You're not in a position to take care of her.' I then say, 'it's ok,' after I hear only silence on the other end of the line, a silence of concern and relief, I suppose. 'You can stop this fighting, you know, it's not good for either of you. You can't let her ruin your life. You don't want to be an accomplice in all the harm she causes you, man, in the way she is shaping your life. Go on practising judo. You'll see, she will be better off under the care of professionals rather than fighting all day with a son who resents her.'

Still the guy doesn't talk. Then finally he says, 'How much I owe you?'

'Ah, it's cool, man, I generally don't do this, how do you call it, I mean phone consultation. Treatments via phone…'

'Distance therapy, my man.'

'Yeah, exactly!'

'Shall I come into the clinic?'

'I suggest it, but maybe after you relocate your mum, you wait and see. The rash should now improve from there on. Then, yes, feel free to give me a call.'

'Cool, thank you very much, I really appreciate your help, my man. I'm looking forward to meeting you.'

'My pleasure, good luck.'

'Who was that?' asks my mother who had been following the one-hour phone call from the sofa, although she doesn't understand a single word of English.

'It was a patient,' I say.

'Did he book?' That was the whole point for her. If I had a good flow of clients in my clinic, if I was doing well, making money. She didn't really care much about the nature of Chinese medicine.

'I don't think he needs to come in for now, he's going to be fine.'

'It's normal he won't book if you talk to him on the phone for an hour. They won't respect you, *ce n'est pas ton ami, eh!* That's the work of a secretary, not of a doctor to talk to them. You need to have a secretary who's nice and talks nicely. That's the way you manage a business. What was wrong with him? Did he catch a cold?'

'No, but I can't tell you, I have this thing of confidentiality I need to guarantee to my patients.'

'Ok. It's cold in this country. More than in France. Whenever I return to France I go back with a cold.'

I sit on the arm of the sofa. I recall the sound of the guy crying and complaining about his desperate relationship with his mother as I listen to my own, talking about her struggle with the temperature, despite, in my experience, there being a miniscule temperature difference between Bordeaux and London, and I sense a mild malaise settling inside me. I'm not sure anymore that I did the right thing advising that guy to send his mother to hospice. It is not up to me to advise patients in that way. I'm just an acupuncturist. I should just stick to the codes of my profession. What if the guy calls the British Acupuncture Council and tells them one of their members told me to put my mother in a hospice? Fuck, I shouldn't do things like that; it even goes against my personal values, to send a poor old woman to a hospice when she has a son willing to look after her. But then I don't know. Healing can come in various ways and forms and may require you to go against your principles now and then. And these principles and values and morality, god, conceptual social ghosts which have even too much weight on us. I like to think that we healers have the capacity to maintain distance from our nominal identities as physicians, acupuncturists, doctors, psychotherapists, nurses and once in a while tap into our shamanic potential to deliver a treatment that goes beyond solely an intervention in the body and the psyche. I like to think we have the power to deliver a treatment that re-establishes a person's life purpose, their *Ming Men,* instead of focusing always on the *de-spiritualised, de-mythologised,* fragmented aspects of life that makes it impossible for one to see the larger picture of a life. Once again, we are back to the theme of boundaries and territories; the sense of viscous safety they provide.

The reason my mother is sitting on the sofa with a gloomy expression etched across her face is because I introduced her to my book project—the novel about my family history. I told her I needed her contribution in the form of an interview, and she dislikes the idea very much. Her face turned sombre as she took some time to consider my request. Then she said, 'I don't want to talk about these things, they depress me. I don't want to.'

This is the reason I sat on the sofa arm so I could look at her sideways, halfway confrontational and halfway friendly, a passive-aggressive stare that should get her to change her mind.

'Look, there is no other way I can retrieve this information. I know it's your life, but it's also a huge big hole in my life that I need to fill up. It can't go on like this. I need to know what happened. I need to know who you are, who you were, who was Dad? You can't refuse to let me know about my origins.'

Suddenly, the talk I just had with the guy on the phone rushes to my mind. A paradigm about life's inherent cruelty: the well-being of one depends upon somebody else's sacrifice. My own ability to understand depends on my mother's renunciation of her serenity. How do we go around this? When she told me she was coming to visit I was not sure I was ready to receive her in my home. I have nothing against her, it's just because I'm becoming a creature of habit. I perceive anyone who comes to visit as a huge disruption. I stare at her profile silhouetted against the balcony window, sulking over this interview issue that is spoiling her day and the prospect of a gratifying holiday here in London, and it occurs to me that things will be fine. With or without the interview, we will both benefit from spending a few weeks together.

She's been here one day. Last night she helped me carry the sleepy kids home from the bus stop in Hackney Central and put them to bed when we came back from the airport. Then she had a tour around the house that she was seeing for the first time and was pleased that everything was nice and tidy. She then sat on the sofa and took some stuff from her carry-on luggage, a little bag of sea salt, a bottle of cologne, a sushi-size plastic bottle of olive oil with a print of a praying Virgin Mary on it. She asked me if I had a lemon and a bowl of water. 'Room temperature?' I asked. 'Yes,' she said. I brought her the cut lemon and water and she squeezed the lemon into the bowl of water, added a handful of the sea salt she had brought from home, and carried out the entire operation while praying. Then she went around the house and sprinkled the walls of every room with her holy water concoction, which was meant to protect the house from malevolent spirits and attract the protective blood of Christ. I followed her during the process and felt a sense of gratitude and affection for what she was doing. She keeps on being a mother despite it all.

I woke up on the sofa in the living room very late the next morning and found my mother and the kids already awake in the kids' bedroom. She sat on one bed watching the two playing on the floor, the boy with Lego and the girl with some stationery. Like the night before, discouraged by the language gradient, the kids made no effort to acknowledge her, nor did they even pretend to be interested in her. And she seemed more understanding. More at peace with the way things were, happy with the simple possibility to be there watching them. I asked the three if they had breakfast. The kids did, mother no; she said she was fasting. We then went to drop the kids off at their mother's, my ex, a twenty-minute bus ride from home, both women enthusiastically greeting each other and chatting in French at the doorstep. My mother was always fond of Ella. She would have accepted Ella's invitation to come inside for a tea if I didn't pull back, I just didn't feel like it. We kissed the kids. Took a bus back. Did a little window shopping in Hackney Central, and now we are here on the sofa with me staring at her in profile.

Yeah, I am. I'm seriously disappointed by her refusal to participate in my project. I don't want to fake her past, like what happened when Brandon Lee mysteriously died during the making of *The Crow*, and the end had to be digitalized to finish the film. This story means a lot to me. I have been working on it on and off at length, with all the work of taking notes, collecting interviews, doing historical research, underlining all the new English words I came across in my reading and repeating them in my mind throughout the day so they hopefully stuck, and here I meet my biggest obstacle, my mother, who refuses to concede a couple of hours of her time for an interview. But I do understand if the past hurts. I also understand if she struggles to see my point. Writing a novel, to her, boiled down to a ludicrous exercise which never did and never will bring me any true financial relief, only trouble. She was of the opinion that being an acupuncturist was the real deal for me; I would have been better off as a doctor, a proper doctor, with a white coat and stethoscope, but in the absence of any of this, a career in complementary medicine, an acupuncturist, a *Docteur da la Medicine Chinoise*, as she put it, this suited her better than the fact that I was a writer. If you add on top of this that as a writer, I had reached a point that I required her confessional input in order to sustain my work, then I see why she was concerned.

It's strange how this thing of being a son works, you keep wanting to please your mother even when you had a poor history of interactions with her. I feel that deep inside me, I long for her to see me, to recognize me, to be proud of me, to celebrate my success as an acupuncturist but the truth is, I am anything but the son who can make her proud. My acupuncture practice is going down the drain. It's been so long since my last research paper. My membership to the *Journal of Chinese Medicine* has expired and I haven't bothered to renew it. The chairman of the British Acupuncture Council is chasing me via email because I haven't submitted my professional development project yet. Nor have I put much effort lately into marketing the practice. One year since I committed to writing from 9 a.m. to 1 p.m., I am now doing it nearly the whole day. It had that effect on me. Writing had the upper hand and was stronger than all my good intentions for the practice. I see less patients now, mainly Harry, and sit more on the green couches of the Hackney housing benefit department, filling up HMRC forms to get the financial help I need to make ends meet. I have a strong feeling that all is going to change once I finish this book. All will fall back into place. Maybe in a new order, I just don't know when.

I try again to convince my mother that I need that interview. She is unmovable. Actually, increasingly upset as I realise I'm blatantly bullying her. So, I let go. *Sarà quel che sarà*. We just get on with our life. I do some reading and check my email and the news on my phone. She goes to pray in her room upstairs for an hour very loudly. Then comes down and cooks a meal which I eat alone because she's fasting during the day, a Christian Ramadan, launched by her evangelical congregation in Bordeaux. She can only eat after 6 p.m., and prays at least three times on an empty stomach.

We go for a walk up to Broadway Market, and along the canal down to Victoria Park. It is a long walk where I let out for the first time everything she needs to know about my relationship with the mother of my kids and the reasons why we broke up. It had been difficult to explain by phone in all these years, but now that she is here, it seems easier, it seems we have space for a conversation of this type. My confession comes to her as a surprise. She had no idea things were impossible between us. Our separation after eight years together upset her very much, even more than it did with me and Ella. I remember the phone calls we had; she had prayed for us every single day to get back together even when I was trying to convince her we were both happier apart. But now everything starts making sense to her. Now that she's here, now that we're walking alongside the canal, she nods and understands. 'I see, it's best for both of you.'

Something has shifted in us both after the walk. We're both more comfortable with each other. But something else must have hit her that I still haven't figured out yet, because she turned very quiet all of a sudden.

She makes small talk, about a shop window and some people's outfits and dinner plans, but she is completely silent for most of the day. We cook dinner together in silence. Take dinner in silence. She just says good night before climbing up to her room around half past nine. I sit on the sofa checking my phone while her praying reaches me from the upstairs room. Then I watch a film.

It's just the next morning, while I'm in the middle of reviewing the case of a patient I'm supposed to see later in the afternoon, that she comes into the living room holding a cup of tea and sits next to me.

GROUND

She carries an even calmer aura with her. She seems rested. I suppose the praying, the fasting, the silence she had sunken into yesterday have yielded to her a level of mental clarity that feels rather powerful to me. I can feel it on my skin. With no preambles, she spontaneously starts talking about her past, when and where she was born, her parents, her first encounter with Dad. It is evident that something shifted in her mind; she had woken a different person and decided to give me an interview although this might cause her malaise. Something in her renewed mood says that she has now grasped the meaning of what I'm trying to do and that she has come to terms with the fact that I'm entitled to know about my past. I grab my phone, tap on the recording app, and start recording.

Benin

My mother gave birth to her first kids, Redeso and me, on the 1st of September, 1976, in the General Hospital of Brazzaville. The birth of twins was traditionally a good omen in our culture, even more so when they were the first born. Parents of twins were cherished, blessed, seen by the local population as people with a good star shining upon them. In fact, twins were celebrated by giving them a set of local additional names on top of their first names: Yambu and Yampy, Sagbo and Sinsu. I was Yambu-Sagbo, my brother, Yampi-Sinsu. Dad named us Redeso and Redesof as an homage to the love he felt for my mother. Both names are a portmanteau of the syllables of their names—*Re* (René), and *So* (Sofie). The *f* ending in my name is to differentiate between us. The *de* in the middle stands for the English possessive article 'of'. (Re-de-So, like Re of So in English). My mother didn't like the idea at first, but my father did. Needless to say, if René liked something, well, there was little one could do to stop him. My mother remembers that at that time she lived in her own house in Brazzaville, in Congo, which Dad had bought her. She had just finished high school, was planning to enrol in a degree in oil management while carrying out a young woman's lifestyle. Things were good for Maman Sofie. She remembers being happy as the concubine of the rich and popular *Man of the Shoes*, despite being home alone with us twins, and Dad often being out of town for work, or with his wife, Maman Natalie. My mother was fully aware that whenever Dad was not sleeping with her, he was sleeping with his wife. And she coped pretty well with it, while we cannot say the same for Maman Natalie, who was not up for seeing her marriage turning polygamous and was having difficult times. Her marriage to my dad was torn apart by fights and arguments that eventually pushed him more and more towards my mother, making Natalie's life even more miserable. Then they broke up. That's when my father's relationship with my mother became official. Yet times were hard. Congo-Brazzaville was going through political instability. On 18 March 1977, with a wave of mysterious closely linked political assassinations, our socialist president, Major Marien Ngouabi, was killed. He died aged 38 after serving eight years as head of state. Ngouabi's assassination remains controversial because the exact conditions of his death are still uncertain. Also because, like President John F Kennedy and Patrice Lumumba, he was loved by the population and was considered a national hero, a young father of the revolution, portrayed as an honest, humble president devoid of that megalomaniac thirst for power and wealth characteristic of far too many African leaders. The problem for my family, and more specifically for my father, was that the Central Committee of the *Congolaise Parti du Travail* elected an army general called Joachim Yhombi-Opango as successor to President Ngouabi. The direction General Yhombi-Opango moved the country was met with widespread criticism across all levels of society. He pushed the country from the left to a martial-style right-wing regime, with curfews enforcement and strong police presence. A number of people who had been suspected of being behind Ngouabi's death were executed (they were later determined to be innocent). He also put in place a series of austerity measures to attract loans from Western donors, then hit West African traders with a mandate that allowed for the expropriation of their assets and deportation. My family's fate was once again at the mercy of a country's political reforms. A West African trader himself, my father saw his assets seized by the Congolese government and was forced to leave the Congo.

At this stage, Redeso and I were about seven months old when my father was stripped of all his wealth. Our older siblings, Debra-Jo, Ocean, Sigmund, Lorenzo and Klaus, were settled in Benin, where Maman Natalie had taken them, supposedly in an anger-fuelled response to the worsening marital crisis she was going through over Dad's relationship with my mother. Just Redeso and I were in Brazzaville at the time these events took place. My mother recalls that we lived between her house and her father's. She says that my father was placed in a sort of refugee camp while waiting for his deportation, along with other displaced West Africans. Then, when the time for his flight came, my father did something completely in keeping with his style. Through his government connections, he found ways to delay the flight and was conceded special permission to be escorted by police car to Sofie's father's house where she was at the time. Olivier was quick to understand what was about to happen as soon as he saw René coming out of the police car. He tried to stop him. He tried to persuade his daughter not to fall prey to a second mistake, but it was in vain. The Principal just entered the house, went to Sofie's bedroom where Redeso and I were sleeping, and picked us up under Sofie's silent watch. A tacit agreement was at work between the two of them. He knew she would have to follow. She took nothing with her, she just left her father's house, following her man to the police car. They were driven to the airport, escorted to the airport gate where the flight to Benin was about to take off.

At first they stayed in Cotonou at Maman Debra's house, my paternal grandmother's house, a house which she remembers being overcrowded most of the time with Rene's siblings and their families and kids. Some were there to visit, others she just couldn't figure out if they lived there or not. Among the dwellers were Debra-Jo, Ocean, Sigmund, Lorenzo and a toddling Klaus. They had been settled in there since the day their mother, Maman Natalie, had brought them to Benin from the Congo a few months earlier as a form of retaliation for her husband's infidelity. That was the first time my mother met them in person. My parents soon rented a house in another area of Cotonou, Saint-Jean, in the north of the city, where they moved with just Redeso and me, leaving my other siblings in the big matriarchal house under the care of Grandma Debra and the women who lived there. My father, starting from scratch once again, embarked in a daily mission of looking for new business opportunities around town, while my mother stayed at home looking after Redeso and me and managing the house.

It was not long before those extended days of maternal solitude awoke in her unpleasant feelings of displacement and grief. Grief for the way she had left her family back in Brazzaville, so abruptly and uncaringly. The poor man, her father Olivier, must have been so disappointed. She felt like she betrayed him at the first opportunity, and now she was left to battle this growing fear that she would not become someone important as Olivier expected; instead she had become a housewife at age 20 and an immigrant as well, a lonely immigrant in a covertly hostile environment. For she wasn't very well received in René's family and the immediate community. She felt that although polite, people were cold and tried little to engage with her and she thought that maybe they were jealous or fearful that Dad's lucrative genius would be driven far from their family interests. In addition, my mum was a foreigner, worse than that, she was from Congo, the same country which had just expelled many of their fellow West Africans.

But she felt optimistic and despite it all, she believed it was just a matter of time before the relationship with René's family would soften and her partner's work would start to roll again. And with money flowing in, they would be able to hire a nanny. She would then return to her studies, enrol in business school, and finally regain the respect of her father by becoming a dignified, emancipated African woman. But facts foretold a different future. Weeks grew into months and despite René's fruitful work that raised their living standard, nothing else had really changed for my mother. She felt lonelier and lonelier, spending entire days home by herself with two babies.

I must say that her personality was a strong contributing factor in her solitude. My mother's shyness and quiet disposition made it hard for her to befriend new people. She'd rather stay by herself at home, sitting outside on the veranda, or go around for errands alone but for the twins wrapped one on her back, the other on her front. Her only visits were from Grandma Debra, her only friend. The old woman had found qualities in Sofie that she liked. In addition, she felt responsible for the new family of her wandering son René. So she'd come home every day to give her a hand with the housekeeping and the kids. Minute and kind, with little glowing eyes, Grandma Debra felt sorry for Sofie struggling to settle in, to see her isolated, in fractious relationships with some of her family. She read sadness in her eyes, yet all she could do was keep her company, a silent company, since she too was a person of little words. They carried their own work around the house in silence, had a meal, put the twins to sleep, then the old woman would return home leaving my mother alone once again.

More days of solitude passed. My mother began to suspect that René was seeing another woman, possibly Maman Chantal, as he hardly came home. The sarcastic grins on some of René's relatives reinforced her fears until, one day, she confronted him directly, asking if he was cheating on her. He denied it and she dropped the topic despite the fact that she knew he was lying.

After that, whenever she talked about her future studies and when and where she might enrol, he dampened the conversation with the excuse that they were not yet able to invest financially in minor matters such as studying, university degrees, and other trivialities; they couldn't even afford to pay a nanny in their current state, how could they be worrying about studying. For him, her priority was to stay and look after the home and us until things got better. Then they would find her this goddam school. Not now. Now was the time for her, he declared, to become a woman.

***

Soon Redeso and I were able to crawl all over the house. One morning somebody knocked at the door. Sofie opened it. Standing outside were René's five children backed by René's cousin, Tantine Ellen, a woman about her age, but whose vibrant and assertive spirit was a marked contrast. The five children—Debra-Jo, Sigmund, Ocean, Lorenzo and Klaus, glared at my mother in bewilderment before their auntie pushed them inside, explaining to my mother that now that she had her own house, it was her responsibility to raise the children of her man. Sofie didn't even try opposing. She knew it would take her nowhere to start a fight with Ellen, and it would only risk further aggravating her position before René's family. She realised that Ellen had a point: tradition dictated that the kids lived in the house of their father. Sofie was acquainted with this custom, as she too was raised by her second mother when her real mother left the household. She took the children in, then went through the incident with my father when he came back late that night. I have no trouble believing that my father wrapped it all up with a sarcastic comment such as, 'And you didn't have time to cook for all of us, I suppose, with all the complications you had today!' He then decided to take us all out to dinner. That's how my family began to take shape. With my mother carrying a twin wrapped on her back, and eight-year-old Debra-Jo carrying the other one in her arms, along with Sigmund, Klaus, Lorenzo and Ocean, we walked out into the night, into the streets of Cotonou.

Monsieur Idrissa Kamosi

One day my father received an important visit from an old acquaintance—the minister of public works and infrastructure of the People's Republic of the Congo, visiting Benin precisely to meet my father. Their friendship dated back from the time my father supplied the nation's public facilities with furniture and headed construction and renovation plans for government infrastructure, under the minister's watch, services that had earned my father the minister's respect and admiration. The two had not heard from each other since the time my father was expelled from Congo-Brazzaville under the government of Yhombi-Opango, the same government that Monsieur Idrissa Kamosi had been serving as a minister for public works and infrastructure. Now they had a table booked in one of Cotonou's top restaurants to discuss a deal the minister had lined up for my father. Each man arrived at the restaurant with their respective wives. My mother told me she was visibly pregnant with Happiness by then, and yet looked more elegant than ever. She remembers that under the fervour of going out to dinner with her man again like they used to in Congo, she had finished off her look with some of the jewellery my father had bought her at the height of their old life in Congo. This included her favourite bracelet, the bracelet he gave her in the fanciest bar in Brazzaville where he first told her he was madly in love with her right at the beginning of their relationship.

The minister and his wife had just arrived at the restaurant when my parents walked in. They sat at their table, ordered expensive drinks and food. All the ingredients for a delightful night were present and the night would have surely been successful but for one incident which took place in the middle of the meal, right when the minister's wife noticed my mother's bracelet. The woman cried in admiration, grasping my mother's hand and drawing it near to get a better look at the piece of jewellery. At that, my father asked her if she truly liked it. Of course, she did, she confirmed. So my father ordered my mother to take the bracelet off and give it to the minister's wife. My mother was stunned. But could she say no to her man in front of everybody, in front of a minister? No, her cultural norms forbade it. She swallowed the humiliation she felt as the table dropped into silence waiting for her to obey her husband. She then took off her bracelet and handed it over to the minister's wife who accepted the gift with no qualms. On the contrary, she looked rather galvanised, as did her husband, who smiled approvingly at the *Man of the Shoes*.

The minister opened the conversation giving my parents an update on the state of the Congo since my parents had left nearly a year earlier. The state had slipped into an insidious political crisis, the minister explained, a crisis of values and ideology, heightened by the suppressive Opango administration. The yet unsolved assassination of president Marien Ngouabi was central to the disorder that rippled across the country. Far too many people were being prosecuted and sentenced to death. Many were still waiting in prison or being held in military court on charges of conspiracy at that very moment. And yet all of them, from first to last, were innocent, the minster told my parents. Former President Massamba-Débat, Captain Kikadidi and Brazzaville's Catholic Archbishop Émile Biayenda, all were our compatriots whose blood had been shed unfairly. He depicted a nation which was plagued with corruption and deception, that had failed like so many other African nations to live up to the expectations the whole world had placed on them in the wake of independence—despite the potential in land, natural resources and the good intentions of the

African people. It broke his heart to see all the heartfelt values of the leaders who had fought for our liberation replaced by the thirst for power and greed of a dubious class of politicians who managed the country as a family-run enterprise. Those people were the real enemy of the revolution, the real cancer. So-called patriots who not even remotely had the well-being of their country and their people at the centre of their work. Being a politician was for them just a lucrative profession, the best way to shift government revenues, state contracts and favourable policies to themselves, the members of their families and their tribes. It was mortifying to witness this all first-hand, he said. Then, after taking a deep breath, he moved the conversation to the reason he came to Benin—the job he wanted to offer my father. A job about road making. It appeared that the International Monetary Fund had finally opened the tap once again now that the new president Opango had pacified the diplomatic relationships with Western countries after his predecessor's very costly insubordination. A substantial budget had already been assigned to Monsieur Idrissa Kamosi's office to invest in public works; among those, the implementation of the road system in Congo-Brazzaville. There was no better candidate than my father to head the big job of building and improving the country's road system in his view. Yet there were some hindrances, he explained. New anticorruption measures pushed the government to partner only with established building companies that were able to prove they possessed professional and technical attributes—including all the necessary building equipment beforehand—to execute the job. Now, the minister was well aware of my dad's financial situation, of all the assets he had lost under the new government, and that he had no means to invest in such a big project at present. He was also well aware that he could do nothing from his position to lift Dad's ban from Brazzaville. His plan to get him back on board relied on the strong feeling that a change in leadership was underway, judging from the general dissatisfaction mounting towards Yhombi Opango. There were indeed murmurs that the Central Committee of the *Congolaise*

Parti du Travail was already paving the way for Major Sassou Nguesso to replace Joachim Yhombi-Opango. The minister was positive that once in power Nguesso would lift the ban on West Africans and allow them back into the country as a solution to the country's economic problems. By allowing West Africans back in, the idea was that they could fuel the economy with an injection of additional trading forces into the domestic market and gain him the electorate. He basically charged my father with the challenging task of setting up a building company from scratch in time for the imminent change of presidency and the subsequent reopening of the national borders to Western Africans.

The minister knew him. He had full trust in the fact that my father could accomplish whatever he put in head. As for my father, who thrived in this type of challenge, he didn't need to think twice before accepting the job.

My mother's experience that night was not as fructuous. While my father left the restaurant feeling he had gained something out of the dinner with the Minister, my mother clambered back into the car with the opposite feeling, of having lost something, something important, something whose value went beyond the bracelet itself and stretched into her dignity, eroding further the trust she felt towards my father. She kept quiet during the car journey home and barely answered to his questions, until my father, unable to ignore any longer that he had hurt her, finally apologized, explaining to her that he acted that way to work up the minister a little. It was an opportunity that could sort them for life, he said, while the bracelet, no matter how you look at it, was just a bracelet. He promised he would buy her thousands more with the money they were about to make from the minister's job. It was no use, however, as my mother knew there was no need to bribe the minister since he had come from Brazzaville expressly to offer that job to Dad. No matter how many times he could purchase the same exact bracelet, all the bracelets in the world wouldn't match the value of the single one he gave her out of love. My father acted that way driven simply by one of his major weaknesses—the compulsive need to give things away.

***

My father met Pino soon after the meeting with the minister. Nobody knows exactly in what circumstances they met, not even my mother. She just claims the two businessmen met during one of Dad's work trips in Cameroon, where Pino, new to Africa, sought opportunities to importing tropical fruits to Italy. They came down together from Cameroon. Pino stayed at ours for a while where he was introduced to my mother and to us kids, who were dealing directly with a white man for the first time. We all felt fond of his jokes in a broken French straight away. Him and Dad got on very well. They would spend entire days together, losing themselves in conversations that would promptly lead to new business ideas. Their encounter was seminal for our future life in Italy, key to the many fortunate and tragic turns our life would take thereafter. Everything we are today was in the subterranean process of assembling itself during those days when Dad sat at the veranda with Pino, drove him around Brazzaville in and out of markets and shops, introduced him to suppliers, buyers and producers of this and that textile, sugar canes, coffee, and tropical fruits, and to his high-ranking friends who might be interested in establishing a tie with a Italian market. My mother sat with them in the veranda the night Dad told Pino about the business deal the Congolese minister had offered him. It was big, Pino observed, it offered unbelievable prospects if the project was to be extended to other African countries. There was nothing else this continent needed more than new roads. What my father needed was just upfront capital to cover the start-up expenses. We're talking about very large and expensive pieces of equipment and the salaries for a good number of the workers. Dad, who had been looking into second-hand machinery suppliers and had gone from bank to bank to evaluate loan and capital possibilities when he was last in France, had calculated that he would roughly need eight hundred million Franc CFA—about one million pounds—worth of capital to initially assemble all the requirements he needed to obtain the contract from the minister of the Infrastructure of the People's Republic of the Congo. In reality, he had nothing. He was financially broken. This didn't dissuade Pino, who, grasping the magnitude of the Minister's road construction project Dad pictured to him, probably the biggest deal he could have in a lifetime, and fascinated by Dad's mind and agendas, dropped his initial plan to flood the Italian market with tropical fruits, and offered to work with him instead. He ensured him he could find all that was needed to start-up at half of the price he stipulated. He knew exactly where to go. In fact, he said, he knew construction equipment suppliers in Italy that could cut him a very good deal.

That was how my father's most ambitious project began. He started working assiduously on it, typing down ideas and the business plan in an old machine at the desk in his room. Pino, assigned to look for opportunities of funding, low-rate loans and second-hand road machinery prices in Italy, left Congo to go back home. My mother was left to look at the big men taking up whatever they could and being free to pursue their own ambitions, while hers drifted further and further away. Her house, her domain. Raising seven kids, her life. And another kid was on the way. How did all this happen? How did she, a young, carefree girl who spent long afternoon studying with her friends at the park near the French embassy, morph into this, a young mother of seven kids, in the space of just a few months? A housewife, the fiancé of a man who she hardly saw, who, according to the rumours spreading in the area, was having a love affair with another woman, right under her nose, while she cooked and washed clothes for him and his kids in a foreign country, amid the adversity of his relatives, with no friends but an old woman? Was it her fault?

Dad's fault? Was the cultural baggage to blame? The example she took from the female figures she grew up with was not to question much, to accept what her culture of submission expected from her with no notion that she actually could refuse it all and be another person, choose a different path. She just went on with what stood before her, but whatever she did she tried to do the best for us kids. She learnt how to treat us equally, addressed us all as her own kids, mediated when we had a fight, treated our wounds, all done out of love, as she truly felt for each of us. Love for us and for Dad, because at the end of the day she genuinely loved him and deep inside trusted he would lift our family out of this situation at some point to a more dignified state as soon as he got back on track.

Life turned brighter whenever my father was back home from his work trips. She felt closer to that weightless Sofie who once used to be picked up from school by René back in Brazzaville. Things began to make sense again; generally, he came back with a large amount of money he earned from a good deal and was able to provide us with a high standard of living. We bought nice food and new clothes, and music played loud in the living room on top of Dad's gushing and charismatic voice that gave us an exciting account of his journey in France, in Holland, in Brazil. He brought with him gifts for us in the form of toys, clothes, and jewellery and perfumes for maman Sofie, took her out for dinner and to the cinema, and visitors returned to our house once again, including more benevolent versions of some of my father's relatives, particularly his favourite cousin Tantine Ellen and older sister Tantine Marielle Tawema. Soon we recruited a servant. His name was Masambila. Dad, a can of Kronenbourg in hand, introduced him to us, saying sarcastically we just needed to snap our fingers to get the man running to serve us. But that was not the case. Masambila never ran. He just walked. He was around twelve then, apparently already experienced at managing houses for better-off people. A khaki shirt with rolled-up sleeves, a pair of overused peasant trousers, and a pair of flip-flops, he left with my mother who gave him a tour around the house, giving him a general instruction of the work that awaited him. Even though we had a new helper, my mother kept on doing a good part of the housework herself. My father was busy anyway; even when he was at home, he often sat at his desk writing down projects. She remembers feeling his eyes on her when he came out of the room, looking at her as she dealt with his progeny. She would meet his eyes and saw a man who was growing in love with her. Sincerely in love.

Maman Sofie gave birth to my younger brother Happiness on the 11 of February of 1978 in Cotonou. Soon after his birth René proposed to Sofie. She accepted. They married in Cotonou's main Church at the presence of only the priest, the witnesses, Grandma Debra, and a handful of friends. Members of both families refused to attend a marriage they disapproved of. However the union was happily sealed by the holy bond of marriage. The only sad note, even sadder than the mutiny of their relatives was the fact that few days after the birth, René flew to Paris with another woman. And stayed away for several months. My mother was oblivious of the details, she just knew that some major opportunities related for the Minister road's job had come up in Paris, and it required Dad's presence in situ urgently. She helped him to prepare his bag and waved good-bye as he was driven away in a taxi. She hadn't the faintest idea that at the airport Maman Chantal was waiting for him with her bag and that they were about to take a flight together to Paris. She just waved good-bye.

Maman Chantal stayed in Paris with Dad for four months, where they rented a flat, enjoyed the life in Paris, with dinners out, cinemas, walks, and visited some tourist sight. I know that Dad also went there for work and managed to strike some deals and did gain some money during the time he was there. I also know that it was during that time in Paris that Chantal had fallen pregnant with my sister Moon. But probably Dad was not entirely aware of that, probably not even at the fourth month of pregnancy; he may have mistaken that faint bulky belly of Maman Chantal with her gaining weight from the saucy French cuisine. I want to believe that he did not know, I want to believe he wouldn't have been so inconsiderate to do what followed.

At the time Chantal was due to fly back to Benin he gave her an envelope full of money that was meant to reach my mother, but he clearly didn't have the nerve to tell the women he just engaged in a lengthy affair with. 'Give this money to my wife, please,' and instructed her instead to deliver it to a friend in a TV Shop in Cotonou to solve an old debt. He secretly called Sofie and instructed her to collect an envelope with some money he had put together for her and us kids from a friend of his in a TV shop in a week's time, counting on the fact that Chantal would have dispatched it by then, ensuring the two girls would miss one another. But that was exactly what didn't happen. The two women met at the shop. It could be that Chantal delivered the envelope some days later, or Sofie went there way too early, or most likely, both variables played a part in this unfortunate event. The fact was my mother had been standing in the shop for a little while when Maman Chantal walked in. Both women stood, staring at each other. With not much surprise as they were not idiots, they sensed what was happening, it was just a matter of having their suspicions confirmed. Now Chantal was sure René had dared to use her as the means to deliver money to one of her arch enemies. Whereas Sofie faced the shattering proof that during all this time she was holding down the fort, René had spent what was meant to be her honeymoon in Paris with the same woman he swore he was not seeing. The same woman whose son she was looking after as a proper son. Yet that was not all. To make things even more sinister was the fact that both women were visibly carrying with them a piece of René at the time of this encounter: Sofie had the newborn Happiness wrapped on her back and Chantal was visibly pregnant. Obviously from her man, Sofie assumed. Chantal walked towards her and handed her the envelope, rather than give it to the shop owner, and walked away.

By the time Sofie reached home, she had formed an idea of how to fix all this mess. She took Debra-Jo aside and explained her that things were not working out for her in this country and she had to go back to Congo, 'I need to bring you back to your granny.' Debra-Jo nodded, conceding. She grasped that something serious and urgent was behind Maman Sofie's drastic decision, and informed the other siblings that they were all leaving and helped them to pack up their things. Maman Sofie drove us all – Debra-Jo, Sigmund, Ocean, Lorenzo, Klaus, Redeso and I and Masambila back to Grandma Debra. She explained to my grandma the reason for her decision, that this was not the life she had signed up for, things had spiralled out of control, reaching a point where she couldn't tolerate it any longer. It was too much. She needed to leave. Grandma Debra understood, kissed her good-bye, and hugged her. My mother took with her only Happiness, and took a taxi ride down to Nigeria, where she bought her flight with the very same money René had sent to her via Maman Chantal. They stayed a few days in a hotel waiting for the flight and eventually took off to Brazzaville. She confesses, she would have left Happiness behind too if he hadn't been so small, for the usual tradition: 'the child stays with their father'. But Happiness was too little. So they flew off.

Keys and Keyrings

At the age of fourteen, Klaus began skateboarding with Tulio, the eldest of the two Italo-German Rullo brothers. They skated at every opportunity, during the two hours of time-off that preceded the beginning of after-school activities, the afternoon break and the evening, the two-hour gap between the dinner and bedtime, and the entire Sunday. The rolling and the strikes of the skateboard hitting the ground as they attempted to complete new tricks had become a daily soundtrack of our days in the courtyard of the Institution of St Catherina. It was not only the practice of skateboarding that was alluring Klaus's thirsty soul, but it was also being part of a movement and a family that went beyond the institution's borders to the urban landscapes he saw in the skate magazines he was addicted to, where kids across Europe were pictured doing amazing things. Along with Tulio, Klaus had become part of the worldwide community of dissidents who plastered walls with stickered slogans to educate people that skateboarding was not a crime. He dug covertly through the charity-given bags of clothes in a dark room of the institution, looking for clothing, which mimicked in the best way possible the ones promoted by his new community. I remember once he found a jumper of the Independent. Another day, his first Airwalks, which he wore around like he was a new man. But, in all this, what Klaus longed for most was to roll out of the institution riding his board, he wanted to take his experience of skating deep into the city, in squares, under porticos, in skateparks, weaving through crowds of real people, like his peers.

He had enough of practising the same old tricks in the structureless soil of the institution courtyard. But the priest would not allow him to go out alone, he wasn't old enough. The priest also disliked skating. So, it came as no surprise that Klaus did not hesitate when Lorenzo proposed that they escape one night to attend a disco night, about which a friend from school told him, which he didn't want to miss at any cost. Tulio and Yusuf joined the small group of fugitives.

The four boys rose from their beds at night, when the institution was deep asleep. They put on their coolest clothes, which they had sorted out previously and hidden under the pillows. Klaus and Tulio grabbed their skates, then sneaked out into the dark corridor to the main bathroom on the second floor. There, they climbed out of the window in the toilet onto the low-to-the-ground awning, walked along its whole length, climbed down into the main courtyard on the side near the car park and football field, and ran crouched down like marines, winding through the few cars parked in the parking lot, until they reached the compound walls. They waited to hear that no cars passed on the other side of the wall, before climbing it. And then, they were out. That was the first time Klaus was outside unsupervised so late. About to put down his skateboard and roll away, Lorenzo stopped him so as not to rouse the neighbourhood with the noise. They were still close to the institution and everybody in the area knew them. They ran off into a nearby lane, where Lorenzo and Yusuf stole a pair of bikes they found locked to a bike post. Opening the coded locks was an easy task for boys from St Catherina—a piece of cake. Two cycled while the other two skated. It was a dream come true for Klaus to finally have the night city entirely at his command, to glide over the street on his skateboard with his friends, riding out of confinement. The warm summer breeze brushed against their faces as they sped through the night. The wide-open city allowed them into its recesses. A whole city with plenty of possibilities to try out new tricks and practise old ones. To fail, fall and try again. Pavements and steps to make ollies up and down, to do flips, handrails to hazard grinds and slides that they had learnt from their peers in the skateboard magazines.

Soon, they arrived at the outdoor disco at Acque Minerali Park. Tulio and Klaus took their skateboards in their hands, while Lorenzo and Yusuf dumped their bikes outside the gate, next to rows of parked *motorini* Piaggio—Ciao, Bravo, and Vespa. Klaus was visibly mesmerised by the scene that appeared before them: lights and people flooding the night. The music grew louder as they made their way towards the hot spot. Among the crowd, they bumped into one of Lorenzo's classmates, Tomaso, who had told Lorenzo about that night. He was glad they made it and led them through the mass of people to a group of teenagers and young adults who sat on the edge of the dance floor stage. It was a mixed group of people, but all white Italian, most of whom were unfamiliar with the four boys from the Institution of St Catherina, except for Tomaso and a dark-haired girl, who had a crush on Lorenzo. All girls had a crush on Lorenzo—he was becoming more and more handsome. Even more so now that he wore a long, thin-braided hairstyle and blue contact lenses. 'You guys are from the institution, aren't you?' said a watchful boy from the group, one who didn't look very much pleased with the idea of a bunch of niggers and a southern-Italian-looking guy coming to hang around in his park.

That was one of the things you had to take on board back then in Italy, to have to deal with people like him. You wouldn't pass unnoticed if you were black, no matter where you went. Mixed reactions that ranged from sympathy to curiosity, horror to hostility were commonplace, but rarely, I have to say, did we meet hatred. Hatred was a step ahead. Hatred required a degree of knowledge. It implied that you'd been directly exposed to the culture of a group of immigrants for long enough to take a consciously developed stand. While back then in Imola, and on a larger scale in Italy, there was not yet ground for this paradigm of intolerance to take hold. Italy was still new to the migratory flux, and light years away from the climate of xenophobia that sweeps across Europe nowadays. There was practically nobody there to practise racism with at the time. The first African immigrants were a sparsely located phenomena of pacific people, innocuous good fellows, at times perceived as funny and a bit silly, easy to pat on the head. There were awe-inspiring Eritreans and Ethiopians from Italy's failed colonisation attempts, and the tall, friendly, slow-paced Senegalese, who sold you imitations of popular clothes brands on the street, cordially named *Vucumprà*—'Wanna-buys', or more friendly *Vucu*. A name that was then applied to all blacks, and in some degree, to low-ranked foreigners in general, before the influx of citizens from Morocco nearly two decades later, which then inspired the Italians to substitute the designation of *Vucumprà* with that of Moroccan. Black Africans, Indians, Polish, the Chinese, and particularly the southern Italians from Rome downwards, the whole lot, we all became derogatorily called Moroccans. As for the rare settlers with a long history in the country such as my siblings and myself, the Italians responded differently to us than they did to the average immigrant. They expected to be dealing with the usual Moroccans when they met us for the first time and approached us with the usual paternalistic attitude. An attitude that would change immediately as soon as we opened our mouths, as soon as they heard us speaking Italian with the same accent as theirs, with reactions that ranged from ones of surprise to slightly patronising, 'Wow you speak my language very well, when did you learn it?' to perplexity, anxiety and eventually camaraderie. The more we went on conversing, the more they would come to terms with the fact that they were dealing with one like them. Our Italian was an example of how trust-inspiring the power of language can be. People level up with you on the spot as soon as they understand that you share the same idiom. The use of insider terminology and the exact accent prompted them to act with unexpected familiarity with us, all the while mulling over the fact that we were part of a new phenomenon—Black Italians. But even though we were accepted, we felt different. We were treated differently than our white peers. Yet we had a hard time recognising that as a form of racism, because the people who called us 'little nigger' were good to us. They were authority figures in our daily lives—our teachers, our parents' friends, caring and loving people from the parish that we were introduced to. For us, the fact that they were not bad-intentioned excused them, because there was little trace of hatred or not at all. For example, in an everyday scene involving us, a mother would say to her child on the street 'Look, a nigger!' I remember thinking that nothing was amiss there because, from Cardinals to the kind local policemen down the road, I was affectionately addressed as 'little monkey!' 'How old are you, blacky?' I would have never called them racist. The old-fashioned Italian racism was in my view just a form of timidity, a stage prior to breaking the ice. Once you got past that point, the racism was over, the racist would give you whatever he could and invite you home to eat pasta all'amatriciana with granny, because that same racist would be the guy that I would meet in church on Sunday or during the processions. It was the parochial Italy. The charitable Italy that looked down upon us, which pitifully stroked our faces and rubbed our afros, implying that no matter what, since we were black, we were in need. Italy—a country of fraternity and equality, of *gli amici di cortile*, of the do-gooders, of the guilty-feelings regime, of the 'undercover friar' mentality, the moralistic Italy, of the quiet noondays in town with la Giovanna and Don Francesco and his mentally-challenged brother and la Piera who says, 'Well…' This was the Italy of the Democratic Christian party. The Italy that had only recently survived the horrors of Fascism and Nazism and vowed to not put up with that same narrative ever again.

But all of this elides one condition. All this 'poor boy' and 'we treat you like one of us,' would only survive if the foreigner behaved well. Like a Christian. Otherwise, even granny would turn up her nose and say, 'I'll send you back to your country!' We, the black and foreigners of that time, were well-aware of this potential threat hanging over us at all times and tried our best to comply with these tacit rules of hospitality. We tried not to misbehave, we cringed at the news of black offenders, felt ashamed by the loud rant of a black guy on the bus getting fined by a ticket officer suffering the crowd's disapproval, their eyes on us as if we too were somehow involved in the incident, even though we sat at a distance from it. In some instances, we were the first to condemn the foreigner who rebelled with his minor crime, or we refused to voice our true opinion in the matter, so that we were certain to be in the good graces of our gentle hosts, the Italians. We didn't want them to think bad of us, to get us deported. Especially, we didn't want ourselves to be the object of our friends' sarcasm. To behave well was a way to prevent creating an environment that kept on reminding us that we were inferior, an anomaly, a flaw of white society, when all we wanted was to be treated as equals. Not as *Vucus*, Kunta Kintes, Bingo Bongos, Boogie Mans, Slaves, Chimpanzees, *Negretto* or *negrone*. So we behaved. And we were accepted.

That was how it was that night, when the boys from St Catherina clicked with the rest of the group as soon as they proved to them that they spoke perfect Italian and that they shared the same cultural references. They chatted away, smoked cigarettes, somebody bought a few beers. Tomaso's group of friends were nothing extraordinary, but just because the night context was new to Klaus, all these people gained a special light and he asked a lot of questions about what they did and wowed at everything they said as if they were some of the most outstanding people in town. In response, these people found this awkward-looking guy who had no hesitations starting a conversation or pumping up your ego with rhetorical questions, who stuttered, and laughed nervously, a very enjoyable guy.

Lorenzo had wandered off with the brunette at some point to a more isolated location around the park, leaving Klaus, Yusuf and Tulio with the rest of the group. What happened next, he just heard it afterwards from Yusuf and Tulio. Apparently, a hit began to play, 'The Rhythm of the Night', and Tomaso's group went all down to the dance floor to have some fun. Tulio and Yusuf followed them, but not Klaus, who refused to join in, despite numerous invitations. He waited alone at the edge of the dance floor, his unfailing cap, skateboard at hand hanging from one side. He was too shy. But, saying that, he was an outstanding dancer. He was outstanding in any form of art in truth. A mess at school, but when it came to creativity, whatever came at his feet or hands, whether it was a ball, a skate, or he was just dancing, Klaus's performance would have without question left a mark on whoever watched him. He was a poet of movement. An incredible brain. I always had the feeling that Klaus was an undiscovered genius. Even that night at the Acque Minerali Park, he could have left everybody amazed if only he let himself go with some break dancing in the middle of the dance floor. But Klaus didn't have the guts for that, so he stood waiting on the margins, looking around, melancholy and at sea, but also at the same time deriving enough enjoyment from witnessing other people amusing themselves, his friends, everyone.

Then he realised his friend Tulio was gesturing him to come over again. Klaus refused as a fight broke out. Apparently, a boy, upset for Yusuf being all over his girlfriend, attacked him. Of course, Yusuf, robust and fight-ready, took it as an opportunity to get some sport and hit the guy back in the face. The backslash was swift. Three more people, friends of Yusuf's opponent, went over the boy contributing to the struggle in the middle of the dance floor. I'm sure it would have ended in a different way if Yusuf was a white guy and not a black Somalian guy, but there is always an extra variable at play if a black person is involved. Perhaps others would have tried to separate the two, or let them fight, trusting that a one-to-one fight was a fair fight, but a nigger who dared to punch back at one of them in public was something they could not tolerate, in any possible way. It required an immediate response. So there they were, four on top of Yusuf. Tulio and Klaus ran straight into action. But it was mostly Klaus, he was enough to change the tide of that situation. He slammed the skateboard in the face of the first one, gave a sound head-butt to the second and then at that point nobody dared to venture any closer. There was something that scared people more than violence: rage and demons. Klaus could evoke both. In a blink. His bursts of anger were part of his talent, as extraordinary as any other discipline he took on. His creative power was directly proportional to his destructive capacity. It was unclear where he drew all that strength from, since he was anything but a tough-looking guy, lean and only of average height. Whatever burned in within him didn't boil down to physical power, but pure rage. Klaus was violently kicking the face of one of the poor fellows, when Lorenzo, emerging from the crowd, rushed to stop him. He held him from behind, yelling at him to calm down and dragged him off. The four ran away through the crowd, as people shouted at them to stop. They got back on their bikes and skateboards and rolled away.

The incident had no repercussions on the Fantastic Four, not that night, nor the day after. There were no calls from the police, and no one noticed that they had escaped. Everything went as smooth as silk. When they arrived home, they climbed back onto the low roof, then the window, and quietly crawled back to their room, got undressed, and slid under the covers. All physical signs of the fight were skilfully masked with caps lowered to the eyes the morning after, jacket buttoned up to the mouth, foulards wrapped around the neck. This only lasted for the morning, as once they were at or back from school, they could blame the broken lips and black eyes on the usual brawl, occurring at school or at the institution.

All turned out well. The injuries healed with time, the mind forgot and days went on with the usual pace. Daylight got shorter, and days grew colder. We were entitled to a new coat if the one we had the previous year didn't fit anymore. Scarves and gloves on and you went for another day at school. At one and something we were back home. Pasta with butter and cheese, and a steak with salad on our tables on Thursday. Fish on Friday. At two hand claps from Don Ettore we would stop eating and walk out of the refectory. As the weather grew even colder, and daylight ran towards its nadir, we stopped going out to the courtyard and instead spent our recreational time indoors, inside a big room in the basement called the 'Under'. Full of columns and equipped with games, a ping pong table, and a few football tables, the space of the Under was a tenth of what we had available outside in the courtyard, but people still enjoyed playing football. The noise was similar to that of a leisure centre, with screeching trainers on linoleum and saturated voices of kids engaged in different activities simultaneously. Then we watched TV in the TV room upstairs for an hour and a half in the evenings. Two hours on Sundays. We saw *The Goonies*. *Indiana Jones*. *Back to the Future*. We saw *Stand by Me*. We saw exultant eastern and western Germans hugging each other after the fall of Berlin's Wall. A man in China stopped a line of war tanks in Tiananmen Square just by standing in front of them.

The days started stretching again with the onset of spring, warm wind crept in, and we rushed back outside to the courtyard, taking up our old positions at the wall near the football pitch, at the bench next to the kitchen, hidden away at the far end of the parking lot, or inside the institution's abandoned bus that smelled even more rotten than the previous year. We watched Tulio and Klaus ride their skateboards with renewed energy.

Then Dad's news came.

I didn't know how far I could trust it, and I dismissed it at first when I heard it directly from Sigmund. He came into our bedroom as we were setting up for bed. He sat on mine and Redeso's beds.

'We are out of here. Dad has bought us a house in Imola,' he said. Ocean confirmed it the day after when we came back from school. 'We have a house.' Then was Debra-Jo, when she came to visit that same afternoon. 'Dad has bought us a house in Imola.' It turned out that it was true, Father had bought us a detached house on the hillside of Imola, in a street called Via Suore on the outskirts of the Tozzoni Area, a hilly area. The conduit for the deal was Pino, as he was for the first house. The big old man had found a good deal from his circle of acquaintances with Dad's remote instruction, managed all the negotiations, paid and now held the keys. The keys of our house. From the night Sigmund told me, although I tried to give little importance to it, I couldn't help imagining Pino holding the keys of our house. I pictured them, the keys, just a bunch of keys, possibly attached to a boring plastic lobster clasp I usually saw around. There was something fundamentally new in the existence of these keys, in the notion that someone close to us had actually held them, as they were the concrete evidence that this news was different from Dad's usual promises. It wasn't like the ones about buying us cars and motorbikes and the plan for the house he showed us during our vacation in Africa that ended up being nothing with nobody knowing where it was to be built. The idea of a family friend living a dozen kilometres from us, with those keys in his hand, proved that this time the news was solid indeed. It was done, accomplished, and after years of institutional life we were finally going to live in a proper house. I caught Redeso getting lost in thought several times throughout the day; at lunch, in the classroom, in the courtyard while playing, his gaze angled upward. I had no doubts that, like me and possibly like our siblings, he was daydreaming about the imminent arrival of his new life, when he would be able to move into the new house and get his room ready. He would fill up his wardrobe with the clothes he'd be pulling out from his suitcase, put a poster up on the wall, park his bike in the garage, open the fridge in the kitchen for a can of coke and a few slices of salami whenever he fucking wanted, and stroll back upstairs to his room to watch TV. It all felt so unreal that we were careful not to speak about it with anybody, not even amongst ourselves, due to the superstition that it could all be jinxed if we spoke about it carelessly. As if the house was actually a tiny house which lay fragile in our hands, a small house made out of a very thin layer of crystal.

Pino's ever-lasting Fiat Uno drove into the courtyard of St Catherina the day after, sometime after lunch, to take us to see our new home. It was a Sunday, we had on our civilian clothes from the mass we had attended in the morning. All seven of us sat waiting on the benches in the courtyard, along with Gabriella, who had driven her own car to help transport some of us to the new house. Still jovial as usual, Pino, the big old man, looked to have aged considerably as he came out of the car and limped, due to a recent knee injury, in our direction. I also noticed that he had a few lumps bulging out from the back of his head beneath his thin white hair. His face was still red like a pepper but his big hands over us as we hugged had become smaller with time. I realised as we hugged that I felt less attached to him, as if I were facing a different man than the old pal I was used to see hanging around the old villa in Zolino with Dad. His feelings towards us, however, seemed unchanged. Maybe he looked more distracted and less exuberant, now that we were not seeing each other as often as we had when we lived in the villa. Still, he treated us as if we were his nephews; he brought each of us a chocolate bar, asked us how we were doing at school and shook his head in disappointment when Ocean told him that both Klaus and Lorenzo were performing very poorly and lectured them, saying, 'This is the most important time of your life, guys. What will become of you if you fail to get your diploma? You don't want to be a factory worker. You know it is a tough life working eight hours in a factory, and it's boring, and the pay is ridiculous! Is that what you want for your future?'

Things were going well for Pino. In recent years, after he stopped working for Dad, he had gone back to his initial plan of trading tropical fruits from Ghana. I heard he had set up a company with some local associates and that they were making good money, bringing fruit like avocado, papaya, and mango—varieties people barely knew—into the region. And yet, not much of his style had changed. He still wore that 70s-style public-servant-type suit and tie that made him look as if he was living in scarcity. He still wore his white hair brushed back.

We sat on the courtyard's long bench with him, eating the chocolate bars. Once finished, we clambered into his car. The manual window handles, the beige felt seat covers, the pop-out ashtray, the smell of cigarettes and the radio with the red pointer set to the same channel, everything was still the same but undergoing the relentless process of yellowing of time. Half of us rode in the car with him, while the other half followed behind in Gabriella's Lancia Y10. We drove for fifteen minutes across the city, past the Pedagna's suburban area and carried on uphill through the sunny rural landscape of open green fields and hilly vineyards.

'There it is!' said Pino, pointing at a house that emerged far in the distance from the green landscape. The four of us—Redeso, Lorenzo, Klaus and I—stretched out our heads to an angle where we could see the house and kept it in sight for the rest of the journey until we arrived. We parked on the lawn in the front of the house. Gabriella parked next to us. The grass was wet from the past night's rain as we walked on it. I could see that Dad went close to his preferred specifications due to the grandeur of the house. The size and style of the property were in some respects similar to that of the old villa we had in Via Emilia. An independent, isolated mansion, but more modest, more agrarian. Unlike the old villa, which was hidden in a court of trees, this one would have been entirely exposed to sunlight if it wasn't for the shadow of a big ancient oak tree towering right next to it. The rest was just lawn. A large lawn with undefined borders. Set apart, on one side of the property, was an auxiliary building that looked like an abandoned barn.

The entire property looked like it had been abandoned for a decade. All the shutters were closed, the green paint peeling off. The yellow coating of the house was also peeling and cracked all over. A big chain locked the front door, most likely to substitute a broken lock. It looked nothing like the bright, welcoming place we had imagined. Quite the opposite, the decaying aura surrounding the house was strong enough to suggest that it would take far longer than what we had anticipated before we could move in. But not everything was bad. The front view was staggering. We could see a large part of the city of Imola from above, with more hills and woodland rising from behind the house. What was most important was that we had a house, no matter how long it would take before we were able to move in, it was ours. We waited for Pino to open the padlock, which didn't open with the set of keys he had, even though he tried three different keys. None of them worked. So, we tried to get in through the back door. It worked. It opened. We were in.

We walked into the entryway, among the stuffy smell and the dampness, until Debra-Jo and Pino opened windows and shutters, letting air and sunlight flood into the living room. Like the exterior, the interior gave the same impression: there was a lot of work to be done. It was completely empty, without a single piece of furniture. All the plaster was peeling and there was lots of dust and dirt. There were broken windows and the old externally applied electric wiring was burnt and needed replacement. Our footsteps almost echoed against the tiled floor as we walked around the ground floor individually, scattering randomly to every room. All looked the same, empty and in decay. The toilet was broken. The kitchen had just a stove and an old sink. There was no running water; Ocean tried to turn on the tap. Obviously, all the amenities were off explained Pino.

'It will need lots of work, guys, that's for sure,' he added. 'We need to rebuild the roof before you can move in, it's all broken. Changing the toilet and furnishing is the least of the problems, but the roof, guys, we need to work on that, you don't want the rain pouring on you while you sleep, right?'

'How long do you think it'll take to repair it?' Debra-Jo asked. We were all climbing upstairs to the second floor, one behind the other, including Gabriella who, like us, looked both doubtful about the condition of the house, but happy for us, happy that we had a solution at least.

'That totally depends on your Dad's timing,' Pino explained, 'It's not cheap at all to rebuild a roof. Whatever he put on was just enough to cover the cost of the deposit and pay the first month's mortgage. If he sends the money tomorrow, we can call the builders, and in less than a month, you're in, my word!'

The whole project kept on taking a different light from what we pictured originally. With each additional bit of new information—the work it needed, the costs, the deposit, the mortgage, Dad's timing—the further off the eventuality of a move was pushed into the distance. But again, we could persevere. If nothing else, we knew we could endure. We had done it for years. We could do it again. We looked around the four empty rooms on the second floor. There was a third floor, an attic, but we didn't see it because Pino discouraged us from going up there, saying it was not safe due to the collapsing roof.

'I know I know, this is not what you were expecting. But you have no idea how little it cost, it's a bargain, trust me, a really good deal for what your dad was able to afford. Imagine it once it's complete! I've seen plenty of houses that looked like this in the beginning, a mess everywhere!—which makes things look way worse—and then you clean up, sort all the things out, paint and you'll fall in love with it. What truly matters is the quality of the building, which I can guarantee, is good. The rest it's just decoration, wait and see!'

***

We left the house with less enthusiasm than we had on our way there. We had little to share on the matter during the car journey back home. It wasn't so much the state of the house, more the amount of time the whole thing would take before we could actually move in. Knowing Dad, the time could stretch indefinitely. Until then, we considered ourselves in exactly the same place we stood before: in the institution. Before we left, Pino gave a set of house keys to Debra-Jo and kept one set for himself. He then gave us a big smile from the driver's seat once he dropped us outside the institution. 'I'll get in touch as soon as I've got news', he said, before driving away.

After consulting each other, Debra-Jo, Ocean and Sigmund agreed we should all have our own sets of keys, so Ocean went to cut more copies a few days later and gave us each our own set. I remember the day as a milestone in my life—the first time I ever held in my hands a set of my own house keys. It was a set of two bare keys held by a metal key ring, the key's edge still freshly sharp from the key maker. I felt a big change was underway. I was getting closer and closer to meeting the standards of a more ordinary life. More similar to one of those kids who went home alone at the end of a school day and were entitled to open their front door by themselves, with their own keys. I stopped with Redeso at the supermarket the day after on our way back from school to buy a proper key ring. We both got one with a rubber motorbike hanging from a plastic loop. We kept the sets inside our pockets all the way to the institution, feeling them in our pockets, then put them into the drawer of our bed table. We got changed into our customary tracksuits and joined the others downstairs in the courtyard. At that point, after seeing the house and getting the keys, we felt we had nothing to fear anymore in letting our friends know that we had a house. So, we did. We told the kids of our group that we had a house now, but of course, aside from a few comments—a 'wow' and an 'I'm happy for you'—as long as we were still hanging around them, keys or not, the event of our house meant little to them. Gino, red hair with the permanent arm cast, deflated the whole thing by casually commenting, 'Then you're gonna burn that one down too.'

I went to sleep that night with a mixed sense of edginess and peace. Ocean was on shift to put us kids to sleep that night.

'Do you have your keys there?' he said when he passed by my bed, a finger pointing at my bedtable.

'Yes,' I said.

'Well, from now on, when things get funny, pull out your keys and give them a good look.'

What I liked about Ocean was that he was a simple person, reserved, kind and sensible. His head was on his shoulders but he had room for humour even if that humour was largely self-contained. I'd say in the environment of endless rearrangement in which we lived, Ocean's plainness came as a much-needed quality that granted a sense of calm and continuity in our lives, much like the neutron that stabilises the atom and prevents protons from repelling each other.

***

June came around. With the academic year coming to an end, both Lorenzo and Klaus failed their respective classes; Lorenzo his third year of secondary school and Klaus his second year. He was to repeat the second year, after having failed the first year once already. Redeso and I, on the other hand, did relatively well; we barely managed to pass and continued to year two. Sigmund and Ocean also did well. Sigmund completed his third year at the Professional Institute of Electro-Mechanics with dignity, and Ocean finished his third year at the accounting school. A few days after the end of school, we received more big news—perhaps bigger than the purchase of our house, at least on an emotional level. Dad was sending us tickets to spend that summer in Africa. The news came from Debra-Jo, which was then confirmed by our parents in a phone call we received on the institution's landline a few days later while we were having dinner. The loud ring prompted one of the supervisors to leave his post at the table and rush across the refectory to go and pick up the phone at the reception hall. He came back after a few attempts at overcoming the inconsistent reception issues of international calls. 'Who is it? Who? Ah, yes yes… *Bonne soirée* … It's your father, guys!' We dropped forks and knives and propelled over to the reception desk as if it was a very serious matter, like the announcement of a death or something.

We grouped around the old-fashioned grey phone on the desk, with its ring-shaped dial, receiver and spiral-like cable, but the line was too quiet for all of us to participate in the conversation simultaneously with the receiver on the desktop. It was more practical if Sigmund and Ocean managed the bulk of the conversation, while Klaus, Lorenzo, Redeso and I tried to gather clues about what was being said through their expressions and comments. We had our turn at the end, with our '*Oui oui, suremant... Oui... Oui... Oui... Moi aussi... a bientôt... Bisous.*' In a nutshell, our mother was coming to collect us in two weeks. We were about to spend another summer in Africa. We came back into the dining hall splitting off to our separate tables, feeling larger than before, larger than usual, as a result of the agreement we had just established with our parents.

***

Some special measures had to be taken specifically for us in preparation for our summer trip to Africa. The institution always underwent some adjustments during the summer holiday, which in Italy lasted about three months. The place emptied of half of the residents, most of whom returned back home, including Tulio Rullo, his brother Riccardo and the three Paroli brothers. Around thirty people remained, those who were stationed at the institution on a permanent basis. The more dysfunctional, the semi-homeless like us, the asylum seekers forced to stay in the country by law, and the immigrants who could not afford to fly back to Morocco, Brazil, or Somalia. With the exclusion of an extra handful of adults who had work commitments in town, the group of vacationers boiled down to about twenty people. Right from the end of June up to the beginning of September, we would spend the whole summer away in the institution's two summer residencies. The first stop was to Don Ettore's native town, high up in the Alps of Piedmont, a very small and neat town called Caprile, where we would settle for a couple of weeks before moving to a second destination. This was another house of the institution, where we would stay for the rest of the summer, without the priest. It was back to Emilia-Romagna, in a small mountainous enclave near Bologna called Monghidoro. We travelled by a van and a few cars. One of the maids and a chef came with us. But that summer, my brothers and I were to skip the tradition. We were to bypass the summer in the mountains and wait at the institution for our mother to come and take us to Africa. I don't know why they couldn't just send us the tickets and let us take the flight by ourselves under the supervision of Debra-Jo, Sigmund and Ocean, but apparently that was the arrangement—we had to wait for Maman Sofie to come.

Klaus was, without a doubt, the most excited about the prospect of the African trip. He looked like another person, as if he had regressed ten years. He was probably the only one who could so readily and swiftly shift from a state of fierce toughness to childish innocence just at a whiff of cheesy news like going home to our family. You could hardly recognise him, the same kid who had no qualms about using a skateboard to strike someone in the face at a discotheque was now excitedly describing to the residents leaving for the mountainside our summer plans. He implied that he was now part of the group of residents who went back home for a holiday when he proudly explained cheerfully: 'Ah no, man, we're not coming this year, be-be-because we're going ba-ba-ba-back home.'

The departure of the holiday-goers' van and cars left the institution as empty as every summer while our luggage lay next to our beds, ready for the African trip. All rooms morphed into something else, widening and sitting more quietly than usual now that it was just Klaus, Lorenzo, Redeso, me and a dozen adults hanging around in there. We ate at the adults' table with Sigmund and Ocean, the remaining tables all empty. There was a nearly spectral feeling of unusual silence we could perceive at our back. We didn't even need supervision and spent time just by ourselves hanging around the courtyard. We'd occasionally come across Sigmund, Ocean and a few of the workers, including Mr P, who was put in charge of us now that Don Ettore had left for the mountainside with the other residents. When we departed, he too would drive to join the others on the mountain. According to our parents' instructions, we were meant to leave two weeks from the day of the phone call, but they didn't specify what date. It wasn't set yet.

We hung around with no clue when we were supposed to leave.

We just waited. A week passed with no updates. Then another week passed and still nothing. And another week. And another. I felt I was sitting again in a very familiar place. Those days threw me back to the climates of solitude I felt during the periods we spent on our own in the house in Zolino and the time in the small clinic, where all that waiting, going through weary, empty days, felt like waiting in a desert to be rescued. It was nothing like the type of solitude of when you are alone—I wasn't alone—but I could still feel it. We stood waiting day after day with no news, the solitude growing on a visceral level. The solitude of being powerless, of being left hanging on with no explanations, when it would have taken nothing for them to pick up the phone and let their kids know that they were running late or whatever. We felt like we weren't worth even this small attention.

The days grew hotter with the coming of July. The empty courtyard and the heat-scorched ground of the football pitch, truly looked like the harsh, arid soil of a desert. I watched Klaus gasping for an update whenever he caught sight of Sigmund and Ocean walking towards us, just for him to spit on the ground with disappointment and resentment when they brought no news, as if they were part of the conspiracy that aimed to keep him in that unnerving state of hold. He passed the time engaging in his solitary activities more than usual. Neglecting skating, he would rather play alone on the football pitch. He'd place the ball at the centre of the field before he kicked it to the goal post. He would then go to fetch the ball and repeat the process, his face showing he was lost in a train of unintelligible thoughts as he walked back to the centre of the field holding the ball in his hands.

We waited. More days. Sometimes, we'd go out for a walk around town with an adult who took pity on us—one of our brothers or another resident—who would take us out for chores with them. A couple of times, we met Debra-Jo. She too had no news but would spend the afternoon with us at the bench in the courtyard.

Soon, another special measure was taken for us when Mr P had to leave the institution to join the others in the mountains. Being in charge of the minors left at the institution, he couldn't leave us there, so he had to take us to join the rest of the group at the mountainside, leaving Sigmund and Ocean behind to wait for Maman Sofie. Mr P explained to us that he would drive us back to the institution when Maman Sofie arrived, trying his best to hide that he knew how this whole thing was about to end. So, we loaded our luggage, already packed for the Africa trip, inside the boot of Mr P's Alfa Romeo. We drove out of the city to the highway and headed on about four hours northward up to Piedmont. To Biella, near Switzerland. To Caprile. To the mansion house on the mountainside on the far edge of the small town of Caprile. People from the institution, brightened and energised by the life at that altitude, were fully immersed in their holiday life and looked surprised to see us getting out of Mr P's car. They were expecting to see us in a couple of months, but there we were, way ahead of schedule, the losers, having to tell to everyone that our stay was only temporary because our parents were just late, but they were still coming to take us home, yes because Mr P would drive us back next week. There wasn't even any point in unpacking our luggage. We just parked it next to our beds and took out only the necessities we needed for the day, putting back what we took out in surplus, and keeping our stuff well organised in the event of our departure. We engaged only partially with the general activities of our peers. We didn't want to get too messy, let alone get injured right before taking a flight. More days passed and we let ourselves get fully drawn into the day-to-day scramble of life in Caprile, joining tournaments of ping-pong and table football, singing sessions and collective games in the courtyard like everyone else. We stopped noticing that our clothes were dirty. As for our luggage, we left them messy next to our beds.

One of the best features of the house in Caprile was the view we had from the courtyard. The courtyard sat right on a clifftop overlooking the town below and other more remote towns lying far in the distance. From there, you could see the small network of streets, including the road which broke off from the town's main road and climbed up to the institution's residence. That was the road I often caught Klaus staring down from the terrace. He stood leaning against the banister that ran along the edge of the drop-off, melancholic eyes staring at the town below, at the many bell towers of the churches, the lake, the mountains on one side and the road, the road that led to us, as if there was a way to figure out amid all the cars driving it which one would drive Maman Sofie here.

Few cars drove along that road. Many passed our house. Some entered the gate, made a U-turn and drove back. Others drove into the courtyard bringing some visitors from Imola, a pair of priests from the parish and a group of the Catholic Action boys with their guitars and grit, but never Maman Sofie. In the end, she didn't come. Somehow, the plans for the holiday in Africa had broken apart without us being notified. Didn't matter. As usual, even Klaus eventually gave up waiting. Our luggage was finally unpacked and all our clothes were sorted into the wardrobes like everyone else's, leaving the space next to the bed nice and clear. We got sucked into our holiday, enjoyed our meals at the small canteen with food that was prepared with more love than down in St Catherina. We helped the cook to pick nettles in the fields for her green lasagne. Whispered at night in our bedrooms. Challenged each other to have a cold shower in the morning. Raced down to the small town below via a steep dirt pathway that cut through the woods for a stroll around the shops in town to buy a Swiss Army knife, some postcards to send to friends, a leather bracelet with our name on it. We walked for half an hour up to a small lake and sat on the benches next to old ladies dressed alike in sugar paper dresses, and walked further ahead, up to a second bigger town, more similar to a Swiss one. We went for a few day trips, hiking over the crest of the mountain and singing at the top of our lungs our moto song, 'And who are we? And who are we? We are from St Catherina! We are from St Catherina!' We climbed up to the top of the mountain where a metal cross sprung out of it and sat down at its feet to eat our packed lunch with salami sandwiches and canned fruit and water that we gulped down from our individual flasks that hung around our necks. Then we marched again, with our heavy mountain boots and the sticks we had carved with our names and tribal patterns, tapping the ground to keep vipers away. Until it was time to move to Piamaggio, the institution's second summer residency for the last month of summer vacation.

LONDON, PRESENT DAY
VI

Dear Telma, I'm listening to the interview I did with my mother on my headphones so as not to disturb her; she's having a nap upstairs. It all sounds different, the recording, now that I replay it, not always pleasant. Some bits are heavy to swallow indeed. Her voice too, the grieving timbre of it, throughout the interview, doesn't help. Perhaps it was a bad idea to drag her into this because she really gets down when recalling her past with my father. She also suffers from heart problems. What should I do? Stop now? How necessary is this project? For her, for my siblings, for me? Would I be able to go on living my life happily if I dump it all? I'm sure I will, but I'd rather not give up now. There are still things I need to know. It's my birth right. The cruel right of a son, perhaps the only inheritance I'll receive from my mother. I listen to the recording. I note down the relevant points on my laptop. Here and there I need to rewind to get hold of some obscure French words. It's not long before I need a break. I prepare myself a cup of coffee which I drink outside on the terrace and find you there, unexpectedly standing on your terrace, you, the strangest thing in my life. Somewhere on the spectrum between a diva and a thug, my neighbour, the foreigner from Portugal, my new most intimate friend. You are in jeans and a blue shirt, resting your back against the wall of your house, smoking a cigarette that seems to taste bitter today. You free a side of your face from a long tuft of wavy hair as soon as you notice me, standing two terraces away from you, and you smile.

'That's a surprise!' I say, 'I didn't know you were back from holiday.' But you don't seem to grasp what I said, the traffic noise on Lower Clapton Road is too loud today. A chord of buses had jammed the road, and horns of fed-up commuters broke through the buzz of the traffic. 'I said that it's a surprise to see you!' I repeat louder.

'The same here. How are you?'

'Good. You look very well. Did you come back today?'

'What?' you shout again. The buses' rumble shakes our windows. You make a sign to me to wait, rest the cigarette on the ashtray on the table and disappear indoors. You stay inside for a little while, probably answering a phone call, or going for a piss, while your terrace, the outdoor table and chairs, remain lifeless. I look at the two terraces in between us. Then I look at the floor that extends from the opposite side of my terrace. All terraces lie adjacent one to another in a long line and are separated just by borders of brick walls one foot high. We are all so close. Technically, we could easily just walk across each other's terraces as if we share a strip of land, like in a housing association, but we hardly interact. The norm is for everyone to mind their fucking business. We all came to London to hide, and we've been lucky. We have found a place where we can ignore each other. Some terraces are always empty, particularly the two that belong to the Muslim families who live on either side of my house. I never see them outdoors. Another terrace has been empty since I moved in. Other neighbours pop their noses outside just to have a fag or make a phone call then they retreat inside, closing their windows and curtains behind them. Abandoned empty flower pots punctuate all terraces alike. Some have deck chairs folded by a wall. A rusty barbecue set rests on the second terrace between mine and yours. That flat has been vacant since I moved in.

You finally come back. You're holding your phone. I go to grab mine from the living room when I hear it ringing. It's you. Your name is on the display. I answer as I move back outside and sit on my low wall facing you.

'Hey.'

'Hey.'

'This is strange,' you say. 'To hear you from the phone while seeing you.'

'Yeah,' I say. 'I can see from your mouth there is a little delay.'

Something about what I just said makes you laugh. A laugh that sets in before I can hear it through the receiver.

'It would take us just a few steps to meet and hug, sit next to each other, but I can't today. I can't see you. He's very upset about our friendship. He is at the post office and could be back any second and would be upset if he sees me with you. Even if he sees me talking with you on the phone. Especially now that we have just come back from a holiday together. Do you understand?'

'Yes, I do. But what's the difference in any case? He's fine with your other your friendships, right?'

'You know you're not just a friend. He knows I have a crush on you… And I missed you.'

'What shall we do then?'

'Let's keep it this way, let's just be friends. Even if I break up with him, I would not come to you anyway, I don't want to have sex with you, it would spoil everything. I'm fed up with relationships. They spoil everything.'

I feel the same way, I say to you, but I'm not entirely sure. I'm fine as a single man, single parent, I'm fine living alone and sharing the kids fifty-fifty with my ex. I'm fine fucking around. It's a privilege, I say. Then we sit in silence for a bit, looking at each other and hearing our silent breath through the phone. I pay attention to the noises in the background bouncing back and forth from your phone, the buses, the indiscriminate voices of people on the street, a howling police siren. Or is it an ambulance? It passes me first and then reverberates through your phone. And then the siren is faintly disappearing, only audible outside of our phones. You're on your feet, head and shoulder resting against the wall, a hand on the pocket of your tight jeans, the other holding the phone. Here, above the high street, suspended over the traffic jam with you, it seems that there is more space than one could possibly think of, around, above, despite the thick grey cap of the sky. This thing of being visible to each other while talking through a digital medium makes things between us, our need for each other, even more urgent than usual. A sort of high-definition masochistic holographic Skype. Both of us are only half-way anonymous to each other. It's a different type of conversation. It is as precious as when you talk with a friend or relative who lives abroad, for you are here, and simultaneously not available. You live in another country. Your terrace sits outside any free movement agreement. All these fucking borders they have set around us. From geographical, to physical, to emotional, a matryoshka of cages. Borders we have erected ourselves, or complied with to the extent that it seems we can understand life only through the logic of territories. And this logic seems to be timeless and primordial. Do you *belong* to somebody, my love? Do you *belong* to him? Do you *belong* to the values of the Portuguese society or the English or any social values at all? Do you belong to your own promises? To your aspirations? To the train of your thoughts? To your job, family, your actions? Do you *belong* to your land? Can we steal each other from others? Are we indeed *stealable*? What is the difference between ground and territory? Where do the boundaries of your territory lie against the ground you're standing on? What is the fucking ground? Where is it? Where does it start and end? Tell me where were you born my love? Tell me where? Where are you truly located if we strip away all the manmade layers of cement that cover the ground and all the geographical borders? If all the pens and offices of the European diplomats were stolen before they could sign any of their fucking international treaties, you and I, would we have actually ever been foreigners?

'My mother is here,' I say.

'Is she?'

'Yeah, she's sleeping upstairs'

'It's kind of strange imagining you with your mother. Did she come from Africa?'

'No, she lives in Bordeaux. She's been living there for ten years. She's a French citizen.'

'And how do you feel about it? About having her here?'

'It's nice to have her around.'

'I was thinking that we might move back to Portugal if things get ugly with this Brexit thing.'

'Really, you're leaving?'

'Why stay? There is nothing of that "thing" of London left anymore. It's getting ridiculously expensive. I see the point of struggling financially. But not in this condition. Not just to stay here and live a pointless life. Even the hipsters that started all this gentrification business have left Hackney. All the artists, the cool people, all gone. I don't find it charming to be living hand in hand with just white collar people, brokers, bankers and millennials.'

'What if there is a second referendum, would you still leave?'

'I don't know. Maybe this Brexit thing is just a good opportunity for us to move on to a more decent life.'

'Will he go with you?'

'Yes, he said he will.'

We stay in silence.

'Don't fall in love with me,' you say.

'I'll try not to.'

'Don't allow me to fall in love with you.'

'I'll try.'

'I have to go now. Ciao.'

We both hang up the phone, the warm closeness of our voices interrupted. But we don't move from where we are. You don't go in, neither do I, we stay there to prolong this moment together. We wait in the realm of visible things only. We stare at each other, split apart by two terraces, suspended over the traffic jam of Lower Clapton. Hanging up the phone to part isn't enough, it doesn't work in the physical dimension. We had to use a different stratagem here, something that works in the dimension of visible things—a gesture of the hands, an eye blink, a smile. And now we can both get back into our flats, to our individual, ordinary lives, as ordinary as they can be.

I bring my cup of black coffee to the table. It is cold now and tastes bitter. I sit down in front of the computer, staying like this in a meditative state for a while, memories of our conversation still playing in my mind—of you leaving, of not seeing you anymore—while taking sips of coffee and wondering whether to write or go back to my mother's recording. I read the news instead. London's Mayor, Sadiq Khan, a radical Remainer campaigner has pledged for a second referendum in an open letter he wrote to *The Guardian*. He overtly supports the People's Vote movement manifesto in that people should have the final say on the country's direction—whether a hard or soft deal, or just remaining in the European Union. 'I don't believe it's the will of the people to face either a bad deal or, worse, no deal,' he says. 'That wasn't on the table during the campaign. People didn't vote to leave the EU to make themselves poorer, to watch their business suffer, to have the NHS wards understaffed, to see the police preparing for civil unrest or for national security to be put at risk if our co-operation with the EU in the fight against terrorism is weakened.'

Then I read on the next page that the number of Tory's cabinet members who feel the same way is on the rise. That the UK should stay and that a second referendum is the only democratic way to pass the deadlock in this new very much unexpected 'catastrophe we put ourselves in,' they say. I stop reading the news.

I'll miss her. My favourite part of UK is leaving. She's moving back to Portugal.

I put the headphones on, play back my mother's interview from where I left it. I cringe at this passage when she gives her account of how, fed up with my dad's cheating and of the Beninese lot, she moved back to Congo leaving us behind in Benin. I cringe again when I listen to it again for the second time. She left us there when Redeso and I were just two years old. It sounds even more sinister to be hearing this event from her digitalised voice. I had no clue I was left at that age. I really don't know how to explain it, if this way of managing things is the African way, as she claims, and African kids don't mind being dropped off here and there because they know they're going to grow tougher. That me as an African man shouldn't feel the way I do. Or is it because I'm a fucking European pussy that on hearing my mother saying casually that she left me when I was a baby depresses me? How many things about my past am I still unaware of, that I would probably die never knowing? Not about her and my father, but about me and my siblings? It's our story. I write down some notes. Then I hear my mother waking up, the floorboards above my head creaking under her steps. She comes down the stairs, leans in the living room from the door, her face rejuvenated from the nap. 'Is it time to pick up the kids?' she asks.

'Yeah, we leave in twenty minutes,' I say.

'So I have time for a shower?'

'Sure, you have time for a shower.'

Around three-fifteen we set off to collect the kids from school. We walk in silence, as if there was a thick sheet of metal between us. I grow nervous, as usual, as we approach the school gate. I have done this ritual for five years, yet I still feel tense. The school parents make me nervous. We pick up April from the entrance of the Year One building amidst an explosion of children of different races and credos, who run into their parent's arms or stay playing in groups. We meet Bernardo coming towards us in the middle of the courtyard. I kiss them both on the head and ask about their day at school while my mother takes the perplexed April by the hand and we walk off. My mother seems very happy, a genuine happiness, a type of happiness that appears all together a mystery to me. What does she like about walking with a grandchild she barely knows? I wonder what's on her mind, what she's thinking about now as she walks with that smile on her face? Can love travel so far through time and space? Is it only God that is the driving force of this woman? I realise that I'm about to spoil her mood, and I'm not even set for recording when I ask her, 'Why did you leave us there?'

She keeps on walking, turning gloomy all of a sudden, as if the question had landed at the worst time.

'I left you all there because I didn't want your dad to claim that I took his kids and use that as leverage to come to harass me. I wanted him to reflect over his actions. If he complained about Happiness, I would have told him: I'll send him back to you when he turns two.'

Big Plans, New Life, the Big Deal

You can imagine how happy Olivier, my mother's father, was to have her back in his house in Brazzaville after she escaped from Benin and her marital difficulties back in the late seventies. He, along with my mother's siblings and stepmother, welcomed her and vowed to give her the support she needed to get through this difficult time.

Meanwhile, a thousand miles away in Paris, René was in hot water. Informed by his Beninese family that Sofie had moved back to Brazzaville, he had a reaction that I wouldn't have expected from the seemingly impervious *Man of the Shoes*. He panicked, fearing that my mother had split up with him. He called everyone in his family and his social circles in Benin and Congo to get more information about the fate of his wife and to attempt to talk to her. The answer was the same everywhere: 'She's back in Brazzaville. She doesn't want to talk to you.' In vain, he called her house in Brazzaville, the one he bought her when she got pregnant with Redeso and I, but she wasn't there, she was staying at her father's house. So, René called there several times, and each time Olivier answered or was passed the phone by one of Sofie's sisters. 'She's done with you, please stop calling,' he'd say. Something inside my father shifted as he grasped that this time he had gone too far with the wrong woman. He was not dealing with his usual women who would stay waiting at his feet, and he loved her even more under this new dramatic circumstance. My father dreaded the possibility that she would drift into the arms of another man, which was entirely possible since Sofie was still young and very beautiful. Then there was her father, a huge influence on her and a significant obstacle between them. It could be that Olivier, who had been averse to him from the very beginning, would now persuade his daughter to divorce and eventually push her to a new marriage to keep René away once and for all.

How to solve this impasse? How to have her back if he could not even enter the country due to the Congolese government's immigration restriction on West Africans? The only way was through his powerful network of acquaintances inside the Congolese elite. He managed to reach the minister of security of Congo, Monsieur Pierre Gizenga. The minster, familiar with my dad's reputation as a great businessman and for the refurbishing service he had provided to the government, listened to him as he frankly explained the reason why he needed to return to the Congo. Minister Pierre Gizenga agreed that the matter was very important indeed and decided to help him. A couple of weeks afterwards, Dad received an official permit from the Congolese government that allowed him to enter and temporarily reside in the country under the condition that he was to report his residential address to the police and that he was not to leave his domicile under any circumstances until he received new orders, a sort of house arrest. So, the Principal took the first flight to Brazzaville, dropped his bag at a friend's house and took a taxi—clearly in breach of the agreement with the office of security—to Olivier's house. My mother, who was sitting on the veranda of her father's house holding little Happiness, was shocked to see him entering the courtyard. After six months of hiding in Paris, and two months after my mother had fled from Benin, there he was—her husband—getting out of the taxi, fresh and sound, as if they both had never left the Congo and the whole time in Benin had been just a bad dream.

No less astonished was Olivier. However much he was burning with anger, Olivier decided not to interfere. He stood up from his Zimbilamba stool with disdain for his daughter's husband and walked inside the house, counting on his daughter's common sense to manage this predicament wisely.

René walked towards my mother. He looked genuinely sorry for how things had turned out, my mum recalls. He apologised hundreds of times, swore that he made a terrible, terrible mistake, and that it would never happen again. He was done with her, with Maman Chantal, once for all. She was out of their life. For real.

'This is the promise of a man.'

Nevertheless, no matter how sincere my dad was in his heartfelt declaration, she felt they had reached a point of no return, and that the relationship was dead for her. She had suffered too much, too much.

'There is a limit to everything. I'm not up for somebody ruining my life, René. I gave you all I could, your kids are in Benin, I'll send you this one too as soon as he's weaned, so that we are even. Now, please, go back there to mess up the life of the woman you got pregnant, not mine.'

Dad stood there, determined to reconquer her heart as he had conquered glory and fortunes throughout his life. He explained to her that it was love that brought him there. True love. For the first time in his life.

'I promise in this very moment, in front of God that, starting from today, our life will change. Listen to me. We're going to be so rich that we won't have any of these nuisances anymore and I will be there, every time for you. Every time. You want to go to university? Well, we're going to enrol you, now, this very moment. You want to work with me? You want to travel with me? Be my associate? If it is yes, you say voila, then you're going to do business with me. We will travel, we will do our work together. Whatever you want. All I know is that I want to take care of you. That's all I want to do. You make me see things differently, in a way that is changing me. Nobody has this power. Nobody. But you. What does it take to give me just another chance?'

My mother was resolute in her position. There was nothing that could make her change her mind. 'It is discouraging to see that we have come down to this so quickly. My real concern is imagining what could be ahead if this is only the beginning. I won't allow anyone to treat me like this again. Never again! I have my aspirations, my integrity, my dignity to preserve. I can't just give it all up, chuck it away, for the use of the first dog I come across. It's my life. Is that important for you? Look around you, look, can you see? Everyone is calm, people want to have a tranquil life, they don't want someone to come and bring a brothel into their life!'

She got up from her stool and walked back inside, leaving my father hanging alone outside. Eventually, he went home, but he was anything but defeated. He came back looking for her the next day, and the day after that, and again the day after that, but it was always in vain. Olivier wouldn't allow him in and Sofie wouldn't come out. So, René had no other choice than to turn to another plan of action. He stopped going to my mother's house and started instead to latch on to Sofie's sisters and brother, whom he'd casually met around the area. Over time, he managed to get in good with them and used them as leverage to persuade Sofie to reconsider her position, to the point where even her brother began rallying for René and promoting him at home. Along with her sisters, they painted him as a transformed man. A man who was now able to see her properly, to see the real woman she had become.

'If anything, this experience helped him to understand how important you are to him. He's mad for you. I never saw him like this, so, so motivated with all the projects he's talking about! He said he'd never go back to Benin and is willing to start from scratch. Give him another chance, would you, or do you want to become the wife of who knows who *babolas*. You are being too proud!'

Eventually, it worked. They influenced and infiltrated her mind, so that even without seeing René, Sofie saw to give him another chance.

GROUND

Simultaneously, there were problems with Maman Natalie, my dad's ex-wife. She had appealed to the court to come into possession of his assets, an appeal that was rejected, as René appeared in court with his powerful lawyer and won the case on the same day. In the process, he got back all his assets, including the business and capital that had been confiscated by the government during the administration of Yhombi-Opango, who had been removed from office by the central committee of the CPT and replaced by Sassou Nguesso. The ban against West Africans was soon lifted, as foreseen by Monsieur Idrissa Kamosi, the minister of the Public Works. Many old traders were able to move back to the country once again and fresh blood moved in too.

My father moved back to his old house in the Diata area. He moved back in with Maman Sofie and Happiness. Around the same time, my mother flew to Benin and collected Redeso and I, both of us two years old by then, leaving the others behind in Cotonou at Granny Debra's under the care of the women in the big matronly house. Those were times of substantial changes taking place in my family. My parents' relationship strengthened, as Dad had promised. His recent experiences had truly been transformative for him. Motivating him to cut his ties with the past, with his ex-wife, the other woman, and with Brazzaville and Cotonou. René decided it was time to move from the continent. He chose Italy because Pino, with whom he'd been in constant conversation ever since they had met, had described to him an appealing market there—a country with a diverse industry, with plenty of trading opportunities. Pino told him he could find him low-interest financial services in Italy, lower than he could ever get in France. He wanted to introduce my father to some people who, he was certain, would serve his purpose of the road construction project in the best way. Above all, he mentioned a man called Alvaro Belluzzi who, according to Pino, could supply him start-up equipment at a wining price.

***

My father flew to Italy alone for the first time. Pino received him at Rome's Fiumicino Airport. He got him a room in the same hotel he was staying at. Toured with him around the Italian capital, leading him through the culture, habits, part of the history he knew and, of course, the market. That was the whole point of their presence there. I can imagine my father listening to him carefully and, securing all the verbal and visual information in his mind, immersed himself in this place that was in some ways similar to Paris but different altogether. Pino introduced him to some of the people he knew in Rome—entrepreneurs and dealers—during lunches and dinners, where he translated Italian for my father. My father nodded, just nodded, each mild tilt of his head showing he had added another piece of the puzzle of this new country that was forming before his eyes. It was not yet the time for him to share his opinions nor even the time to employ his winning humour, rather it was a period to gather information. A couple of weeks later, they travelled to Bologna, then to Imola, where Pino was from and where he navigated the market with extreme confidence. There, as in Rome, he introduced my father to key figures in the industry. They travelled a lot in Pino's Fiat Uno to assess local manufacturers and farms, making contact with possible partners. All of them seemed interested in the possibilities my father described to extend their markets to African countries. You need to consider that most of those Italian traders Pino introduced him were the heads of family-run, middle-to-small businesses that counted on a local or regional output, and in very rare cases, national. For a black man in aviator-style sunglasses and a suit, with sideburns and a moustache to step in and get his translator to tell them that there was a high demand for their respective products in his country—that he could make them rich in no time—was quite an attractive prospect. My mother told me that my dad finalised some of those meetings by purchasing stock of their products right on the spot, such as the shipping container of ceramic tiles he bought from the Coperativa Ceramica di Imola that he would later ship down to Congo. Now that I'm digging deeper into my father's life as I go on listening and transcribing my mother's recordings, I see that my father's persuasive power went beyond the sole fact that he was a charming and very engaging man, as my mother put it. It was not just because he had a knack for business. I think at the heart of my father's success was the fact that he was born as a powerful person full stop. For some reason, it is human nature to place trust in powerful people. People are eager to associate with, depend on, and stick with powerful people—in politics, the markets or socially—virtually everywhere people need someone extremely confident to lean on. The more powerful you become the more dependents you have on your back. The flip side of this exercise of power is that some of the dependents, if not all of them, will naturally reach a point where they will attempt to reclaim the power they gave away to their leader. I say naturally because, in some ways, what they do is simply take the leader's blood to refuel their emptied veins—a natural redistribution of wealth. So, here it was that Pino arranged a meeting for my old man with one of the men he had told him about, Alvaro Belluzzi.

My mother describes Alvaro Belluzzi as a short, middle-aged man, with a beer belly, dark-greyish curly hair, who reminds her of that actor, she says, Danny DeVito. He was one of these new rich men from the fields who had made their fortune riding the wave of the postwar economic boom. Despite owning businesses and properties, men like him had never stopped working their own lands themselves. Alvaro Belluzzi was involved in providing building equipment, not as an owner, but as a middleman, apparently a very well-connected middleman, the man who was certain to lead them straight to the best deal in the region. My father and Pino met Alvaro Belluzzi at his home, a manor house in the countryside of a little enclave called Casal Fiumanese. Alvaro's wife topped up the spread of freshly cut

Parma ham and Pecorino cheese at the table. Alvaro, with his fieldboots still on, topped up their glasses with his homemade Sangiovese wine. My father trusted him because Pino trusted him. Apparently, in the history they had of doing business together, he had never let Pino down. So, my father went straight to the point, with the premise that there were great chances for everyone to get a share of a colossal road-building project if they all played their cards right. He first illustrated how, historically, the problematic road system in Africa had hindered its economies. Domestic and regional trading routes of African nations were already hampered by geographical limits—the Sahara Desert, the jungles and the long, swollen rivers, made even less navigable because of their many waterfalls. Most of these obstacles had long been overcome but the communication networks between trading countries were far from optimal. Add the mismanagement of existing roads and there was still a lot to do.

'I'm saying we are in the beginning of the '80s and still too many African countries are isolated from each other and from the rest of the world. Many have no or very problematic roads. The cities of some key nations are not even linked by road or railway or anything. We've got a huge market there.' Dad's master plan encompassed two stages, a short-term project and a long-term one, both quite pretentious in my opinion, but both perfectly in line with Dad's style. The short-term project involved him carrying out Monsieur Idrissa Kamosi's job of building and repairing roads in Congo-Brazzaville. The second project—my father's true aim—was to extend Minister Idrissa Kamosi's project to include other African nations, if not all of them.

'By the time we complete the first job, we will have built a strong reputation and we'll be investing the profits in new equipment and on scaling up. Then we point high, very high. From a national to a Pan-African infrastructural project. What I'm saying is, let's get African countries mutually involved in an unprecedented step to build mega projects that can benefit the whole continent's economy. Imagine a highway from Brazzaville to Djibouti, from coast to coast. Through the Red Sea and the Suez Canal, the western coast and central African countries would gain access to the Asian and European markets. I'm not talking about dreams, but real possibilities. The whole project has been drawn up with all the estimates and evidence supporting it. But it is secondary. For now let's focus on the smaller one. The road in Congo-Brazzaville. What I need is highly reliable second-hand equipment. Durable machines like trucks, excavators, bulldozers and road rollers. I will provide you with a comprehensive list, you get them shipped down to the Congo. I'll need quite a lot of them. Hey, are you sure this guy will be able to get all this?' he asked Pino, who was translating for both.

'Don't worry, I know this man. He'll get you all you need!'

'Now tell him,' Alvaro Belluzzi said, 'this, what he calls the short-term project, building roads on a national scale, is no doubt an exceptional deal in itself. Of course, I will get a hold of the best machines you can possibly get at a price you can only dream about, but I just want to be sure your friend is well aware of the cost we're talking about for such an ambitious project. How is he going to pay? With his own money? Loans? Government subsides? I'm not an expert on African affairs, but are we sure his government has budgeted enough to fund just project one alone? Just the shipping of all these machines will be nearly as costly as buying the machines. Add the border tariffs, and you'll need experts, mechanics and engineers to assemble the entire plant. You might need to train lots of people, I know once I get paid, it's no longer my business to handle the administration, and I see you have a good brain in there, but be careful, man, not to be too overly optimistic. It's a really huge sum we're talking about here.'

The road-building projects were, in my opinion, my father's most ambitious projects and the most important for him, not only for its profitability, the prestige, and the pleasure of being responsible for its grand execution, but they were tied in with something deeper. An irrepressible side of my father that was more idealistic. The reformist side of him that had always been sensitive to the political and social problems of his country. These projects reawakened memories of the old principal of the school in Nigeria, the one who had put his school at the service of the Igbo refugees who fled the pogroms in northern Nigeria. Dad truly believed that he had a part to play in the commonwealth of his country, helping the economy and uniting African countries in close co-operation to integrate them all into the global market.

Dad came back home enthusiastic about his trip to Italy, my mother recalls. Enthusiastic and full of big plans and with plenty of things to say about the food and the friendly people. He told her that she was going to love it there, that she was to work as his associate and that everything would be nice from then on. Italy was the hot place now. He wanted to move there straight away. So, preparations for the big move began. Dad's plan was for them to settle there first before bringing the children. And so it was.

My parents decided that, as a temporary measure, Happiness, who was still a baby in need of personal attention, would go to the village of Sibiti where Granny Aminata—Sofie's biological mother—lived. They dropped off Happiness there to live temporarily under her care and took Redeso and me back to Benin. We reunited with our siblings at Maman Debra's house, so that when the time came for us to leave we would all be in one place. Almost all of us.

My parents sold most of my father's financial assets in order to have enough liquidity to invest in their new life in Italy. Finally, they took a flight to Italy. It was November 1978. They lived in a hotel room in Imola for a while. Then, again, it was Pino who found them a house. The right house. Our house. The villa in Via Emilia, on the outskirts of Imola. My mother said she wasn't entirely convinced about the house when she first viewed it with Pino, my dad and the estate agent. She was concerned about the price and the size. While it would certainly suit a large family like ours, it was maybe too much at this stage and to buy it would put them straight into massive debt. Pino also had doubts and assured Dad could find something still suitable for a large family but perhaps more affordable. But then there was my father.

'What's wrong with you?' he said appalled. 'Did we come all the way here just to waste this gentleman's time?' That meant the choice was made. There was no point trying to persuade my father to take a couple of days to think about the deal and maybe see a few more houses. Although we were not financially able to afford a house of that magnitude, my father, who was not up for putting his family in one of those common flats where most people lived in Imola, bought the villa, putting down a substantial deposit and committing to pay a hefty monthly mortgage. He was positive, he said to the director of the Bank of Imola, that they could avoid going through this petty paperwork for the mortgage since he would be able to resolve all house payments with three instalments. Not content with the already generous concession from the bank toward a stranger with no credit or work history in the country, he borrowed more money to furnish the house, to open the utilities and bought a car, a brand-new Jaguar.

My parents stayed in Italy for about a year alone. I was three years old when they returned to Africa and four when they took Klaus, Masambila, Redeso and me from Grandma Debra's house in Benin to live in the villa in Italy during the winter of 1980. I don't know why they only took us three from the kids, I assume for financial reasons, as they probably could not afford to buy tickets for all of us in one go at that time and opted to split the trip into two groups. Both Redeso and I have retained very few memories of our first arrival in Italy. We supposedly reached Imola by train from Fiumicino Airport in Rome with Klaus, Father and Maman Sofie. Then we took a taxi to the new house. The first thing that comes to my mind when I attempt to recall my first impression of the villa is the silence, a constant, widespread silence throughout the whole house, almost like a living entity. The silence was due to the large size of the house, the lack of furniture, the isolated location and the wall of pine trees that enclosed it, creating a buffer around the house. Silence because nobody had lived there for a while. Silence that was a direct contrast with the busy life we had back at Grandma Debra's house in Benin. The fact that it was just Klaus, Redeso and me during that first year didn't help. My mother set us up in the same bedroom, bought us some toys, and for months, life inside that house was all we knew. We played with the new toys our parents bought us. Hung around in the front yard and explored the lawn and the bushes at the back of the house, but, beyond that, I don't remember that we did anything else. We had not started school yet, so our parents probably took us out for errands around the city whenever it was possible, although most of the time they were away for work. In those cases, we would be left under Masambila's watch. I remember seeing snow falling for the first time in my life with Klaus, Redeso and Masambila. The four of us stood watching it from our doorstep. I have a memory of my father returning from one of his trips, the noise of his car wheels crunching through the snow. He got out with some presents for us, including a trio of remote control cars that kept Redeso and me busy for days but did not interest Klaus at all. He played with them for ten minutes at the most the first day then never touched them again. Unlike us, and even though he was only a year and a half older, he had no interest in playing with toys. It was around that time he began playing alone with the tennis ball. He happened to find it under an old cupboard in the dining room, presumably belonging to whoever had lived there before us, and picked it up, bouncing it with his hand up to the attic, where we usually played. There, he would go on playing peacefully at length, throwing the tennis ball against the wall and catching it. Sometimes with a smile on his face. Or staring at the void beyond the window. Or humming an African song. Masambila's quietness added to the silence streaming from the walls of the house. When our parents were away for work, he was put in charge of us—preparing meals, eating at the table with us and putting us to bed. His routine became where we began to find safety and a sense of continuity, more than we found with our parents. My twin brother and I looked at him whenever we needed a wee or a snack, or when we were under the drive of our first life investigations and needed answers to existentialist questions such as, *How come birds fly? Why is the water in the glass not blue? Why is the climate so different here? When will we become grown up?* We begged him to sing us 'the twins song' every night and sat on the floor while he accommodated us and sang in his low voice as he kept on ironing, the vapour of the steam iron escaping as his hand gently pushed it back and forth over our clothes.

In the space of a year, Debra-Jo, Lorenzo, Sigmund and Ocean made it to Italy too, and they brought a whole new dimension to the house. Things changed for the better. Their presence filled up the house. That sense of isolation and the intensity of that ubiquitous silence lessened. Days turned brighter. We finally felt plugged into a more dynamic, wider, fulfilled existence that was starting to bring Italy to life. The dinner table was now set for eleven of us when you included our parents and Masambila. Up in the attic, down in the living room, in the courtyard, and in the back lawn, where we had been hanging around for a year just us three, there was lots of noise now that the full gang of siblings was together playing, all seven of us very much eager to spend time together. Our catchment area widened from our premises to outside into the neighbourhood, now that we could go out for walks with Debra-Jo. We rarely took the way from the main gate to go out, which went straight to the very busy road of the Via Emilia—the historic Roman-straight road that connected Rimini on the Adriatic coast to Piacenza, on the north-western border of Emilia-Romagna with Piedmont, cutting across the whole region. So, we usually left home through the backyard, which led to a small suburban area called Zolino. Soon, we became familiar with the neighbourhood shops and some of our neighbours, but we still could barely connect with them. The locals, intrigued by the new and recurring sight of a group of black kids strolling in area, stopped to get to know us, asking things like, *I noticed you guys moved into that big house there, what's your name?* But we could hardly hold a proper conversation since we were still entirely French speakers. The arrival of my older siblings also prompted some logistical changes around the house. Debra-Jo moved in to sleep in the same room as Redeso and me, while Klaus moved in with the boys. She also took charge of our lives whenever our parents were away for work, replacing Masambila, who remained predominately in charge of the housekeeping. As for my parents, well, I don't know, I don't remember them being part of the picture very much, and my mother didn't add anything relevant to this story during our recent conversation, except that she and my father were travelling extensively, to Congo, São Paulo, Cape Town. They were the Bonnie and Clyde of the business. At this point, my mother had put on hold her study plans once for all. She had let my father lead her into the art of trading, so that she was soon able to do her part in bringing home an independent income. They split their work tasks; she was in charge of providing quick money for our day-to-day subsistence with the profits she made from sending cargo of unsold clothing, shoes and belts she'd buy from factories and suppliers in Imola and surrounding areas, down to Brazzaville. Meanwhile, the *Man of the Shoes* took care of negotiations with buyers and sellers, did market research and laid the groundwork for major and long-term partnerships in various places, like Khartoum in Sudan, an attractive gateway to the Arab countries and the Middle East. My mother recalls in particular that although René's work was more diplomatic in essence, he never travelled empty-handed. Wherever he went, she says, 'he'd get shipped a cargo of goods—from Italy to Khartoum, and vice-versa, from Congo to Senegal, from Senegal back to Italy.' My mother learned to do the same. Never leave a country empty-handed.

Another big opportunity to turn Dad's work around arrived from the Ministry of Public Works and Infrastructure of the People's Republic of the Congo. My dad's friend, Monsieur Idrissa Kamosi, the minister behind the road construction project, had offered him two new state commissions in order to unlock the bigger road implementation job. One was to refurbish the National Assembly House, the other to rebuild a garrison, both projects to be set in Brazzaville. The plans were funded by money from Structural Adjustment Projects, a monetary reform programme enforced by Western countries to indebt African governments as a solution to boost their economies and get returns on their loans. The problem was that this scheme gave a way to foreign banks to directly manage the monetary policy of the debtor countries with authoritative hands that were strongly opposed by many African leaders. But not by ours—not Sassou Nguesso. He actually welcomed the imposition of the neoliberal formula of austerity, privatisation, deregulation, and trade liberalisation on a country that was still deeply anchored to the socialist ideology of his forefathers and gave the green light to the Americans and French to put their hands on our mines and oil fields. But as the minister put it to my father, 'C'est une solution que nous donne a manger.' To him, the country finally had the means to invest in public works, thus the building of a garrison and the refurbishment of the House of Parliament—jobs that would generate roughly a million Euros of net profit for my father. The building work started with a small team of builders and a small provision of basic equipment my father had purchased locally. That was when he established his building and trade enterprise, the WAT, World-Africa Trade, Congo Corporation.

Now we were getting rich again. The Principal bought a second brand-new Jaguar as soon as he came back to Italy. A month later he bought two Land Rovers and two Mercedes. He hired a personal tutor for us to help us learn Italian, a chef, a secretary, and a chauffeur. It was around that time that our home turned busy. Attracted by my father's success, many people from Africa, particularly my dad's relatives from Benin, began coming to the villa, crossing national borders that back then were permeable. Some stayed for just for a short visit, while others would make themselves more comfortable and present my father with their own business projects, all of which needed a financial blessing from him to start. But they also looked for his highly valued opinions. All were now in admiration of my father's international achievement. It was one thing to make it in Africa. Another in Europe. And Dad did it. He was living like a nabob in Italy, in a big villa with four luxurious cars and a huge sum of money in his bank account that swelled day after day. Those were lively times in the house, times when Pino and his family would come on Sundays to join us for barbeques, when my father opened a branch of the WAT Congo enterprise in Italy and came home one day carrying merchandise he bought at the Mercatone Uno, including a box of microphones and a sound system he set up in the room he named the Conference Room. We followed him inside the room, intrigued by the occurrence, the big man pretending not to be overexcited when he pulled out all the gear and set it up with the help of our Italian tutor, Martino. He tested it himself with few casual, pretending, murmurs. A few days later, there was an influx of the worldwide businessmen's diaspora. A large majority were from Africa, but there were also a minority of others from different places that were operating in Africa—all connections my father had made during his business trips around the world. Everything seemed possible then; it was a shared feeling that my father's affairs were at a turning point. I remember a specific day when Debra-Jo called us all to come and see Dad being interviewed on Tele Sette, on TV. We crammed on the sofa to watch him answering a young journalist's questions about himself in his broken Italian. About the vision of the WAT Congo enterprise and a new plan he had of opening a new regional TV channel. His name was growing. Our family name was growing. This was the time when I was the son of a millionaire. The time when my parents took photos of my mother with braided hair and my father in a cowboy hat that was then hung on the wall in the living room. The time of the African masks and the small statues and the djembe, which we banged on and sang with for days, brought as gifts by one of the many visitors enriching the house. The time we posed, the seven of us plus my parents, Pino and some of the African visitors, for the family photos we took in the front yard next to the hammock and next to my father's cars. Other photos showed just the seven children standing in our karate stances. It was the time we started attending at Italian schools. Redeso and I went to nursery. The others went to primary school, Debra-Jo to secondary school. It took some time and the dedication of our Italian tutor before we could keep up with the pace of our classmates, but we eventually managed to get there. It was the time of our first Italian friends coming to visit us at home, the time of racing down the stairs riding cardboard sheets. The time of the sofa-song jumping game. Although we had never celebrated Christmas before and had little knowledge of it, that year our parents bought us Christmas presents. There were seven bikes. We assembled them ourselves with Masambila. All of them had stabilisers since not even the oldest amongst us had ever cycled before. I remember we spent Christmas day and many days thereafter cycling around the courtyard in a circular motion around the fountain, like a clock, the seven siblings on their shiny bikes, Dad and Mum looking at us from the front door.

Pride

My father's work commitments in Brazzaville, besides having considerably lifted our living standards, also led to a situation where our parents had to spend more of their time in Congo than in Italy. That meant that my mother could look after Happiness herself now. So, they brought him back from Granny Aminata in Sibiti to Brazzaville with them. Around that time, Maman Sofie also became the stepmother of Moon. Born in Benin to Maman Chantal, a year after Happiness, Moon came down from Benin to join her father's household. My mother placed both Moon and Happiness at Charle Magne, a top French private school in Brazzaville. In the space of a short amount of time, my mother became pregnant gave birth to a girl, Mavie. She had three children on hand in Africa and seven in Italy at the age of 25. Then my parents, weighing whether or not to send the three left in Africa to Italy to join us to establish our primary domicile in Imola, chose to wait. My parents' demanding commitments in Africa forced them to cut their business relationships with other countries, leaving intact only the ties with Italy.

My father's renewed popularity came, however, with a harsh price as one might expect, and two problems swiftly arose. The first one was that among the people who were coming to visit were Dad's older sister and cousin, Tantine Marielle Tawema and Tantine Ellen. They were of course part of the group who were more likely to stay for a long period of time each time they came, which gave them plenty of time to exert their vicious influence on my father. The second problem concerned my father's behaviour. He had changed. All those ego-affirming achievements went to his head. He became overconfident and difficult to deal with, a hundred times more so when he was under the psychological influence of his relatives. My mother says that their marriage was catapulted years backward into the old environment of disagreements and mistrust they had back in Benin. The alliance my parents had only recently formed started gradually deteriorating. No more Bonnie and Clyde during the time the Tantines were visiting, but just their voices, the Tantines' voices, trying to persuade my father to manage his talent and assets in the direction of his Beninese family. Not always convinced of their views, doubly so when it came to his wife, whom he knew they disliked from the start with no sound reasoning, my father would initially stand up for Sofie. He was not a wimp—I'm sure you've got that straight by now—but it is widely known how persuasive the force of manipulative talk can be. Moreso if the victim is prone to the influence of the manipulators' will in the first place. If they have a single-minded agenda, they will eventually manage to change your viewpoint on matters you thought you had under control. My mother remembers that Dad started looking at her differently and stopped listening to her in the way he used to. Her words were worth nothing now. She was suddenly just a kid whose opinion was irrelevant, if not irritating, in his eyes.

Now, during all this time, while building the garrison and the National Assembly Home, my father never put aside his major ambition of driving WAT Congo to take the lead in building roads on an international scale. So, now that he had over one million Euros, the prospect to start it up became possible. He discussed the idea with his sister Marielle and cousin Ellen the time they visited us in Imola. Both women agreed with him, it was a huge deal with large profit margins, that was open to large opportunities for expansion, he should absolutely embark on it. Investing one million Euros in supplying first Congo and then Africa with a desperately needed road system would perhaps be the greatest thing the *Man of the Shoes* has ever done. My mother was the only sceptic about the deal. She looked at it more objectively, without letting herself be carried away by my father's boastfulness, concluding that he was about to put himself into a risky financial situation. Not that the deal was flawed per se, no, she too believed it was good, but not if it was executed on the terms that my father had in mind. It would indeed turn into a complete suicide if he decided to invest all his capital plus loans into a single deal, with no backup, no guaranteed margin of success. They could lose everything if just one little thing went wrong. That was not a sound business in her opinion, it was simply gambling with his family's money. It made more sense to her that my father should first secure this money, invest it safely into the property market and buy the house in which we were living for his children. 'You even claimed to the bank you'd be able to settle the house mortgage in just three payments.' She reminded him. 'And now that you have the money to buy it all, what do you do? You want to invest in something uncertain? Listen to me, buy this house. We put a foundation down, solid concrete walls, if anything should happen we are covered, at least we are sure the kids will always have a place to stay. Then you are free to invest whatever comes after in whatever you want.' But as I told you, with my Tantines around, the success getting to his head and his own ambitions blinding him, my father found my mother's discourse simply very irritating. You can imagine his answer: 'So now, just because I let you do a little business with me and taught you few tricks you think you are better suited to this job than me! Who established WAT Congo? You? Then take the lead. Or else move aside and let me do my job. I'll buy each of my kids a house like this within the next year. End of conversation.'

Work began. The contract for the implementation and construction of a pre-set number of roads in the southern region of the Republic of Congo began and was put on the table and signed by my dad. My father invested all the money he earned from the two building jobs in buying the road-building equipment and setting up a quarry. He had to add a further half a million to complete the purchase, which he obtained from the Bank of Imola, in the form of a second loan on top of the one he had asked for when he moved to Italy and on top of the costly mortgage he had just started paying back. René was already drowning in debts the day he climbed into Pino's Fiat Uno to be driven to meet Alvaro Belluzzi. The big meeting took place one morning inside a warehouse of second-hand road construction equipment, in the industrial area of a small town neighbouring Imola called Castel Guelfo. With them was a quarry engineer who was to guide them through a thorough evaluation and selection of the machines needed for my father's project. Alvaro Belluzzi introduced them to Giovanni Bevilacqua, the business owner, who lived with his wife and two kids right above the business premises and who had been dealing with Alvaro Belluzzi since he was a young man, according to Pino. They only dealt with top-quality second-hand equipment, all of the products working perfectly. Papers for newly-made revisions lay on the table, plus the legal documentation of each machine. It was not by accident, Alvaro Belluzzi claimed, that half of the region was supplied by them. Giovanni and Andrea took my father, the engineer and Pino around the warehouse's parking lot, where a wide range of industrial machines sat, all nearly new-looking. Many were trucks, but there were also wheel loaders, excavators, road rollers and motor graders. The stock didn't even remotely reflect the amount and diversity of the products that were needed for the road construction project. They mainly had earthmoving equipment. Bigger machinery, such as the components for a fixed plant, crushing plant, asphalt mixing plant, hammer mill impactors and parts for the conveyor system, they would get from other dealers, Alvaro Belluzzi said, according to my father's requests. Giovanni's machines were to be seen more as samples of the quality-for-price deals Alvaro Belluzzi intended to serve my father. If the Principal was then happy with them, Alvaro Belluzzi would set up a supply chain for the remaining machines from a network of dealers and ship them to Congo. Alternatively, if my father or the engineer who came with him to check on the machines were unsatisfied, their partnership would end there, Amen. Dad let the engineer do the work of assessment, trailing behind him as they toured around the machines, Pino and Andrea accompanying them and Giovanni doing the talking. They had one of Giovanni's employees manoeuvring the machines under the instruction of the engineer, ensuring both the engineer and my father were happy. The whole committee then moved into the office to finalise the deal. René signed the agreement to buy just half a million Euros worth of products at first. Then he spent another million on more products, shipments, border charges and bribing customs officials once he was in Africa, after he had the chance to test the quality of the first small bloc of earthmoving equipment on the ground. He was truly satisfied, my mother recalls; all machines worked perfectly fine. All of the products were shipped to Congo at different stages in line with my father's purchasing timing. He made sure he would be at the port to clear the products through customs once they arrived via sea and to organise their transportation to the quarry in Point-Noir. His dream was turning real at last.

PART III

Foster Home

One day, one of the chefs from St Catherina, a stocky woman called Tonia, left the kitchen in a fury because 700,000 lire—about 350 euros—went missing from her wallet. She accused my brother Lorenzo of the theft, threatening him aggressively that she was going to press charges if he did not return it. Despite Lorenzo denying his involvement, the matter went to Don Ettore, who confronted him, 'did you steal that money?' Lorenzo swore he had not stolen it. The priest paid the chef back the money from his own pocket. However, the incident was not without repercussions for Lorenzo. He was summoned by social services to discuss the occurrence, where again, he swore he was not involved in the theft. Nevertheless, our social worker Ursola Delrio decided to take action. Lorenzo was relocated from St Catherina to a different institution, one run directly by the AUSL, the regional social services department. This institution was in another city—the hilly and remote, ancient town of Verrucchio in the Province of Rimini—about half a day's trip away from us. Life at St Catherina ended for Lorenzo. All of us, his brothers and the people he had lived with for the past few years, watched as he and his backpack were bundled into Mr P's car and driven away.

A few days afterwards, Klaus, Redeso and I were summoned to attend an audience at the juvenile court of Bologna for a case review. Debra-Jo, Ocean and Sigmund were not included because they were of age by that time, and as such legally independent. As for Lorenzo, I didn't know why he was missing, whether it was because he was passed to another jurisdiction or if there were other reasons. The judge reviewed our case in front of us, reading through a series of documents that Bologna's legal and social services had amassed over time. The paperwork dated back to around 1983, after the night our house had burned down. With an eye on the report, the judge asked us individually about our lives. 'Redeso, how do you feel about this and that event?' 'Tell me, Klaus, how was it for you? And you, Redesof, what do you have to say?' These were questions aimed at understanding how we had been coping, living in the institution and away from our parents for so long. Each of us gave our own account. The judge listened carefully.

One of her last questions was directed to Redeso and me only. She asked us if we wanted to consider undergoing adoption. We were thirteen years old. In the context of our family constellation, this event seemed just another surreal prospect. We were sitting there with one of our brothers, had two more at St Catherina, one in Verrucchio, a sister at Oasis, and a flock of siblings spread across Benin and Congo. And there we were, facing a stranger representing the law of a country that we didn't quite yet know was ours or not. How do you answer such an intimate question in that context? And then what? Do we get adopted only to be more dislocated than we already were? We had spent many weekends, sometimes even the entire winter holidays, with other peoples' families, including some of the benefactors that habitually hung around St Theresa, and yet we had never gone as far as considering to permanently adhere to another family unit that was not ours. The idea of it felt anything but appealing; on the contrary, it felt dark. Seriously dark. We both said we preferred to stick with our family. The judge consented and wrote something down on a paper. The meeting's final outcome however, devised a solution that technically became another form of adoption. Facing the evidence of our parent's repetitive failure to meet their parental responsibilities, the juvenile court of Bologna decreed that they were unfit to fulfil the task of parenting, and permanently stripped them of their parental rights over Klaus, Lorenzo, Redeso and me. We became, legally, sons of the Italian government.

Translated in practical terms, the court ordinance meant we were moving under the control of social services and away from the religious institutions. I think this gain in executive power over our lives motivated Ursola Delrio to try out a second manoeuvre after the one she tried with Lorenzo. For Klaus, she arranged a viewing at a foster home, named Casa Famiglia, in the deep countryside of Toscanella, just 15 kilometres from Imola, and asked him if he would like to live there. Klaus fell in love with the place at first sight. So, it was decided and a few days after he was transferred to this new place.

Those of us who remained in Imola went to visit him some weeks later: Redeso and me, Sigmund, Ocean and Debra-Jo, who also brought her boyfriend. We drove there in two cars, one that belonged to Sigmund and one that belonged to Debra-Jo's boyfriend, Ugo, a 21-year-old carpenter, who was a kind and amusing fellow. Toscanella was another of the small towns set in the Via Emilia's straight trajectory, like Imola, Castel San Pietro, Bologna, Modena, Parma and, Piacenza. Sitting halfway between Imola and Bologna, Toscanella was one of those small, working-class places with a relatively recent history, a couple of bars facing the busy main road, a pharmacy, a petrol station and a church. Arriving at the town, we turned off the Via Emilia into a secondary lane that deepened into a late August countryside. Fruit-bearing orchards and crop fields extended on both sides of the road. We stopped at an old-fashioned level crossing with the red-and-white-striped bar that lowered with the dinging warning of a bell. We waited silently in the short queue of cars and bikes until a slow-moving cargo train passed by breaking the quiet, bucolic landscape. Then the bell rang again, the bars lifted.

We drove for another couple of miles, up to a lone-standing building on a generous and peaceful pasture with a large vineyard and acres of surrounding fields. That was the Casa Famiglia. The main building consisted of a two-storey house and the rest of the property was divided into three attached habitations. A huge, empty barn sat on the far end of the tenure, next to a lawn. A small, one-storey auxiliary building stood next to the entrance of the main building. The closest neighbour's house was on the other side of the street and there was nothing else within a mile radius. The whole property seemed to have been newly refurbished, and was well-kept.

Debra-Jo's boyfriend, Ugo, parked his car at the edge of the lawn. There was a hammock hanging under a big oak tree, a swing, and a small, nervous black dog pawing at the feet of the swing. Klaus came out from a section of the main building followed by another man, presumably one of the people running the place. The guy appeared different from the type of supervisors we were used to, as if from a new generation of supervisors that boasted an improved quality of humanity and were more at peace with themselves. Klaus looked different too, positively different. You could see right away that the climate of the new place had already begun having an impact on him. He received us with a bright smile as we got out of the car, as if we had arrived at his house and that the supervisor next to him was more a flatmate than a carer. I felt there was something in him with which, while we'd lived in St Catherina, we had lost touch. How odd it was to meet Klaus in the midst of a healthy, beautiful, countryside idyll, and him coming to receive us, so at ease, from his new home. He introduced us to the man who accompanied him, the head manager, a man in his thirties, named Franco. Franco, Klaus said, was a big shot in the Boy Scouts universe of Imola, he was also an associate of a charity and ran a mountain-trekking gear shop too. Franco gained our friendship right away. As he led us inside he briefly introduced us to other residents of the foster home. A girl who was watching TV in the living room said 'hi'. Another girl who was coming down the stairs shared a few timid niceties with us. From the dining room, a guy who sat curling his hair with his fingers waved to us. Next to him a rebellious-looking kid only glanced up from the bowl of milk and biscuits he was having for a snack and smiled, amused by something he found in Redeso and me, maybe our twinness. All were white Italians. And everyone in there gave a strong aura of normality even though they were still under care. You could see straight away that the policy there was nothing like that of St Catherina. The residents there, as Klaus reiterated time and time again with enthusiasm, were free to do whatever they liked, like in a family environment. He himself opened the fridge in the kitchen to give us a demonstration and picked up a slice of ham, and explained while chewing it, that he could take anything he wanted. He could also prepare his own food if he didn't like what the supervisor had cooked for the meal. He said he was free to watch TV. 'Hey, li-li-like a family,' he said. 'It's amazing.'

'So, you don't miss us?' asked Ocean jokingly.

'I-I-I stopped missing you a l-l-long time ago, you in-in-in particular!'

And we laughed, in the way only Klaus could make us laugh. He was, without trying, spontaneously amusing.

He said that there were of course, obligations for the residents, such as doing homework and housework, and the carer would encourage them to meet due diligence, but nobody would stand breathing down their neck, or smell armpits and feet, and scrub ankles and back of the ears when they came out of the toilet. It was up to each resident to keep up with his own responsibilities.

'If I-I-I want to go to bed dirty, fuck it! I do it. It's my life! Do-do-do-do you know I have a motorbike? Co-co-come, I'll show you!' We followed him back outside. Again it all felt unreal, once we stepped out again, to be walking with Klaus in the middle of all this green landscape and the fresh open air of his new house. The sense of peace, the smell of ripening grapes of the close-by vineyard, I could hardly believe that life could change so drastically. We walked along the white, gravelled pathway, our steps cracking over the pebbles, the clear, wide-open sky all around. A song by the Beatles played out of the window of one of the tenants' rooms.

We reached the barn. A few pedal bikes and motorbikes were parked under the roof of the barn's side porch. One of the motorbikes belonged to Klaus. It was a College, an affordable 50cc motorbike, the kind in use among working-class teenagers, that the social services had bought for him. He used it every day to go to town. We wowed at the motorbike, and to everything he explained to us about it: that it was fast, that there was a guy in the neighbourhood, a professional mechanic, who offered to paint it red for him, and that the social service will fund lessons for him to learn to drive higher-calibre motorbikes when he hit sixteen. We went back inside to see his room, but soon we came out again, and spent the remaining time with him chatting outside, around the hammock and the swing.

Life seemed resolved for Klaus. The resentment he felt toward our father had subsided into the tranquil environment of his new residency, along with all the rest of our family troubles, including our new house in Via Suore. It wasn't his business anymore, whereas for us it was still an ongoing issue; we counted on it, but it looked like it was going nowhere. As usual. It had been nearly a year since our father put down the deposit and we had entered the home for the first time with Pino, but there hadn't been any progress yet. He had not sent any funds to start the refurbishment. The house was simply sitting there on the hill with the roof collapsing. From time to time, on a casual ride in cars or on bikes we would go to look at it from the outside. Once Redeso and I cycled there with a couple of friends from school to show them around. We proudly opened the door with our keys and led them inside the house on a tour of the decaying space, still covered in dirt, dust and cobwebs, and showed them its empty, ancient and dark rooms and collapsing facilities. What were you supposed to do in such circumstances? Ok, you say this is my house, and then what? Could you offer them a glass of coke, and get all of them in your room and play video games? Could we have listened to some music? Cooked ourselves something? We couldn't even sit anywhere. Not even on the floor, so unattractive as it was. My classmates walked around the house with a combination of care, politeness, and fear of offending us at every turn, in case they revealed what they truly thought of this place. They were right. What makes a house your home is not the structure. Day after day the place sat there neglected, like an enormous crow dying on top of a hill. Debra-Jo learned from Pino that small chunks of our father's money was coming in now and then, but just enough to cover outstanding mortgage payments. That was all. Aside from that slow repayment, our house was hypothetical, an idea which we could access with our keys, but not in any other way.

We spoke about Lorenzo there at the swing with Klaus. Debra-Jo and Ocean who had recently spoken with him on the phone said he was doing very well in Verruchio. He took the whole thing around his expulsion positively. He even became mystical about it; he believed the incident had happened because he was the one chosen by higher sources to fulfil a sort of family mission that wasn't yet very clear in his mind. We ended that day with the plan to organise an expedition to visit Lorenzo. Then it was time to go. We left Klaus's foster home sometime before dinnertime. The nervous black dog scuttled back and forth across Klaus's feet. He turned his back to us after he waved goodbye a few times, his smile shy and awkward as usual, and walked away across the gravelled pathway toward the entrance of the Casa Famiglia, while our cars drove out of the property.

***

Debra-Jo's life, to everyone's surprise, had also, unexpectedly, flourished into a dream. She was the girlfriend of Prince Charming. Handsome, tall, funny and good-hearted. A well-intentioned man. But above all, a man she loved madly. For whom she could finally feel that fulfilling emotion that is love, after all she had never managed it before. Many other things had changed in her life, but let us go in order.

It all started after her second night of somnambulism that had taken place about a year before. Debra-Jo woke up the morning after, clearly oblivious to what happened. She couldn't explain to herself why there was dirt and grass in between her bed covers. Then she noticed there was a letter on her bedside table addressed to her. She opened it and read it. It had been written by Sister Gaudenzia and dated from the night before. The letter started by informing her of the reason why she was dirtied with soil and grass. Then it went on to announce that Sister Gaudenzia was leaving the institution. Debra-Jo read the letter to the end, then rushed to wake her roommate Gabriella and told her about the letter, reading some of the passages aloud, going over the part more carefully where the Sister said she was leaving. Gabriella hopped out of the bed and rushed with Debra-Jo to the nun's bedroom. They knocked at the door. There was no answer. They opened the door. The room was empty. The bed was intact. Everything resting perfectly in peace. They checked in the toilet, went downstairs to the living room, to the kitchen, calling out her name and awakening the other girls with the noise. Learning about what had transpired, the other girls joined in the search. They looked for the Sister everywhere, including outside and then waited in the living room, speculating about all sorts of possible scenarios. Maybe she had gone out to complete her chores somewhere. But she hadn't. The letter was clear. She had left.

Eventually, the girls called the institution of St Theresa of the Child Jesus, which was affiliated with Oasis and the headquarters of the congregation managing both places. Their call was handled by a few different nuns before it finally reached the head of the congregation who calmed them down, reassuring them that she had the issue in hand, and who arranged to come and see the girls in person later in the day.

 She came late in the afternoon. The Superior Mother of the Congregation of the Little Sisters of St Theresa of the Child Jesus was a nun from Argentina with a penetrating stare, and a very thin voice. She called the girls to sit down with her in the living room. She took a deep breath before saying,

'We are in the process of finding you a substitute, since I'm afraid to say, you won't see Sister Gaudenzia any longer. She has permanently renounced her vows. A suffered-over choice, she told me, which I'm afraid we need to embrace, although it is very painful for all of us. We will certainly miss her. I know you are all shocked and possibly hurt by this event. It was unexpected, especially that her departure would happen like this in the middle of the night without notice, but this is the way of the Lord. What He gives, He takes away. I'm sure she loved you very much even if she didn't take time to say bye. You see, some people struggle to say goodbye because they can't bear to say it to people they love.'

'But where did she go?'

'I'm afraid I have the responsibility to protect her privacy.'

'But is she well?'

'Yes, yes of course, she is well.'

'Did you talk to her?'

'Personally.'

At that point there was nothing else to add. Sister Gaudenzia was gone.

The new head of Oasis made her entrance the next day, led by the Mother Superior, who took her to her new room and then around the house, giving her instructions and introducing her to the girls. She was different from Sister Gaudenzia in every way, the girls observed, but she seemed okay.

As for Debra-Jo, who was now aware of being a sleepwalker, Sister Gaudenzia's departure made it clear to her that she had to take some measures to deal with her problem. First, she let all the girls know about her condition, including the new nun, so that everyone could keep an eye on her. Then, Sister Piera, the new head of Oasis, decided she would hide the keys every night. They also decided to tie a little bell around Debra-Jo's ankle to play it safe. She was checked on through the night by Gabriella or by any of the other girls who passed by her bed on their way to the toilet, but nothing ever happened. Many nights passed this way. Debra-Jo never sleepwalked again. The fact of this suggested to Gabriella and the other girls that the whole phenomenon of Debra-Jo's somnambulism was unequivocally connected to the nun, since the only two known episodes she had experienced in her entire life happened during the time she lived under the care of Sister Gaudenzia. She had never had it before, and not after, at least for all Gabriella and the girls knew. 'Maybe they are two witches, Debra-Jo and Sister Gaudenzia,' Gabriella told her friend Sabrina, the diva, one night at Oasis, when they were sorting out the kitchen together. 'Witches in the good sense,' she clarified, but the meaning of the pact the nun talked about, 'the witches' pact', still remained obscure to her. What was that all about? '*The tigers that can't share the same hill… I leave you my kingdom.*' What kingdom was the nun talking about? Indeed, the letter seemed to deliver some hidden messages. Debra-Jo had read it many times and was not as surprised as the others to discover an occult essence inside the otherwise ordinary-looking nun, but she too struggled to decipher what the Sister truly meant in some of her wording. When she talked about her kingdom, what kingdom did she refer to? Could she have been referring to Oasis? '*I leave you Oasis?*' No, that was out of question. That was a nun's business. She must have been alluding to something else. What was this metaphor about?

There was also the other passage that impressed all the girls: '*I promise you will heal now my child, now that I take my own path, you will heal, you will sense life running through your veins once again and love and trust in the goodness of people will flood you. I give you back what you deserve. What was taken away from you by the worst side of humanity.*' This passage proved to be very powerful, since it ended up describing the transformation Debra-Jo began to undergo soon after the departure of the nun. It happened slowly, taking days and days, but it was undeniable to everyone that Debra-Jo was changing right in front of the other girls' eyes. Her mood changed, so did her personality, something from her core opened up to the outside world like a flower blossoming and showed all her hidden beauty. Presence came forth through her eyes. Some parts of her personality grew firmer while others softened. Her attention to details expanded in a way that things she could not see before were now in plain sight. It was like she was going through a second adolescence and falling in love with life for the first time. Many things that were once out of reach, or meaningless, or incomprehensible, now made perfect sense. The sermon to which she used to pay little attention was now a full sensorial experience which she could perfectly relate to, with tears of commotion. Every time the priest pronounced 'God', or said 'because God wants', 'because God did', 'because God', it was God speaking directly to her heart. She was now able to clearly see what had actually brought all these people to spend an hour of their Sunday morning in a church.

And so it was with people. She sensed communion, their quality, and she felt empathy and a desire to reach out to them and talk to them. It was in this receptive state of mind that Debra-Jo met Ugo. He was a handyman, the handyman that Sister Piera had called to start working on small jobs, which had been neglected by her predecessor, in order to refurbish the institution. They started talking while Ugo was putting up some new cupboards in the kitchen. He was funny. He made her laugh. She felt at ease with him. They went on interacting any time they came across each other, whenever he came by to sort out new repairs for the nun. Then one day she found a rose laying on her bed. She looked at Gabriella, who sat on her own bed with an I-was-here-when-it-happened sort of look on her face. Debra-Jo too knew who the gifter was. 'It's the most beautiful thing,' she said holding the rose.

A few days after, as she was hanging about in the living room with the rest of the girls, she heard from the window Ugo's cheerful whistling as he entered the gate and walked across the courtyard. She understood then that she was in love with him. She stood up and walked across the living room, while he entered the building wearing his white denim dickies, carrying some planks on his shoulder. She walked through the corridor. He walked up the stairs. She came to the landing and met him. 'I want to be with you,' she said. They kissed. And this time it was different.

Either because he had work commitments there, or because he went there to see Debra-Jo, Ugo soon became a habitué of the Oasis as his love story with Debra-Jo grew stronger. He would come to pick her up in the day and bring her back at night. Sometimes he would stay for tea at the Oasis with the girls and he would even go out with the whole group for walks or nights out at other venues.

Although the girls missed Sister Gaudenzia, her absence didn't impact their lives in the measure one would expect after such a long cohabitation. Things stayed more or less the same, even though some girls left and others moved in. The new nun, however, was more reserved and did not like to take part in the mundane narrative the girls used to share with Sister Gaudenzia. Sister Piera ran Oasis with a more pragmatic and traditional hand, which at times could even be too strict, although the girls with their 'please please please' were able to bend her will when they really wanted.

Ugo, who liked Oasis and its people, noticed that Debra-Jo was growing too dependent on that place. He brought up the issue with her several times. He was of the opinion that as a 21-year-old, and free now to go her own way, she should take a big step and move out. Debra-Jo was aware of this, she said to him, but she was just taking her time with the prospect. She had presumed that soon she would be able to move into the new house, the house in Via Suore, with her brothers. To take care of them. But meanwhile, time was passing and nothing was changing. No work had started since Pino had shown them the house for the first time, a year before and it still remained uninhabitable.

There were, however, other reasons contributing to my sister's reluctance to leave Oasis. She had lived there for so long that she had grown very attached to it and to the other girls, and she feared being alone outside in the world. But she needed to try, Ugo insisted. She was a woman now, a very strong and capable woman, she should trust herself. He had just bought a house with the help of his parents and a few months after they first met, Ugo asked my sister if she wanted to move in with him. My sister accepted. When she left Oasis she also left Imola, since their new house was in Bologna.

Like Debra-Jo, both Ocean and Sigmund had reached an age where they were technically free to move out of the institution any time they wanted. But it seemed that moving out was not a priority for them. Not so much because they were waiting to move into the new family home in Via Suore, but because they too were dependent on St Catherina, like Debra-Jo had been on Oasis, like any typical, Italian, young adult would be in their parents' house. They felt no pressure to give up the comforts and the affections of the house in which they had been raised. They had roots in St Catherina, made strong bonds with people who had taken the place of their family, had enjoyed the privileges of being senior residents, and had the love of Don Ettore. In fact, the priest loved them as if they were his own sons. And they loved him back as if he was their father.

In terms of education, the two brothers went different ways. Sigmund, tired of studying, dropped out of school in the third year of a five-year electrician's course. Ocean on the other hand persevered with his plan to conclude the five-year course at the Commercial Technical Institute so as to gain a diploma and hopefully work in a bank as an accountant.

While Debra-Jo moved to her new house with Ugo, Ocean, nineteen years old with an ever-present Grace Jones-like haircut, was attending the last year of his studies. He had dropped basketball to switch to a less team-oriented sport, kickboxing. His first proper job was to serve as a supervisor on a part-time basis for St Catherina, looking after us, the youngest residents, from late afternoon until bedtime for a weekly salary of, what would be today, 100 euros. He also started working as a model for commercials and fashion events around Italy.

As for Sigmund, he had made friends with a man named Alfonso. Alfonso owned a workshop of antiques in Imola, which Sigmund had started frequenting, until one day, he started working as an assistant for the man. He learned to restore pieces of furniture among the smells of the solvents and the chemically-treated wood. He then opened his own little shop in the warehouse that stood on one end of St Catherina's courtyard. The warehouse had previously served as a depot for furniture and general junk that the institution had collected from the house-clearing service it offered to the public. Sigmund also ran the service. Any antique he brought home, he would then refurbish himself using the techniques he had learned from Alfonso and he would put them on display in the warehouse.

News of Sigmund's projects spread quickly, and antique dealers and traders began to frequent the warehouse in St Catherina. It was then clear to Don Ettore that Sigmund had found a purpose. He just needed specialisation. The priest enrolled him in a three-year professional course for restoration, so at the time that Klaus moved to Casa Famiglia and Lorenzo to Villa Verucchio, Sigmund was steeped in study and work, both for the Institution and Alfonso.

***

One day, while Redeso and I were hanging around with our gang in the courtyard, our social worker, Ursola Delrio, the same woman who had just recently transferred two of our brothers to their new foster homes, came over to us. Wearing her austere brown skirt and long-necked, white woollen jumper, she said she wanted to talk to us. We took a little stroll with her across the courtyard away from the rest of our gang, with her walking between us, talking to my brother and then turning towards me.

'Twins, soon you can drive motorbikes!' she said, I think, referring to the fact that we were turning fourteen in only a matter of days, and probably also trying to pique our interest with a rebellious topic she thought would impress us.

'What do you want to talk about?' we asked her.

'Nothing alarming. I just want to make you an offer. Feel free to take it or reject it, totally up to you. I know you have been visiting Klaus at the Casa Famiglia recently. How did you find him?'

'It seems he's doing well.'

'What about the place? What's your impression?'

'People there enjoy a great deal of freedom,' Redeso said, kicking away a stone from his path. 'There is a lot of space. The garden, the dog, it's cool down there. They have a vineyard, motorbikes and stuff.'

'I mean how do you like it? Would you like to live there?'

We kind of felt it had something to do with moving out as soon as she said she wanted to talk to us. Once moving around becomes part of your life, once your nomadic gene has been activated, all the relevant sensorial equipment that comes with it enables you to foresee when the next move is underway, like those animals that can anticipate the onset of an atmospheric or geological event. But still, despite the number of times we had been standing in that place, I mean, standing before someone informing us that we were about to move house, it always carried with it such a strong force that it always felt new to me. I would feel butterflies in my stomach. My mouth would dry up. I threw glances in the direction of the guys of my gang, who were messing around in the distance, wearing their tracksuits and laughing at some of Gino's typical bullshit. I looked at my twin brother to check if he felt the same way as I did, and then glanced at the place around us. I noticed how my perception of it all intensified and became dense, vivid and clear, more detailed, as if I were actually seeing it all for the first time from an outsider's point of view, now that I had this new option of leaving, in hand.

I looked at the epic football match being played on the football ground. At the long benches stationed between the kitchen and the main entrance where Don Ettore sat chatting with one of the chefs and a few people from the Catholic Action Group. I looked at the decaying basketball court and at the bike shed, where we watched older kids repairing their clunky motorbikes and learned tricks to open combination padlocks.

We left St Catherina a couple of days later. We didn't receive the warm kind of leaving party with assorted pastries and Coca-Cola, but it was meaningful all the same. Everyone we came across during our last two days stopped to wish us good luck, including the chefs and the cleaners. Mr P gave us both ten-euro notes directly from his wallet as a farewell gift and told us to come and visit sometime. To the boys of our gang, we promised we would keep in touch. Only Don Ettore seemed unhappy, somehow annoyed by the event of us leaving. I would learn later that he took it personally, as a rejection of all the good things he had done for us, that we had voluntarily chosen to leave his institution at the first opportunity. Still, he approached us after dinner and wished us good luck with a sincere smile.

I remember Ocean coming to our dormitory on our last night while we were getting ready for bed even though it was his day off.

'Hey Twins, ready for a new life? I've come to say goodbye now for tomorrow I'll be away, working at a fashion event in Milan. What to say… It was nice, this time together. Try to behave there at the foster home and say hi to Klaus!'

'Ok. Thanks, Ocean!'

A handshake the American way, as we used to call it back then, was the closest we could get to a proper hug.

Trees

Franco, the head of the Casa Famiglia carers, came to collect us from St Catherina on a Monday in early September at the wheel of a burgundy Fiat Uno. We drove along the straight trajectory of the Via Emilia and had a glimpse of our old house as we drove past it. The villa—the villa which had burned down eight years ago, which lay at the edge of this road and was one of the last houses you could see before leaving town. You could hardly miss it if you travelled eastward away from Imola. So it was today, on our way to Toscanella, that the old villa came into sight on my right.

It stood quiet as usual. The iron gate was closed and the front railing through which you could have a glimpse of the main façade was still there, with the gravel front yard amidst the semi-circle of pine trees. The burned top half had been repaired so that there was no trace left of the accident. But it still remained unclear who lived there, if anyone lived there at all, since we had moved out so long ago. Sometimes, on other occasions, I saw a car or two parked in there. But never a single soul. It looked like the house with its garden lay suspended in a timeless zone. As though it was something, something more than a house. I don't think that any one of us ever enquired about what had become of it, we just knew that the Bank of Imola had seized it at some point in the past, since my father had never managed to buy it nor to solve any of his debts. But still we thought of it as our house. More than we felt about the house in Via Suore. I imagined Sigmund and Sigmund's relationship with this house that he might have been seeing nearly every day for years, every time he drove out of Imola to go to Dozza, Toscanella, Castel San Pietro or Bologna. What thoughts did he have at the sight of it, which had become unavoidable. The house belonged to such a distant past but was still so relevant, so symbolic to all of us, to each of our destinies, as he himself had observed once, since the day he had accidentally set it on fire. How did you feel brother? Did you ever take secondary roads to avoid passing by there? Did you proclaim anything to the house when you passed it? Did you sometimes pull the car off the road, stop and look at the house and let your memories and imagination run? Did that house become your urban shrine? Or had you grown so used to seeing it that you just drove by it without paying any attention? I don't think so. I have the feeling that as long as that house lay there, we would all be subjected to a feeling of one kind or another as we drove past it.

Franco talked to us just to make us feel comfortable during the car journey to Toscanella.

'How do you feel moving out?'

'Cool.'

'I hope you guys are sporty, 'cause you'll be cycling on country roads quite a lot to get to town and get the bus to school every morning.'

'You guys will give us the bikes?'

'Yep, we can get them at the Mercatone Uno. Do you have any preference yet?'

'What about mountain bikes? Is there cash for them?'

'I think so. We may need to go with the affordable ones if that's ok with you.'

'Fine with it.'

The sign saying Toscanella appeared at the edge of the street as we approached the small town. We passed an industrial area, then a night club, then a petrol station. We turned right past a church, feeding into the lane that we had taken the last time with Debra-Jo and Ugo, the lane that led away from Toscanella's tiny urban area into the open countryside. Houses appeared less frequently. Orchards and fields lay on both sides of the road. A few dogs barked somewhere in the background. We stopped at the ringing level crossing at the end of a queue that was longer than the last time to wait for the train to pass. Some drivers, to kill time, waited outside their cars smoking cigarettes. Some others just left their doors open, letting music play on their radios. Then the slow freight train crawled by in front of us. Then bars lifted, and slowly, like one of the processions we were used to back in St Catherina, the homogenous line of cars and bikes drove forth, hurdling over the bumps of the railway tracks as we crossed, and all the vehicles dissipated as they scattered away at different speeds. We turned left on Via Capitolo. We stopped in front of the green gate of the Casa Famiglia. Franco got out of the car to open the squeaking sliding gate, then came back into the car and we drove into the courtyard. The small, nervous dog bounded over to us and stayed playing at our feet as we got out of Franco's Fiat Uno.

'This is Dog,' he said.

'Dog the dog?'

'Yeah, Dog the dog! It was on the folks to give it a name but as you see no one seems to care.'

'Dog's a cool name,' my brother replied. Then Klaus came out to receive us.

'Hey Twins!'

'Hey Klaus!'

'You take them to their room?' Franco asked him.

'Yes, le-le-leave it to me.'

We followed Klaus inside the house carrying our sports bags on our shoulders. We came across two of the tenants in the hall, the girl who we had seen a few weeks before heading to the kitchen, and the guy with the mental problems who was just standing on the hall by the stairs, twirling a tuft of his dark hair with an unreadable expression on his face. Both greeted us, but the mentally unstable guy with his thick, black glasses, face full of acne and a pair of Franciscan sandals, followed us up the stairs to our room and stood waiting and watching over us by the door while we settled in, fingers still twirling his hair. We just ignored him as we looked around our new room. It was a three-bed room with two beds lying perpendicular to each other on one side of the room, and a third, against a wall on the opposite side, right next to a window. Klaus had been sleeping here alone for the last four months, which indicated that the Casa Famiglia was a relatively recent establishment if he had slept alone all this time, and that it had just reached maximum capacity with the addition of us twins. We were seven overall, including us. Three boys in one room, two in another. And two girls in another. Another clue suggesting the place had been just recently opened was the brand-new look of the furniture. The colour-coordinated wardrobes, desks and bed frames all seemed recently bought. I was probably about to be the first person to sleep in my bed. The differences between St Catherina and this place were so extreme that I felt like I had been living in a staged reality for the last few years by contrast. I had moved to a place where I had my private desk lamp and bed lamp on my colour-coordinated bed table and matching, empty bookshelves. I would not have to walk six beds down the room to reach a goddamn, broken, metal locker that lay at the far end of an army hospital-looking dormitory, but just take one step from my bed and I would reach my brand-new wardrobe and my sleek and shining desk. The window beside my bed overlooking the side of the garden that held the oak tree and the swing, and extended to overlook the vineyard, had no safety grid.

'This is freedom, guys,' declared Klaus, guessing what kind of internal thought process Redeso and I were going through. 'If you w-w-want to go out in the courtyard you can. T-t-t-there is no such a thing like a scheduled time for st-st-studying and that type of shit. Take your bike and g-g-go exploring the area around, man! You can. This is f-f-fucking freedom!' He was standing in the middle of the room while he said that, his bed all done and neat behind him, partially hidden behind a corner of his wardrobe. There was not a single poster or decoration in the room. Klaus had chosen to leave it clear.

'Come and see my room,' said the mentally ill guy, who I'll call by his name, Telemaco, from now on, and who was at the door still twisting up his hair, his face with the same blank gaze. We went to see it. It was about the same size, with the same colour-coordinated furniture, with just one bed less, and, in contrast to our bedroom, was covered in posters of racing motorbikes and metal bands, mostly hung up by Telemaco's roommate who was out at that moment. Telemaco then took us down to the kitchen to have tea with biscuits. We met another supervisor there, named Valeria, who was just starting her afternoon shift. She was a scout too, she explained, like Franco.

Later on, Redeso and I were drawn into doing some gardening labour with Franco. Not that we were supposed to do it; he could have managed it all by himself with no problem as he was one of those types of handy guys who could build himself a house. He had also helped to complete the construction of this foster home. It was just because he caught us wandering outside in the garden looking lost at sea, that he got us involved in some gardening work that, as he said, would connect us more to the spirit of the place. He showed us the work that needed doing. One thing was to help him build a front garden, a rustic, wooden fence around the little plot of lawn that edged the gravelled driveway. The other was the planting of some trees by the front gate. He assigned the first job to Redeso, while he would show me the other job, he said. He explained to Redeso how to place the wood rods in the holes he had already dug, secure them with rocks placed around the rods at the bottom of the holes and then pour in cement to fill it up to the surface. Then he led me over to the front gate, where a line of holes on the ground dotted the front perimeter of the property and a number of cypress shoots lay flat on the ground with their roots wrapped inside earth-filled bandages. The work was similar to the one he had assigned to Redeso. I just needed to put a small tree shoot inside each of the holes, keep it straight using the same technique of using rocks as stabilisers, then fill the hole up by shovelling in the earth that was piled beside each hole. He then went to finish the stockade with Redeso, which required more work, while I carried out the tree planting by myself. There were eight cypresses. I planted four in a line on one side of the gate. Another line of four on the other side. Then I walked to the middle of the road to see my work from a distance and felt an immediate sense of connection with those small tree shoots. Two lines of four with a green gate in the middle, forming a symmetrical composition. My hands, shoes and trousers, were dirty with soil. And then I realised something. I looked at my hands and then at the trees and took a deep breath. There had been three significant events in my life where I felt I was inside my skin. One was the night of the fire, then the night outside my father's house when we returned to Africa. The third time was right now. Staring at those trees made me feel I had actively done something meaningful for the first time.

'You guys are going to grow big,' I whispered to the trees.

I shifted my attention to the calm expanse of green scenery surrounding me, at the elements of my new life, the sky, gratifyingly wide and blue. Far in the distance, I caught sight of a figure on a bicycle turning from the main road onto our street. As he approached, I recognised him as the same kid who had been drinking milk and who found Redeso and me funny, when we came here to visit Klaus with our siblings a few weeks earlier. His name, I would later know, was Nicola. He was Telemaco's roommate. Wearing a Ramones jumper, jeans and high-top Nikes, with straight, corvine hair covering his eyes, he circumnavigated me riding a BMX, greeting me with just a nudge of his chin, and entered the foster home's gate.

LONDON, PRESENT DAY
VII

I will stop here today. This project can be draining at times, with a whole, large family of desperados to follow over three different planes, and the fucking limitations of writing in a foreign language that makes me feel dumb some days, twice as much if I had one of my sleepless nights.

What the fuck.

Why on earth have I thrown myself into this project? I shouldn't even be here, feeling the draft from all the windows and doors and the damp smell of this shitty Victorian house. I should be in Italy. Getting my load of sun and *aperitivi* on the squares with friends and siblings and entrenching my small place in the Italian literary universe that I had conquered with ten years of hard work and three publications. But what a dick instead.

A fucking dick, as they say here.

A wanker they say.

A prick.

Prick.

I like the word 'prick'. It should be something of national pride in my view. The supreme insult. Sharp, nearly vowelless, incredibly degrading, in that you use only the further end of your vocal apparatus. It sounds like someone spitting with an 'r' in the middle. It leaves no space for reconciliation. 'You Prick!' And argument done, solved, whatever it was. Whatever it means. Only a prick could have let his career go and watched it dying. A promising career thrown down the drain, when I had been once well advised by a prominent Bolognese writer of my acquaintance to never let more than three years pass without putting anything new out into the market if you don't want to be forgotten. It's like any other business, he'd said. That is exactly where I had failed. It has been nearly eleven years since I published anything in Italy, not even an article, nor a short story, not a single interview on the radio nor a talk at a conference. The last talk I held was here in England, at Oxford University, where I gave a lecture on my adaptation of Shakespeare's *Romeo and Juliet* for a literary festival about Shakespeare adaptations across Europe. But in Italy, dead silence. I bet nobody remembers me anymore. I bet there are countless authors who, despite moving abroad, have managed to keep their career intact in their homeland and now are receiving royalties, fame and tonnes of kisses from home, while me… Why didn't I do the same? Laziness? Negligence? Arrogance? Or is it because at the end of the day Italy was not my homeland?

Fuck it. Maybe that's all it was, my Italian has declined along with my professional life. This may be an explanation. It went this way as a logical, if not natural, yeah, natural, consequence of who I was—not a native. My life there, my presence in the territory, since the very first day I had set foot in the country had always been the precarious presence of a passenger. You want to travel light, if you are on a lifelong journey, just with the essentials, just with what truly belongs to you. In any case, I need to admit that there is more to it. There is me refusing to accept an identity, rejecting my Italian identity, my Italian past, memory, conduct, which perhaps shows the crude truth that I am just ungrateful for all that the country had meant to me. Someone told me it was just anger. 'You are Italian, Red. You are just angry. Just come to terms with it. Where do you belong otherwise?' It may be true. My veins are indeed filled with anger. I am misanthropic to the core, Amen. Tomorrow it might be different, but today this is all I have, all I can give you, my daily, absolute truth. I am here. Now. Stuck in my own writing. That is enough for me.

GROUND

I sense that my English vocabulary is swelling and taking my writing far from the tedious process that it was at the beginning of this project. Unfathomable ideas take shape. Partially thanks to you Telma my love, I must confess. With the way you give yourself to life, you inspire me. With you I understand the relativity of our own pain, we give too much weight to things when ultimately, nothing really matters. I wake up here. I eat here. I work here. I fuck here. I die here while dreaming of high-rise buildings, robots, spaceships, whores and bands of idiots at the bar and me fucking you to soreness.

Telma, Telma, Telma, tell me three things. The first three that come up in your mind. I desperately need to hear them in this everyday grey afternoon. What would they be? Mine are Wolves. Bones. Socks.

Telma, I know who I am. I can't be done yet. I know who the fuck the guy who is sitting here actually is. I don't need to try. This thing doesn't die out, the writing I mean, you have it or you don't have it. And if you have it, it stays with you for life. Despite years of dormancy and struggle, this voracity is still here, alive and strong, it pours out of my fingers with more vehemence than before, like tree roots digging their way through layers of earth to reach nutrients, or wild plants springing out of the concrete floor, writing finds its way through. It pushes out and eradicates all the barriers no matter how high they are, like the revolt of nature. I am the revolt of nature. I am the unforgiving river that deviates onto another course if it finds obstacles in its way, cost what it may; I will reinvent myself if I have to, remerging from the depth of the earth under a different guise, or a different form, with a different pull, different motivations, in a different language. I will win regardless. Because writing is far from being a skill one possesses. It is not my job, it just happened to me once by chance, as the rest of my life. And since then, it has been the itinerant land where I permanently locate myself regardless of the external changes. If I had to answer the question, 'where do I come from?' I would confidently answer: 'from my own process of writing.' That is the only country I hold all the right papers for and there is no officer at any fucking border grunting at me or stopping me to search me on the street. This, what I am doing now and here, writing while the Polaris star shines on, it is my fucking ground and nobody is going to yell at me 'Go back home you fucking nigger!' Not from here.

***

A few months after the UK-EU divorce deadline, with Theresa May's withdrawal agreement being rejected over and over, a hard Brexit seems to be the only option looming. The Tory cabinet slipped into a britches warfare. The House of Lords should have a say in this but not the Queen, and all the good kids are leaving the Labour party which is, allegedly, infested with anti-Semitism. And despite the Labour-induced vote of no confidence and the repeated humiliation, Theresa May keeps on fighting for, what, nobody knows… maybe her own name, for the best interest of her country and some corporate lobbies, for the snipers, the Templars, the Zionists, for the dark money of the Fundamentalist Christian, the Radical Right and for Steve Bannon's passion for travelling around the world. The foreign investment rate is slowing down and EU immigrants are leaving the UK. But my mother, the most foreign of them all, is still here.

She stands there, by the living room door, staring at me while wearing a well-fitting denim jacket. Like she is about to go out. Which makes her look even younger than usual. She actually looks younger every day, as if time runs the other way around for her. Like in the *Curious Case of Benjamin Button*, who was born as an old man and aged backwards, growing younger and younger. She is a mystery to me.

'Where are you going?' I ask her from my desk.

'To meet a friend of mine.'

'That's a surprise. I didn't know you had friends in London.'

'Yes, I knew her from the Congo. I'm going to pray at hers.'

GROUND

'Where?'

'In Brixton.'

'Oh wow, and you'll go all the way there by yourself?'

'Yeah, I checked on the internet. Then I have my phone. It's easy. I take the Overground, then the Victoria Line at Highbury and Islington and get off at Brixton. My friend is going to pick me up at the station.'

'Ok, have fun there!'

'Don't wait for me for dinner. I'll be late.'

'Ok.'

She checks to see if she has her keys in her bag as she walks out and closes the door behind her.

It has been nearly a month since my mother came to stay with me in London. Probably the longest period I have spent with her that I can clearly remember. I am sure I will miss her when she leaves. I go for a little walk myself too. Up to Hackney Downs Park, I stroll around the empty field looking up at the night sky clogged with clouds and take a few deep breaths. Then I walk back home, make myself a tea, grab a book by Augustin Fernandez Malo, sit on the sofa and read it while sipping the scalding, liquorice tea, until there is a knock at the door. I wonder who that can be. It cannot be Mum because she has got her keys. Could that be the milkman? I go to open it.

It is you. You and your boyfriend. Standing at my front door, you are holding a bottle of wine, him, standing behind you, is the first to explain.

'She really wanted us to come here and have a drink with you! Can we?'

'Sure,' I say, leaving the door open for both of you to come in. It is clear that you have been already out drinking for a while. You left your daughter with a babysitter, you explain, and you were drinking in a nearby pub when you had this idea, at the peak of your drunkenness I suppose, 'Let's go drink a glass of wine with the neighbour! Let's buy a bottle and take it there.' And that is exactly what you did. You convinced your boyfriend on your night out together to leave the pub, go and buy a bottle of wine and see if I was at home.

'I tried to convince her not to,' he says 'but she really wanted it. I don't know what's wrong with this woman!'

I sit on the sofa mildly nervous. He looks around the living room trying to immerse himself while you go to fetch three glasses, as if you are in your own house, open the wine, serve it, bringing it to each of us, 'Cheers!'

'Cheers!'

We lift the glasses up and drink.

'Where is the music?' he asks, this man from Slovakia, looking with surprise at my only standing amplifier and speakers. 'Don't tell me you're one of those who uses Spotify.'

'Yes, of course, I listen to music from my phone.'

'Or laptop,' you add.

'Ah, what a disappointment from an acupuncturist!' he says.

'And an author,' you add.

'Yeah yeah, even worse! Everything traditional, all ancient choices, but when he comes to music, badabooom, there you are, the donkey falls into Spotify.'

'He's a music fanatic,' you say to justify.

I think about his dubious use of 'donkey' that in Italian is usually used in derogative terms, but maybe not in Slovakia. We never know in London. Cultural differences justify a lot of strange things you hear.

You show me one of your best smiles standing next to the table with feet set wide open like a ballerina.

'He listens only to vinyl,' you clarify. 'But he doesn't like latte!'

'Unfortunately, I don't have any vinyl my friend, only Spotify or YouTube.'

'Of course, that's ok, Spotify is fine,' he says.

I plug my phone into the amplifier and allow him to take control of the music since he is the expert. I like him. He is a cool guy. There is a twist of cynical irony in whatever he said that gave me a taste of how you ended up with him. He is charming and good-looking, and he clearly loves you very much. You make a good couple. But you have told me many times that you don't love him anymore. That you want to break up with him, but you can't find the strength to do it. Although you tried a few times, you got back together. Was it a sensible choice you made to bring him here? Was it smart for me to let you in, to persist in hanging out with you? Who do we belong to? How is this thing going to end? I just know that I love you. And I know you feel the same way. This shit is tedious. I fill up another glass for myself. I top up yours. And I thank you both for having thought about me tonight. 'My pleasure,' you both say. The Violent Femmes he has chosen feels like the perfect choice.

'Explain to me,' I say to him, 'What's wrong about Spotify?'

He argues that it is the most disengaging way to listen to music, while with the old-school vinyl it was real. It was authentic. There was an exercise of will, you were physically and emotionally engaged, while with Spotify, 'what is that! Do you really care about music any more with Spotify? Before there was all the waiting to get paid to go and buy your new album, there was the visual and tactile thing of the cover art, and pulling out and handling the vinyl, putting on the record, setting the arm upon it, and listening to that purr sound at the beginning of each track. Do you want to compare this with Spotify?'

I agree with part of his argument. 'Yeah, you're right,' I say, 'it's shit nowadays,' and we go on talking and laughing. I open another bottle of wine as the one you brought has finished and we talk about our favourite cycling routes in London. By the canals, through the Liverpool Street area up to South Bank. To Holborn via Hoxton and Clerkenwell. He illustrates his preference for the Docklands and as we talk you gradually zoom out, observing us both from afar, at times looking bored.

You lie down on the carpet, on your belly, the glass of wine next to you, your face flushed from drunkenness. Now and then you roll from one side to the other. And I don't know how aware you are of how intimate and sensually charged this gesture is, rolling like this, on my floor, a step away from my feet. I need to make an effort to stop staring at you while I am talking to him. He is clearly unhappy with what you are doing and growing impatient. But this is the problem with free-spirited people like you; you are barely aware of boundaries. Of what you are doing. As I am. We would make a very problematic couple if we were together. We need counterparts that ground us, not that trigger us as we do to each other. But at the same time not counterparts that would do whatever it takes to cage us.

'Why are you doing this?' he now vents it out. 'Why are you rolling like this in front of him?'

'What's the problem? I'm just rolling like a bear.'

'Yes, but this is not your house, it seems like you live here.'

'So? In some ways, I live here. I'm very familiar with this house.'

'Do you feel at home?'

'Yes of course!'

'Do you feel at home with this guy?'

'Of course I do.'

'Can you stop rolling please?'

'OK, ok, wow!'

I serve myself another glass. Now it is Iggy Pop singing, '*I'm gonna be your dog.*' There is the rattling of keys coming from the front door before it opens and my mum walks in in her denim jacket looking like she's been a bit chilly out there on her way back here. She looks surprised to see drunk people in the living room at this time of the night.

'This is my mother, Sofie.'

'Hi Sofie, It's a pleasure to meet you!'

'Hi, it's my pleasure!'

'Can I serve you a glass of wine?' you ask her.

'What?' she stares at me confused as though she needs translation and permission to join us and wonders who you both are, anyway, all at the same time.

'*Tu veux du vin?*' I simplify.

'Why not, a little bit!' she says.

'*Oh, c'est superb!*' you exult, and stop to kiss her on the cheek as you rush to the kitchen to find her a glass.

The Big Road Construction Project Begins

On a winter day in 1982, my father left Italy never to return. That was the day that stuck in my mind as *the day* my siblings and I were abandoned by our parents. 'We were abandoned by our parents,' I used to explain to people when they enquired about our life. I even shared this same narrative with my audience in a few radio interviews and book launches when I gave a picture of my family history. Not with the intention to build a persona or to move my readers; I was being genuine, I truly believed that I had been abandoned. And nothing ever challenged this belief. I would have even sworn to have known the reason why they left and to have seen them from the window of my room while they furtively snuck into the car and ran away into the night. What I knew was that something went wrong during the process of a business deal they were doing in Italy and that my father was then facing legal consequences. In the frenzy to escape the police who were coming to arrest him, he and my mother roughly packed their possessions in the middle of the night. Masambila helped them through the preparation and put the luggage in the car and the chauffer drove them to the airport where they took the first flight to Congo. The problem here is that you don't just catch a flight at the last minute in the middle of the night from Bologna to Congo without booking a ticket in the first place. All I needed to do was to sit with myself and go through the whole incident rationally, to see that it was a story that I made up, pure science fiction, another gap-filling trick of the mind.

There was nothing dramatic in my parents' departure. Nobody woke up in the middle of the night with police after them. My siblings and I had never been abandoned. I would learn from my mother that we had all been given notice, as usual, by our parents, in person, that they were soon to set off on one of their regular business trips to Congo. Because that is what it was. Just the usual business trip to Congo with plans to return in a couple of months. It was not night and I had not been looking from the window of my room because they left in the morning while we were all at school. They were travelling to Brazzaville to receive the quarry equipment Alvaro Belluzzi had shipped down, ready to start the Big Road Construction project. They had entered the chauffeur-driven car, my father, cheerful as usual, with the prospect that he was at the dawn of the greatest quest of his life and would come back as a winner, with new presents for us, and would finish the house payments and put more work into furnishing it. My mother was still doubting it was a safe move.

Work at the site of the WAT Congo quarry in Pointe-Noire started. The first shipment of machinery was assembled by local engineers. Offices and worker facilities were built on site. New cargo of trucks and earth-moving machines were driven to the sites from the port. My father and the site manager moved from workplace to workplace to supervise and orchestrate the activities. Then the rock extraction operation from the mountain began. There were explosions, the collection and transportation of rocks, stone crushing plants operating. Taking place simultaneously were road planning and site surveys with road architects and regional councillors and my father. If anything, my mother says, it was something to see him back to his old self, at the top of the game, revived and focused. But he was also very nervous. This project truly meant a lot to him. All the money he had invested in it, the pressure from the Minister's expectations, my mother's qualms, us kids in Italy and in Africa, his own reputation, and the potential this project could unlock if it all went according to plan. A lot was at stake.

Problems began emerging just a couple of months from the start of the project, when the machines began to break right in the middle of the work, which was expected to a certain extent on a project of this scale. I'm sure my father and his team had factored this into the equation, as much as they had calculated there would be some damaged product, possibly from transportation. Hitches they would be able to solve, however, with just a call to the mechanic. But they were facing a larger problem than the few isolated episodes of faulty machines. Works were often and regularly suspended, from days to weeks, because the crusher had broken down again, and the excavator had died while they were laying the foundation of a new road, and the mechanic, short of a replacement piece, had to order it from Lagos with unbelievable waiting time. Similar issues were occurring to trucks while driving on the roads and the same thing happened to many other pieces of equipment. They did not need the mechanic's opinion to figure out there was something wrong with many of the machines from the beginning. The quality of the second and third shipments were even worse. Most of the machines were faulty upon delivery. Some would not even turn on from the start, while others fell apart while they were being assembled. Not all, but too many. Enough to hinder the production, to even arrest it completely. Soon it was the case that the workers spent more time idling while waiting for the mechanic to fix the machines than actually doing work.

My father furiously complained to Pino and Belluzzi on the phone several times. Pino was as stunned as my father was. 'How was it possible? We saw the machines, they were working perfectly. Let me talk with Belluzzi.' Belluzzi blamed it on the African way of working, because his equipment had never let anyone down. Never in Italy. He could not do anything if his machines had ended up in the hands of incompetent, unqualified engineers who assembled them with their asses. Poor Dad, powerlessly watching his big project sink. The work was in a swamp. The cost of keeping the whole apparatus together, and paying for the repairs and salaries surpassed any profit and put them in a deficit. Ninety percent of the car machines had died. There was no way to resurrect them. This was the reason why my father could not come back to Italy. Unless he paid back his debts to the Bank of Imola he would be sent to jail.

What was meant to be his triumph proved to be a crushing defeat. His Waterloo, as they would say here. The result was that WAT Congo was unequipped to be able to fully operate at a competitive standard. With just under half percent of its capacity, my father's enterprise could not build new roads, nor improve old ones. Work halted and the WAT Congo quarry looked like a cemetery of industrial machines with a stream of life running through it. My old man was devastated. It was hard at this point not to suspect that he had been the victim of fraud at the hand of Alvaro Belluzzi.

We ignored Pino's involvement in the scam, if we can, in fact, talk about it in the terms of a scam rather than the grimmest purchase my father ever happened to pursue. Because it could simply be seen as a bad move from the start to buy a plenitude of second-hand industrial machines that were supposed to undergo intercontinental shipping and a high degree of mechanical stress. The you-get-what-you-pay-for rule might be applied in this case.

Or my father was right to believe that this whole affair had been consciously orchestrated by Alvaro Belluzzi. Maybe he and his umbrella of dealers had made a substantial profit by selling a shipment with only half of the machines fully working, while the other half consisted of broken equipment that was put into the containers as filler, just to make the full quantity. The point was that such an operation could have been either the work of an organised crime syndicate, which would mean something, or just a series of unrelated incidents involving lazy suppliers, which meant something different. It was difficult to say. Very difficult to get to the bottom of it, as Pino explained to my father. The only way would be to go legal, but again, it would take years and lots of money for a transcontinental trial of this scale, with Italian specialists that would have to come to the work sites to check the veracity of my father's claims and so on, and after all, Alvaro Belluzzi was able to provide all the legal papers to prove each machine had gone through revision by certified car repairers and national regulatory bodies, papers that he, Pino, had checked himself one by one, when he went to Alvaro Belluzzi in person. Pino was furious as much as my father was. But as soon as he received my father's complaints, he had concluded that there was nothing illegal in the deal as all the machines were fully certified.

Alvaro Belluzzi too reiterated, when he spoke again with my father, that he was able to prove that the equipment he had sent down was fully working at the time of shipment. He stressed the fact he was not responsible for any damage that could have occurred during the transportation, the unloading, the assemblage and maintenance due to third-party incompetence but he was willing to double-check with the umbrella of his suppliers for any fault. Despite the months of negotiation, not one viable solution emerged. There was nothing Pino could do for my father to get his money back. It was all gone. His biggest dream, and the million and the half of the bank loan he had put into it. All gone, for machines that were, for the most part, useless.

To aggravate things further, he could not even go to Italy to face Alvaro Belluzzi in person because he feared he could be held liable in Italy for the bank loan he was unable to repay and that he may even face arrest. Who knew? And what did he expect to resolve by going there anyway? Whether or not it was a scam, Alvaro Belluzzi knew how to protect himself in his domain from a lone Congolese immigrant. Bottom line, the failed road project and the ensuing bank debt discouraged my dad from returning to Italy. That was the real reason behind his absence in our lives, the reason why he did not return to the villa in Imola after that last trip to Congo. It was anything but an intentional abandonment, simply the result of an unfortunate cycle of events.

Following the catastrophe, the WAT Congo enterprise remained operative just enough to run a quarry, thus turning into a service of rock production. The minister passed the road deal to a French enterprise to whom my father was in part able to supply rocks and derivates. All the dead machinery meanwhile came in handy to the poorly-paid and unpaid workers and the diverse population of external smugglers that breached the quarry in the night to steal parts from the machines. My parents had become gravel sellers now, my mother told me. They had no money to pay our workers and the people in Italy, our chauffeur, the Italian tutor, the servants. My parents' life was further shaken the day they received a phone call from Pino announcing that the house in Imola had gone up in smoke. My mum says she was in pieces. She was desperate to come to Italy on the first flight but, for reasons she never specified, she was unable to. Maybe there were financial reasons, or they just got lost in planning for the trip, until they saw, since we were safe after all, that it wouldn't be of any real practicality to have my mother in Italy during the resolution of the incident, other than simply adding to the number of homeless people. My parents followed the development of our misfortune from afar through Pino's calls, about our move to the small clinic, then to the institutions. At that point, they made a conscious decision to take some time to think through the best possible way forward to relieve the plight affecting my family while we were under care. The main question, whether to take us back to Congo or to leave us in Italy, created a split between them, with my mother wanting us back in Congo while my father began thinking that we may be better off in Italy. In the meantime, my father committed to pay an annual fee to the priest and nuns for our accommodations, which he only maintained for a couple of years. My mother began coming to visit us in Italy from the time Klaus, Redeso and I stayed in the institution of St Theresa of the Child Jesus and kept the tradition of coming once or twice a year throughout our life there, even though her visits became less consistent once she had Mavie and then Monique. Time passed and the choice to let us grow up in Italy came about naturally as the most sensible option for us. We just needed a house. A house for us, and for them, and our younger siblings in the fortunate case that things turned out positively for my father, should he clear his debts and move to Italy permanently.

From a work perspective, my father's business never picked up again. It fluctuated between a bad and sustainable performance. His friend, Monsieur Idrissa Kamosi and other contractors and business partners, slashed him from their contact lists. News about the failure of the WAT Congo spread fast, costing my father credibility. Eventually, facing financial difficulties, my father stopped sending money to Italy to pay for our stays in the institutions. We were kept there out of the arbitrary choice of our carers.

Then came the house in Via Suore. The first real possible solution to our long-standing family crisis. Here I am tempted to believe that my father had always believed in Pino's non-involvement in Alvaro Belluzzi's equipment scam. It is the only way I can justify why he chose, again, to charge Pino with the task to find a house and to manage the negotiation. Which, apparently, Pino did very well. He found the house my father could afford, explained to him the work the house needed and gave him a quotation. My father put down a deposit, then paid off half of the amount in one go and set up to pay the rest through a mortgage in my mother's name. He arranged to send money to Pino to start the work of refurbishment, the priority being the repair of the roof. But that money never came according to Pino. The house preparation never went past the first stage we saw it. We waited for years, our keys ready, but no work started.

One day Klaus, despite being in a better place there in the countryside, perhaps the most serene we had ever seen him, asked Sigmund again, 'Why did Dad abandon us?' And this time Sigmund, tired of Klaus's struggle, tired of the struggle of each one of us, and of our lifestyle, witnessing the house in Via Suore going nowhere, decided it was time to face Dad. He called Africa. Things were not right, he told Dad. We needed to sit down and talk. The *Man of the Shoes* agreed with Sigmund and vowed to send the tickets for us all to come down to Africa to discuss the issues as a family. No one believed him after the experience we had just had the previous summer, when the same promise had gone up in smoke. And yet, it happened, we received the plane tickets for us all for a trip to Congo, including Ugo. I was fourteen by that time, and I had already been living for a year at the Casa Famiglia with Redeso and Klaus. Lorenzo had been living a year in Villa Verrocchio. Debra-Jo had settled in Bologna with Ugo. Sigmund and Ocean were still in St Catherina.

The Meeting in Brazzaville

A border officer at the Brazzaville Maya-Maya airport leered at me and my siblings as we checked in our passports. 'I used to wear your father's shoes,' he claimed as if it was of national concern, upon recognising our surname on our documents. 'I hope you guys will be able to look after him one day when he gets old with your jobs in Europe because no one else will do it here.'

'Sure. It will be on us,' Ocean reassured him, but the truth was that none of us had ever thought that we might have to provide for Dad one day. Nor had we believed that a hardass like him would even grow into a little old man, let alone die, or ever need the support of a bunch of hopeless kids, who, if they even managed to achieve a tenth of what he had achieved in a lifetime, God would bless. Besides, the officer wrongly assumed that we were straightforward economic migrants, whereas we were more accidental migrants, unlike the migrant stereotype anyhow, who consciously seeks a better life abroad and is willing to pick up any shitty job to provide for his family back home through Western Union. Our case was not even that of a rich family from a poor country sustaining their kids' education in a rich country. No, at this stage, it was something specific to our family only, something that could only be read as miserable parents in a poor country not being able to provide for a set of miserable, half-way migrant progeny, waiting in the limbo of a not-so-rich country, who had not developed the emotional bonds—or had broken them over time—that would enable them to respond to the eventual cultural obligations of caring for their poor, ageing parents one day.

This internal call to care for someone has to emerge from something that has a shape, a frame, a well-defined identity. While us, who, what were we? Italian? Beninese, Congolese, orphans? Sons of the *Man of the Shoes* or sons of the Italian government? I do think that the officer's comment caught us all unprepared. I believe we felt all the same way—blank—before the border checkpoint officer. We collected our passports, passed the border, walked through the airport. All was unchanged. The same people. Same heat. Same music. Same smells. We stayed a little while waiting at the luggage collection for ours to come through. Then we walked to the exit. Dad was there on the Congolese side of the arrival gate, still looking the same but different. Not as old as the border officer's words might have suggested, but he surely looked more mortal. In flip-flops, plain trousers, a white shirt that was open at the chest, showing a thick golden necklace hanging over his bare skin and his usual moustache, but without sideburns this time, without a cowboy hat and without the same glow.

He gave us a shy smile as he caught sight of us coming out of the arrivals. Hugs, kisses, taps on the shoulders, then he was introduced to Ugo and shook his hands, entertaining him with some foolish banter to which Debra-Jo, Ocean, Sigmund and Lorenzo joined in with nervous euphoria. Klaus and us twins stood quietly looking from the side. There was another man with Dad—a new chauffer, wearing a short sleeve, floral, dashiki-style top, who took charge of our luggage, carrying away as many pieces as he could while Dad helped with the others. We went outside the airport. It was a plain afternoon. The wraparound, scorching heat of Brazzaville hit me, but the impressions I had originally had, of the multitude of black people for example, had faded. Things were different this time. We were different. Inside and outside. We received Brazzaville through the eyes of people whose lives in institutions and family problems had hardened them, leaving us with little room to respond in a healthy manner to the wonders of our homeland. It fills me with sorrow to recall that it was nothing like the summer vacation that we had had a few years before.

GROUND

Whatever reason brought us home this time distilled the experience to something practical, something stronger than the impulse we had to reunite with our family and our disappearing life in Congo. We had come to sort things out. And our father, who was aware of this, was receiving us with a very similar frame of mind, hastier and colder than usual. We had no idea of the many ongoing life challenges and the defeats and grievances he endured that had hardened him too, all the energy he had dispensed trying to lift himself over and over again out of poverty, and the awareness, that weighed heavily in the back of his mind of repeatedly failing us, knowing that we were here not out of a genuine desire to spend time together but to understand why his obligations towards us were in deficit.

As we approached the two Mercedes cars, visibly in bad shape, I felt pity for my father. He looked to me now more like a caricature of a gypsy, with the same moustache and the golden necklace on his bare chest, that had once made him look so grand in my eyes, as he carried our suitcases toward the decaying, tacky and dated black Mercedes. He helped the chauffer load our baggage into the car. Then he walked to the driver's seat, hands in his pockets. A man and his kids. We got into the two cars, Ugo journeying with us. My father wanted him to sit in front with him, since he looked at him as the guest of honour, his daughter and firstborn's man. But he was also the first official white member of our family. In the back seat, Debra-Jo, Redeso and I, listened to their arduous conversations, with Ugo communicating in extremely basic French to which our father compensated with clunky Italian.

I noticed various signs of wear inside the car: a back door was held closed with a metal wire coiled around the front and back window frames. Window handles were missing. The one on my side did not work at all, so I could not pull down the window, which was stuck at the top with only a thin rectangle for fresh air. Fortunately, cooler air rushed in through the passenger window in front of me. The view was still eye-catching but more banal, for the same reasons I mentioned above; the discontent, disenchantment, the perspective of a fourteen-year boy. I soon became intrigued by something new nevertheless, something I began noticing in the expressions of the people I saw outside on the street, in their eyes: a severe, impassive stare. It was in everyone's eyes, including my father's, when I looked at him in the rear-view mirror as he stared at the street ahead. Then I noticed it was not just in the eyes of people, but in everything else as much, in every element of the landscape, in the architecture, and vegetation, in the streets, even in what meant to display amusement, harbouring in the picturesque, hand-painted billboards, in the biblical-sentence-long names of buses and shops, and in people gaily hanging together outside the bars. A degree of hardness lingered underneath the surface of everything in my old town, Brazzaville. And maybe it was solely determined by my own emotions during that car journey home. Or maybe not. Maybe it was there from the dawn of time. Fuck it.

The car ride was long. We got stuck in an epic traffic jam, father's car engine groaning like a tractor, and the smell of the exhausts of thousands of cars getting denser. Green and yellow taxis and hordes of motorbikes crowded. Street sellers took advantage of the traffic jam to wind around the lines of cars to sell goods—food, drinks, ivory and wooden statues, shell-bracelets and shell-necklaces. Some stationed at the edge of the road displayed their wares, such as a lone pair of djembes and some bottles of fuel. The smell of fried food rose up with the smoke from the cauldrons of street-food stalls. That same severe stare showed in the eyes of the sellers who leaned on Dad's window pushing their products forth. Dad bought some dried fried plantains and some cold coloured drinks in plastic bags, the ones you need to pierce with your teeth and drink straight from the bag.

I spotted my brother Happiness hanging about with a group of friends outside on the street by our house. I could make out some of the kids we made friends with three years ago among his group, all teenagers now, doing nothing in particular but just strolling in the middle of the empty street. Happiness looked as if a piece of sun was hidden within him, so glowing was he. When father stopped the car alongside the group to tell him to go open the gate, his big eyes on us filled with joy, hands stretched through the window to grab our hands. '*Les jumeaux!*' '*Ca va mon frère! Et tois ca va?*' We held hands. We greeted the other kids too, all cheering and tapping their hands on the car and trying to get them through the car windows to greet us. "*Ca va, les jumeaux? Tantine Debra-Jo, Bienne arrive!*' And things started to take another perspective. I saw that in the end we had space for more than just anger.

Dad drove into the driveway, Happiness on one side holding the gate open. Mavie and Moon stood up from the edge of the black-and-white, mosaic-style, tiled veranda floor where they presumably had stayed playing while waiting for us. Maman Sofie came out to the veranda, followed by Monique, who was no longer a baby but a little kid. So much had changed in the space of three years, even their stance of deference toward us had lessened. They all seemed more at peace with themselves, more defined, at the centre of a life that had continued parallel to ours, despite three years of silence in between, with as much force as our lives, with as much entitlement.

Things were more or less the same as the last time we had been inside the house of Rue Massembo Loubaki. The same Afro-Danish décor, the long, brown, L-shaped, velvet sofa, the wooden tea table, and the Hi-Fi–TV station. I was also noticing new old things, the presence of which I could not make sense of; pieces of furniture that I saw there the last time, but now when I looked properly looked as if they were part of the décor in the old villa in Imola. The globe bar that opened up in two halves was certainly the same. Even the sofa we had sat on three years ago was actually the same sofa with the integrated hi-fi system that was in the villa, so were some of the sinister and intricate, totem-like, wooden African statues and Dad and Mum's picture, both looking very young and beautiful, she in thin braids and he in that cowboy hat, seemingly safe there hanging on the wall, far above the dystopic family reality.

How could all these relevant details have escaped me the last time I was there? And how did they get there anyway? But again, never mind, nothing surprised me anymore about my parents' life. I mentioned it already, I was fourteen now. I just assumed they had asked Pino to dispatch all the things that had survived the fire. Maybe when we were ensconced in that small clinic or when we were at St Theresa. Maybe my mother managed the operation during one of her later visits to Italy. Maybe it was Maman Sofie who went to inspect the villa, who then hired a house-moving service to send everything to Congo, all the valuable things which she managed to save from the ashes. I am sure that all her jewellery had been saved. And maybe more stuff, maybe our father had got back the microphones and sound system from his conference room and set them up in a new office here in Brazzaville. It then occurred to me that the Mercedes cars in which we had just came from the airport, were most likely the same pair of cars that used to be parked in the villa's front yard. What about the two Jaguars and Land Rovers? Probably sold. Anyway, I didn't care. Those same objects were not the same objects any longer, regardless of the house they were now in. As much as we had changed, those objects too had morphed. They were things that no longer held the same charge, their meaning had changed and so had their beauty and the glow they had had back then. It was as if the clock in the house in Brazzaville had stopped at the glorious time Dad enjoyed in the seventies; a time that no longer felt glorious.

Two young servants, whom we had not seen before, pretending to finalise some cleaning in the living room, came to sneak a look at us, then rushed away giggling. New to me, or better, unusual, was to feel such a quietness in the house. There were none of the people, the Tonton and Tantine, I was expecting to see waiting to receive us, no other people than my closest family, my parents and their kids and the servants.

GROUND

We went to settle in our room. Redeso and I were still in the room with Happiness. As we pulled our stuff from our bags, Happiness sat quietly on the bed, watching with curiosity over this pair of enigmatic brothers of his, whose culture and aesthetics differed so drastically from his, even more so now that Redeso and I were developing our own tastes in terms of looks. My hair style, for example, short dreadlocks springing up, were unthinkable to him, since these were socially unacceptable in Congo and associated with some sort of dysfunction, like mental illness, drug abuse, or it was assumed you were a jerk. People laughed at me on the street, to the extent that I had to wear a cap. Redeso was more stylish, wearing a black trilby hat, his distinctive John-Lennon-style sunglasses, jeans rolled up at the ankle over black palladium boots. Happiness got even more puzzled when we pulled a Sega Master System console out of our bag. Coincidence had it that he had his own TV in the bedroom, a small black-and-white piece of electronic junk, but with all the ports in place for us to plug in the console. We set up a game, *OutRun*, the one about the blonde and dark-haired couple racing in a red Ferrari. We showed him how to play it. Then my little sisters, Mavie, Moon and Monique, came in, the three of them, first standing and contemplating for a while behind us, letting the sight of Happiness playing the game on the screen do the talking. Then they sat on the mattress next to us. Then the kids from the neighboured started showing up outside our window; they had climbed over the backyard wall of the house, first one, then two, three, four, until the window, a jalousie window with a few glass sheets missing, was saturated with faces and fingers gripping the grids, to peer in at this unusual happening of a video game Happiness was playing in his room. All of the kids watched in silence so as not to be caught and kicked out by Dad or a servant. Some of them did not know what a video game even looked like. Eventually we heard a servant shouting in Lingala outside the kitchen while running in their direction. All the kids, like flies, dispersed, climbing back over the wall disappearing out of sight.

We had a nice family dinner that night. Nothing special. But it was alright. Yes, it was fine. We stayed until late chatting on the veranda with my parents and Ugo. Then father sent Happiness, Redeso and me to go and buy some ice cream, because he felt like ice cream, because we should celebrate somehow with something Italian. We walked a block away in the semi-darkness, stopping to greet people on our way. Then Happiness asked us, as we entered the gate of the ice cream man's house, 'Are you sure you guys want to talk with Dad?' obviously referring to the big meeting we, the angry Italian siblings, had on our agenda. He posed that question in a way that showed he knew a few facts about Dad that we were overlooking and that he knew him better than us. He had grown up with him, after all, and saw him every day, in his various facets, for years and years consecutively. He knew him in a way I did not.

Later I understood that Happiness did not ask out of innocent curiosity. He was indeed worried and sorry for us to have come all this way here to sort out things with someone like the Dad he knew. He was also concerned by our urgent desire to settle matters, which he may have considered inadequate and selfish to some degree, even narrow-minded, since we were not taking into account the fact that although our family was drowning in mess, on both the Italian and African front, we, the Italian siblings, were the ones that were better placed in their eyes. Simply due to the fact of growing up in Europe, no matter the kind of lodging we had, we enjoyed a huge spectrum of opportunities they felt were unavailable to them so long as they remained in Africa. They would rather live in an institution, they suggested a few times, which was not a big deal for accommodation after all in their view. Nothing so remote from boarding school in Europe, a boarding school, which, again pointed out to them that we were part of an elite. What Happiness meant with that question was simple, at least from the standpoint of a kid raised in Africa. Firstly, it was a lack of respect and gratitude to call into question the man who gave you life. Secondly, having difficulties was not a prerogative of the seven of us from Italy, but rather the fundamental condition of existence. I am sure my little brother, when he asked us, 'are you guys sure you want to talk to Dad?', spoke from a place where he witnessed hardship everywhere he looked. It was all around him, on every corner, in every life, and no one in his entourage ever complained about not having enough food, having to live in a dump that lacked basic amenities, seeing their own kids dying from flu. The concept of moaning about problems was absent. He was surrounded by a specific African stoicism where people coped with whatever situation they were presented with, never able to opt-out from a difficult situation but yielding to it without question. My brother Happiness, I supposed, would look with no surprise at one of his classmates that had given birth at thirteen and who was forced to beg on the street to provide for her baby. He would not be surprised if she did not go to the police to report the man who raped her, nor if her parents did not encourage her to do so. Parents would not complain about miserable conditions in their workplace, nor did they complain about their son who had died in the civil war. The amputees in the street would not tell you they should have received a better education about the risk of diabetes from the council. Happiness was growing up in a country where for most people life was a life sentence from day one. There were no petitions to sign. It was then difficult for Happiness to understand parental neglect if we had plenty of food to eat and the opportunity to take advantage of an otherwise bountiful life abroad. Asking 'are you sure you want to talk with Dad?' was another way to test if we were willing to swap lives and live in Africa to be subjected to an authoritarian man like our father. But we missed the point of what he was asking, we just proudly answered, 'Of course we want to talk to him!' And he did not touch the subject again.

The ice cream man, a boy from the block we knew from our last holiday there, opened the door and let us into his house. After greeting us, he took us to the kitchen and across the living room where his family—parents and kids, and girlfriend—were watching TV in the dark. The guy pulled few boxes of different flavours of ice cream out of a meat-freezer, put a few scoops on a container according to the amount of money Happiness gave him and led us back to the door. We walked back home, handed the ice cream box to Debra-Jo who went to the kitchen to prepare cups for everyone. All the flavours, even the chocolate and lemon, tasted of vanilla but just with different food colouring. Yet father deemed it the best ice cream of his life as he scraped the last bit out of the box. We went to bed.

We had the meeting the morning after. First thing in the morning, soon after breakfast, the whole family—Debra-Jo and Ugo, Ocean, Sigmund, Lorenzo, Klaus, Redeso and me, Happiness, Moon, Mavie, Monique, Dad and Maman Sofie—sat in the living room on the L-shaped sofa and added some additional chairs. Fourteen people, members of the same family, chose their seats according to where they were most comfortable sitting, so that at the end we found that we had accidentally ended up sitting in three different groups: the Italian delegation on one end of the sofa plus a few chairs, Dad and Mum sat together taking up most of the other side of the sofa, while the four youngest sat at the junction between the two sofas, in between their biological carers and us. You can kind of see it as the youngest playing the role of the witnesses in a historic kid-parent confrontation. Among the little witnesses the most alert was Happiness, the most aware, and most interested in what was happening, his stare swinging back and forth from our group and our parents, while the other three sat looking less engaged. I threw a look at Sigmund, our spokesman, the one that started this extra-domestic revolt with a phone call to father, once he had had enough of all our problems. My big brother was getting ready to be the first to take the word. I could see he was mentally going over his points, focused and determined, exuding confidence in what he was about to say. After all he had no doubt that he was on the right side of the conversation, the charity clothes and toilet roll the priest had supplied him for ten years were already a good motive to start and win the battle.

It was sad, to notice how divided we were. On the one hand, we from Italy could not see that we were privileged. On the other, my younger siblings and my parents to some degree, could not see that having a higher quality of life and being better located geographically was not necessarily a recipe for happiness. The perception of suffering was a relative concept that changed from culture to culture. Other peoples' worst lives should not be a good reason for us to keep quiet and accept terms that were harming us. We simply could not let other peoples' suffering overshadow our anger, more privileged or not, holding on to promises of change and solutions that were never delivered, waiting for nothing, for the sake of being disappointed time and time again, with no explanation given. The house rotting away on the hillside of Via Suore year after year was having a deep, if not permanent, impact on us, on a practical level. On an emotional level, there were things we were entitled to bring to the table, regardless of how pathetic they sounded. These were things that Sigmund, however, would have never allowed himself to bring to the surface, not in the context of this meeting, not even within himself probably. Looking back, I understand he did not know, and so we did not either, that all we truly wanted to convey that day to our parents was that growing out of their sight, without their physical contact, without their practical and emotional support, with no ongoing conversation, not having them there when we needed them the most, undermined our sense of integrity. But of course, even if we were to assume that we were aware of this pain growing like a cancer, it would not be the right time and place to discuss this type of argument.

Dad. The *Man of the Shoes*. His sunken head in between his shoulders suggesting he was not as relaxed as he wanted to show us, his arms hanging, one around Mum, the other over the sofa's back, like a big man. He opened the meeting by saying 'So, what is this all about?'

That was enough to scrape the first layer of confidence away from us. Sigmund's speech began to sound less certain than the one we had practised on the plane together. However, he went on, his voice cracking a little. He covered the primary issues and also added more, to my surprise, like things specifically related to Redeso and me, things like we were too young to grow up without parents, and that we had mentioned a few times to him that we did not look at our parents as our parents anymore. He mentioned the parental rights withdrawal order from the court of Bologna, that we were living apart from each other, with Lorenzo living miles away while Redeso, Klaus and I had been placed in another town again. He spent some time over the issue of the house on Via Suore, arguing that in the two years from when we had gotten the keys not a single part of the work had started, due partially to lack of funds which we understood, but also because of pure misconduct. It was, in our eyes, a massive blow to learn that Maman Sofie had bought 10,000 euros of Italian spaghetti to sell in Congo during her last visit to Italy, when that money could have paid for repairing the roof, which could have allowed us to move in. Until this point, Sigmund was doing very well, but from then on, when he started talking about the house in Via Suore, he got so carried away that he made the mistake of referring to Maman Sofie's spaghetti trade deal as a stupid manoeuvre. Dad frowned a little at the sound of the word stupid, but he said nothing. He waited in silence for Sigmund to continue to the end. Now that the boy had finished and stood there, looking a bit confused and drained in the face of Dad's indifferent silence, the bravest and most together of all of us now did not sound as persuasive as he had before, nor as relevant. Further, the few things that Ocean and Debra-Jo added in support of him, though calmly and respectfully presented, sounded rather blunt. Dad's indifferent reaction, or perhaps the eyes of our little siblings looking at us like we had some mental problems, or a microscopic realignment of the universe playing up, in the light of this new context, where we had finally pulled out all these years of covert grievances, made us feel we actually would have done better to keep it to ourselves and spare our family all this spoiled nonsense. We felt that the energy in the room had shifted, now turning against us.

'I guess it's my turn now,' Dad said looking straight at Sigmund in the eyes. 'Well, first of all, you will never address your mother in these terms ever again. I don't want to ever hear you refer to your mother as stupid. Am I clear?'

'Yes, Dad,' Sigmund complied, his voice tight.

'If I hear you talking about your mother in these terms again, I'm going to break your legs. Did I make myself clear?'

'Yes, Dad.'

'As for the twins' senses of abandonment, from now on, they're going to stay with us, and live in Congo with us. This is their house, with their brother and sisters, I don't want to hear about this nonsense anymore, did I make myself clear?'

'Yes, Dad.'

'And now the meeting is over, get out of my sight, out all of you!'

That was all. What could be termed the quickest planned meeting in the history of humankind accounted for perhaps five minutes. The whole point of our presence there, arranged upon our request, to open up the way for a fair dialogue with our parents, and discuss the problems we had been facing for nearly ten years and to hopefully find a way forward, had been nipped in the bud five minutes from the start of the meeting. Just because Sigmund had used a word that sounded offensive to Dad to describe Maman Sofie's inconsiderate financial operation. Even though it was absolutely right to call it for what it was, a stupid manoeuvre. Just a very *stupid* manoeuvre, I mean, we couldn't think of anything more badly-timed, and in more bad taste, than Maman Sofie coming to Italy and shipping down to Congo ten thousand euros-worth of spaghetti under our nose, while we were waiting in the institutions for funds to repair the roof that would end, once and for all, our time in institutions. What we got was that after longing for years for an opportunity to speak face-to-face with our parents, after Dad had invested an additional 10,000 euros for our flights, that once we finally spoke out, the meeting was over without any resolution. It literally landed on nothing. It ended up aggravating Redeso's and my situation if anything. I looked at Redeso as soon as father declared that we were to remain in Congo and saw reflecting in his face the same terror I felt. Then I looked at Happiness's gaze of disbelief. In disbelief not because of father's decision, which, he expected would roughly be something along those lines, but rather for us, for the way we had ruined our life with our own hands. It was the expression you give to a friend who had gambled away all he had and had fallen into poverty right before your eyes, or was nearly run over by a bus because he crossed the road without looking. I knew at that very moment what he truly meant with '*are you sure you want to talk to Dad?*'. He meant that this guy was able to threaten his own son with breaking his legs for nothing, even if the son was on the right side of the argument and could change the course of mine and my brother's lives with a snap of his finger. With '*are you sure you want to talk to Dad?*', Happiness was introducing us to a man who didn't care at all about Italian legal papers stating he had lost the paternal right over us, here he was still the absolute voice of authority on any matters that concerned our lives.

We were all disturbed by the result of that meeting when we powerlessly left the room. Dad went back to his den. Mum, who looked even more concerned than before the meeting, followed him soon after and I supposed they had their own private review of the incident, with him, I guess, winding himself up with anger and her trying to deescalate him and soothe him to common sense. I remember that day we were all wearing traditional clothes, the sets of colourful boubou our parents had tailor-made for us in keeping with tradition and that we wore during the first days we arrived home as a way of celebrating both our arrival home and re-Africanisation. Ugo, too, wore one that matched Debra-Jo's suit in pattern. Redeso's and mine were identical. The others were all different. Dressed in those boubous, we left the living room in different groups. Most went outside, some others, like Sigmund, frustrated and humiliated, chose to withdraw into his room. For us twins, what should we make of Dad's decision to keep us there? Did he mean it? Were we about to start all over from Brazzaville? All my life in Italy passed in front of me like a film as if I were dying. My room in the foster home, with my desk and lamp, my bike in the bike shed, my friends, my girlfriend—I had a girlfriend at that time, a girl whose mouth tasted of salt when we kissed for the first time outside school—my CDs, the Saturday afternoon strolls in Via Mazzini, the real gelato, the snow, the Piadina Romagnola. I was not ready to give it all up, I did not want to live with my father or with my mother. The house in Via Suore—fuck it, fuck that and the roof! I had no more problems I wanted my parents to solve in Italy. After all the shit we had gone through, I could not believe that Dad was about to inflict this new blow. I had a storm raging in my head. I didn't want to live in Africa. I did not want to be severed from my whole life in Italy and forced into a culture that I did not perceive as mine anymore. However, eventually at noon Mum came downstairs to talk to Redeso and me after we had been subjected to Ugo and our brothers teasing all morning—'Are you going along with the Lingala class?', 'Oh Twins, come on, don't be upset, they have nice pizzas even here, you know!' Mum came over while Redeso and I were grieving, sitting outside on a rock on a little alley on one side of the house that led to the backyard. She sat next to us. The ten thousand euros-worth-of-spaghetti woman. Who, to be honest, since the meeting didn't really take place at the end, had not told her side of the story. There was also no concrete evidence to determine what had truly happened, if things had really gone the way we believed, or if she had acted in lieu of our father, or if the spaghetti deal had been intended to finally generate the funds we needed to get the house fully sorted. We simply did not know the full story. My mother sat next to us. A mother and her sons. The chronicle of some people's life. It was noon, as I said, the smell of lunch being prepared steamed out of the kitchen behind the corner. The sun over our heads laid short shadows of the three of us onto the floor, us on the rock on the side of the house, our electric blue boubou patterned with some tubers, turnips or parsnips. Redeso with his Lennon glasses and trilby hat on and me playing with a Red Sox cap in my hands.

'He didn't mean it, he was just very angry,' she said referring to Dad's decision to keep us there. 'He knows that you don't belong here anymore. You're now Italians, he would never dare to do this wrong to you, to unroot you again, interrupting your life in Italy like this just out of anger, and I would never allow it, unless you want to stay here. Do you want to?'

'No.'

'Well, then you're going to go back home with the others.'

'Are you sure?'

'Yeah, we sorted it already, there is nothing you have to worry about.'

Again, there were underlying truths in between her words we could not grasp at that time. Ours was a tragedy which could only be understood retrospectively, probably due to the functioning of our coping mechanisms. In order to endure life's recurrent shocks, we had been closed off from what was truly going on inside ourselves.

It is only now, after time has loosened things up and I am going through this episode once again, that I see that my mother was actually muffling her pain that day as she was reassuring Redeso and me, her first set of kids, whom she saw drifting further and further away from her. I have come to believe that most likely, deep within herself, she had hoped for a different answer when she asked, '*Unless you want to stay here. Do you want to?*' But back then we could not fathom that the person standing by us, speaking those words, cared for us. Who was she? Beyond the woman living in the shadow of my Dad, who came to visit us in Italy and stayed in that hotel in Piazza Matteotti and made lots of business calls and took us down to the restaurant to eat expensive, succulent steaks with fries. Who was the woman I imagined walking through the ruin of the villa in Imola, preparing to move some of the valuable relics to Congo? Who shipped the ten thousand-euros worth of spaghetti down to Congo? How did she live through all of this? What was her role?

I began to see that she was not just a passive figure in Dad's backdrop but rather had some influence on him, possibly more than any of the other women did, I suspect. Even more than Dad's sister and cousin. Big decisions affecting our life for the good or the bad may have been conceived by her mind also. But I do not know to what extent. And I do not even know whether I should investigate any further, if it is truly worth it, if I will ever get to get a comprehensive and reliable account of our story.

***

Masembo Loubaki, our street, was still there. It was one of the streets my father would have paved at some point if the WAT Congo project went as planned, with its mango trees sticking up here and there and the usual street dogs lying barely breathing, on the edge of the street, flicking their ears to rid themselves of flies that eventually returned to rest on them.

Occasionally a car, a motorbike drove by, slowing down to carefully dodge some large puddles of water in the potholes in the street. Otherwise, it was dead-quiet, with residents going about their daily grind. It felt nice to see all our friends once again. They seemed to be shaping up, physically, intellectually, but also in terms of the place they occupied in society. Pelé, for example, the outstanding football player, possibly with a great career ahead if he had lived in a different place, hardly touched the ball now and worked until late in the night as the local barber, his business consisting of just a chair, a table and some basic barbering tools set at the edge of his street.

Slim worked full-time for my parents as a servant and as an errand boy on the bike. Another of our friends had become a seasoned circus athlete at fifteen. Another went to join a mercenary group to fight a war on the eastern border of Congo-Zaire with Rwanda. Other kids made ends meet the way they could, taking up different small jobs, helping their parents at garages, and in market stalls. Childhood had ended for all of us.

We spent quieter days. We did a lot of walking, sat down in places, chatted with people in the area, made our first approach to the local girls, and watched, mainly watched at what was going on around us. I began to realise that I was in a whole different place, unlike that beautiful, idyllic place from few years ago. Some elements of the culture that had passed unnoticed before now hit me in the face. The level of poverty some people lived in, the number of ill people suffering from some mysterious diseases that I never came across before, with unexplained lumps covering their bodies, deformity and mutilations, freaks lingering in the shadow of the area of life.

That summer, since there was space available and our older brothers preferred to hang out with their local girlfriends and friends, Redeso and I had the opportunity to join some of Tonton Martin's jeep expeditions with Debra-Jo and Ugo. We drove south a couple of times, down to the seaside in Pointe-Noire, to paradisiac beaches. Beaches of fine, white sand and crystal-clear waters, palm oases all around, empty and uncontaminated by human activity for miles, like a white, sandy desert. Microscopic transparent crustaceans hid in the sand around our bare feet, as we stood with our trousers rolled up to the knees, and we were graced by the western winds of the Atlantic Ocean, which propelled waves to the shore and blew through our clothes. It was as fascinating for Ugo, as it was for us, to see such a scenario, Africa and its vast, open spaces, its natural landscapes so clearing and regenerating, and breathable, for the first time in his life. It was without a doubt the perfect spot for the couple to honour their union, walking hand in hand on the white beach, behind Tonton Martin, Redeso and me.

GROUND

I am sure Debra-Jo was well aware that she was walking now with the love of her life, so much as the space she found in within herself lately, sinking into the experience of love, the 'kingdom' Sister Gaudenzia had mentioned in her letter. *You need plenty of space to awaken from a long sleep my darling, and I am giving you all the space you need, I leave you my kingdom, with my departure.* The legacy the Sister had left to Debra-Jo with her departure and pursuit of her own dreams. The kingdom, which at this point she understood, was nothing more than the experience of being. Of loving. Of being one with God.

Places like this beach had been the context in which Debra-Jo had symbolically been living since, regardless of where she was located geographically. In fact, there was a noticeable difference between the girl who took this outing with Tonton Martin a few years ago and the woman walking hand in hand with Ugo now. This was a full-blown woman, well-rooted within herself and her relationship. She was present to herself, alert and responsive to the transformative motions of life, now acting from a place where the poison Masambila had ushered in was cleared out of her system, and substituted with the certainty that there was nothing she possessed that could fundamentally be lost, nothing at all. Moreover, there was no place she could fall from, since her feet now walked on the firm ground of the path to the fulfilment she had been entitled to from birth. That is the only way I can explain her reaction of indifference to the way Dad managed the meeting. She did not even look that sorry for Sigmund, and for neither of us being repeatedly subjected to these rotten predicaments, but was just positive; positive, with the Mona Lisa's smile, that in one way or another things will work out.

Gerard paid a visit at our home a few times with his newly acquired wife and a two-year-old boy, in the guise of a man who was now completely resolved with my sister. He seemed to be doing pretty well, financially, well-dressed, driving a brand-new Golf he had bought with his work as an assistant for an engineer at a Chinese company that, in partnership with a private local firm and a government agency, was renewing the Moukoukolou Hydroelectric dam, 400 kilometres away from Brazzaville. My mother sent a servant to buy some Fantas and few beers for the guests because we had not a single drink at home. Those were times of scarcity. The fridges that were full to bursting point upon our arrival had gradually emptied and were not being refilled. We had no hot water at all and there was a shortage of running water throughout the day. We had to flush the toilet with buckets of water which we fetched from the well and fetch more water from the well to heat up on the stove to bathe ourselves with. Once in a while, we drove to have a proper shower in the public toilet on the periphery of Brazzaville, where you were provided with a stone to use as both a soap and a sponge that you were supposed to hand back at the end of your session.

One day, early in the morning my mother woke up Redeso and I, stroking our shoulders gently. We were going to take a trip with her to visit our grandfather, Olivier, a man I had never met before. Not consciously at least. We had breakfast with bread and butter and hot milk that she had prepared in the dead-quiet kitchen. Then we drove to the station by taxi and took the train with a few early-morning commuters and traders transporting goods including livestock such as caged chickens and a pig and a goat on a lead. More travellers got on at each station as we journeyed across the rural Congolese landscape, loaded with their animals and more goods. In less than an hour it was daylight, and the train was so full that some passengers found no other space to travel than hanging on the sides of the train and on top of the roof. We disembarked at our station in a small town, the name of which I have forgotten. We took another taxi and drove down a road lined with palm trees and sparsely-situated houses that seemed to be part of the flat landscape and occasional shops alternating with shacks, where local people waited outside their premises busy in manual work. A kid in shorts came running up the middle of the road shortly after we drove past his house. I turned to look at him from the rear window, as he stood expressionless in the middle of the road, making a bull horn's shape with his fingers and gesturing it in our direction, a gesture whose meaning I was unable to decipher but is seared into my memory. Finally, we arrived at our destination, a small village that appeared to sit at the end of the world I knew, where a group of huts made from red clay and large grey bricks stood, with some distance between each other. My mother paid the taxi driver as he dropped us in front of an isolated hut. The soil we walked on was dust of the same red hue as the huts. My mother preceded us, dressed in a light blue tonality. Redeso and I wore some smart clothes which she had bought specifically for this occasion. We entered the hut through a curtain door, allowing the sunlight to breach with us, into the otherwise dark interior. An old man with white hair sat alone on a wicker mat on the floor of the main room. His eyes were entirely white. As soon as I noticed them, his white eyes, I sensed that I had reached the most remote place I could have possibly ever thought to go to, not just in terms of geographical distance but also in relation to my origins, and the distance between my life and this reality, and the distant emotions it invoked in me.

'This is your grandfather, Olivier,' my mother said. We sat in front of him on the mat. 'He had an illness that made him blind, come closer so that he can touch you. Dad, here are the twins, Redeso and Redesof.' A faint smile and few wrinkles lifted the face of the old man as his ancient hands reached Redeso and me. '*Bonjour grand-pére!*' we said. '*Bonjour les jemeaoux, bien arrive!* You bring joy on my heart today. You're turning into two young men. How old are you now?'

'Fourteen.'

'Is life in Italy good?'

'Yes.'

'I'm happy to hear that, my sons. Very happy. Very happy today.' He nodded in the direction of my mother as if to approve of something she did. I do not know quite well what it was, maybe the choice she had made of bringing us there, which had made him happy. He returned to us, his blind stare hovering somewhere above our heads and beyond us as if he was waiting for something, maybe for us to say something, or he was listening to our inner dialogue, I don't know.

There was nothing we felt we could say to him nonetheless, so unfamiliar was the situation. We sat in silence, the four of us, a little longer until, still smiling, the old man turned to my mother, and addressed her in Lingala. She responded in Lingala. Then, 'The *Aremo...*', the old man pronounced solemnly. Redeso and I turned to our mother in need of a hint to decipher the old man's words. She nodded to encourage us to wait and trust that Olivier was about to feed our curiosity.

The old man told us about the origin of our surname, not from his lineage, but from my father's lineage. Facts that I now find interesting, considering that my grandfather, Olivier, had been opposed to my father his entire life, based on what my mother told me. I reckon he felt the need to tell us because he sensed we had reached a point in our life where we ought to know why we were always in transit.

He told us the story of a young man, long, long ago, in the times when the Oyo Empire reigned the territories of West Africa. A young man who was the successor to the throne of one of the empires in Nigeria. I cannot recall which one exactly, it does not matter. What I know is that this young man was an Aremo—the king's firstborn. The Aremo were not as lucky as any other crown princes of other kingdoms who were bound to rise to the throne following their father's death. The Aremo was destined to follow his father to the grave, to be killed and buried with him. This tradition went on generation after generation; firstborns were sacrificed and buried once their father, the king, had died and the crown was passed to the second son.

Yet our hero refused to die for his country's traditions and escaped once his father fell ill. The Aremo found refuge in the neighbouring country of Benin where he settled and found work in the port. Since he never revealed his name and origins to anyone, local people named him Big Bracelet, for he wore a Big Bracelet. In the Beninese Fon language, Big Bracelet translates into our surname. This man was supposed to be one of our ancestors. I did not know what to make of it, if I should regard it as a local myth or if it was the account of a real event. I just found it fascinating back then. It is only now, looking at it retrospectively, that I see that my grandfather, with the story of our deserter ancestor, had given us a clue that could explain why we were living a life of exile, uprootedness and displacement. Perhaps the restless spirit of this mutineer Aremo lived on through my paternal lineage. Perhaps we were not even meant to exist.

It was then time to go. The taxi which had taken us there had been waiting for an hour. An hour that felt like a dream once we were driving away from the village, back to the real, busy life in Brazzaville, never to see Olivier again. The hut. The blind man inside. All just a dream. My mum said he died five years afterwards of old age, under the care of the other villagers.

A couple of weeks from that day, we left Congo to go visit my father's side of the family in Benin. To save money, the trip was reserved only for the eight Italians, including Ugo, and my parents. The youngest remained in Congo. We said bye to them definitively, since after the visit we were to fly back to Italy directly from Benin. Redeso and I gave our Sega Master System to Happiness as a present and my older siblings distributed most of their fine clothing and shoes to the friends and girlfriends they had made there. Colonel Tawema, my uncle, came to pick us up at the Cadjeoun airport of Cotonou, Benin, in a turquoise boubou with matching kufi hat, black pointed shoes and mirrored aviator sunglasses. He was waiting for us outside a beige Mercedes leading two taxis, his hands hanging by his side. A thin smile formed on his face as he caught sight of us exiting the airport. We greeted him and drove to the Tawema family home in three cars. The view I had of Cotonou through the taxi window was that of a tidier city than Brazzaville, with more paved roads, nicer houses, taller buildings, more greenery. I noticed several construction sites operating but despite them there was a sense that the city and the streets were empty.

'It's a bit of an enigma this place, right?' Redeso said to me during the taxi ride, looking at the scenery outside the window. 'If a war erupts here at some point, we have the legal obligation to come here, to this place to serve as soldiers, since this is our true homeland. Not Congo. Not Italy. So weird.' He was right, in that Benin was our homeland on paper, while Congo was just our birthplace.

The taxi stopped at the entrance of a huge, walled mansion in an area that looked more like Cotonou's Beverly Hills compared to Diata, our area in Brazzaville. One of the colonel's sons kept the gate open. The taxi drivers unloaded our luggage from the boots of their cars. They waited for the colonel to come out again and pay them once they had carried all the luggage inside the house. The Tawema house was brighter than our house in Diata, at least from outside, with lots of shining tiles on the veranda which was flanked by the lush, green leaves of tropical plants, banana plants and mango and papaya trees, and a big courtyard on one side, which housed the servants. The interior was oppressive, with the choice of dark mahogany furniture and the multitude of statues and masks adorning the house, and for something else, something sinister I could not figure clearly, like a phantom, but that was very close to the quality of Colonel Tawema himself. Madam Marielle Tawema walked down the stairs dressed as if she was attending a gala and gave us all soft, enduring warm hugs. This was my father's older sister, the one who based on my mother's account, used to have a great influence on my father, who to me seemed like a sweet and a well-intentioned person.

The pleasantries went on for a while as we all stood in their spotless reception room, the colonel with his arm around his wife's waist, his wet and self-piteous eyes in plain sight now that he had taken off his sunglasses. Their three sons, aged fifteen, sixteen and eighteen who stood on the periphery of the gathering, seemed like they were raised in such a way as to never look their father in the eyes even when he questioned them directly. Two of them led us to our rooms. Then we had dinner at home, with Italian food that Tantine Marielle Tawema had delivered from the restaurant of her hotel expressly for us. She was one of those middle-aged women who looked like the most well-intentioned people in the world and seemed extremely wise and calm. A presence that you perceived in a distinctive way as soon as she was nearby, like she was able to read you without you being aware of it and able to provide the peace of mind you needed. How her and my mother's relationship had evolved over time from the period my mother had lived here some fourteen years ago, I could not say. I only saw two women getting along quite well that night. They sat next to each other at the table as my father's voice dominated the conversation as usual, the two of them laughing in complicity at his irreverence. So too did the other few guests there, my father's other siblings with their families, so distant from me that I won't even bother introducing them. At some point during the dinner Tantine Ellen, my father's cousin and best friend, made her entrance, bursting into the room like a bomb with her two young kids and her husband and her sensationalism and glamour, setting fire to the party. She threw astonished comments everywhere, and loudly kissed her way from person to person around the table, with the collective vocals reaching a paroxysm in the room, and then froze up in disbelief when she reached Ugo. 'Eh! No way! Debra-Jo sorry, but this handsome guy come with me now!' She forced Ugo up and pretended to run away with him only to stop at the door, and clapped her hands and laughed with everyone, punch drunk with euphoria.

We drove by car continuously during the time we stayed in Cotonou with our parents going to visit my father's friends and family. We went to the zoo, to the swimming pool, to visit Dad's high-ranking friends and to some local tourist attractions. The older ones went on a safari one day with the colonel. But mostly we hung around the area with the Tawema boys.

I personally do not have many interesting memories of that time, save for the fact that time in Benin soon grew boring for everyone alike. I guess we felt the holiday in Africa was stretching out too long and we were growing homesick. Literally sick. We spent days in a state of infirmity, hanging around the house and the little area around it, feeling drowsy and depressed, with no drive to engage in anything other than waiting and longing to go back to our life in Italy. Did that mean that we were Italians if we felt so homesick for Italy? But home was far. Far as hell.

Apparently, there were some problems with the tickets and my father was struggling to get the necessary amount to pay for flights back for the eight of us, which might lead one to wonder why he had paid for the trip to Benin in the first place. As pleasant as it was in the beginning, the holiday had turned into a torment, with us lying in painful anticipation for news about our flights, day after day, waiting. We killed time rereading the Marvel comics which Sigmund had brought from Italy, exchanging the same three or four issues between us over and over to the point where we had them memorised. Finally, the news broke that the tickets had come through. But my father had managed to buy only four, which of course went to the oldest: Ugo, Debra-Jo, Sigmund, and Ocean, who gaily and rashly, prepared their bags and left, leaving Redeso, Klaus, Lorenzo and me behind.

If before I had felt I could not cope anymore with this stretched staying, this time I felt as if I were dying. I let myself go to the symptoms of a severe case of homesickness. I had hallucinations of my friends in Italy eating *piadina* with Parma ham, *stracchino* cheese and rocket and stretching their hands to me to go on bike rides.

My girlfriend appeared to me and we kissed and fucked and I felt again that unforgettable taste of salt filling up my mouth. Then, a few days later my mother came with the news. She had managed to buy our tickets. Finally, we were going back. We said goodbye to the

GROUND

Tawemas and the rest of the Beninese family, including Tantine Ellen, who came by with her kids to say goodbye to us. We said goodbye to Dad. My mother, who drove us to the airport in the Tawema's car, explained to us that we would fly to Italy by ourselves, due to lack of funds to purchase her a ticket, I think.

'It will be easy,' she said, 'just follow the signs.'

'Ok Mum,' we agreed without even thinking about it.

'Here are your documents, present them to the officer at the border control, when you arrive,' she said, handing us a plastic envelope with all our documents inside.

She found a parking spot in front of the airport entrance and we got out of the car, taking our luggage. Just as we were about to walk into the airport, we ran into a commotion taking place in the parking lot. A crowd of furious people were running after a man, shouting, 'Thief!'. More people joined the human hunt, including some travellers, who dropped their luggage in the fervour to take part. They quickly brought down the thief and suddenly the man was being beaten with shattering cruelty. There was also a kid of my age among the punishers. The metal rod this kid was brandishing, stained in blood, rose against the midday sun, and struck the poor man on the ground time and time again.

At that sight, the meeting we had with Father at the beginning of the holiday came to my mind. Concepts like different perspectives, privileges, priorities, opportunities, dead ends, ramped up in my mind. That same hardship my younger brother Happiness implied when he had asked *Are you sure you want to talk with Dad?* was embodied in this kid. I was not standing before an assassin, but just a kid, a kid striking another human being in the head with a metal rod just because that man had stolen a wallet or something. None of the adults around him stopped him. How far could he go? Could he kill him? Why was he there and me here?

My Friends

Lorenzo had his first encounter with the law when we arrived at Milan's airport. Our documents were being checked at the border counter when the border officer said to Lorenzo, 'Your residence paper is expired, I can't let you in.'

I will never forget Lorenzo's face at those words. *I can't let you in.* What was this now? He had been suffering from homesickness for the past few weeks like the rest of us and was desperate to return home, to Italy, but now that we were home, the door was shut to him because of an expired date in a document. What was this document anyway? What was it saying, this document that my mother gave us and said that we had to present at border control? I had never seen it before. It was a thin blue paper bearing our photographs and all our details with the heading of 'Resident Permit'. A thin piece of paper that had left Lorenzo standing in dismay and terror in front of the officer's counter, in the middle of the airport of Milan, surrounded by a mob of travellers that were all of a sudden all white, whiter than the whitest thing I had ever seen in comparison with the African black reality we had just left. White people who were waiting in the queue behind us, this white border officer presiding at the counter, those white people who were carrying their bags past the counters and beyond. Just white people. And us four, the only black people, in the middle of them, with Lorenzo waiting in fear of a resolution. After a phone call, the border officer confirmed that he couldn't let him pass and that a police officer was underway to deal with the situation. He ordered the remaining three of us to move on, saying that we couldn't just wait there. We left because we were ordered to do so, because he was the voice of authority and because we were confused. Whatever was holding Lorenzo back was something with which we didn't want to identify though we knew it was in us, under our skin. It was something that said that we were different from all those people passing through the border checkpoint with no problems. It said our passports were not enough to grant us entrance home and that we needed an extra paper to prove that we were ok and eligible to come back home or else we faced law enforcement.

We left because we were used to strange things happening. We left because we were used to being split up. We left because our life was all about borders. We left without looking back at Lorenzo, we just walked through the gate and kept on walking, just imagining the police approaching Lorenzo to take him away.

We were just three now. And none of us had a clue how to navigate an airport. We had never been alone before. We were suddenly subjected to a completely new world with people coming and going in every direction and plenty of options of where to go. I remember Klaus looking bewildered. 'Where d-d-d-do we go?' asked the genius, who could navigate all sorts of creative disciplines with outstanding ease. Then Redeso and I remembered mother saying to follow the signs. We looked for the luggage collection sign. Found it. We followed it until we arrived at the luggage area. Our belt was already running. We picked up our bags, including Lorenzo's, looked for the exit sign and left.

What happened back there? Back then, I was unable to make the connection. I knew I held a Beninese passport, but still, as a kid growing up in Italy, it never occurred to me that my siblings and I were so different from our Italian peers to the extent we could be denied entry to the country we called home. I was not even familiar with the term *immigrant*.

The people from our foster home stood waiting for us at the arrival exit with Franco, the head carer. I was glad to see them. It meant a lot that they all came. We hugged and kissed. Telemaco, the mad guy, clung to each of our arms in turn and squeezed them tight, jabbering 'Friofriofrio!' a nonsense he used to express contentment which translated as 'I'm very very happy.' Nicola, the cool dark-haired boy, the youngest of us all, just smiled. The girls gave us each a kiss, while Franco asked us all the questions. 'What about Lorenzo?' He was supposed to give him a lift to the station from where he would take a train to Rimini to go to his foster home in Verucchio. We explained what happened, about the border control officer, 'His paper has expired!' Klaus concluded, bored and annoyed.

'Oh fff... fabulous!' said Franco 'They held him?!'

'Yeah apparently.'

'A kid?!'

'He's not a k-k-kid anymore,' corrected Klaus still annoyed. Annoyed for the fate of his brother but also annoyed with him for somehow contributing to his own ruin. 'He should be looking a-a-a-after his own documents!'

'Shit. I can't believe it.' Franco continued, hardly listening to Klaus. 'This is the direction this country is taking. Ok, ok, I will talk to your social worker as soon we get home.'

We walked out of the airport with our housemates asking us about the trip, about Africa and about our family. I felt like I'd been away for a tremendous amount of time as soon as I stepped outside into the air and under the Italian sky to walk to the foster home's van. I could not tell whether all that I saw before me, these people from the foster home, the familiar Italian landscape unfurling outside the window as the van drove home, were real or a memory, whether or not they had simply paused where we left off. This was home to me, regardless of what happened to Lorenzo. Italy, Bologna, the Via Emilia to Toscanella, Imola, it was my home. I loved it here. My mother was right when she said that day in Congo, '*You're now Italians.*' I felt it growing at the centre of my chest, a sense of satisfaction and pride at understanding where I belonged. I have no doubt Redeso felt the same. So did Klaus. These guys in the van, riding with me along the highway to Toscanella, were our family.

The van was a white Fiat Ducato van bearing the acronym of the Italian Regional Social Service on the side, AUSL—*Azienda Unita' Sanitaria Locale*. The sixteen-year-old girl in the front seat next to Franco, wearing a pair of skinny jeans and a large woollen jumper with long, blonde curly hair, was Livia, the oldest of the gang. Next to her was Denise, fifteen, with flat dark straight hair kind of printed onto her gaunt face. She looked pathologically thin and withdrawn but could reveal a very sweet and witty personality when she opened up. As for Telemaco and Nicola, I have introduced them already.

We arrived home. Fiorenza, the supervisor who was on shift in the afternoon, came out of the house to welcome us, along with the nameless, overexcited little black dog that we all ignored. Redeso, Klaus and I went to settle in our room. We put our bags down, sat and lay on our beds, familiarising ourselves with it once more, and finally, we relaxed, though not completely because of what happened to Lorenzo. I called my girlfriend a few hours later from the phone stationed in the hall. Her dry voice answering '*Pronto?*' streamed through my senses like both the most unlikely phenomenon and the most beautiful thing that could happen to a person. A month felt like a year of silence.

'It's me, Red,' I said. 'How are you?

'I'm well, how are you, how was Africa?'

'Cool,' I said. 'And Rimini?'

'Very good,' she said. 'Look I have to tell you something before we carry on.' And I got it. She was my first girlfriend but I was not stupid. I just had to put together her voice's cold tone and this premise to foresee what was coming. She had found another boyfriend, she said, at the beach, and wanted to break up with me.

'Is that ok?' she asked.

'Of course' I said. 'Well then... I'll see you around.'

'You were cool!'

The use of that *were* puzzled me further. I guess she meant to say 'it was cool to be with you' but it came out awkwardly. What can you say? I just said, 'Hey thanks!' Then we hung up the phone. I felt at odds with everything after the call, with the silence, with the desire I had held on to for a month to see her, with the change, of course, my own imagination had to take now under this new order of things, and with the prospect of not being able to try that salty kiss of hers once more in my life. I went outside in the garden and lay down on the hammock by the oak tree. It was the end of August 1990. My fifteenth birthday was in 2 days. The dog was halfway to his den having a nervous rest. 'My name is Luka' played out of the open window of the girls' room. The vineyard, with grapes ripening, stretched as far as half of a football pitch behind me up to the road. On one side at the far end of the courtyard, beyond the little fenced field, was the barn we used as a bike shed. On the other side of the gate, stood the line of cypress trees I planted a year ago.

I slept very badly that night. I languished between feeling hot and cold. In the morning, I couldn't get up. I had a 39-degree fever. Klaus was lying in bed in the same condition I was in, sweating like a pig. The fact that we were both ill simultaneously in the aftermath of our trip to Africa rang no alarm for the supervisor on shift. She gave us some medicines to calm down the fever. It was in the afternoon when the thermometer hit 41 and we were both in the grip of delirium, that she called the doctor. The doctor drove to our home immediately from town and checked on us just like the old times. He diagnosed malaria. They called the ambulance straight away and Klaus and I were carried to Bologna's St Orsola Hospital. Malaria was, without a doubt, the worst illness I ever had. I became so weak that I barely had the strength to move, yet I had to as I was in desperate need of a comfortable position. I also had to hold my arm still to not mess with the IV drip. To make it worse, at the peak of my delirium and agony, the nurse mistakenly injected me with a solution that served to induce vomiting, when my stomach had been empty all day. I spent at least a couple of hours in the grip of dry heaves, with the idiotic apologetic nurse holding my hand. 'I just noticed it's your birthday, darling, today!' she said, and in my eyes, there was Pelé's dog lying on the floor next to my bed and my blind granddad Olivier with the Aremo sitting next to the nurse and I was, despite it all, fascinated by the advancement of medicine that possessed solutions for inducing any natural physiological process. That all this new technology was handed to nurses like mine. In the middle of puking nothing, I imagined their pantry in the back room as an armoury of injections ready for every use and I told my granddad that the nurse had a solution that could get a paraplegic up on his feet and one capable of accelerating bone repair at light speed if a patient slipped over and broke his bones right at the end of a nurse shift. 'Here you go, sweetheart!' But there was no easy way to stop the heaving. It went on until I fell asleep.

After a couple of days weaving in and out of feverish sleep, I began to recover and to feel lucid again. I sat up on the bed and saw Klaus, who had recovered earlier than me and was healthier, eating his lunch on the bed in front of me while watching TV and chatting with a neighbouring patient.

'Still alive, Twin?' he said. 'Ma-ma-malaria is cool hum! I'm going to-to-to tell my friends I got f-f-f-fucking malaria, Jesus! I had Lorenzo on the-the-the phone earlier, he called the hospital, do you know? He-he-he says hi, he slept in the airport, do-do you know.'

'Where is he now?'

'Back in Verucchio. The social w-w-w-orker ma-managed to get him through the b-b-b-order. He-he-he-he slept in the airport.'

'Poor guy,' the patient next to him interjected. 'I bet it must be horrible to sleep in an airport, in Milan, to boot!'

'He de-de-de deserved it,' said Klaus. 'You don't know my brother, he-he is an idiot.'

A few days later, we were discharged. Franco came to collect us from the hospital, and soon we were back to our lives once more. With the onset of autumn, all of the residents joined forces to prune the vineyard from morning until early in the afternoon. Two full crates of grapes were to be kept for us, while a larger quantity was sold to local winemakers. School began too, for Redeso and me, Nicola and Denise. Telemaco worked in a nearby nail factory. Klaus, who by then had been out of school for two years and now worked as a labourer in a metal mechanic factory in the industrial area of Imola, set off to work on a motorbike. Livia was the only one who went nowhere in the morning, afternoon or evening, never. For reasons I haven't understood quite well—I overheard about drug abuse and a toxic relationship with her mother—she wasn't allowed to leave the foster home without supervision. Hers was more like a home detention. She just stayed there, in her bedroom, in the kitchen, or on the swing outside in the garden, smoking two packets of cigarettes a day.

We all met up again at the end of the school and workday. There would be things that needed our attention, like attending to house-cleaning schedules, doing homework if we had any, tending the little vegetable garden we all took care of, feeding the dog, or just hanging around, watching TV and listening to music. In good weather, Redeso, Nicola and I would get our bikes and cycle around the countryside. The three of us had become thick as thieves, riding along fields and orchard roads in sparsely inhabited areas. Some days we cycled into town to Toscanella where we hung outside the bar with local teens, played video games and cycled further down the road to see the guy who worked at the local petrol station and knew a lot about motorbike maintenance. In winter, not even our best gloves could help hold against the burning cold and humidity of the countryside. We'd ride as fast as we could to warm up and would challenge the level crossing, accelerating even more when we heard the bells and saw the bars lowering, either managing to slip through the crossing just in time, our heads ducked down to the handlebar level, if we had luck, or we had to pull the breaks with a sideways drift at the last minute.

One day, we stopped at an abandoned quarry. An extraordinarily quiet and beautiful place that we found by chance. It was deserted, pieces of abandoned old machinery lying around, rusting away. The orange hue of the sunset made the entire scene look like the setting for a film on Mars. We dropped our bikes on the floor and rested on the bonnet of an old truck, watching the sun going down on the horizon. Then Nico pulled out a packet of tobacco from his pocket and made himself what I thought in my naïveté was a cigarette, but would learn afterwards was a spliff. The sunset light cast over his face when he lit it.

'Are you guys seriously aiming at becoming two chefs?' he said, somehow amused. He always gave the impression he found amusement in something about the person he conversed with.

'Yeah, all points in that direction,' we said.

'Is that cool?'

'What?'

'The prospect of working in a restaurant.'

'Not bad. You, what do you want to be?'

'I don't know. Maybe a lorry driver, a taxi driver, or a bike racer. But it seems so unlikely that you can just say I want to become this and you just become it. We are sons of the eighties, after all, what's the fucking point in becoming something? And then what, you gonna show to the world what, that you had become what, someone? Or you did something... how do you say... you know what I mean?'

'Something meaningful?'

'Yeah, that thing!'

'Why not?'

'Us? People like us? No chance. We're going to be disqualified at the first round. The real world shit on people like us. Better keep a low profile. Don't know why Livia is so desperate to go out. Way better in care. The real world's fucking full of sharks; eat you alive. There are no real friends out there.' He took a big drag and resumed his talk. 'You guys want to have kids in the future?'

'Can be cool. You, you don't want them?'

'Maybe. It's the only thing that could make sense to me. Getting a house in the countryside with a girl that has a fucking head on her shoulders. You know, the type who doesn't like bullshit. You know. I'd work my land, she'd cook, and we raise our kids and give them what I didn't get. You know, like smiling at them, answering all their questions, you know what I mean. I would cultivate my own grass, but hey, I'd stay out of any other types of drugs. That's all bullshit. I don't think it'd be fair on them.'

I never knew why Nico was in care, I never asked, and he never told me. All I knew was that his uncle, fed up with the kid's situation at home, called the social service. The social service paid a visit to Nico's parents, found the environment at home unsuitable for the kid and put him in care. This was the second year he spent in the foster home.

He was originally from a small town near Imola. An interesting kid. I always felt he was years ahead of Redeso and me, both in terms of physical development and behaviour despite being two years younger than us. At twelve, he already had some experience of life: he smoked cigarettes and weed, drank alcohol covertly and would habitually vanish for some time; no one ever knew where or whom with, and would stay away for hours or days until a police car would bring him back in the middle of the night. I remember being awakened by the noise of a police car entering our courtyard, the car doors opening and closing, the supervisor rushing down the stairs to open the front door, Nico slurring a 'fuck off', possibly to both the police and the supervisor, before teetering upstairs to his bedroom, leaving the police officer to report to the supervisor where they found the boy drunk and what he was doing.

GROUND

Sometimes life could get messy very quickly at the foster home. You had a furious Klaus giving a head-butt to a supervisor who was trying to deal with him, and then had to be locked out of the house until he calmed down. There was Livia, a twenty-cigarette-a-day smoker, throwing things out of her window and shouting at the top of her lungs that she wanted to get out. 'Let me out of this shit! I want to get fucking out!' You had her again squirming with her helmet on, the carer physically holding her at the gate as she attempted to escape on her motorbike. You had her again holding a hammer and threatening to smash her own face with it if they tried to stop her. Then eventually things would settle. She'd let go of the hammer and let one of the supervisors take her back inside. Klaus's breathing would gradually ease out, and slightly ashamed for having disproportionality lost it once more, he would say sorry and would be let back in. We would then have a snack of tea and biscuits in a strange atmosphere of things that were only partially resolved. Redeso and I would go to our room, do homework, listen to music, chat or read. I was into Stephen King at that time. Redeso was being carried away by Herman Hesse, and he was talking to me a lot about it, about all the findings and teachings he was getting out of his reading. To me, Redeso's essence was that of a radical. I remember looking at him with admiration for the stylistic choices he made, like when he spent an entire day bleaching his hair and dyed it blue, or when he got himself some tartan-patterned red trousers and paired them with a long brown corduroy coat, his favourite outfit for a while. To finish off his style was a sentence he wrote himself that Nico tattooed on his arm, despite the kid having no previous experience with tattooing and wasn't even that good at either drawing or writing. I remember them carrying out the operation in our room sitting on Redeso's bed, the stereo playing some of Nico's metal bands—Skid Row or Pantera—Nico using a needle he dipped in a Bic pen's black ink to undertake the two-hour work of tattooing my brother. The result was terrible, of course, but at least Redeso's sentence was there. *Keep your head up, my friend!* That was a time when Redeso's mind was stirring with ideas, theories, discoveries and epiphanies about life's social and existentialist mysteries. He would discuss them in his typical high-spirited manner—'Because you know this.' 'If you think about that.' 'The real dilemma is that.' 'And yes, because I truly believe that this is possible to be accomplished!' His friends at school loved him. They all gathered around him when he arrived at school with lots of 'Hey Redeso' here, 'Redeso' there, and were buzzing around him when we left school, exchanging feverish talks with him and hugging and slapping his shoulders. Looking back at him during that period of our life, seeing him riding on his college motorbike while yelling his observations to me as I rode my motorbike next to him, I can see that that black kid with blue hair and safety pins on his tartan trousers was already a seeker.

One day, Redeso brought home a Casio keyboard he bought with his savings. He placed it in our bedroom. Plugged it in. Turned it on. Regulated the volume. Started playing some one-finger-based random tune over one of the beats stored in the keyboard. He played the whole day. The day after. And again, and again, every afternoon after school, he sat at the keyboard experimenting, until he was able to put together some melodies like Talking Heads' 'We Are on the Road to Nowhere' and Beatles' 'Obladi Oblada'. Then he started to make his own songs. He would select the keyboard's basic rap beat. The scratching effect, the clap and the Yo! all attained by pressing the effect key. He would try out his first lyrics, write them down, rap them and all of sudden something new was filling up the air in our room. I could do nothing else but join that little revolution Redeso had just brought into our lives. It was not long before we started producing tonnes of hip hop songs together, inspired by Public Enemy, Run DMC and Beastie Boys, writing, editing and trying different sounds. Sometimes Nicola joined us. Sometimes Livia would come into our room to listen or just to hang out with us. She'd sit at one of our desks, drawing while the three of us played around with the keyboard, her blonde curly hair brushing the paper, her lips cracked all the time, her face halfway absorbed in her art and halfway in building her own opinion on our music.

It felt nice to have her around. Me and her had become good friends. Like a little brother and big sister. It always pleased me when she came into my bedroom with her smell of cigarettes asking me to go for walks with her. Since she was restrained from leaving the premises, we just walked outside in the garden, through the vineyard and sat on the swing next to the oak tree. And stood there, lightly swinging, sometimes holding hands. I can say Livia was the first person I loved unconditionally. I'm sure she felt the same for me. The music she listened to—Toto, Susan Vegas, Joy Division and Patti Smith— reflected her spirit. She led me to discoveries as she talked to me about all these new things in the region of building your own values, the amplitude of love, what respect meant for her, and sexuality, freedom and authenticity, which were unexplored themes to me. I remember one day, in particular; she told me about finding beauty in things around me even when things looked ugly. And I remember wondering within myself, 'What does she mean by beauty? Is it something you can see if it's not there?' I sat quietly, listening to her. Listening. Absorbed by it all. Trusting that whatever she was saying to me was important and would stay with me over time and hopefully get more accessible to my mind one day. She spoke a lot about freedom, I guess, as a direct result of the condition of confinement she was living. People end up in places like foster homes for all sorts of reasons, some reasons more serious than others, but I think ultimately it comes down to freedom, to people hindering your freedom. The freedom to live in a healthy family environment, the freedom to grow into beautiful, strong, self-worthy people, the freedom to not be assisting your parents to inject heroin all day and the freedom to not be asked to help them because they can't get the right vein, the freedom to not to be forced by your parents to prostitute for their clientele.

'It's not a utopian concept, Freedom,' she told me one of those days in the swing. 'It's something we can achieve now in this world.

Something we need to fight for. The problem is when you go after the wrong freedom, the fake freedom, the freedom you've been sold, like everybody's freedom. No. That's shit. They're selling you that shit for you to not see the freedom that matters. Mr Redesof, you have your own unique freedom to find. Mine is different. It's different for everybody, depending on what kind of freedom you were born for.'

***

At some point, a new carer turned up. His name was Filippo Averna, a very friendly-looking guy. One day, during one of his first shifts at the foster home, Filippo Averna stood at the door of our bedroom, listening for a little while to Redeso and me playing music.

'It's good stuff,' he said. 'How would you feel playing in front of people, having a concert I mean, a proper concert, in front of an audience?' Redeso and I, who had never considered such a possibility, that is taking our rudimental music to a different level, to a place outside our room, could hardly grasp the meaning of it, and took his question as a compliment. No more than that. But apparently, he truly meant it. He was offering us the opportunity to have a gig. It turned out that Filippo Averna was a big shot in the Imolese rock music scene—he was an ex-drummer for a rock band and now worked as a manager of a prominent local rock band. He saw that we were something new in a provincial local music scene saturated with rock and metal bands. Twin black teenagers playing hip hop in our province was something he had never come across before. One week later, he came to us with a date set for our first concert at a music festival in Imola's Covered Market, where we would open the festival along with three other local bands. We just needed to get more professional, he said. So he introduced us to a professional keyboard player who would help us compose the beats for our songs. We met the guy once a week at his house with lyrics and all and got the job done. In the end, we produced a series of professional tracks and burned them onto a CD.

Then we thought that it would be a good idea to add a third element to our band to make it more dynamic. Nico was not available; beyond having fun with us the time we rapped together, rap was not his thing, and moreover, he was busy taking heavy metal drumming lessons. So, we talked about the band project with one of our classmates, Gennaro, the only connoisseur of black music I knew—jazz, blues and rap—the guy had so many tapes by black musicians whom I had never heard of, and he was also an excellent saxophone player, aside from being a nice kid. He enthusiastically joined the band. Now we were three, with a band name formed by our initials RGR. Gennaro had the perfect place we could rehearse, the garage at his house, which his parents let him convert into a rehearsal space. There was a small sink and an old sofa, all we needed to wee and chill out, a sound system and three mics we bought together with our savings. After school, we'd meet in his garage two or three times a week to rehearse over the pre-recorded material we received from Filippo's friend, with some of Gennaro's live saxophone added in. The three of us took turns singing the lyrics Redeso and I wrote. We added elements of synchronised dance as it was in vogue at the time. We rehearsed and rehearsed, polished and polished.

Then the big day arrived. Flyers and posters for the event had been delivered around town, advertising RGR among other local bands, so the night was bigger than I thought it would be. The room was full. I remember at some point dreading the idea of having to go on the stage and sing in front of an audience. I asked myself, 'What if I don't make it? If I froze in front of everybody. If they don't like it?' But we couldn't go back now.

We went on the stage after the first rock band had finished. Yes, Filippo Averna was right, we brought something different to the scene with our baseball hats, New York Yankees, Chicago Bulls and Red Sox T-shirts and Jordan trainers. The public, which had come mostly for a rock night, looked puzzled at this trio of colourfully dressed kids in basketball garb, but there were people in the audience who had come specifically to see us, like some of the foster home kids and staff, and some other friends, including a takeaway pizzeria owner whom we had befriended recently. My voice trembled and cracked when I held the mic to introduce us, even though all I had to say was, 'We are the RGR.' And then Gennaro turned on the beat. Redeso took the word first. I was amazed as he started to rap confidently, gesturing with his free hand to the audience. Redeso was a born innovator, pushing his voice to new boundaries. He had charisma, grit, ideas and talent. It was something to be watching him. I felt my legs trembling and I had to struggle to stay put and not run away the whole time my brother sang. My mind fought to stay clear, not to be blank until it was my turn. I managed to get out of the danger zone and keep it up. My rap loosened as soon as I noticed from the eyes of the audience that they liked what we were doing, their eyes glimmering as they nodded to the repetitive beats and our rhymes. That night I had a crystal-clear conviction that not all life was shit. It was not all about lagging, not having a place in society, being the worst at school and having parents telling their kids not to play with us. No, it was possible, possible to stand up on stage and get people to listen to what we had to say. Possible to make it right.

Music became our thing and Filippo Averna, our manager. He would arrange concerts for us and drive us around to have gigs. We would get paid at each gig. Plus, each concert offered an opportunity to establish new ties with other musicians and get inspired by their music to improve our sound. Then Aerosmith and Run DMC featured together in 'Walk This Way', smashing down the barrier between the urban and rock scenes and opening the way to a new genre. Then 'Bring the Noise' followed in 1991. It was another huge hit as well as an extraordinary celebration of an alliance against the status quo, with Anthrax making a cover of a Public Enemy song featuring Chuck D on vocals. Redeso, Nico and I would call each other when the video was on, '"Bring the Noise' is playing, man!' and we would dance and mosh like three furious idiots in front of the TV at maximum volume. 'Bring the Noise' was the voice of our generation poking through. It was huge, bigger than 'Walk This Way' for us because it went beyond rock and rap fusion and was thrash metal merging with hip hop. We just could not resist the temptation to rethink our band, adding rock elements to our music with three additional players—electric guitar, bass guitar and drums. We twins remained on vocals and Gennaro did some extra at the sax and console. The game rose to a different level. We became more aggressive, more shouty and even more lyrical, creating a new sonority, which reflected our personalities more and brought into the pot the variety of music we liked, such as a tribal imaginary of Arrested Development, Bob Marley's Rastafarian rhetoric, mixing it up with rap and the culture of punk rock music that filled Imola such as Pantera, Ramones, Faith No More and Anthrax.

Our look was hybrid as much as our music, with long dreadlocks and ripped or patchy punk jeans, and calls to our African roots such as a boubou top or African necklaces. The no-man's land we had been living in all our lives had brought about something different from what was expected, something altogether different from the first source of inspiration we meant to replicate. It was specific to Redeso and I. In some way you could see our music and look was eclectic, reflecting our lack of adherence to any specific culture and subculture, or to the crossover of the diverse realities that each played a part in shaping us. These different realities we met across our lives had silently seeped into our soul, brewed for years and reversed their courses into an active, outpouring, torrential force. It was now our turn. We were being made. We were becoming the new protagonists of our time. From the music festival's main stages to polished music venues to the dusky and sticky stages of squats, we juddered and shouted out rhymes about racism, social issues, parental negligence, animal rights and people's empowerment. Disillusionment, our hopes, our fears, our physical yearning for space, the muscular urge to break free from containment that we had built up over the years, our love and pain, our need for individuation and affirmation, our need to be perceived as good at something and our anger, lots of anger, all was released out on the stage. Our lyrics were good. Our musicians were good. We knew we were leaving a mark on our audience because people were talking about us. I remember, in particular, a progressive audience in a small remote village that we went to play in one night that knew all of our songs by heart. They had made copies of our demo to give around town and sang along with us, '*There is no difference! There is no difference!*' moshing and pushing each other throughout our concert. We ended up in a couple of national music magazines with favourable reviews and then began being called to be the opener for some semi-underground bands in the scenes of Bologna, Rome, Napoli and Milan.

At the centre of our support was our closest circle of friends. A kid who jumped out of a moving car one night when we were out drunk called Arturo; a red-haired Sicilian copy of Kurt Cobain named Andrea Mancuso; Franz, a mixed-race guy who had recently moved to St Catherina; Gennaro, Nico and a respectable-looking guy from a nearby town called Ferro. That was the core of the gang. We were called the Obelisk because we used to meet up at the obelisk monument at the Piazza Matteotti in the centre of Imola on Saturday afternoons with our motorbikes parked against it. Each one of us with a Vespa Special or a College, or a bike if you were younger, like 13-year-old Arturo who hung onto our arms whenever we rode off.

Life rolled on. We'd ride around Imola and the surrounding areas, the fresh breeze of freedom upon our faces as we rode across town to each other's houses, to parks and to the rivers flowing through nearby hamlets. We would camp out for a night, swimming in the river, grilling our meat and vegetables on a fire, chatting, getting drunk on our first bottles of vodka and listening to Andrea Mancuso play the acoustic guitar he carried with him everywhere we went. Not only did he resemble Kurt Cobain, but he sounded like him as he sang '*Polly wants a cracker…*' or '*I'm so happy, cause today…*'

GROUND

Andrea Mancuso, my best friend, was another important person in my life. He had inherited strong ethical and moral values from his father in which he firmly believed. His family were the first people I had met who practised vegetarianism and alternative medicine, who treated themselves with herbs and fasting and campaigned against the use of pharmaceutical medicine. It was at their table during edifying conversations with his parents and sister that I first heard about organic food and animal rights, the numerous and readily-available effective natural cures for illnesses typically considered untreatable, such as cancer. They told us about a case they witnessed of a controversial Spanish healer who had on his record many cases of so-called incurable diseases that he had cured with just the use of natural remedies, and who was therefore harassed and eventually silenced by the trillion-dollar-worth pharmaceutical industry. There was a motivated, thoughtful and well-mannered boy beyond the scruffy-looking grunge persona of Andrea Mancuso, a different genre than the average Imolese, but also from the rest of our members in the Obelisk. Unlike the rest of us, he was a bright student, from a functional family and always played fair no matter the circumstances. He encouraged us to do things in a different way or at least reconsider our actions when we undertook acts of vandalism or breached the rules unnecessarily, at least *some* rules. It was, in fact, his combination of integrity, sympathy, generosity, positive attitude and assertiveness that made him the centre of our group. No matter what, you knew you could rely on Andrea Mancuso.

Meanwhile, there were some important developments at the foster home. A major one happened somewhere around November 1991, when MTV played 'Killing in the Name' by Rage Against the Machine. And that, again, was another score for us, this time from a band that was born hybrid and was completely natural in its ability to flood our living room with an unbelievable combination of musical subtlety built on a blues scale and one of the most balanced distortions I ever heard, and yet so potent, a new politiciszed band that knew how to stretch our nerves to an explosive end.

Then one night at dinner a few weeks later, Livia, who had just turned eighteen, announced that she was leaving the foster home. It was so upsetting for everyone that even a sulky, careless person like Klaus looked lost upon receiving the news and admitted that he would miss her. The night before her departure, after dinner, after we had watched a film together in the living room and put on our pyjamas and were ready to go to bed, she came into our room and asked if I were free. I was. She took me by the hand down to a room on the ground floor, to a second living room in a wing of the house we rarely accessed. The room was fitted with a little sofa and a round table and we sat quietly under the dim light of the table lamp. The quietness of the room combined with the quietness of the still, dark countryside I could see outside the window. We stepped over a toy train track that was lying on the floor to sit on the sofa. I was aware that she wanted to carve out a special moment with me to say goodbye. I was aware that Franco had tried to persuade her to stay an extra year. A probationary year, when, from the safe environment of what had become her home, she could enjoy some free mobility while remaining monitored, instead of breaking into the world so abruptly, with so little preparation. Both carers and her social worker believed that she was not ready to leave, but they could not force her to stay anymore, and perhaps if they had detained her less in the first place she might have remained longer. But of course, at eighteen, gaining the right to choose for herself, after all those years of detention, it made perfect sense that Livia just wanted to leave. I just wished that I had been more persuasive too in making her stay longer. Fuck, if only had I been more there, more present, I would have loved to have known her plans. Was she going to stay with her mother? What if it went all wrong and they picked up their fight and her mother kicked her out? Did she have a plan B? What about a job? What was she planning to do? What if she got back to that shit she was taking? Didn't she want to stay with us an extra year? No, in keeping with her many lectures on freedom, Livia wanted to live her life more than anything. Her bags were already packed in her room. Her new car, a second-hand Citroen Deux Chevaux, was parked in the courtyard and ready to lead her to her fate.

I didn't ask her anything. She was the only one talking but, as usual, I was listening. I was taciturn in nature. Withdrawn, often apathetic. Her lips still cracked, her light grey eyes at times looking at me, at times drawing inspiration from a vague space in front of her. Our bare feet resting on the floor next to each other. That night Livia advised me how to carry on alone without her. 'Just observe the fundamental rule,' she said, 'and you won't get it wrong. The rule about fear. Get to know fear, learn how to navigate it and how to not give in to it. You do that by remembering things. Remembering what happened. Remembering who you are, where you come from and who you met along the road, no matter what they try to take away from you they will never be able to take away your history. The thing is that all your people live in there, in that history, and will rise up for you if you call them. They're going to fight for you. And you will find me among them.' Then she added, 'Remember me, Redesof, I'm your ground.' That was a germinal night for me. I pictured her words as if she had extended her hand into my chest and buried a little seed, a seed that contained inside of it all the solutions I would need throughout my life journey. To this day, I just need to connect with that seed to find the strength and trust I need to push through very difficult times. Livia taught me to reach my inner power with those words, my power that was my history, my people, all the people I met. She better summarised the ten years of empty religious rhetoric I had received from all the nuns and the priests.

I slept strangely that night. A light sleep. Then woke up in the morning, feeling sad at the idea that my friend would be leaving that day. I had breakfast. Then Livia was bringing her stuff down the stairs. The general mood in the house was down when we all stood outside in the courtyard to kiss her goodbye. We stood watching as the Citroen

Deux Chevaux set off through the gate along Via Capitolo. Her hand waved goodbye through the car's window and that was it, another great person had gone.

Life Lessons

Debra-Jo's first son, our first nephew, was a mixed-race boy named Elia, who was born on a winter morning in 1991. My siblings, Ugo's parents and some of Debra-Jo's ex-mates from Oasis, including Gabriella, were all present when I went to visit the hospital. Suddenly, there was a new being in the world, all wrinkles and a full head of curly hair, taking up his own real yet tiny place among us, nestled in Debra-Jo's arms. My sister's eyes filled with maternal love for her new little creature. Debra-Jo. Now a mother. Who would have ever expected this from that little girl who escaped the fire many years ago? She had come a long way. And now baby Elia, the crowning achievement of her life. The picture of her holding her baby, her family and best friends all around her, perfectly represented the stage at which my sister was in her life. I don't think she could have felt happier. She regained her place at the centre of our lives and it was like the old times in the villa when she was directly taking care of us. We spent so many weekends at Debra-Jo and Ugo's house in Bologna, dining together, celebrating Christmas, Easter and birthdays, serving each other roast chicken and fried piadina and ending with her unmissable mascarpone with amaretti. We were all at the table, all happy, engaging in effervescent conversations. Some of us turned into adults, some introduced new girlfriends to the family, Ugo and Sigmund kept up the mood with their jokes, Lorenzo would bring fresh air from the Adriatic Coast when he would visit from Verucchio and tell us about his life and the people of the village. Our little nephew passed from arm to arm. By opening the doors of her house to us, Debra-Jo gave us something more than dinners together, making up for the home we didn't have or the one which had been slipping out of our hands. All this wouldn't have been possible without Ugo's support. He made us feel welcome at all times, although I bet it must have been challenging to have such a big family around so often, no matter how subtle we tried to be. The bond we had back then was so strong. We were happy together. Discussions about the house in Via Suore or any other thing we were expecting from our parents were not as relevant any longer. Since the meeting in Congo, we had given up hope. We had given up hope for our parents, our homeland and our house but Debra-Jo showed us that, despite all, we could still be together and be a family.

It was on one of those days in her house that my older siblings gave me ugly news concerning our beloved Pino. One day Father called them and they learned that he had sent the money to repair the roof. He wanted to know how the work was going, but nobody had known that the work should have been started. My brothers went to ask Pino about the money, but it seemed he did not know either. My brothers reported back to Father, who swore angrily that it had been sent. Now we began to understand that it was not a coincidence that whatever financial action my father undertook with this man turned into a disaster.

Gradually, a new picture of Pino came into focus. We had no physical evidence to incriminate him, but the world was small, and Imola was even smaller. Through St Catherina's network, the parish and Sigmund's antiques business—a perfect location for unexpected encounters—people who had dealt with Pino started to disclose despicable facts about this man that we had once considered part of our family. Beyond stealing the money needed for the roof, we were told, Pino had been hindering our life in different ways: siphoning the monthly mortgage my father sent to pay for the house in Via Suore, pocketing my father's money regularly since the beginning of their partnership, even stealing my father's Land Rover and Jaguars and the other valuables in the house after the fire. Along with Alvaro Belluzzi, he was fully involved in the scam of the equipment for the road-building deal that brought my father to his knees. But again, we would have needed to get legal proof to incriminate him, but we could not be bothered, we didn't care anymore and we just felt like leaving behind the past. We had baby Elia now, Debra-Jo's house to meet at for Christmas and open our presents under the tree. Whatever happened before and whoever fed himself from our misery, fuck them, we still had a full life ahead that we wished to live without resentment. Pino died of a heart attack. Sigmund gave us the news, driving down to the foster home specifically for this purpose. None of us flinched whatsoever on hearing about the end of Pino. 'Don't t-t-t-take it too seriously, Sigmund,' Klaus commented while bouncing a tennis ball against the wall outside the foster home. 'Only an animal ha-ha-has died.'

Another piece of big news concerned Lorenzo. He had been relocated again, this time to the foster home in Toscanella with us. During a social services reassessment of his case, as he had turned eighteen, he was asked what he intended to do now that he was legally free to choose for himself. He was offered the option to use the government structure for longer if he thought he would benefit from it and so the decision was made. With nowhere else to go to, no savings and no imminent work, Lorenzo accepted the social worker's offer to spend a further year under care, so that he could have the adults backing him as he tried out his first moves in the outside world as an independent young man. During the assessment, the social workers also found out that he was no longer happy at Verucchio and had expressed the desire to return to Imola. That was how, through our social worker, Ursola del Rio, Lorenzo was brought back to Imola. I mentioned previously a second living room inside the foster home that I went to with Livia the night before she left, the room with the toy train track on the floor. That was part of a separate, fully-fitted two-bedroom flat that was supposed to foster more kids but had always been vacant. Lorenzo was moved in there. Klaus soon joined him, as he was transferred there a few months later just before his eighteenth birthday. The arrangement came with a new set of regulations that they had to abide by in order to live alone. For instance, they had to consider the main premises as somebody else's house, which they could not access without the carers' authorisation. They were required to cook their own food in their flat, do their own washing and look after their house, providing for themselves as would be expected from two independent adults.

Contrary to everyone's expectations Klaus's life, with all that talent the boy had, didn't take off. He enjoyed a very prolific life as a skater soon after leaving St Catherina, taking his practice far beyond the level of what he was able to when he was blocked inside the courtyard institution. With a plethora of options available to him now that he was free to skate around Imola and Toscanella with other skaters, he was finally one of them, through and through, wearing his own fitted Santa Cruz, Independent, Powel Peralta skater outfit. And he was free, free like the kids framed in the skate magazines that he used to envy. Then, right when he gained notoriety as one of the best skaters in Imola and the surrounding areas, he stopped skateboarding. It was the same way he dropped the breakdancing he was doing back in St Theresa, way before taking up skating and then rapping. Hard to say if out of boredom or something else, but Klaus would just habitually give up things. It was around that time that something inside him began to falter, taking him more and more away from the imaginative boy he used to be and closer and closer to a common, haggard, disenchanted young man. At the age of seventeen, he took high-cylindered motorbike driving lessons. With some difficulties on the theoretical part, he managed to pass the exams and obtained a licence to drive high-cylindered motorbikes. He then bought himself a second-hand Cagiva Elephant and changed its colour patterns himself with spray paint. He painted over a carton board stencil with oversized clothes on, a cornrow-braided hairstyle and his ever-present Walkman playing French and American hip-hop, and that was it, any interest in expressing his talent had died. You could say that his life became all about driving that Cagiva at dawn through the countryside roads to reach his workplace and riding back again in the evening to the foster home.

Klaus's happiest time was during meals, particularly when he was served his favourite dish: pasta with sausages, peas and cream, which he would bury in a spoonful of parmesan. He would hum a random tune the whole time he ate, his head resting sideways over one hand like a melancholic dreamer, while the other hand held the fork the way a baby would. Once he had consumed his meal and left the table, he would fall back into his usual self, grumpy and frowning, essentially dealing with everyone from the least hospitable state of mind. Klaus was an enigma to everyone. Looking back, I can't really say I knew him, even though we went through many things together and shared a room in the foster home for years, we were never on the same page, not open to each other's lives and not even that interested in each other. I think Redeso and I looked to him more than he did to us. His life unfolded from a different plane in a stunningly incomprehensible way, like that passion he had for pornography. I never understood it, I enjoyed my time with pornography, but I have never seen anything equal to Klaus's veneration and deep understanding of the pornographic scene. He had a big suitcase full of adult material sitting on top of his wardrobe. It was common to catch him in his time off reading one of his magazines while listening to some classical music like Chopin and Beethoven. He leafed through it analytically like he was reading the *Economist* or something, an inquisitive smile etched on his face, in the sense that there was no sign of sexuality involved in what he was doing. I never noticed him being aroused while reading one of his magazines or masturbating or going to the toilet with the magazine, he just lay reading it in the open, nodding and commenting to himself. Did he see something beyond the repeat of those penetrations that we couldn't? I often wondered if Klaus wasn't, in fact, seeing an entirely different world altogether, like he was in a perennial state of hallucination.

At some point, he went through a Nazi stage. It all started with an editorial covering the problem of an emerging Italian Nazi group that he had read. *Something* about the radical ideology, the brotherhood, the cool aesthetic of gangs of young men posing in front of a Nazi flag, explaining why they went going around beating up foreigners and advocating a racist manifesto, said *something* to him that he suddenly identified with very much. He looked for more material and showed it to us, with as much adulation as he had felt once for the skaters in the skating magazines Tulio used to show him. He now called his brothers dirty niggers and gave us the Roman salute whenever we came across him. 'If you were white, you'd be a racist,' Debra-Jo told him once. He answered, 'I-I-I am a racist, nigger.' Then one day a strange accident happened. It was during a day trip to Firenze that we, the foster home residents, were about to undertake by train. With us was Fernando, one of the supervisors. As we were standing and waiting for our train to come to the platform of Imola's main station, there was an announcement warning people to stay away from an incoming 'special' train, which was to temporarily stop on the platform where we were standing. The stadium-like chants sung by a multitude of hooligans preceded the arrival of the special train. As the train slowed down and stopped at our platform, you could see it was packed with football match-goers, most likely heading to see their team playing in the Bologna stadium. They all sang out loud and hung out of the train window, all styled like Nazis, shouting their slogans, and flying the flags of their team, forcefully gesticulating with their hands, some sticking the Roman salute out of the window. The level of violence they were subjecting everyone on the platform to was almost physical. But not for Klaus. It wasn't violence, not in the same way the rest of us witnesses perceived the whole thing. The world he was seeing seemed to not reflect in any possible way the one the rest of us were dealing with. He was intrigued by this special train carrying this unusual aggregation of young protester-like people. His eyes shone like he was seeing a band of old Nazi friends he hadn't seen in a while, and now they were here, in front of him, entertaining the whole station with some breath-taking choreography and boasting the best display of racist chants he had heard in his life. Unable to resist their call, he got up from the bench we were sitting on to go to them. He walked across the platform to reach them, intending to gang up with them, and he was possibly convinced they were going to laugh together like in the past when he had easily made friends with other strangers. He wanted to be loved by them. He wanted to hear them say he was not like any other nigger. He went after their love to prove to himself that they had nothing against him personally; it was a way to not understand that there were people around the world who hated him unconditionally and would do whatever it took to get rid of him. In that short march towards the train, Klaus was going straight to enter the grace of those guys. As soon as Fernando, our carer, realised where Klaus was heading, he rushed up and grabbed his arm, pulling him back, 'What are you doing, Klaus!' But the attention of the train hooligans had already turned to Klaus by then. They hurled violent racial insults, raised their hands in the fascist salute and called out to him with all sorts of death threats. Their faces deformed as they lurched and leaned out of the train windows, wishing they could get out and beat him up. I can't forget the bewildered look in Klaus's eyes as he withdrew with Fernando under the shower of insults from the hostile crowd. They were only prevented from attacking Klaus because the train doors were locked, and they had the prospect of the game in their hearts before anything else. But Klaus's look, the look of a fool walking away from rejection—I will never forget it, it was clearly saying, *what did I do to them? Why are they acting like this if they don't even know me?* That was the first time I saw Klaus being so small and insignificant. I guess he had learned something new, that he had to live with the idea that those people could attack him one day and that he could experience hatred he had no control over.

It hurt him, it hurt Redeso, me and, to some extent, the other kids from the foster home, to witness firsthand that somewhere out there, there were people or associations where hate towards us, black people, was a main constituent of their ideology.

Some weeks after the train station incident, Klaus, Redeso and I learned another important lesson regarding racism. We were summoned by a foster home carer named Giorgio to see something on TV. He called us three because he knew whatever was happening concerned us directly. The TV was showing what looked like at first a folkloristic assembly of people dressed in green attending a festival in a rural area. But they were actually talking about politics, reforms, devolution from Rome's central power, secessionism, federalism and anti-immigration policies, all wearing the same green bandana around their neck with no exception, each bandana bearing the symbol of the Sun of the Alps. Some held up green flags with the same symbol on them, with a figure of a knight pointing a sword upwards against the inscription *Lega Nord*. A middle-aged man, with glasses and a coarse voice, talked in the foreground over a small number of media microphones.

'This guy is called Umberto Bossi,' Giorgio explained. 'He's the leader of this new party called *Lega Nord*, a right-wing political party. Look at them properly. Try to understand what they want.' We stood looking, the three of us and our carer in front of the TV, hearing the political rhetoric of Umberto Bossi, I could barely understand, with the group of hopeless-looking middle-aged countryside people existing in the background.

'They are a very marginal regional phenomena,' Giorgio went on lecturing, 'they are largely looked at as a group of isolated buffoons, but, you know, the same was said about the Fascist and Nazi parties, people looked at them as just a bunch of clowns and then.' Giorgio's intention was to give us a little taste of the type of resistance we could be facing out there, with a first introduction to our institutionalised enemies, so that we could start formulating an idea of what we were and where we stood based on the external environment's response to our presence. Then we began to put things together and understand that it wasn't just an impression, that we truly had enemies and those enemies were growing in numbers. The presence of people like us in the country was controversial, giving room to debate and fuelling burning sentiments. We were not just people, not like my Italian peers I grew up believing I was the same as. The *special* train of hooligans insulting Klaus, Lorenzo's detention at the border control in Fiumicino airport due to his expired residency permit, the verbal abuse yelled at us from cars, graffiti on the walls saying *Dirty niggers get out of my country*, some hateful stares on the street and public transport, old classmates now teasing us saying we stole their girlfriends and jobs, the news of a black man thrown out of the moving train, the news of another black man set on fire by a group of Nazis and now the political rally of this Northern party wanting us out the country, all of this pushed us to understand that we were not just people. To force us to question our identity and place in society. I was finding it hard to think in a convincing fashion that I belonged to this country when it was indeed evident that my siblings and I were receiving different treatment from what we thought was our country. I mean, how could I feel I was like them, one of them, if I was not treated like it? Was my subjective perception of Italy changing as I grew up, forming a more realistic picture of the society I was living in, or was the provincial Italian racism, that I had once known as a friendly, innocuous, *ice-breaking* type, giving rise to a climate of proper racism? What could I expect as a black man living in Italy?

No need to say Klaus's affiliation with the Nazi skinheads stopped at Imola's train station. He did not perform a Roman salute after that, and he chucked away all his racist propaganda and, most importantly, he stopped calling us and Debra-Jo dirty niggers. As he was about to come of age, he was transferred to the independent flat next door to the foster home to start an independent life with Lorenzo. Then appeared a girl from Imola called Samantha. Lorenzo met her one night at the Parco delle Acque Minerali outdoor nightclub. The same venue he had escaped to years before from St Catherina, with Klaus, Tulio and Yusuf and ended up in a fight. But this time, Lorenzo went alone as a proper young man, charming as usual, with his long thin-braided hairstyle like Terence Trent D'Arby, green contact lenses and early nineties pop-ish look. He was chatting with a friend when a very attractive girl approached him. They hung out together throughout the night in the venue, then, as they were having an intimate conversation before he attempted to kiss her, she said to him there was something he ought to know. She was ill, she had AIDS. Lorenzo's first reaction was to zoom out. The way he looked at her changed immediately. No more fervour. No more urge to grab her and kiss her. Instead, he made it clear to her that he wanted nothing more from her in that sense, but would she accept a friendship? Her crush on him, however, meant she would not accept no for an answer. He got trapped in her mind. She would call and she would drop love letters at his door at the foster home once she found out where Lorenzo lived. Sometimes she'd ring the bell but there was never an answer, until one day Klaus opened the door. This is where their story began.

Klaus opened the door to Samantha. A boy opening a door to a woman who was hungry for love. A boy with a sinkhole of unmet emotional needs within, opening the door to his fate. The perfect alignment of two unfortunate souls.

'W-w-who are you?' he asked her.

'I'm Samantha. And you?'

'My n-name is Klaus.'

I remember from the many times she drove her white Citroen BX to the foster home to pick up Klaus. She was white as a ghost, which stood in stark contrast with her dark hair, and she had something very sweet, melancholic and lonely glimmering in her eyes. I could see what Klaus found in her beyond her scruffy-looking reggae style. She was another one of his favourite kinds of outcasts in his extensive study of humanity, but an even more radical subject this time because she was terminally ill. Ill with one of the most socially stigmatised disorders, which was believed to be transmitted in unorthodox ways like junkies with infected syringes or by a fuck in the toilet of a night club. That was bread for Klaus's teeth. Besides, she was clever, funny, pretty, a few years older than him, and part of a life-breathing imaginary, an opportunity for Klaus to extend his knowledge to the darkest corners of life, which he simply could not turn down. Klaus entered a full-on friendship with Samantha, which eventually evolved into a love affair, and then partnering. Lorenzo was no longer of interest to her now that she had found Klaus to come and pick up in her white car and drive around Imola. She fell in love with him. At that time I was uneducated about HIV/AIDS and I only knew a few facts about the ways you could get it and then you would just die because there was no effective treatment available. I didn't even know what HIV/AIDS symptoms looked like. Nor what people affected by it looked like. Not certainly the way Samantha looked, the first person with the illness that I had knowingly met. No, she was not the way I imagined them. She looked healthy and vibrant to me, which led me and probably everyone else to believe, along with the fact that Klaus had consciously chosen to be her boyfriend, that AIDS was not so bad after all, not so serious and deadly as they had pictured it. I thought to myself, you get HIV because you don't know the other person had it, no one would be so inconsiderate to transmit it if they knew they had it in advance. And I was sure that there were safe ways around it, let's say by having protected sex, or having asexual relationships and maybe, I thought, the medical establishment might have finally found a cure. They find a cure for everything, why on earth should there be an illness lingering forever without a solution being found?

I never worried about Klaus, nobody truly did. Then Samantha died, a few months after they first met. There was an article about her death with her picture in the local newspaper. Franco, the head supervisor, brought it to us, dropping it on the table. I guess they felt like writing an article about her death because it was still a big deal to hear about people dying of AIDS in our provincial reality. I barely saw Klaus in those days. I saw a fleeting, lonely figure who would leave home only to go to work. When he returned, he'd park his motorbike on the barn's porch, walk across the gravelled courtyard to his flat, exchanging no words but a bitter smile with whoever he came across, enter his house and lock himself in his bedroom for the remaining of the day. He didn't appear as sad as one would expect from someone who had just lost his girlfriend. He looked to me more confused—if anything, disoriented and disappointed, yes, disappointed, as though he had picked up something he deemed would last him longer and not crumble in his hands so quickly. But there was also a trace in those eyes of someone who had a glimpse of the oblivion that lay under the surface of everyday life and was suffering heartbreak and loneliness. Still, I don't think he ever opened up with anyone about his feelings for Samantha's death. Not even with his closest brother, Lorenzo. One could sense what he was going through because he had more difficulty articulating his words than usual in that period and was stuttering to distressing levels. But across death and illnesses, life carried on.

Klaus and Lorenzo lived in the flat next door for a year-and-a-half overall, after which they were taken out of care and provided with an affordable council flat in a dodgy area of Imola. Lorenzo debuted in his first artistic profession as a nightclub performer at the age of twenty, while making ends meet building shop carts in a trolley factory in Imola. Then he was introduced by Klaus to three performing artists from Bologna—Marvin, TJ and Max—with whom he formed a boy band called the 4-More. They were four good-looking and talented young men with a shared dream to make it through as dancers and singers. Their popularity picked up quite rapidly. The 4-More, with

Lorenzo, the charming leader and the audience favourite, left their mark wherever they played and became increasingly requested in the nightclub scene across Italy, from north to south, playing both as a band and as backup dancers for bigger names.

Meanwhile, Ocean had graduated as an accountant and continued to work as a supervisor in St Caterina, where he still lived and tried to make it as a model at the age of 23. Sigmund completed the three-year course of furniture restoration, funded by Don Ettore. By the time he turned 23, he had made himself a good circle of clients around his antique shop. As for Debra-Jo, she had found a job as a cashier in a supermarket. It looked like all of us had a vision or aspirations of some sort. Even Debra-Jo, with her simple job as a supermarket cashier, was working on her and Ugo's project of building their family, but not Klaus. Klaus seemed to be the only one among us who had no direction or drive. The most talented sibling had stopped researching. He had given up.

LONDON, PRESENT DAY VIII

Dear Telma, it's me here. I am here. I seek myself in the bathroom mirror as I wash my face late in the evening. Young and then old. I'm forty now, fuck. This shitty time truly is something we need to confront. I'm going to die at some point and yet I barely know if I am a decent person or not. After what happened today, I cannot be sure.

I've seen only one patient today, at 7 p.m. Then I had dinner, a takeaway. After, I decided to go for a walk. Just a walk. I didn't feel like going to a pub or to drink today. I want to take it easy. I run into Luke, the beggar stationed in front of the Sainsbury's at the end of Lower Clapton Road. He is the most stylish beggar I have seen in and around London and also the friendliest, with a sunny smile, worn grey dreadlocks sticking out of his mariner's cap and leopard-patterned Clarks. He engages in the usual chat with me, speaking with his strong Jamaican accent and I can make out one word out of a hundred. I give him the coins I have in my pockets, which amount to £1.20. I carry on and continue walking.

This is possibly one of my favourite activities. Just walking, for the sake of walking, passively absorbing the narratives of the environment around me. I walk to Dalston Lane and then to Ridley Road Market, where the last remaining market people are closing their stalls amidst the acrid smell of rotten fish. I hit Dalston, the sharp streetlights, car lights and the glow from the ultra-modern skyscrapers of the city on the horizon, blinking. It seems as if every time I come around here, something is being built or closing permanently. South Asian people sit inside the tiny phone and computer shops working late hours. The Turkish waiters in formal attire, serve customers and glare out of the windows of their restaurants. Eclectic Dalston kids hang out in groups, the girls in crop tops even in winter. I walk northward and turn back toward home, crossing Hackney Downs Park and ending in Clarence Road I come across a meeting point of some local Caribbean people who regularly cluster around old cars blaring reggae, drinking ginger beer and smoking spliffs. We greet each other, and I carry on walking.

My dear Telma, there is a degree of humiliation that plays out whenever you endure an episode of racism, which it is easy to deny before acknowledging it. Because the last thing you want on your mind at the end of a day is the emotional stain of humiliation. All anybody wants is to reach home, watch some shit on Netflix, read a book, have a chat on the phone with a friend or your kids or whoever and try to hold on to normality. You hope that no one will question who you are, that they will trust you on the spot when you say that you are ok and that you are just a person. But that doesn't always happen.

On my road, two blocks away from home, a police van passed in front of me and stopped abruptly. A group of six police officers stormed out of the van, running towards me in a kind of 'It's him!' state of mind as if they were dealing with a terrorist attack and I thought, fuck, I know this shit, I know they are coming for me. I've grown familiar with this 'Hey you, stop where you are!' It always happens very quickly. The alarmed look on this blonde police girl's face as she approached me whizzed through the air passing by my eyes. Three or four of her colleagues overtook her, grabbed me, forced me to turn over and handcuffed me.

I say, 'What the fuck is going on?'

And immediately, I felt extremely disappointed so much so that I whispered, 'Not here. Not in London.' Not so much because I was being treated like a criminal, but rather because there was a reason I came all the way here, there was a fucking valid reason for me to leave all I had in Italy and move to London. I had grown fucking tired of shit like this, of having the police stop me at every turn to question and search me and I naively thought that London, Hackney, would be different, that here I would be just a guy like any other, like the black guys I saw on my first days here in the library, driving a cab, or the 48 or the 242, the many black guys I saw behind the Hackney Job Centre counter, one of the guys whom these policemen I stupidly believed were familiar and friendly with. But this was the third time I have been stopped by the Metropolitan Police in the ten years that I have lived in Hackney. All those guys I mentioned might have been suffering the same fate without my knowledge. I am simply shattered by how pathetic and small the fucking world is in the end. These guys are saying to me that, we, black people, are fucking hopeless, regardless of where we go, in Bologna as much as in London.

I feel the handcuffs tightening around my wrists as I try to shake them off. I turn to face them, and one of them points pepper spray right in my face. 'I'm going to spray you with it if you don't stay still,' he says. At this point, the neighbours have come out on the street. They are at their windows and at their doorsteps. It's Hackney, what is left of the old Hackney, the mixed pre-gentrified Hackney. Residents who know all too well of policing ineptitude, and they know me. They know me as the guy who often goes for a walk alone or with his kids.

'Leave him alone, he's cool,' they shout.

'He's done nothing, we know him!'

'Where are you going?' the policewoman asks me.

'I'm going home. I live just there, two blocks away. What is all this about?'

She takes notes on a pad of paper transcribing whatever I say. A few of her colleagues are busy talking in the street by the van on their radios and searching around for anything I could have allegedly dropped on the street. Another one holds me by the handcuffs, while the other guy keeps the pepper spray pointed at my face, ready to spray if I dare to move. Another is searching me.

I never stole and never assaulted anyone. I did use drugs but never sold any. Why such a blunder on their part? What is their mistrust founded on? Maybe I'm telling this story for them too, especially for the guy who was holding the pepper spray at my face, his eyes filled with hatred. I've been here training for four years as an acupuncturist, I have my own clinic now and I'm doing my best to heal people. I dress decently, I'm forty and yet I see that I still belong to the restless, chaotic, class of people that roam this world in the roles of losers, guests, customers, renters and labourers, their land and dignity stolen and their bodies left to bleed or to drown in open seas or flee wars, crying to the sky to be seen as humans. But we are guests even in our native countries, only breathing and giving birth to new scum to be placed at the service of the true owners of this planet.

All my pockets were emptied. My wallet, documents and phone are in their hands being checked with a torch. They probed my back looking for something incriminating and I see it in all of them. A gradual pitiful realisation creeping in: *we got the wrong guy*. We stayed there trapped in that depressing joke for about ten minutes more with them droning on with questions, about who I am, where I have been in the night and all of that, but they were now less sure of the legitimacy of their intervention. Yet, they carried on, more out of duty than anything else, while the people of my street were still there making noise. After a few crackling sounds from their radios, one of the police officers was allowed to take the handcuffs off me; the guy with eyes ignited with adrenaline put the pepper spray back in his belt.

'Sorry,' the young girl said, 'We are out on the look for a black guy going in the area with a knife who matches your description.'

The pepper spray boy, a twenty-year-old guy, suddenly became my best friend, justified the search by saying, 'the problem is that in this area you all look the same, particularly at night.'

GROUND

But that was not the worst thing. It was not him or them. No, it was not. The worst thing was my calmness. Yes, I was deeply calm. I waited for the police van to drive off. Then I walked home.

I opened the front door and closed it behind me. As soon as I walked into the living room, turned on the light and looked around me, I felt extremely lonely. My flat, the dwelling of a single man with no attachment to it, sat so quiet and looked so bleak tonight, more so than usual, that I felt I could not bear to stand in there by myself and needed to see you. I needed a voice or a little text message saying 'I'm coming over there.' I pulled my phone out of my pocket, a gesture that took me back to the earlier hand of the policeman searching and emptying my pockets. I scrolled down to your contact. I was about to call you. Then opted to text you instead. Then I changed my mind again, and then I could not decide whether to call or text you. Then I said to myself that the worst would be if you say no. I would not have been able to bear it should you have told me you were not available, and I thought about going for a pint with a friend, and I was about to text him and your face emerged again, and I said fuck, and dropped the phone on the sofa.

JADELIN GANGBO

My Parents

Looking back, I think the saddest point in the whole story was the way the failed road construction project permanently changed my father. I mean we are all the same in our need for inspirational role models, people who inspire us and give us the courage to dream big and pursue a meaningful life. A light in the darkness and a hero to believe in, yes even if it sounds pathetic, we all need to believe in someone. That someone for my siblings and me was our father. For better and for worse, we believed in him. Despite the clump of absurdity he had in his mind, and all the problems he caused us, he at least gave us the impression that we were the kids of one of the greatest men in the world. We could bear the depressing life he abandoned us to because we woke every day believing we were part of a special family and we were simply on an extraordinary journey. My father inspired us to take risks in life and be imaginative. He was the man in a faraway land, the voice at the end of a phone, the man in a cowboy hat waiting at the airport exit in Brazzaville who became a millionaire with a cigarette trick and earned widespread notoriety as the *Man of the Shoes*. Our problem was not that Dad neglected us. We were in the hands of a man with a big heart who would go to the moon for us if he could, he'd give us everything we wanted if he could. Our problem was that he couldn't because he was delusional. He genuinely believed that everything would fall into place one day soon, that he was always on the brink of restoring his wealth, finding new markets, signing new trade deals and getting us out of the institution and into a dream home when in truth the mess kept growing day after day until it spiralled out of control. My father was like a kid who was set on building a sandcastle on the seashore just as the tide comes in and destroys the castle and the kid starts building a new castle, just a few feet out from the shoreline, that will eventually be crushed by the tide too, yet he continues the process of building on precarious ground. In the same way that the kid has little interest in the sandcastle itself, Dad cared little about the results of his labour. He was so focused on the process of his work that everything else slipped out of his field of vision.

Many people had prospered through his work, especially among his relatives. Nowadays, some occupy influential positions and some are millionaires because they once had the good luck, whether in the form of loans, gifts or stealing, to find themselves in Dad's proximity when he was at his best. From Benin to Congo to Italy, they all had a share. If my siblings and I believed you could point high and achieve anything you wanted, it was because we heard stories about our father's life through a variety of people in Congo, Benin and Italy, who had come across him in their lives and had been marked by him.

But then, even that small thing fooling us to keep going, withered and died off when my father lost his power. There were no survivors of the road construction project, just an abyss of debts and dead machines rusting around a desolate quarry. All of us were forced to come to terms with the fact that even our Dad, *the Principal*, was subject to defeat like any other being. Confidence, power, vigour, luck—just one bad turn had washed them all away.

My mother told me he fell into depression for the first time in his life. He hardly left home and refused to take jobs. My family in Africa faced food scarcity. The kids' head teacher would frequently call my mother because their uniforms were dirty and because they had always the same packed lunch with saca-saca and manioc. Moon and Happiness were eventually downgraded from a private to a public school. Mavie and Monique, often home from school, were neglected because my mother, having to make up for my father's idleness, took charge of bringing home some money.

She started trading building materials, first on a regional level and then with bordering countries, while also managing the quarry. With the quarry experience, she got the hang of dealing with building materials and it was not long before she became acquainted with the construction market. If there was something she learned from my father, it was the art of trading. The first rule of never travelling empty-handed, for example, she told me, stayed with her. Whenever she travelled to a different city or a different country, she would always carry something from the place she was travelling to sell in the city or country of destination and vice versa.

Despite her best efforts, however, things hardly improved at home and certainly not in her marriage. In fact, they were getting worse between her and her husband; they were fighting all the time. At the centre of their quarrels was my father's infidelity. My mother had become accustomed to finding him in bed with other women whenever she got back from her work trips. However, that was still bearable, in a larger context, due to the degradation of their lifestyle. My parent's relationship reached the point of no return when my father started dating his niece, a girl who was the same age as Debra-Jo. Her name was Nicolette and she was the daughter of one of my father's cousins. This affair was hard for my mother to take in, too much for her to acknowledge in the beginning, and she really didn't want to think and understand that her husband was cheating on her with their niece. My father tried hard to hide his incestuous relationship when my mother was in Brazzaville, trying to fool her into believing that Nicolette hung around her house innocently like any other relative or friend that would visit. It was when she was away, once she came back from her business trips, that she would learn from people that the two had been acting like a couple and that Nicolette had slept in her bed every night and ruled the house like a governor.

GROUND

In addition to this problem, a major one was mounting: the problem of selling my mother's only property—a house in Pointe-Noire. A house my mother had bought herself with the revenue she earned over the years from doing business both on her own and as my father's associate. She decided to buy that house around the time my father showed his first intention to gamble all his capital in the road construction project, as a shield against what she predicted would be a financial disaster. It was an inevitable decision, she said later, to invest in that house, after watching my father's business style. Even at the peak of our wealth, little belonged to us, most things we had were temporary possessions. She was of the opinion that he should have saved, securing himself, and invested in something concrete and stable such as real estate, which we could always rely on and rent out in times of difficulties. But my father had reached a point where he no longer cared about my mother's opinion. He found her only irritating, this woman who, as his cousin, sister and lover had warned him, was always going against him. She was even more irritating now that she refused to sell the house in Pointe-Noire when my father, her husband, who was desperately in need of money, was begging her to sell. How dare she buy a house with the money that belonged to their family in the first place? And how could she be so selfish and stubbornly refuse to help her husband and her kids who languished in poverty? At this point, my mother began rebelling against my father and his family. Whatever they had to say, there was no intimidation that could be held against her anymore. Too often she had seen the same thing happen and she knew it would happen if the house was sold. The revenue would do nothing to alleviate her children's suffering and would only be used to back another of my father's wild financial adventures. She would not allow this to happen again. Not on her watch. It was on these terms that the house in Pointe-Noire turned into the subject of the fiercest fight between my mother and my father.

In all this, my father's family backed him against my mother. They labelled her as selfish, an opportunist and an ingrate, after all the things they had done for her. They looked down on her as just a poor girl who had made her fortune because she met my father, not because of her merits. I have reason to believe that something larger than the family's financial management issues was at play in this contingency because technically speaking my father did not need my mother's assets to start up another business or feed the kids. There were countless other ways he could generate the capital he needed, he still had assets, lands across the country, possible creditors, and the quarry—if he put the effort in managing it—which after all, was still operating although at its lowest productivity.

Regarding his side of the family, if the kids starving was, in fact, of major concern to them, they had two options: lend him some money, or even better, relinquish whatever money or business they had stolen from my father. But they went for neither of them. Nor did they mention my father's promiscuity and incestual relationship, nor did they consider how my mother felt about all this. They rather stood barking at her, demanding that she sell her only possession. I agree with my mother when she says that the challenge of her house was a contention of power and pride between my mother and my dad and his family. As a matter of fact, what was at stake was the dignity of a man socially expected to prevail over his wife for the sake of his family name, even moreso when such a family name had long gone down the drain. In other words, my father and his family were angry because my father had become half the man he used to be while my mother, in contrast, had quietly, on the side, and in a small way, begun to become more than the woman he had married. She put good ideas on the table, she was clever and she always managed to make her point amid the family mayhem. She had gained inner strength. This was the most intimidating development. She had finally come out of the background and was determined to run things in her own way from now on. No more smiling here and there, pretending that everything was fine. She spoke about everything that she felt was wrong in her house, including my dad's mistresses, his relationship with his niece, his role in his family and his mismanagement of the family assets, all of which infuriated my father even more. In retaliation, he burned her clothes publicly or gave them away to whoever was out there, servants, neighbours, anyone. He gave her jewellery to random kids to go and sell at the market and threatened her he'd bulldoze her goddam house down. Despite the pressure my mother was under, she maintained her decision not to sell the house in Pointe-Noire. That piece of paper my father kept on trying to claim, the property deed, meant far more to my mother than the house itself. It was the deed she signed to get back her dignity, to end the cycle of compromises she had to comply with when she gave up her life, including her studies, to suit a man who never demonstrated he was worth it. No, this time no, she would not live for him, no matter how angry he'd got. She would escape to find shelter with her father Olivier whenever the fights escalated. She told me she'd stay there for days. The only reason she would go back to my father and put up with all their problems again was for the kids— Happiness, Moon, Mavie and Monique. She was frightened to leave them with him. Finding a way out of the impasse was imperative, even more so now that the country faced political upheaval.

The elections of August 1992—the first multiparty elections since independence, forced in large part by the Western democracies—put an end to nearly three long decades of single-party rule, including the thirteen years of Denis Sassou Nguesso's administration. The new democratically elected president of the Republic of the Congo was Pascal Lissouba. However, Pascal Lissouba struggled to maintain control of the state when the allied Parti du Travail redrew from the coalition, leaving the presidential tendency without a parliamentary majority. Therefore, Lissouba dissolved the parliament and called for a new election in May 1993. Lissouba was victorious again against former president Denis Sassou Nguesso and Bernard Kolelas, a prominent politician. Kolelas and Sassou Nguesso's opposition responded to the election result with a claim of fraud, fuelling long-standing ethnic and regional tensions between the three parties' supporters and respective rival militias—the Cocoyes, Cobra and Ninja. The civil war of the First Republic of the Congo ensued. It erupted in Brazzaville, with Diata, our area, being one of the three main zones that was controlled by a militia group. All of a sudden, Brazzaville had a curfew in effect and gunshots could be heard across the city every day. Every day there was news of arbitrary arrests, detentions, the torture of civilians and murders. There were rapes, looting, arson and summary executions at roadblocks.

Brazzaville was burning and so was the climate in our home. My parents' relationship had reached a tipping point, with my mother staying more with her father than at home with her family. The kids left with Dad were neglected. Whenever my mother returned the shouting, insults and fights over the deed to her house resumed. That was until the day my mother, unable to take anymore, brought the whole issue to a different level. She went to see a Congolese lawyer, Madame Trevie, about whom my mother had heard good things.

Madame Trevie received her in her office in the centre of Brazzaville. She was intriguing looking, the portrait of a liberated woman. She was a reflection of my mother, showing who she may have been had she taken a different path. They were both around the same age and Madame Trevie was the kind of woman Olivier had once longed for my mother to be. She had studied in France, married a Congolese writer and was known to be a pioneer for women's and children's rights in the country. My mother had no clue what to expect from the meeting. She didn't have sufficient means to afford a lawyer. Fortunately, Madame Trevie was used to cases like hers and felt sympathy, reassuring my mother there was no need to think about money for the time being, and that she could pay incrementally whenever she began to earn again. With Madame Trevie my mother, for the first time, saw that there was a way out of her problems. She was inspired and motivated to speak up about the conditions she had been living under and told her all about her ordeal, that she was being manipulated daily, that she wasn't like herself anymore and was depressed. She told her she thought many times about divorcing Dad but was frightened to be left with nothing and to lose the kids. She dreaded thinking what could happen to the girls if he took them to Benin. Were they going to be happy? Would he be able to look after them? What if he made them marry against their will? Would she be able to see them again if they got pregnant? Boys and girls were not the same in our country, she stressed.

Madam Trevie knew this very well. First, she reassured my mother that asking for a divorce was indeed the right step to take in this instance, and second, based on my mother's declarations, my mother would retain custody of the kids under the current Congolese legislation and she would maintain her right to keep her house in Pointe-Noire. Madam Trevie told her there was a good chance that she would gain ownership of the house in Brazzaville too if she won custody of the children. From Madam Trevie, my mother learnt that she had rights as a woman and mother and that there was an entire functioning legal apparatus that ran parallel to the ignorant, popular misconceptions that had dominated her adult life. For those who knew how to navigate the law, there were several little-known articles that protected people like her against people like my father and his family. My mother learned that she didn't have to fight this fight alone. Indeed, she could fight, win and finish with my father once and for all and start a new life. The lawyer was confident in the outcome of her case because she knew my father by reputation and was familiar with his misconduct, as well as with the pile of cases that had been filed against him in the tribunal over time. After a series of visits, my mother told me she felt relieved when the lawyer told her, 'Now you don't have to put up with him anymore. I will take it from here and get you divorced. I just want you to take your kids and go to your mother for a while.'

Madame Trevie sent her to her mother because she lived in Sibiti, deep in the rural inland of Congo, which was hostile to foreigners and even more so in times of ethnic- and regional-based wars. Given the political circumstances, my father, a Beninese, would have never dared to venture to look for my mother in the middle of nowhere unless he was up for getting slashed with a machete. So it was. My mother went back home to her kids. She spoke with them about her plans. Both Happiness and Moon turned down her invitation, choosing to remain in Brazzaville with Dad, while Mavie and Monique accepted to escape with their mother. She waited for night. Then, with Monique and Mavie, she set off from the house. She helped the girls to climb the house walls since the main gate was locked, and only Dad had the keys. My mother and my two sisters climbed over the house walls and none of them saw my father ever again.

The reason behind Happiness and Moon's decision to stay in a city that was being ravaged by a civil war has always remained obscure to me. It was only in my mother's account that I understood a bit better about what caused the two kids to remain in Brazzaville, even though her story really only applied to Happiness, as she didn't mention Moon at all. According to my mother, Happiness chose to stay in Brazzaville because my father would take him to Canada as he had promised. As for Moon, we don't know. Maybe my mother didn't even ask Moon to come with her, who knows? Perhaps, as a result of gaining her legal rights, she felt that she no longer had the same obligation to the daughter of another woman, or at least felt less compelled to care for her. What we know for sure is that Moon and Happiness stayed in Brazzaville with my father during the early stages of the civil war. We have no record of my father's reaction to my mother's flight with the two girls, nor the way he went about the divorce trial, apart from the fact that a decree of divorce between my parents was indeed issued in February 1993 by the court of Brazzaville. We know that Nicolette became his official girlfriend and moved into their house, taking up the role of mother for Moon and Happiness. Things were not the same anymore. The climate in the house had changed. Life as they knew it before the war was gone. Now, it was just isolation and the struggle to put enough food on the table every day. Our area was the centre of one of the anti-government forces and thus heavily targeted by the national army. People they had known had been killed and gunshots were heard day and night, making sleep impossible. Things burned in the street. People's homes were raided and destroyed by the militia. My father decided to send Happiness and Moon to Benin for their safety. He managed to get them onto a plane to Benin along with his girlfriend Nicolette while he decided to remain in Brazzaville. In Benin, they were lodged at Tantine Marielle Tawema's house.

It is strange to imagine our street, Massembo Loubaki, the same street my gang and I had hung out on, hunting for wild animals, building metal wire toys, watching my friends do acrobatics stunts, playing football, had become a war zone. I had accounts of the way the civil war permanently changed the lives of these old friends of mine, lives that back then I imagined were unchanging. Slim, the guy who worked as a servant and errand boy for my parents, joined, with his family, the members of local minority ethnic groups fleeing the area for one patrolled by their own. Another one joined Kolelas's Ninja Militia and went around with a machine gun. Others were left homeless as their homes were destroyed during an insurgency. Another died, an accidental victim of a random bullet. Pelé, the street barber and old football player, died as well. He was killed while trying to protect an old man from being pushed around by a group of officials. He put himself in the middle and was beaten to death. He died on the spot, right there in the dirt of the street where he was born and lived all his life, like a character from one of those American TV series I used to watch as a child, the ones with kids that enjoyed a full and wild life outdoors. Pelé died fighting his own local fight. Died, his mouth open over the dirt. A true patriot.

PART IV

Redeso and I

If there was anything more ridiculous than the idea of the civil war in Congo my mother depicted, it was the gap between us. It was not just temporal and geographical. It was a complete disconnection between two realities. How could it be that members of the same family could endure the conditions of a civil war unbeknownst to the other half of the family, while my side of the family was having a life, easier in comparison, in one of the most opulent and rich regions of Italy? I was living in Emilia-Romagna, home of the delicacies for which Italy is known around the world—Prosciutto di Parma, Aceto Balsamico di Modena, Parmigiano-Reggiano, Grana-Padana, Ragu Bolognese, and pasta varieties like Tortelloni, Ravioli, Tortellini, Cappelletti, Lasagne and Tagliatelle. I could ride my Vespa across the tranquil, fruit-bearing countryside of Toscanella on my way home, free from nagging thoughts. I would park the Vespa at the bike shed of the foster home and walk across the gravel driveway, perhaps whistling. I would go into my room and play one of my favourite bands on the stereo. I could do all of this while my younger siblings were fearing for their lives, living in poverty and witnessing their friends being killed by guerrilla groups.

While they were living there, we were living in Italy, and all the changes at the foster home had turned it into a whole new place. After Livia, Lorenzo and Klaus left, Denise also moved out. So did Telemaco, the guy who used to come by and squeeze our arms when he was happy.

New kids moved in, two young girls and a ten-year-old boy. Among the carers, half a dozen had quit as well, leaving the place to new ones charged with the same enthusiasm the old ones displayed at the beginning. Then, around the age of fifteen, Nico left. His mother had got her head straight and bought a house in a bucolic town in Imola province, which Giorgio, Redeso and I helped to paint one day. After several failed appeals to the tribunal of minors, she managed to gain the concession to have her son back. She drove the boy's stuff away in a van, including his drum kit. He followed her, riding a new racing motorbike his uncle had bought him. Except for a couple of times when he came to visit the foster home, I stopped seeing him, same with our gang: he came out with us less and less until he didn't show up anymore.

During our time in the foster home, Redeso and I attended a three-year professional chef's school in Castel San Pietro, near Toscanella. We also worked every weekend as commis chefs in a chic restaurant in a small town called Dozza on a one-weekend-each-shift basis, while keeping up with our band commitments. That summer, the supervisors decided that we could remain home alone, unsupervised, while the other kids went on holiday to Sardinia. It was an unprecedented decision at the foster home, to leave two minors alone for two weeks. This came about in part as a practical solution to deal with the fact that Redeso and I had started working in the restaurant on a full-time basis for the summer season, and partly because they were happy with our general conduct and consistency in managing both our work and our band. We had just opened our bank account with a good amount of savings and had proved to them that we were capable of keeping up with our responsibilities. It's easy to imagine our social worker at a meeting with the carers saying, 'let's give them a trial for these two weeks in preparation for when they're going to start living alone.'

Those two weeks went by fairly quickly. It was the first time we had been home alone. However, as nice as it was to be by ourselves, we didn't have much time to enjoy the house except in the evenings after work. We would hang out a bit, chatting and listening to some music, then fall asleep and go back to work the next day. The two weeks moved quickly.

The foster home bunch came back at the end of their holiday. Then school started again. Then it was winter. Then springtime. One day, the foster home's social worker and psychologist, Dr Randazzo, took us for a walk. It was a slow walk around the gravel driveway, alongside the fenced garden that Redeso had built with Franco on our first day there, some years ago. She walked standing in between us, talking cautiously, much like the other social worker, Ursula Del Rio, did at St Catherina and Sister Domenica did in the main toilet of St Theresa. The subject of the conversation was the same, as you can imagine, the difference being that the news was conveyed with a strong southern Italian accent rather than a northern one from a woman who had lingered in our imaginations for years. Dr Randazzo, with her glasses and red lipstick and always in a mini skirt had frequently been the main subject of our erotic fantasies. She said, 'So, Redeso and Redesof, it's time we start thinking about you going your own way very soon. I had a meeting with the educators last week and we concluded that you are ready for the big step. What do you think? You demonstrated last summer that you are mature enough to take up the challenge of gaining our full trust.'

'Ok,' we said.

'So, here's the plan. We'll provide you with a flat in Imola where you can stay for a year. Rent, bills, all will be as low as possible, more symbolic than anything. It's not really about getting money out of you, it's more about getting you into the habit of doing these kinds of grown-up things. You need to consider this as a preparatory step before you get fully out of care, as we did with your brothers, but in this case, you will be living away from here rather than staying next door. However, this still isn't a clean break from us. You will be still under our watch until you turn eighteen, so you will still benefit from our full support whenever you need it, and we'll ensure a supervisor will come to check on you regularly. Let's be clear, it's going to be a huge change. How are you feeling about it?'

'Ready,' we said.

'I'm pleased to hear.'

Redeso and I left the foster home a week from that day. We were seventeen. Giorgio, the new head carer, drove us to our new accommodation, a five-storey building in a quiet residential area of Imola, near the historical centre. The building, just an average building, was privately owned. Only our flat was the property of social services, as Giorgio explained. 'A family of refugees from eastern Europe lived there last,' he said. 'It's a big flat for just the two of you, you're going to see, but it was the only option available. The one we meant to give you just got flooded by the upstairs neighbours and will take time before it gets all sorted out.'

He was right. The flat was big. Designed for a big family, not for two kids. There were three spacious bedrooms—two singles and one double—a big living room with a sofa and a TV, a round table and a balcony. There was enough space for a dining table to comfortably fit in the kitchen, which also had a balcony. There was a storage space, a laundry room and a bathroom with a bathtub and a window overlooking the garden.

Finally, we had a house, like normal people, yet it was also the most depressing place I had ever set foot in. I couldn't explain why, but that was how I felt, very depressed. Maybe because it was so big, so unfamiliar and impersonal. It was a signpost of another big change in our life, but one we had to undertake alone this time. Maybe it was because it was the most normal place I had ever lived. Maybe it was fear. Maybe it was the pain of all that we had left behind. Maybe it was the sensation of stepping out of a shitty situation to another shitty situation. Whatever it was, something about that place brought me back to the same feeling I had when we had entered the small clinic for the first time many years ago—a sense of entering a place that was not designed for my brother and me. I could feel the presence of the last family who had lived there for a few months before they were relocated somewhere else. I imagined them eating at the table and walking down the corridor, sitting on that depressing sofa, watching a depressing TV show of which they couldn't understand a single Italian word. Yet, part of the way the place felt was that nobody had ever lived there. There wasn't a single trace of recent human activity. Just the skin-tingling sensation of ghosts having preceded us.

What would the future the social service workers were preparing us for look like? We could not even imagine it. Not because we lacked imagination, but because that the idea we could choose a future for ourselves did not cross our minds. We just went along with whatever we were given. We were attending culinary school just because our teachers, seeing no other professional outlet for us, convinced us and our carers that getting into one was the best choice for us to get decent work in the future. They even organised a day out for the whole class precisely to take the donkey twins to see their future in the kitchen. It was no use taking us for a day trip to the Liceo Classico and Liceo Linguistico, the specialised grammar schools. Learning how to chop vegetables was the farthest we could go with our education. Culinary school, believe me, was not as fancy as it might seem now, with all those hipster-chef lifestyle shows on TV. No, back then it was just a plain, dirty job for low-skilled people. But we took our teachers' suggestion without question. We reacted to our new living situation in the same way.

We left our bags in the corridor once Giorgio left and went to sit on the sofa in the living room. The space was furnished with just the essentials. There was an oval dining table rimmed by six chairs. Facing the sofa, pressed against the far wall, was a TV stand with a TV and a video player. Blank walls and empty shelves surrounded us. We sat on the sofa, one next to the other, silent for a while with our dreadlocks, ripped jeans and 'fuck-the-system' grunge style. This was us making our entrance into society. And now? Where should we go from here? What is the first decision we should make on our own? Our rooms? Yeah, we chose our rooms. Redeso didn't mind that I got the double room. He took a single room, which was big anyway. We dragged our bags over and started sorting out our clothes. We had a pizza takeaway for supper that we ate at the kitchen table while looking at the view outside our window: a cluster of buildings amidst a few trees. We watched TV, then went to bed.

As soon as I lay down, I felt uneasy in my room. Maybe it was loneliness. Redeso felt the same. He came into my room and asked me if he could sleep with me that night. 'Sure,' I said. We had shared rooms since we were born after all. He lay down next to me, and I set the alarm since we had school the next day.

I don't think Redeso and I ever fully adjusted to the new flat. The whole time we lived there nothing felt like ours, and we continued to feel disoriented, no matter what we did to try to make it more ours. Of course, we were both still excited at being independent, managing a flat, and being free to do whatever we wanted, but that nagging sensation of abandonment lingered beneath whatever we did like a sort of parasite.

Now and then, we had visitors. Sigmund came by with one of his antiques—a coffee table—as a gift for our new house. We gave him a tour around the house and had a snack together in the kitchen before he left. A few days later, it was Ocean's turn. He arrived carrying a huge box of something like forty ten-packs of Kinder Delice, part of the unsold stock that supermarkets used to donate to St Catherina. Debra-Jo came to visit with Ugo and their son. So did Lorenzo and Klaus, with Klaus becoming sort of a regular, though we didn't have much to say to each other. He just sat there on the sofa, questioning us in his nonsensical way, subliminal investigations like, 'Do you think they're talking about important things?' referring to the lyrics of an American rock band we were listening to. Since we could not understand English, we could not really say whether the Faith No More and Primus lyrics carried as much weight as they seemed to, but for us, the aggressive tone of the music we were listening to suggested that indeed those bands delivered an urgent message. The thing was, we were atypical in Klaus's eyes, with our taste in rock music—for him nothing more than indistinct cacophony—rather than hip-hop, reggae or RnB, along with our unusual dress code, mindset and habits. We never turned on the TV, for instance, while at his house TV shows of all kinds were the background to his and Lorenzo's daily lives. Redeso and I actually stuck a poster of Alice in Chains on the TV screen as a political statement, which stayed there nearly all the time we lived in that flat. Plus, we were vegetarians and advocates for animal rights.

While Redeso was, for me, an open book, I could not say the same about Klaus. Although we were quite close in age and had lived together for many years, Klaus's inner world remained largely elusive to me. I don't think it was simply due to our difference in taste; there was something else, something about Klaus, a depth, that was naturally unreachable to me as much as it was to most people. However, he continued to visit regularly for a while. He sat on the sofa in his oversized clothes, sporting a cornrowed hairstyle, asking questions with a stutter amid conversations that were broken by long gaps of silence.

Other guests along with Klaus were constant friends like Andrea Mancuso, Gennaro and Nico. As for our band, we kept rehearsing at our drummer's private studio and performing under the management of Filippo Averna, although with less fervour, in part because there was something no longer appealed to Redeso and me in the overall sonic experience of our band. We felt it was dated in places, with the guitar too old-school rock-metal like Guns and Roses. We were after fuller sounds like the Rage Against the Machine and Deftones. Essentially, we were facing intergenerational discrepancies, as the other musicians in the band were ten years older than us on average.

In addition, Redeso and I had become more apathetic in general. I suppose that it is normal to have a drop in motivation when you're left suddenly to navigate life on your own with no direction and guidance. We soon understood that we had nobody to turn to. The supervisors, contrary to the reassurance of our social worker, Dr Randazzo, were part of the past; not once did they reach out to check on us. It was easy to conclude that all the love they said they felt for us, those stable conditions we enjoyed during our time at the foster home, the perception we had of being surrounded by people we considered our family, the safety net they embodied, the dog and the swing in the garden and the orchard, were all just transient. There was no point in pretending we had more than what we had. We had to come to the reality that these people, like the many others we had met along the way, the nuns, the priest, the supervisors and carers, were all just people involved in the temporary machine of care provision. They were not there specifically for us. They had their own lives. Once their job was done, all that remained was just my twin brother and me. What struck me most was to see that this depressing, true world they had tried to shield us from all this time was, in the end, a lonely place. Vaster than I thought.

But at least we were twins. Each other's best friends. From our mother's womb, across Congo, Benin, at St Theresa, St Catherina, at the foster home, Redeso and I had always had each other's back. Being a set of twins is like being a superhero, you double up in strength and perception and you can shield yourself from the toxic influences of the external world by disconnecting from everything, functioning and existing solely on a frequency that works just for two. In each other, we found the strength to cope with that sense of abandonment that followed us like an obscure triplet throughout the vicissitudes of our lives. However, sometimes that sense of abandonment was so strong that even our superpowers could do little against it.

We soon found out that the most challenging aspect of living alone at school age was to keep up the motivation to go to school. You miss school one day, and the week after you miss two days, and since no one is there to check on you, before you know it, you have fallen into a pattern of taking more and more days off until you miss a whole week in a row. We slept through half a year, stretching our hands out of the bedcovers to turn off the alarm in the morning, and then we would grab some food from the kitchen only to return to bed in a state of lethargy. Often the efforts of one of us to force the other to go to school, like, 'Come on man, otherwise we lose the year, get up!' were met with little success. The bed's grip was so strong that either Redeso or I would turn down the other's invitation, preferring to sleep while the other reluctantly set off for school alone. On successful days, the lazier one of us might find the strength to respond to the call and have a shower while breakfast was prepared by the more motivated one, and we would eat together. We would walk to the bus station from which we would take the bus to the culinary school in Castel San Pietro. There was always the possibility that on our way to school, we would come across a group of friends who, in the mood to ditch school, would ask if they could go to smoke spliffs at our house. Sure. We would hand them a pair of our keys and tell them to leave them on the table when they left. We spent mornings learning about food theories and then about more serious subjects, like history, chemistry and a foreign language that nobody cared about learning or paid the teacher any attention. Less than a school, ours was more like a daycare centre for losers. One of my classmates would have a wank in the last row of desks and clean his dick on a paper towel. Half a dozen of my classmates would spend almost half an hour of the lesson chatting outside in the corridor so loudly we could hear what they were saying. My desk mate, a neo-Nazi in training, spent mornings cutting out Nazi articles and listening to electronic music with the earbuds he shared with me. On Tuesdays, we would go down to the gymnasium to have a couple of hours of physical education. On Thursdays and Fridays, we had kitchen practice all day. We would put on our chef's uniforms, gather in groups around working tables and learn how to skin still wiggling eels and practice cutting meat with half of a cow. Then we would go back home in the afternoon. If the group of school ditchers was still there, half dead on our sofa, we would have a puff from their last spliff and hang around with them until they left.

Our house turned out to be a resourceful place for many of our friends. We found Gennaro inside a few times after school; he had broken in using an X-ray sheet to open the door. Sigmund would come by regularly with his new girlfriend to spend the whole day in one of the rooms in an environment that I suppose was cosier than his room at St Catherina. Another day, we found Lorenzo in the house, eating our food and watching TV. He said his band, the 4-More, was about to record a single and he asked if he could come write lyrics and rehearse here in the morning since it was empty and quiet. For a while, we also hosted a hippy guy who had escaped from home until his dad, an eminent officer in Imola's police department, came to force him out.

Then one day, Redeso and Andrea Mancuso went for a night out in Bologna. They went to a venue called Ca de Mandorli, a place that would become our first choice for dancing to music like the Pixies, dEUS, Sonic Youth and Violent Femmes, plus all our grunge heroes—Nirvana, Soundgarden and Alice In Chains—and some punk like the Ramones and Green Day, and some bands like the Beastie Boys and Cypress Hill to fill the hip-hop slot. On that first night, they met Gerda. It happened at the bar in the outdoor garden, she was drinking with a goth girl and a grunge kid. Gerda, a fellow product of Seattle's musical revolution, instantly liked Redeso and Andrea Mancuso and approached them. She introduced them to her other two friends as well. That night was the start of a very important chapter in our life.

I was lying on the sofa in our home in Imola after my night shift at the restaurant when I heard the clatter of people walking up the stairs of the building to our door. I could hear Redeso and Andrea Mancuso's voices among the effervescent chatter, then the sound of the key opening the door and Andrea Mancuso and Redeso with a dozen other people poured into the room. I was introduced to them. There was a couple in denim jeans. A kid with a horned Jamiroquai-style hat who we obviously renamed Jami. Then the goth girl. A hippie rocker copy of Jesus Christ with his best friend, a long dark-haired, Peruvian-looking boy. There was a pretty, coquette version of Courtney Love, and, of course, Gerda, the leader of the gang, her magnificent smile and ever-enthusiastic deep green eyes lighting up as if she saw shiny diamonds wherever she looked.

'It's a joke that you're called Redesof and him Redeso, right?' she asked me, leading me to believe my brother and Andrea Mancuso had tried to convince her all the way here that we had the same name. She shook her head in disbelief when I confirmed I was indeed Redesof.

'These guys are fucked!'

It was new to me, I'd say subversive, and even encouraging, to go from complete silence to have a group of noisy drunken people in the room, with Andrea Mancuso and Redeso interacting with them as if they had been friends forever. Something in our life had just shifted. In our living room were suddenly a group of artistic dissidents with multi-coloured hair, like-minded people. People you'd be hard-pressed to find in Imola back then and who could only have come from the underground scene of Bologna. We had fun that night, hanging out until the early hours of the morning chatting and listening to our favourite music. In between the three bedrooms and the sofa, we sorted everyone out for a sleepover, and when I woke up, many had already left. But what started there was something meaningful for us. Our new friends from Bologna began to come to our house frequently and each time brought someone new with them. We reached a point where people would settle into our home on a random basis, with some who would stay there all week, some who came and went, and some who came for an evening or just the weekend. There were always people. They would sleep at ours and go to school the morning after, most of them at art school in Bologna since we were all kids still. The oldest of us was twenty, and the youngest was Jami, who was fifteen and had parents who were cool enough to let him sleep wherever. Gerda stuck a sign saying 'Melrose Place' outside the door and with it our council flat had turned into a little squat. Everyone contributed in their own way to manage the house, by cleaning, shopping and cooking, all done spontaneously. It was our small revolution. I remember people bringing their own musical instruments, like guitars and djembe and we made the downstairs neighbours' lives hell as we all sang 'Desire' by the Smashing Pumpkins, Soundgarden, Nirvana, Alice In Chains and early Red Hot Chilli Peppers and danced to Dinosaur Jr, Faith No More and Suicidal Tendencies. We enjoyed our time bouncing on a bed frame with metal springs that somebody had dragged from outside on the balcony. We travelled together to see Primus in Rimini, and The Ramones and Skunk Anansi in Faenza. Redeso, wearing his trusty Jim Morrison t-shirt, climbed onstage to hug Kurt Cobain at a Nirvana concert in Modena, dodging the security and throwing himself to the crowd below. Andrea Mancuso sang 'Smells Like Teen Spirit' at the top of his lungs, along with his living legend.

We would bring beers back home and tap drumsticks on every possible surface we came across. We would make up games and debate our theories on life and the ideal society, while Jami would read some passages by the Beat Generation under the table in the living room, his favourite spot. The goth girl would paint something on the floor while the Courtney Love double, often a bit down, would draw her own world in her diary. We were all rebels being educated by Kurt Cobain, while he shouted from the top of his lungs to rape him. Kurt Cobain told us about the animals he picked up on the street to bring safely home. He told us about the blurred spaces in life when he would dress like a woman and go to school. He screamed. Hung and swung from a chandelier. He threw himself against the drum kit, played guitar crouched down over the stage speaker like he never had enough of the sound his band sent across over the audience, like he wanted to hear it himself too with the same intensity his audience perceived it, even louder in fact, so that he could be flooded with his own nirvana.

One of the last additions, another friend of Gerda, was a big-eyed art student with a buzzcut, who went by the name of Miriam. She wore a mini skirt and Dr Martens the first day she came around and stole Redeso's heart on the spot. He doubted that she felt the same for him.

It was late in the night when everyone was collapsing to sleep wherever they found space, after another day of partying and chatting, that he was walking to his room and she came with him.

'I think it's not the best idea,' he told her, 'for us to sleep together since I don't feel indifferent toward you.'

'Why do you think I'm here?' she said.

They kissed. Their relationship started.

Miriam was my twin brother's first long-term relationship, the first in which he felt very much involved and experienced for the first time what was possible to feel while simply taking a walk and holding hands with another person or sitting with them on benches at the park. He paid visits to her house in Bologna holding a bouquet of flowers, where they would dive into conversations in her bedroom about music and whatever came to their minds. She, like Redeso, performed in a band, as a singer, and it turned out she was also a compulsive drawer. She drew all the time and showed Redeso her works, mostly done in pencil, with lots of portraits and sketches of people in their daily lives. She was very talented. Once Redeso was introduced to Miriam's family, a younger brother and her single mother, he became a regular presence in their modest flat in the historical centre of Bologna. Yet Miriam's mother, resisting the idea of her daughter making out with a black guy, never accepted him completely, never addressed him nor introduced him to others as her daughter's boyfriend. He was only 'her daughter's friend', despite Miriam's repetitive pressure and the arguments the issue created at their table.

'Mum, he's not my friend!' she'd freaked out. 'He's my boyfriend! Say it, M-y-b-o-y-f-r-i-e-n-d!'

Her mother never complied. Still, Redeso didn't mind that much;

he had grown indifferent to the reactions his blackness could arouse in people like Miriam's mother. In addition, the novelty and the passion of the relationship with Miriam were strong enough to minimise any undesired background noise. And there was Bologna, a place we were familiar with from our days out on the weekend with our friends. It was the next big city, our escape from the provincial life of Imola. But we had only known it as visitors. Whereas now, navigating it with Miriam who was originally from there, Redeso could live the city through the eyes of an insider. She'd give him rides on her scooter around the beautiful city, over the cobblestone lanes of the city's old town, past shops, *osterie*, bookshops, ice cream parlours, along with a horde of other scooters and *motorini*. They rode down to the university area of Via Zamboni, past Via Irnerio, and then westward, where they left the old town, passing through Porta Zaragoza and carrying on via Porettana. They then took a turn away from the urban area and rode alongside the extended uphill Portico di Via San Luca that led to the Santuario di San Luca—the church that sits on top of a hill overlooking Bologna. On one edge of the churchyard, they stopped, got off the scooter, took their helmets off and looked at the staggering view of the city from above, with its typical orange hue as though it was permanently brushed by the light of a sunset. The red brick Two Towers stood up from the city centre next to the grey dome of the Basilica of San Petronio in Piazza Maggiore.

On one trip, galvanised by the marvellous view, Redeso crouched down on the floor with a smile.

'I'm reading this book,' he said. '*Jonathan Livingston Seagull*. Have you ever read it?'

'Yes, I did, the seagull who experiments different ways of flying.'

'It would be nice to be free like him, right?' he said. 'To spend the day trying new things out. To improve oneself, to try and try different things until you get them right.'

'Or simply for the sake of flying!' she added. 'Think if we could just take off now and fly over Bologna.'

'Just for the sake of it?'
'Yes, for fun!'
'We are becoming adults, right?'
'Yes, so weird. What would you like to be Redeso?'
'Me? I don't know. I don't think I have many alternatives other than becoming a chef. I mean, I wouldn't mind doing more studying.'
'Seriously?'
'Yes! You know, go to university and learn important things, not just how to cook!'
'But you told me you were average at school.'
'But university is different, you know. I could choose to learn what I want.'
'And what is that you'd like to learn?'
'I don't know yet, but I'm sure I don't have a bad brain!'

Then, like it often happens at that age, after about a year of the relationship, Redeso and Miriam's love story came to a dead end, largely because Redeso's sentiments toward her had changed. He had fallen out of love, turned colder, and found himself being increasingly more interested in other girls, to the point he wasn't able to hide it. Miriam had begun noticing that he had become more responsive to others than to her. She slapped him in the face one night in frustration for his sudden detachment.

'Why are you so cold with me? What's happening to you?' she asked with apprehension, but he didn't know what to say; he just sat in silence next to her, the slap he just received still burning on his face. He broke up with her a few days afterwards by phone. I was there with him that day, standing in the corridor of our house where the phone was, when he told her. Once he hung up the phone, he stood in silence for a little while, my brother, looking at me with regret for what he had just done with the vacant expression of a boy who had just sold his soul to the devil by mistake. He crouched down along the wall and cried.

'Why do I feel like I've been abandoned when I break up with people!' he told me in tears. 'Do you remember Marco, that kid in St Theresa we betrayed?'

'Sure, I do,' I said.

'What if it's going to be like this forever, that we go on feeling no attachment to nothing and no one?'

I let him cry for a little while and sat next to him on the corridor floor, back resting against the wall, facing the entrance of our living room.

'About Marco, you know,' I told him. 'I think it is the thing I regret most, the way we let him down. I wish we fought for him. What do you think is doing now?'

'Maybe he became a priest!' he said still in tears.

'Yeah, it suits him. *In nomine Patris, et filii et Spiritus Sancti*. You know, Redeso, I admire you, you're strong. I'm sure that we're going to make it right at some point.'

Redeso and Miriam's breakup set the stage for other major changes in our home. The *Melrose's Place* situation was fading away. Slowly, people stopped coming due to changes in interests, internal diatribes, boredom, all the most common human reasons. By the time we reached the end of the propaedeutic year we had agreed with social services, visitors to the house had dropped to the levels of the period before the activity of Melrose Place.

The end of the year also meant that we had to leave the flat. We received notice in person directly from the head of Imola's social services, on a day he came for a visit. Mister Grignani. With grey curly hair and a suit under his Montgomery coat, he grabbed an apple from our fruit bowl while asking for permission and sat at the table with us, 'I see you kept the house in great condition, twins!' He said while taking juicy morsels of the apple. 'So how did you find it living here?'

'It was good.'

'You know we have reached the end of the term we agreed for your stay in this flat. You have reached an age where you are entirely independent now. We are ready to discharge you from care, unless you need an extra month or two to find a new home for yourselves. Do you?'

'A couple of weeks would do.'

'Deal! Redeso and Redesof, I want you to know that even if you are leaving us, you can always come knock at my door whenever you need. Can you promise me?'

'Sure, we'll do. Thank you.'

It was the summer of 1995. We were eighteen when we left care permanently and moved to a new flat that we rented ourselves. With that, our teenagerhood ended, and so did all the time at Melrose's Place and all that had been significant in our recent life.

LONDON, PRESENT DAY
IX

Myself, I know now for sure that I cannot do it alone. So many times, I have tried to rebel against the *Word* and to adventure through the psychedelic forest of possibilities with my own lantern, to unravel myself from God's net, I deserted his churches and Him, yes Him, in different ways, by attempting to shape my credo into a practice that was free from any structure. I rethought it as a spiritual practice, I de-gendered it, de-goded it, I called it Being, Universe, I stopped praying for a length of time I thought would be forever, but in the end, I kept falling back to the same place. A point in my life where as soon as I allow myself to invoke *Him*, to talk to the man with a white beard, as I sat on my bed, or on the bus, or walking through the aisle of a supermarket pushing a cart, the power, the warmth of my conversation with Him spreads around my body, instantaneously establishing ties with my surroundings, unlike anything else I have ever experienced. Therefore, I give in to my newfound love for Him and I cry. Then, in turn, I feel the Universe the Being, the absence of duality and find that I have been praying all along to no one but a gatekeeper. And I say why don't you let me go, God. Because I'm still here, nothing has ever changed, despite the numerous mutinies I have carried out, I'm still a fucking Christian. By means of education, sure, but this is what I am. I need to come to terms with it. I am one. No matter how far my fight against my credo will go I will always believe in that which I am fighting against, in God, since you can't fight against something you don't believe in, as the quests of Don Quixote taught us.

It's another day at the desk. Black bitter coffee next to my laptop. Mental inertia gives way to fresh thoughts. Me and the anti-me sitting in the same place.

Diritto. Droit. Direito. Derecho.

It has been already a while since my mother returned home to Bordeaux and I still expect to see her come down the staircase from the bedroom she had used in the month she stayed here. 'Life wants us apart from each other, son.' These were her last words at Gatwick airport.

Madre. Mater. Mutter. Mother. Matter.

Diritto. Droit. Direito.

It's happening again, which means I'm off the right way or perfectly on it? Writing, or something about writing, or something in the way I write, has led me to this place I can't quite define, whether it's where I am meant to be or whether it's just a total disgrace. My acupuncture practice has fizzled out since I lost interest in the administrative and marketing work that is essential for any business to perform decently. The clinic's website has expired. I receive the occasional enquiries now and then, like one every other week, and they don't book. This is a type of practice where potential patients feel it if you are not in the zone to treat them, not just through your voice, but through the quality of vibrations your energy emanates. As my teacher of Chinese Medicine told me once, you need to be available, your qi has to be vibrant for patients to reach you. She was right. We are animals at the end of the day, with more senses than we think. My main concern now is purely financial. Both my current accounts are in the red. One quite a lot. Thousands. The other one is just overdrawn, plus, the Universal Credit claim I recently applied for had been rejected. I received the letter a few weeks ago. It said:

> We're writing to tell you that unfortunately you're not entitled to Universal Credit. This is because we have decided that you are a jobseeker. For Universal Credit purposes you have a right

to reside as a qualified person as defined in Immigration (EEA) Regulations 2016 but that right is excluded for the purposes of awarding Universal Credit. This means that you are a person who must be treated as not in Great Britain. Therefore, you do not have any entitlement to Universal Credit at this time. If your circumstances change, you can make a new claim to Universal Credit.

I went through the letter a few times but I couldn't grasp the full meaning of it, in particular, the part where it says I must be treated as 'not in Great Britain'. What should I make of that? What is it suggesting that I'm not here? Where am I then if I have been living here without interruption for nearly 12 years? It was not so much the fact of being refused financial help that has put me off, I'm ok with that, I've already had my time with benefits. I was more intrigued by this piece of information that suggested that I wasn't there. It intrigued me because it echoed a similar experience I had in Italy where, for some reason, I disappeared from the system. Was this the case again? Or was it just a reminder of the possibility? Or a little breakthrough into my underlying, fundamental state of nebulous location? Was this again a case of the Aremo messing things up?

I wanted to investigate it further, so I took the letter to the Job Centre. At least half a dozen Job Centre officers read it because no one could decipher it, officers who seemed less in control now with the introduction of the Universal Credit scheme. They passed the letter around to each other, clueless. One pretended he did get it but then was disproved when another one challenged him to a sort of hasty bureaucratic duel.

'Are you sure you haven't been abroad for a period of two years recently?' I was asked. I said no.

'Did you not go back to your home country at all, to visit your mother?'

'Yes, just for a couple of weeks.'

'What about your father, perhaps you stayed working with him.'
'He's dead.'
'So you went to the funeral!'
'That was fifteen years ago and, even though, the funeral took less than two years.'

'Right, I see.' Finally, the only way they said they could assist me was to give me a direct number to the decision-making team, since they were now, with the introduction of UC, stripped of the authority for final decision-making. They gave me an additional number for the Citizen's Advice Bureau, just in case, you never know.

I called the decision-making team. A girl answered from what sounded like a call centre in the north of the country. I explained to her that the letter I had received lacked any detailed explanation of why my application was unsuccessful. She read the letter through her terminal and, like the other Job Centre guys, agreed that the language used in this context was obscure and couldn't make anything out of that me 'not being in Great Britain'. I should have indeed been given a clear reason why my claim was rejected. However, the only thing she could do for me was to send a notification to the decision-making team so that they would review my case and answer me with more orthodox wording. She added at the end, 'Bear in mind, though, that with Brexit the government is getting tighter with immigrants.' That's fine, I said. Four weeks later, technically today, I received the new reward letter from the Universal Credit decision-making team that is meant to be clearer, but says:

> We're writing to tell you that unfortunately you're not entitled to Universal Credit. This is because we have decided that you are a jobseeker. For Universal Credit purposes you have a right to reside as a qualified person as defined in Immigration (EEA) Regulations 2016 but that right is excluded for the purposes of awarding Universal Credit. This means that you are a person who must be treated as not in Great Britain. Therefore, you

do not have any entitlement to Universal Credit at this time. If your circumstances change, you can make a new claim to Universal Credit.

Well, I have to just let it go. Fuck it.

I check the time. It's time I get ready to go and see your show, Telma, at a theatre in Bethnal Green which you invited me to. I take a shower. Get dressed and leave the house. I reach the place after about twenty minutes of walking. The event takes place in a sort of underground venue that has turned into a performing space for this one-night festival featuring several artists, including you. The room is full of creative people from and around Goldsmiths University. I watch a couple of Yes And shows before it's your turn. Standing on the stage alone, wearing a paper bird mask, with just your words and your presence to grab the attention of the audience.

It turns out you are an outstanding performer. A natural storyteller, set apart from the conventional and unconventional radicals and from the traditional performers alike. Yours is a different narrative. Unique to your face, both thug and diva, from Portugal. A bird in the wrong nest. The story you tell, a biographic excursion of the life struggles of an ordinary immigrant mother in London, is conveyed by a monologue and a degree of public engagement. You ask questions from volunteers in the audience. You invite them to sit next to you, to play with toys by your side while you encourage them to talk about their own childhood. As they talk and play toys with you, they fall into the role to an extent where they actually regress inadvertently. It's only when you switch into a controlling mother and shout at them to tidy up their room that they realise where they are standing and that they have been exposed and snatched out of the illusion of being in the comfort zone of their childhood bedroom once again.

I wasn't expecting to see a credible performer at work tonight. I thought I would see another pretentious performer; I always assume that real artists are other people than my friends or next-door neighbours, but there I was, staring at you, amazed. I'm seriously impressed at how you managed to deliver a strong and engaging performance with simplicity and playfulness.

I wait for you drinking a Becks in the middle of the socialising at the end of the event. I make eye contact with you now and then while you spread your charm around, talking and drinking a few glasses of white wine with people in the room. Then you come to me with your backpack on your shoulders. 'Shall we go?' I wave bye to the couple of people I befriended during the night, and we leave the place, both already tipsy.

'I had underestimated you,' I say. 'I thought you were average and it turns out that you are not just a real one, you're an outstanding performer. I mean, you controlled the audience with your will like the Pied Piper.'

'Oh, thank you, I'm glad you like it.'

'How can you stand in front of an audience and go on talking for half an hour, making them laugh and cry and all of that?'

'You just use techniques you learned at school. Anyway,' you add, 'I'm giving up, I don't want to perform anymore.'

'No way, people love you,' I say.

'I don't have what it takes. With my ineptitude at doing marketing and networking, I'm sure this is the furthest I can go: performing for a small audience in funny places!'

'Oh, come on, the room was full!'

'I knew all of them, we are all friends. There were lots of people because it was a multi-performance night, so everyone brought their friends. If it was just me there would be only a handful of people. I'm getting old.'

I feel shattered to hear you say this. 'And what you are going to do?'

'I don't know, I wouldn't mind just doing an ordinary job.'

'You wouldn't mind?'

'I don't think so.'

It's the first time that we are walking alone in the middle of the night. Here we have a sample of what our time in Bristol could have looked like if I had come with you that night, last winter. We would have journeyed there together by train, seen your show, had dinner out, drank beers sitting by the river and slept in a boat. But we chose not to. Where would we be if we had made another decision? Would it have been like this? Because this, what we have now, in this very moment, is nice.

The night gets tighter around us. Tighter and more beautiful. Cars and buses pass Cambridge Heath Road at the crossroads with Hackney Road. Fried chicken and kebab shops are halfway full. We walk next to each other, my hands in my pockets, yours in yours.

Then you say, 'It's summer already.'

'Yeah,' I say.

'When I think that I'm really living here in London it feels unreal.'

'I know what you mean; I often feel that I'm a copy of myself when I think that I'm here. Do you miss home?'

'Can't quite figure it out.'

'Your family?'

'Don't know.'

'Are you ok? You seem a bit down.'

'I'm fine.'

Then you say, 'It's not that we know each other. I mean you have become one of the closest people I have here but I can't say that I know you.'

'What do you want to know, things like my favourite book?'

'Yes, for example.'

'Maybe the *Karamazov Brothers*? But I'm not sure, I don't know how I'd feel about it if I read it now. What's yours?'

'It's called *Apparicao*—Apparition. By Vergilio Ferrarra, a Portuguese writer. But, like you, it's an old passion that might not feel as strong now if I read it.'

'What does it talk about?'

'It questions the condition of being human. From the perspective of a girl who's never satisfied.'

'Right.'

'What about bands? What's your favourite?'

'Are you sure you are ok?'

'Yes.' Then you say, 'I broke up with my boyfriend a few nights ago. He moved out.'

It comes as a surprise, though I expected it would happen sooner or later. But now that it has happened, it feels odd. And I don't know what to say.

'How do you feel?' I ask you.

'Relieved, at the moment.'

'Do you want to go home, or do you fancy a drink?'

'Let's have a drink.'

The Dolphin Pub is right there, and it's open and looks quiet tonight, with some boring music playing that sounds like it's for karaoke and the floor is wet. We order two lagers. We stay at the bar, both standing up. I feel very strange. Suddenly cold, distant. Is it because you are free now? That is horrible. I am standing here measuring you in terms of availability or not, instead of focusing on how your emotional landscape might be looking in the wake of the dissolution of an eight-year relationship. And now that you are possibly free, I feel I just want to finish this drink and go home and see you less.

What is this? What the fuck is this? What game is this?

Is it that caustic Self-Regulating Love-Mechanism Redeso and I have borne since childhood, opening and shutting to loving people according to how close they come to us? Please not this time. Not to you.

Then I realise that you're feeling the same. Empty and distant, like you had come out of two big illusions in the space of a few days. Where did all that passion go?

We have our cold beers at the bar and then I ask you if you want to sit at a big table with five drunk guys; they have two seats available. You're okay with it, so I lead you to their table and ask them if we can sit. The five conservative-looking guys, unmistakably part of the new gentrified Hackney, look at us, sinking in a perplexity of drunkenness.

'Where you guys from?' one asks.

'I'm from the Congo, she's Portuguese.'

The reaction is positive though one of them, overexcited, yells, 'Come and sit down, guys, feel welcome in my country!' And repeats it a few times when he calls for a toast to us two, 'Guys, feel welcome in my country! You can stay as long as you want if it depends on me!' I never thought I would hear someone saying something like that in Hackney; Brexit pride has unleashed a curious class of people.

Despite this, the guys are fun. We join their conversation, hardly interacting with each other, until you tell me that you're going home.

'I'll take you,' I say.

'No, I prefer to go by myself,' you say.

I insist, even though I'm slurring my words out of drunkenness and am not convincingly capable at all. You refuse more firmly and grab your backpack, prompting comments of disappointment from the group that had been enjoying your sense of humour, and walk off. I stay longer, for a few pints more. Then I head home too. I fall asleep on the sofa with shoes on and all, shreds of the night I spent with you sluggishly seeping through my dreams.

I hear the jingling of my son's key opening the front door from the outside the next day, and the two little people come into the living room with backpacks on and the green jerseys and grey trousers of their school uniforms.

'Hey, Dad!'

'Hey, kids! How're you doing?' I hug them and have them sit next to me to get an update on the four days they had been at their mother's.

Now, if the Universal Credit team is right in doubting my presence in the territory, who the hell are these kids talking to? However, maybe I should concede one aspect to the decision-making team. Maybe I am nowhere. I mean, what is the place these two kids come to when they come to Dad's? I feel like they come to stay in a bleak, depressingly flat version of Never-Never Land when they come to Dad's after they have been with Mum. At Mum's, an English woman with a large English family, there are no doubts they are in England. They enjoy a sense of continuity in dealing with elements of white English middle-class culture in a large English basin of English artistic friends of their artistic mother and artistic aunts. She even owns a car to take them out for the weekends. They have an exciting, eccentric English granddad who is also a great composer and known pioneer of electronic music, who always gives them fancy English presents. My kids speak enthusiastically about their granddad's machines and computers when they come back from a weekend at his in Cambridge. With their English granny, life is always an adventure. She comes to collect them at Paddington station to take them to her house in Exeter. Granny's life on her English farm, walks at the English seaside, summer camps, choirs and crafting. Splendid Granny singing English carols at Christmas with Mum and her sisters at a fireplace. Then there are weddings and family gatherings at Windsor, and summer with an English uncle on the Isle of Raasay in Scotland. They practically immerse themselves into the sea of their own culture when they are with Mum.

As for Dad? At Dad's, they experience an interruption of that cultural swimming they were doing. In fact, the water dries out drastically. They enter the door and see a lone depressed-looking black guy sitting on the sofa with dubious connection with that world they have just left outside the entrance door, or to his own African or Italian heritages. Dad's house is devoid of any references. The walls of his house are blank, not a single painting or poster, or photos showing him in other contexts, say, him as a young person posing with members of his African-Italian family, his friends from Italy or the Congo, anything that could prove he had a past too before raising them. On this side of the family, there is no spending weekends at their paternal grandparents' house because grandpa died long before they were born. They know nothing about this man. As for their grandma, the same woman who has just been here for a little and tried to connect with them, she lives in France, and they can hardly communicate in the rare instances they meet. There were a few occasions where they met the rest of my family. Bernardo first met my siblings in Bologna as a toddler when we paid them a visit on a summer vacation. He saw them again a couple of years after, at my sister Mavie's wedding in Bordeaux. This was the first time he had a broader sense of his black family, surrounded by his uncles, aunts and little cousins. April went to Italy with Bernardo and me for the first time the year after, she was two; we spent two weeks of our summer holiday in Turin with Redeso and his family. We had a great time. Bernardo and Redeso's daughter, Ilaria, who was two years younger, bonded incredibly. Funnily enough, they look remarkably similar, almost like twins. I remember the girl looking for Bernardo's hand while we walked around the streets of Turin one day. Once she grabbed his hand, she looked in the direction of her father victoriously as if she had accomplished the long-pursued task of finding a missing piece in her life. Or a link to her dad and uncle's life. I remember carrying April on my shoulders that day. Redeso's second child wasn't born yet, and he walked next to me, chatty and joyful as usual. We stopped to get ice creams and ate them on a bench. It was a beautiful day, like the rest of the vacation. However, memories of our stay in Italy rarely came into conversations with my kids once we were back in England and had resumed our lives. There might be some recalling during the days soon after our return, there might also follow a couple of video calls until, eventually, everything would fade away and fold back into its natural course, and it would feel like we hadn't ever left London. Sometimes, I even question whether Bernardo and April have retained or revisited any of those holidays in Italy at all. Maybe privately? Do kids care about these things? All I know is that they never talk about any of them and I don't talk about them either.

I was reconsidering these thoughts, when, out of the blue, at dinner, Bernardo said to me, 'You and Redeso are atypical twins, Dad.'

His own experience of twins, he says to me, is one where twins cannot live without each other. Whenever he comes across twins, young or old, walking together, sometimes dressed the same, like the pair in their sixties we regularly see sitting outside their front door, on our street, who are together every single day, he gets the impression they wouldn't survive without the other. 'How can you and Redeso stay apart so much?' he asks me.

'I don't know.' I say to him.

'Wouldn't you like to live closer?'

'Of course, I would love to have him at arm's reach and go for a walk anytime I want, but sometimes life takes you away from what you want, and you need to adapt to the new.'

'Do you miss your mum, Dad?' My daughter asks me.

'Yes of course I do.'

'How was it to be her son for a little bit? Was it good?' the boy asks.

'Was it like it is for us with Mum?' the little one adds.

'It was good in a different way. I mean I like to stay with her when we are together, and I like to think about her when she's not here. You do the same with your mum, right?'

'Hm,' the little one nodded, pulling up some broccoli with her fork.

'What about you?' I turn the question to them. 'Did you enjoy having Grandma Sofie here?'

'Yes,' the older one said unconvincingly, while the other just shrugged her shoulders. It's an understandable reaction since during the whole time they spent with my mother they didn't manage to have a proper conversation once. As for me, I do miss her after getting used to having her here for an entire month.

Then I had an idea, I decided to play to my kids a passage of my mother's recording as part of her legacy and translate it to them live from French to English, so they can get to know her a bit more in-depth. Her digitised voice breaks into our dinner from my laptop:

'We were rich and we all ended up in poverty. Now I live in a small flat in Bordeaux. Not having much of an exciting life. I'm quite lonely. That's fine, God is giving us other things. Whenever we fall, we will start from scratch. All the experiences we have, feed us with intelligence and wisdom. This is our new wealth. We have always been wise and clever people in our family, but we need to know how to use it, like many things. The only thing I chose is the spiritual. If I didn't have God in my life, I would have killed myself, with all the problems I have faced. It was too much. It's when things are hard that He brings something that will dignify you. He brings the light. If your dad did everything right, you would be cashing in one million every month from your estates. But God didn't want this for you. He had other plans for you guys. He wanted to teach you about real values. He wanted you to use your own head to sort out things for yourselves. To have experiences, to be desperate, to work, to work things out, you needed hardship so that you could find solutions for those problems. I have to fight to make my ends meet now. I buy my merchandise, second-hand electronic goods that I ship to Congo, and I go to Congo myself to sell them. I sit outside there, selling TVs outside with the sun burning me. In the evening I bring any earnings I made to the bank and I start all over again the day after. I have a couple of people helping me to sell. Once we finish, we go home.'

I realise something has shifted in them at the end of the recording. There is a glimmer in their eyes as they stare at the void, transfixed, typical of kids after you have read them a story and they feel connected to the characters of the story, maybe more so than usual as they have had those characters sitting there with them. It's a connection that only distance creates. I see that they finally get my mother. They got closer to her. I also realise at that moment who the true recipients of the story I am writing are. My kids. It occurs to me that I have something to give to them in the end; that heritage void I fear they experience every time they enter my house, I can now fill it by preserving a record of my side of the family story for them.

The Real World

Redeso and I were out of care at eighteen, when we left our temporary accommodation social services had provided us, for a privately rented two-bedroom flat. We moved in with Nico and another friend, Ferro. Being that Nico was still a minor, his mother signed the contract on his behalf. She threw a threatening glare at the four of us and said, 'You're dead if you mess up,' before she left. This new life proved to be something different again from what we were used to, now that we had to play by society's rules, outside the universe of care. All things considered, I have to say we started pretty well, at least for half a year, like four most respectable tenants. We paid our rent on time and managed our bills nicely. If extra expenses emerged, like some maintenance job that was on us as tenants, we sat down at the table, the four of us, to discuss it. Ferro, my roommate, a respectable-looking boy from a nearby town and freshly graduated as a waiter from the same culinary school Redeso and I had attended, was the most responsible amongst us. He was always on our case if things were not right, I suppose because he was the only one coming from a functional family where certain things were common sense. For example, dirty dishes can't stay in the sink for days. It's not a surprise that the washing smells damp if you wait two days to take it out of the washing machine. It would be Ferro who finally replaced the light in the toilet when it had stayed broken for a week. If it was for Nico and us twins, we'd carry on urinating in the dark for an undetermined amount of time.

Time in the flat in Via Cornacchia was technically spent drinking beers shirtless, playing acoustic guitars, watching MTV, fighting for fun, chatting and hanging around with our group of friends who'd come visiting daily—Gennaro, Andrea Mancuso, Franz, a mixed-race guy from St Catherina—and Aster, a 17-year-old Eritrean girl from Bologna I befriended one day on a train journey to Bologna. She was the most classy and exquisite girl I could have possibly come across. Aster brought a feminine touch to our otherwise hopelessly masculine group, prompting us with her presence to act less barbaric and explore deeper conversations, expand our vocabulary with more courteous words and put more effort into cooking and housekeeping. She'd come and generally stay over the weekend, or sometimes for longer if she had no school. I would sleep on the sofa and leave her my bed, or she'd innocuously share the single bed with me when more people were sleeping over and the sofa was taken, our heads resting on the opposite ends of the bed for as much space as possible. She was like my sister. She would then pick the first train in the morning to return to school in Bologna. The others went to work.

We were all skirting the edge of adulthood. None of us continued studying beyond high school, no one went to university. Not even Andrea Mancuso, the better positioned in our circle in terms of personality, family and education status; he had been to a grammar school and we all thought it guaranteed that he would continue along an academic pathway, but he began working as a salesman for his family's water purification company as soon as he graduated. Gennaro took a part-time job as a school janitor while keeping up his own musical projects. Franz ended up being a builder. Arturo, the kid who threw himself out of a moving car, we lost sight of. As for Nico and Ferro, both worked full-time; Nico was a mechanic's assistant in a garage, and Ferro was a waiter in a bar. Redeso and I didn't take any jobs yet, relying mainly on the robust savings we had grown during the intense summer season of culinary work we did. With the rest of our free time we just lived the day, working on our creative projects. Music-wise, we had changed the members of our band again for more like-minded people from Ravenna, including Andrea Mancuso as one of the lead guitarists, finally attaining our ideal sound.

In that period Redeso and I started working for a TV music programme on Italia Uno—Berlusconi's main TV channel. We were approached by a talent scout on the street on our way back home from the supermarket who found something interesting in us, took our photo and our phone number and called us a few days later to arrange a meeting in Milan with the producer of this show called *Jamin'*. *Jamin'* was a big show in Italy at that time, one of the very few Italian music shows that brought national and international mainstream artists to play live in the studio before a young audience. Mine and Redeso's task was to present the top ten charts from different clubs across Italy as external correspondents. All clubs were part of the Heineken circuit, which was the show's major sponsor. So, every weekend, we would travel with our three-man film crew by car to different Italian cities and different venues where we'd record our ten-minute act in a couple of hours. Then we'd have some time off to enjoy a little of celebrity life, eating and sleeping in expensive places, accessing VIP areas and meeting celebrities and figures of the entertainment scene on the backstage or at dinner parties. I remember greeting a young Damon Albarn from the Blur, and hanging with his band while they set up for their sound check in the TV studio in Milan. Or having Jovanotti ask Redeso if he could borrow his jumper for a camera shot, or seeing one of the Oasis guys getting upset because the sound engineer told him he was an idiot in front of everyone. All appeared dull and normal under the studio's artificial lights, and all these people came across to me just as people doing their job, so much so that I never brought anything special back home with me from those experiences.

The best parts were the car journeys with our film crew to the new locations, Redeso and I sitting in the back seat of Eugenio's, our team's boss and director, car. He was a hard-line communist with a barbed sense of humour that entertained us all when he went on his flat-toned, vitriolic rants about Italian politics and the placidity of the same music industry he served. Besides, he loved Redeso and I. We all became good friends on those hours-long car trips across Italy. Eugenio became kind of a coach to Redeso and me as he believed the Italian entertainment scene and culture was in desperate need of people like us—young, fresh, different and black, to shake up a landscape that was dated, tacky and tragically provincial. Through the kind of direction he gave us, I had the feeling that he was leading our performance to become increasingly more provocative and was using us as an instrument for his own internal revolt against the Italian show business. Unfortunately, he lost the battle. We lasted only a season, because we didn't sit well with many of the show's audience. In the producer's words: 'We have been swarmed with complaints about you guys,' he said. 'Italians are still not ready for two black kids presenting their TV shows. I'm sorry, guys, as much as I like you, I can't renew your contract.'

Eugenio drove us to the Milan station for the last time, furious, naming and insulting each member of that industry from the top to the bottom all the way to the station. We thanked him and the team for the experience we had in those three months we worked together. We didn't feel like we lost much, however, and went back to our life to find peace and comfort and familiarity in our day-to-day life in Via Cornacchia.

In that same year, in that flat, I began to write properly for the first time. Up to that point, I had only written lyrics with Redeso and a short story during my last year at the culinary school. I was the only student in my class who submitted a short story instead of the usual essay for a literacy class assignment on poverty. That was my highest success ever in all my years at school. I received top marks, and my literacy teacher read my work out loud to the class, getting emotional here and there throughout her reading. That was when I discovered something new about myself. I was a writer. I had it inside me.

I wrote another story, this time longer, on a notepad with a pen when I was eighteen, which I then gave to a friend of mine as a present. Then I found an old Olivetti typing machine in Sigmund's warehouse, the kind that would trap your fingers in between the keys as you typed and required you to type xxx over mistakes. Eventually, I got the hang of it and spent days writing short stories, poems, thoughts and new lyrics for our music. Then I moved on to an electric Olivetti I bought second-hand. The difference with this Olivetti was that your fingers could no longer get trapped in it and it had an integrated delete function that worked by overlaying the error with white ink. Then I met a girl who owned a computer, back then very rare, and she would allow me a couple of hours at night to transfer all my writing from paper to digital and save it on floppy disks. However, in all this, during all that time, it never occurred to me that I could take my writing to a different level. I never contemplated the possibility of getting my work published. I never dreamt about, nor considered being a peer of other published writers. In my simplistic view of the literary world, it worked like a caste system, where people like me simply didn't publish books. People like me didn't go as far as doing readings and speaking at conferences. You were either born as a published author or not. You needed at least a university degree, a chair at a university, you needed to have a special brain and be at least forty, while I was young and just a chef. And I was okay with it. Okay to just write for the inherent pleasure of writing itself. The world outside disappeared. And I remained alone with my imagination.

The only true big difference between life in care, semi-care and out of care was that once you were out, you didn't really know what to do with the freedom you had gained. Livia, my real-life mentor in the foster home, was right when she tried to give me the notion that freedom was not a straightforward concept. It was not a fixed condition that you passed into once you stepped through the gate from confinement. Freedom, I remember her saying, was specific to each individual, a unique freedom.

I didn't find mine outside of confinement. Nor did Redeso. It was not long before I had come to the understanding that freedom depended on the type of past you had and the way you had lived that past. Ours had created a vacuum that had sucked out a great deal of motivation to see through our options. We didn't know how to live. We didn't have enough training in living in the real world, no role models and not enough backup when the time came. Ironically, we had to do the same as when we were in care: fend for ourselves with no parents around. It was exactly the same shit, but we were on our own when it came to detecting the warning signs of when things would start to go awry. But we didn't have enough experience to effectively do so. We slipped into quicksand inadvertently. We sank without realising we had been sinking for a while. That was what happened with the flat in Via Cornacchia.

It turned out to be harder than we thought to keep up with our own responsibilities around the house so that throughout the year, the ship started sinking. We gradually let go of the meetings at the table and the communal shopping, nobody cared anymore about cleaning, cooking or whatever. Even diligent Ferro, in order to survive the mess, had to adapt and became a first-class monster of the likes of Nico, Redeso and me. We had corrupted him so thoroughly that he could find comfort in living in a trashed house, dirty clothes and empty beer cans scattered everywhere, broken wardrobes and a broken washing machine. The carpet in the living room was fucked, burned and stained with beer and wine. A side of the sofa had gotten crushed from our wild pogo dances. The balcony window was smashed too. The kitchen, well, it was more practical to just order pizza every night and the cardboard boxes piled up day after day over the stove and on top of the fridge. And of course, we made enemies with all the building tenants. They all hated us and saw us as delinquents. Soon our finances ran out entirely because of pizza. I remember withdrawing my last note from the ATM in a complete state of apathy and disinterest toward the implications of having drained my savings. A couple of months from the end of the tenancy agreement, our gas and electricity were cut off for unpaid bills. This was not much of an issue, since the flat at that point was empty most of the time. Ferro had moved back to his parents' house. Nico back to his mother. It was mainly Redeso and I occupying the house in the dark. We didn't even bother to buy candles, since that period coincided with springtime, so it was light until late. It amazes me to think how we literally did nothing every day for some of the last weeks in that flat. Nothing except for going for strolls, walking back home and sitting on the sofa, often with no money to buy food. I remember getting used to one or two days without eating, to opening the fridge, although I knew it was empty, in the hope of miraculously finding a slice of ham or something, until someone, like Andrea Mancuso, would buy us a pizza, or one of our brothers lent us some money. We ate the pizza on the sofa, watching the house fall into darkness.

We left the shared house in a disastrous state on our official last day, and we didn't even bother to ask for the deposit back since, as I would later learn from third-party sources, the cost of repairing the damage caused to the flat exceeded our deposit significantly. With no plans, no funds and nowhere else to go, Redeso and I started living in our car. It was a Renault Nevada station wagon big enough to provide room for us to both sleep and store some of our basic belongings from the flat. Sometimes we drove around town just for the sake of driving. Usually we drove at night, around the city, to the hills, in the countryside, listening to music and enjoying the view and then we would park the car wherever we felt like it and slept. It was an easy life. We managed it well when we had nothing to lose, we just lived day by day without expectations. We knew it could get worse or better, we just didn't know when or which turn it's going to take so we didn't think about how to get out of it. A little money soon started flowing in from a shit job of giving out advertising material door to door that we both started doing. We got paid in cash at the end of the eight-hour working day and we would spend half of our pay on a dinner out in a good restaurant, put some petrol in the car and drive around at night. Funny to think that we were meeting celebrities and sleeping in lavish hotel rooms across Italy not long ago.

One night, when we were parked in the parking lot of a supermarket, Redeso pulled an ID photo out of his wallet. 'Look,' he said, handing me the photo under the dim light of the car cabin. It was an ID photo of our father. It seemed to have been taken for the purpose of documentation, judging from the serious straight stare and the formal clothes our father displayed. He looked older than how I remembered him, wearing a blue tweed jacket with a black bowtie, his face fully shaved. In the place where we were, parked in a car with our belongings stored in the boot, the picture seemed so out of context, but holding it, and looking at it, also gave me a sense of continuity.

'Where did you get it from?' I asked Redeso.

'I've had it since the last time we went to Africa, many years ago for that holiday with the meeting, do you remember? I found it on a table in the living room, and it's been with me since.'

'Do you think we're going to see him again?'

'You can never say. Life's strange, right?'

I gave him back the picture, he put it in the wallet. We stayed listening to the radio until he piped up again, 'Do you remember when we used to play the bells at St Carmine church? You started first with the small one, then progressed to the heavier ones until you reached the heaviest of all, do you remember? We had to squat down to pull that one!'

'Yeah, I remember, it was so heavy!'

'Then, once it picked up, we'd let ourselves be dragged up and down with the pull of the bell! I mean, it was great, right! We have this on our record. We have done this.' He went on overexcitedly. His eyes glimmered. His smile, beautiful. 'One day if someone dares challenging you like: And you, what did you ever do in your life! You say, You kidding? I fucking played the bells of the churches of this fucking country, man!'

Another night, as I was at the wheel, we passed by a figure who stood waiting and smoking at the edge of the street at night, wearing a handbag and a mini skirt, waiting for a client to pick her up with a car. You couldn't mistake prostitutes back then in Italy. I don't know now, but at that time, street prostitution was quite common, most were exploited Nigerian immigrants, dotting some streets and standing a few metres from each other, but sadder than the fate of this mass of women who had left their country in the hope of more dignified lives was that we knew the one we had just passed. We had shared with her a few important years of our life. It was Livia, my best friend and mentor in real life at the foster home. She still had her blonde curly hair but none of that rebellious spark, only the death of her soul emerged from her grey eyes as she stared into the void. This corner of the city was as far as she got with her Citroen Deux Chevaux in her quest for freedom. What was the purpose of all the time we had spent in the foster home anyway if everything we had just came down to this: her selling herself to sustain her heroin addiction, and us living in our car with no purpose?

And her words, where were all her good words? Her values, the freedom, the beauty, the fight. As we drove past her and continued in silence, I felt that all that she had told me was wiped of meaning and power. With a mix of sorrow and anger and resignation, I felt that the only possible truth I should have taken away from our conversations was that there was no way out for people like us. Wherever we went, whatever we did, we were just lining up to inevitable defeat, never to find any freedom or redemption.

We lived a car life for a few weeks until Andrea Mancuso, who had talked to his father about our rough lifestyle, proposed that we come and live with his family. We accepted. Thinking back to it, I have no words to express enough gratitude for what they did for us. They let us into their home and gave us a room with two comfortable beds where we finally had fully rested nights. His parents treated us like adopted sons; our clothes got washed by his mother and put to dry on lines in the garden and our bellies were filled with warm and nice and healthy homemade soups. Naturally, we repaid the courtesy by taking up chores. We helped around the house, went out for wood with Andrea and his father, cut and stored and prepared it for the winter. During the quiet evenings, we'd play board games together and had engaging conversations before warm cups of herbal infusions. They were incredibly united, an amazing family, the Mancusos. However, it was anything but easy to cohabitate with Redeso and me. They had habits that Redeso and I were simply unable to pick up, like cleaning up after ourselves if we dripped on the toilet floor or over the toilet seat, things that angered Andrea's sisters hugely.

But the real problem was more with our general attitude. Instead of understanding and accepting any attempt they made to negotiate with us, we responded with arrogance. Whenever Andrea Mancuso's sister freaked out for one of our misdoings, we just sneered at her. If his dad, an amazing giving man, tried to give us sound advice we argued with him over it. We were always defensive somehow. In the end, we felt the climate became too paternal and restrictive for us. We decided that it was not working for us. Full of ourselves with ungratefulness, we left right in the middle of a meal Andrea's mother had prepared. We went back to living in the car, but this time far away from Imola, in Bologna.

The split between Redeso and I, after about twenty years of living in symbiosis, came about more or less organically during the time we were roaming Bologna. There was not a specific point when we decided or talked about going our separate ways. We didn't have an argument or anything. It just happened that Redeso found a girlfriend and began spending some nights at hers. I would drop him there by car in the evening, spend the night alone in the car and then collect him in the morning. At first, he would only stay there occasionally, then it became more regular until I didn't need to come and collect him anymore in the morning. They both asked me a few times if I wanted to stay for a night, have a shower or a warm meal, standing at her front door, the light of the house's interior shining at their back. But I always declined their offer. I would return to my car and drive off. I didn't resent him for leaving me alone; we reached a point in our life where we had to leave each other, just like we left everyone else. And like it had been with Marco, my love-coping mechanism allowed me not to feel pain, not even when I was separating from the person with whom I had been the closest.

Redeso was at a turning point in his life and it could be that our split allowed good things to move into his life. He settled in. His girlfriend helped him find a nice room in a shared house with four university students, he found himself a job as a chef, and his relationship with his girlfriend grew stronger. Her name was Daniela. She was a brilliant person with a beautiful attitude to life. Daniela worked casting people for TV and film productions and she was a key figure in the long spiritual path my brother would take throughout his life. It really started back at the foster home, when one of the educators gave him three books to read. They were *Siddhartha*, *Jonathan Livingston Seagull* and *The Little Prince*. He read the first two in the foster home and they had always remained in the back of his mind. Then he read *The Little Prince* in the last flat we lived in, a book that apparently changed the course of his life. That sentence, 'the essential is invisible to the eye', turned his brain on and awakened his interest in reflecting on that concept. To him, it meant that there existed a world other than the one that he routinely perceived where he could find true meaning and that the world he had been living in all this time was illusionary, a form of distraction from what truly mattered. What he found even more compelling was the fact that this egoless world was not at all far from us, but was right before our noses. Redeso was now eager to access that higher realm.

So it was on that day he was explaining his transcendental discoveries to Daniela that Daniela told him that his findings were like part of the teachings of her Raja Yoga teacher. She asked him whether he would be interested in meeting him and Redeso was. Daniela took him to her next Raja Yoga class. She introduced him to a man called Matteo. Redeso was deeply marked by his teaching. He decided to enrol in his weekly courses. Matteo's school of esoteric therapeutics was called Energeia. It was a school Matteo founded himself, where he taught themes concerning spirituality and the practice of meditation. The purpose was to gain awareness of oneself and of what dwells in your consciousness, your feelings, your masks and the motivations behind your behaviour, with the intention to transform them. For, according to the esoteric theories my brother was studying, every person has the power to modify their own behaviour, and eventually the power to touch their own spiritual essence and to change their life for the better.

Now that the process of big transformation was underway in Redeso's life, it was, of course, not free from side effects. He quit the band since he felt it didn't work for him anymore; our musical stylings clashed with the values of his spiritual work. Even his style underwent some form of cleansing. No more ripped jeans and rough shirts, but plain, clean clothing. He became quieter, in general, as a person, but somehow more present to himself, more adult.

With Redeso gone, the band began to stumble. A big void in the vocal dynamic ensued that I wasn't able to fill alone. The same songs we played with fervour together now rang out sloppily and unnecessarily dark when it was just me singing them. I lost the drive to make music over time and I took Redeso's departure as the final blow. Morale went down. Eventually, our drummer quit and with that the whole band project was over.

I was a single individual now, driving mine and Redeso's car and looking through the window at the world I had to face alone. I didn't have a job or close friends in Bologna yet, the city was still new to me and I didn't have much to do. I would park the car on a back street behind Bologna central train station, go to grab a sandwich or something and some fruit juice at a nearby supermarket for my lunch or dinner and eat it on a bench. Then I would walk around the centre of Bologna.

Unlike Redeso, it would take a little more before I settled down. After about a month of living in the car, with Redeso's consent, I sold the car to get some liquidity. I couch-surfed for a length of time at strangers' houses at night and roamed around town during the day with no specific purpose. This was the time I was being stopped by police on a regular basis and searched and commanded to show my residency permit because they had no shadow of a doubt that I was a foreigner. Black guys were just foreigners, not Italian, and they were right, as my residency permit proved, I was a foreigner. They checked my papers and then gave them back with the usual footnote: 'Boy, behave, or else we send you back to your country!' One day, they pulled me out of a friend's car, pointing a gun at me, just to dismiss me ten minutes later after checking that my papers were fine and that I had no drugs with me. Another time I was walking out of Bologna station when four policemen started walking closely behind me. I could hear them teasing me and sneering and it didn't bother me at first. I was used to it. It was only when one of them said, 'We should take this guy away and beat him up, for fun,' that I saw red. I turned to them.

'What did you say?' I said. 'You are policemen, representatives of the law, and you want to beat me up for fun?' I was dealt a good hand because we were in a public space and people had stopped to witness the incident. I repeated my point louder so that everyone could hear. At that point, one of the officers, without shame, apologised mockingly and dismissed the whole thing as just a stupid joke from one of his colleagues and they walked off. But something was chilling about them, the way they walked off giggling and tittering like a bunch of kids who just got caught doing mischief.

Another day, I was strolling around the historical centre with a drug dealer I met that day. He took me to his house, a studio flat, where we spent some time smoking pot. Then a girl showed up to buy some weed from him. Her name was Letizia. She was fun. Always laughing about something. Besides, there was something deeply sensual in her bearing, with a leg always resting sideways. And she was pretty. We got on straight away during the time she stayed there smoking with us. Then I walked out with her, talking and laughing. She asked where I was off to. I said I didn't know.

'I'm around, don't have a place.'

'Why don't you stay at mine tonight,' she said.

'Why not,' I said. Letizia was a student from Trento sharing a house with five other students from Trento. She shared a room with another girl, but still we fucked every night in her room trying to be as quiet as possible so as not to wake up her roommate even though she suffered from insomnia. With time, I settled in her house. None of her flatmates minded having an extra tenant as long as I shared the expenses and paid a little rent for half the single bed I shared with Letizia. We were all a good bunch. We made dinners together, played board games, watched films, smoked weed and went out, it was like a big family. Then mine and Letizia's insomniac roommate, possibly tired of hearing us fucking every night with whispered live sexual commentaries, left the flat and I took her bed, and finally we could both enjoy full stretched-out nights. Between me and Letizia, things were clear from the beginning, we were just fuck buddies, nothing more, and we were both ok with it. She actually had a long-time on-and-off boyfriend to whom she was committed back in Trento.

It was time now that I got a full-time job. I found a position in a few days as a chef in a restaurant in the centre of Bologna. With my first paycheck, I bought myself a PC, which I set on the desk in my room. I got Word installed by one of my flatmates, an operation that took an entire day, before I was ready to go. I transferred to the PC all the writing material that I had saved on the floppy disks some time ago at the house of that friend of mine. I started working on a novel. Life with students gave me access to university student life in Bologna to the point that I sort of became one of them, a para-student. I actively took part in their academic conversations when my flatmates received their friends from university at our house and we debated certain philosophical ideas or a certain semiotic analysis of, say, Kieslowski's *Three Colours* trilogy. I attended student assembles, political rallies and marched with thousands of other students in communist-led protests, although I didn't know quite well what we were fighting for. I hung out a lot in the student library and even sat in on some lectures when I accompanied one of my friends there. A few times, I went to a lecture by myself. My closer circle of fellow students, like my housemates, were part of the Trentino community, which, I discovered, was quite a big community of kids who had descended from the mountains to pursue a degree in science and arts and have a taste of metropolitan life in Bologna. It was at a dinner party in an affiliated Trentino house that I met Margherita, one of the tenants. I liked her at first sight, with her long brown hair, wearing glasses and a singlet and a hippy-esque flower-patterned skirt. She approached me while I was looking at a picture hanging on the corridor wall. We discussed the picture, what I was seeing and what she was seeing in it. It turned out that she was a photographer and the picture we were commenting on was hers. We laughed, and at some point in the following weeks, we started dating.

Margherita opened her life to me in a way that was a total relief to me. A fair analogy to describe what meeting Margherita was like would be that of a stray dog being allowed inside a house to finally receive care after a long period of hardship. Margherita's home, her calmness, her embrace and her eyes on me, treated my wounds, physical and emotional. She had me take a bath repeatedly throughout the week to eliminate that filth that had become part of me during the last years of unattended life. And there would be essential oils in the bath—lavender oil, almond oil—and music playing from a small radio by the door. Sometimes there would be candles, sometimes her, naked in front of me. We chucked away most of my clothes because she couldn't manage to get rid of the stink despite running the machine repeatedly, so drenched in it they were. Boxers and socks and some t-shirts I wore weeks in a row went directly into the bin. And we bought new ones. My belly was filled with warm, healthy vegetarian food she enjoyed preparing with me, like her pea soup, her homemade seitan stir-fried with veggies and soya sauce, her homemade jams and fermented vegetables and her blends of herbal teas. It was a new world for me. I felt like I was in a quiet place and at peace for the first time in years.

We started living in symbiosis, in desperate need of each other; I couldn't even go to the toilet without her. I have such good memories of our trips to her homeland in the mountains of Trentino, high up in the Alps, the winters with her parents in the mountain house in Pejo, her dad preparing his rustic orangey polenta on a copper pot over a traditional stove. I remember excursions in the snow-covered forest, both of us wearing thick woollen hats, me a pair of waterproof gloves and her bare-handed, sanguine hands, being more accustomed to the winter cold.

The rides in her Fiat Panda. Our domestic times when we moved in together to our cosy one-bedroom flat in the Zaragoza area of Bologna. Me working at the restaurant and on my novel when I came back home, she preparing for her exams and printing her photos in the darkroom in the cellar, the music of Goran Bregovic playing in the background '*Erdelezi, Erderlezi, Sa o Roma Daje!*' Or else it was a tarantella, her long hippy skirt spinning around as she danced, or Alpha Blondy, and then The Notwist. I remember the six-hour-long version of Kusturica's *Time of the Gypsys* we watched at an independent cinema. And all of the Peter Greenways and Fellinis and Viscontis. When she needed help typing her essays, I typed under her dictation because I was faster. I also gave her my opinion on her work, whether it was the university assignments or her photography, and she did so with mine. She read and commented on my writing and she was the first person who asked me this simple question: 'Why don't you try to get your stuff published?' Aside from the vast love I felt for her, the presence of Margherita was of great importance in my life, especially as she asked that simple question. As I mentioned before, I never considered myself fit for the universe of published authors. I was just twenty years old. I was working on this novel with no expectations, more like how a kid creates his own comic book. However, from the way Margarita put it, it seemed possible, the most obvious thing I could make of the material I produced. She demonstrated to me that the world was not as binary as I believed it was. We were not living in a caste-system-based society. She said that the quality of my work was absolutely at the level of a published author and I should try to give it the visibility it deserved. I trusted her.

Once I finished the novel, I sent it out to a small selection of medium-to-small publishers. I waited a few months before the first answers started coming into my letter box. All negative. They all rejected it very politely, some minding to note down the reasons why they thought my novel was not ready. Based on their observations, I wrote a second version and sent it back, but again it was rejected. At that point, I gave up, so unnerving and demanding it was, but not Margherita. She had the business card of an editor at a small press called Portofranco that she got at a book fair. It was a relatively new publisher with a focus on experimental, playful writing that was growing very well. She sent the manuscript to them herself. A few months later, we received a call on our house landline from the editor. He said he loved the novel. He wanted to sign me.

Sibiti

I hadn't seen my mother since our last trip to Africa when we had that tragic meeting with Dad. I hadn't seen her since I was fourteen. I had spoken to her on the phone and received some letters initially, but then we had separated as never before. Six years of complete silence had passed. In many ways, I had let go of the notion of her. The idea of her was wiped from my mind. Not with resentment, sorrow, or struggle, I would simply never catch myself thinking about her, nor about my father or about my younger siblings. If I did think about them, it was with disinterest, a remote memory of an African family that would come to me like fragments of an old black-and-white film I saw many years ago. Under these circumstances, I could not know what my family in Africa was going through. It is only now that I can reconstruct my siblings and my mother's life. Around the time Redeso and I had left the foster home, the lawyer representing her in her divorce instructed my mother to take Mavie and Monique to her mother's place in the Congo, Sibiti. Maman Sofie had to climb over the outer walls of Dad's house with her two girls after Happiness and Moon refused to come with her. The civil war in the Congo was raging at that point but there, in Sibiti, my mother began a small business. She started it with money she had made selling her jewellery, which came up to about 400 euros. Her business consisted in buying the stock of salt fish in a neighbouring village where production was favourable and selling it to another village where there was a high demand for salt fish. My mother started trading in other commodities too; she mentioned some sugar cane and some wicker products she purchased in a village on her way to Sibiti. This woman from Brazzaville, who walked miles from one village to another to trade local goods, soon became sought-after by the villagers. So it was that some civil servant of a province council came to see her to offer her work. They needed products to build a hospital and houses for civil servants under state infrastructure spending. It was ironic that Maman Sofie was being offered a type of job that was typically offered to my father. Like him, she had to put some money upfront to start her business. The four hundred euros did the trick. She recruited a carpenter and a builder, found a cheap cement seller in a far-away village and started the work. As the work progressed and money began to flow, she began to recruit more workers, buy more merchandise and diversify her business so that she could provide more than building materials. Her life improved significantly. Although grateful to René for teaching her the art of trading, she was happy to be free from her ex-husband's grip and proud to be self-sufficient.

But life seemed to have other plans for her. All of a sudden, my mother fell ill, severely ill, from a mysterious condition that no doctor could diagnose. She lost her strength, could barely walk and had pain everywhere. Even though she underwent test after test, doctors could not find the cause of the illness. She was taken to witch doctors to be prayed over but none of this brought any relief, In fact, she became worse. She lost weight, began to feel as if snakes were wriggling around in her stomach and her body was giving her electric shocks everywhere. It was unbearable, she said. She cried and cried. The pain was compounded by her conscience, the pain at seeing her sickness through the eyes of Monique and Mavie. After all that the two teenage girls had seen, they had to witness their mother wasting away, fearing for her life. They watched, powerless, when she couldn't walk, lying in bed day and night cringing with pain, tended to by other people.

As if this was not bad enough, the civil war in the capital entered a second stage of conflict in 1997 after three years of ceasefire. It is also known as the Second Civil War of the Republic of the Congo. It was fiercer than the first and spread far beyond Brazzaville, extending to the west and northwest of the country. Angola had entered the conflict to support the French-backed Sassou Nguesso's return to power and the result was a decisive surge in deaths amongst civil servants and civilians and the displacement of ten thousand people. Fearing torture, rape and murder and witnessing looting and summary executions at the hands of guerrilla groups in rural areas, civilians fled to the forests. Some intending to reach bordering countries, like Sigmund's mother Maman Chantal, contracted febrile diseases during the crossing and died. Sibiti too was invaded by the gunshots of merciless guerrilla groups, prompting villagers to flee and leave everything behind. My mother, still very ill, had to get herself on her feet and escape into the bushes with Mavie and Monique.

Here is when things became grotesque. My sister Mavie also fell very ill. She had already been sensitive to asthma since she was little, but now, in the woods, with the running, stress and fear of the war, her symptoms worsened. Once the only inhaler she carried with her ran out and without any means to find another in the bush, she had to endure the crisis wheezing and gasping for air. With both my mother and sister severely ill, they found shelter in an abandoned little hunter's hut, feeding on whatever was available in the bush, but food was not guaranteed each day. In the best-case scenario, they bumped into abandoned cultivated fields and dug out root vegetables like manioc and sweet potatoes. They didn't worry about poisonous animals, like snakes, in the situation they were in. My mother had to get her mind around the fact that in a situation where you are severely ill and caring for a severely ill daughter, with scarcity of food and militias ready to kill you on sight, any extra day you spent alive was already a bonus. My mother lost hope; she thought her daughter might die right there in front of her. And then she would die too. She had to come to terms with Monique having to fend for herself. Her thoughts went to her kids in Italy as well, to Redeso and me, and Klaus, Lorenzo, Debra-Jo,

Sigmund, Ocean and those in Benin, Happiness and Moon. She was sure she wouldn't see any of us again. She was sure that even the two little girls wouldn't see us again and was haunted by what we would imagine about her. That she had abandoned us, that she had disappeared from our lives without a word. After all, she had not heard from us in years. She cried, wondering what wrong she must have done to deserve all this, what debts was she paying.

Many other people were hiding in the bushes. Single families like hers, some bigger groups, some lone individuals, each separated by distance, lacking organisation. They were fortunate once to meet a woman who had a little knowledge of the therapeutic herbs that could be found in the area and she ameliorated Mavie's asthma attacks with decoctions she made. But still, my mother told me, they were all aware that Mavie's time was up. So was theirs. It could have been the end of all of them at any time there in the bushes, if not directly through the illnesses then by a guerrilla mob passing through. It was hard to read the intentions of random people they met, who might fetch water from a stream, or linger there by the bank to wash themselves. Anything could happen, it was just a question of chance, somebody with bad intentions could come at night, rape and kill without anybody flinching. They were in the hands of God, she told me.

One of Us

In Benin, Happiness was as much in the dark about our mother and his two little sisters as we were. He had had no news since the night they left Brazzaville. He was now eighteen, living alone with our father and his young fiancé Nicolette. Moon had just moved to Italy, thanks to the joint efforts of Debra-Jo and Sigmund, who had found her a job as a secretary for a friend's business firm, where her extensive knowledge of Lingala did the trick to overcome the new draconian immigration laws. For Happiness, there seemed to be no way out. All the promises our father had made to him, including the one to take him to Canada that had convinced him to stay put, had fallen away. He had to accept his future in Africa.

I was 22 when I received a phone call from him on my landline. He had eventually moved out of our father's house to live with a friend and started his first job trading clothes with Ghana. Eventually, this failed and again left him with no prospects. We hadn't talked to each other in seven years, so I was unprepared to hear his voice from the other corner of the world saying, 'It's me, Happiness.' The same boy who played the Sega Master System for the first time in a room many years ago in Brazzaville was now talking to me with the deep, calm voice of a man.

'How are you, brother?'

'Happiness! How are you?'

We chatted for a while, filling each other in about our lives, the line from the call centre he was calling from crackling and intermittent.

The more we talked the more I felt like I was talking with a real person, who in all these years of silence had been growing parallel to me in Congo. He had turned into a young adult, studying and trying his luck around the streets of Diata and then those of Cotonou. Like me, he too had laid on his bed and dreamt about his future, but unlike me, he had endured war, scarcity and that demeaning sensation of living in a country that offered only dead ends.

'I really need help, brother,' he told me. 'There is nothing for me here, nothing. You need to help me come to Italy.'

It was odd how, until that very moment, Happiness had meant nothing to me. He didn't even exist in my thoughts, and now his simple call for help reawakened the older brother's instinct of protection in me with a magnitude that shook me down to the root. I felt angry with myself for never having actually considered that my younger brother could be struggling in Africa alone.

The day after I met with Redeso to talk about Happiness. He agreed it was time we did something for him. We committed to working together on a way to get him settled in Italy. Using the same route Sigmund used for Moon was difficult; we had to find an employer who was after someone with Happiness's specific skills, like a translator of French and Lingala, but no one was pressed for another Lingala speaker, at least not around our circle of acquaintances. Neither did we have any employer friends who were able to manufacture a fake hiring. We made several visits to the immigration office to understand what options we had.

Those were not the best times for visa applicants. The immigration laws in Italy were worsening, largely for non-EU citizens. Romano Prodi's centre-left Ulivo party was in power. However, the opposition—the centre-right and right coalition of Silvio Berlusconi's Forza Italia, Umberto Bossi's Lega Nord and Gianfranco Fini's Alleanza Nazionale—influenced the direction of the immigration policy and shaping public opinion on the subject. Italy was going through a major transformation. The makeup of the immigration landscape, until recently consisting of just Filipino nannies and street vendors from Senegal and North Africa, had exploded to historic levels. The national picture had become multi-ethnic. In streets where you were used to only seeing white Italian shops, you could now see Pakistani and Afghani men with flocks of kids and wives in hijabs running food shops, new cheap call-internet cafes popping up like mushrooms full of immigrants of all nationalities. The black-and-yellow Western Union Logo entered the collective imaginary. And of course, these changes influenced the national immigration narrative. You would hear everywhere about immigrants and immigration, often in generalising and negative terms. The daily reporting of *extracomunitari* committing crimes became commonplace and created new stigmas, the media exploiting fear and turning public opinion against immigrants. Then came the wave of boats in Lampedusa. In Otranto. In Crotone. Thousands of people were killed on the open sea by bad weather, unfit boats or unscrupulous smugglers. The crowded refugee centres and the surge in demand for residency permits manifested in large crowds outside immigration offices. In such a climate, getting papers for Happiness would prove difficult.

I'd been giving Happiness updates every time he called me, which would be once or twice a week. His voice from an internet café in Cotonou soon became familiar to me, as my voice was for him. At every call, we got to know each other more as adults. I learned that he was religious, about his dream to go to America, about the fate of our old friends in Brazzaville and that he was not in touch with any of them. He hadn't had any news of our mother and our sisters in a while; it had been six years since they escaped from the Congo.

Finally, Redeso and I found a way through. He could apply for a student visa if he were offered a place in a school, so we went to talk with our ex-head teacher at the culinary school. Agreeing to help, the head teacher wrote a letter to the immigration office of Bologna where he stated that he offered a place to Happiness. It worked surprisingly well and Happiness obtained a student visa. We pooled money together to pay for a plane ticket to Italy. The last time I talked to him in Benin was the night he gave me the details of his flight to Milan. We arranged to meet at Bologna station where he was set to arrive by train. I remember that day, Redeso at the wheel of his blue Renault Kangoo, me in the passenger seat, driving to the train station.

Looking at my brother's sober look, at the neat interior of his car, the Arbre Magique hanging next to a picture of the Indian god Ganesh, it seemed hard to believe that we were the same rough kids sleeping in a Renault Nevada three years ago. I had changed too. Still quite scruffy, but cleaner. Both of us fully working, both living happily with our respective girlfriends. Sometimes I wonder how it was for Redeso when we split apart. It never emerged in our conversations. Possibly the closest we went to touching the topic was when, one night he and his girlfriend drove me home after we had dinner together at theirs and she said to me from the wheel of her car that Redeso talked a lot about me, that he missed me and would like to spend more time with me.

In fact, we didn't frequent each other very much, at least not as much as one would expect from a set of twins who had spent so much time together in the past. Still, we did see each other for walks around the city, drinks alone or with our group of friends, at mine, at his or for the yearly spiritual events his spiritual group organised for the community, which I attended every year. It was strange to imagine that the wild, blue-haired kid climbing on stage at a Nirvana show to hug Kurt Cobain and then throw himself to the audience below to be crowd-surfed across the room had become so responsible. Could it be the sobering effect of joining a spiritual group? Or maybe he had been like this all along but the type of life he was subjected to never allowed that side of him to emerge. Was he in less pain now?

Whatever the answer was, I liked both versions of Redeso. I sensed that the sober one was heading somewhere. Besides, his becoming a responsible person came in handy to me many times—all the times I was in trouble with money, when I would get fired and seek a new job or when I had fallen into depression and needed someone to talk to, I'd call Redeso. He would always come down to see me. Of course, it wasn't only me who benefitted from our relationship. I knew he received something from me too, every time he said, after we hung out together, 'Thanks, I always feel better after talking to you.' What I liked about Redeso was that he always had lots of things to talk about, and he talked openly about his life, his relationship, work and spiritual practice. Whereas myself I never had things to say.

Finally, we arrived at Bologna central train station. We easily found a free parking spot, got out of the car and walked across the street into the station, both of us feeling a strange fuzzy sensation of heading toward something previously thought to never be possible; we were about to see our younger brother Happiness.

We didn't have to wait for long in the station hall; suddenly he was there, carrying just a sports bag with him as he emerged from the crowd. A tall man, he had grown way taller than us, but his face, his bright eyes, were exactly the same as the boy who, holding his own luggage, had once tried to sneak through the departure gate with us at Brazzaville's airport. I did not doubt that this young man was Happiness, and he smiled as he recognised us too. After all those years, all those phone calls, after all that distance, we hugged.

Escaping Reality

My first book was published in 1999 when I was 23 years old. A small publisher published it. A one-man-run publishing house. His name was Paolo Marchesi, a well-known former radio presenter who was active in the 1970s, and was now an editor in his late fifties. I consider Paolo Marchesi a legend. He had to go through the editorial process in three days because he scheduled the book release too close. So, I had to drive to Turin where he lived. I spent three days in his house, editing my novel with him all day until late at night, while his wife served us meals and snacks and woke us up in the morning with coffee. His publishing house was really his flat. Piles of unsold books from earlier writers he had published were stacked in the kitchen and bathroom because there was no more space available in the storage room, which was filled with boxes containing even more unsold titles. During that first experience of editing my novel, I learned many things I didn't know about writing, like the right punctuation and when to break a paragraph, there were many words that I thought were proper Italian but were slang or local sayings and I made plenty of grammar mistakes. That was also when I learned I had dyslexia.

'Hum, a dyslexic writer. Interesting!' he said. We stayed there in front of the computer screen, smoking like two neurotics, and made decisions to cut, add and rewrite. At the end of the process, he was pleased with what we had attained. Mostly for finishing the editing in time to meet the publication schedule.

It stayed with me when he said, 'Well, now, you need to detach from this book. It doesn't belong to you anymore but to the public.' It gave me the impression that I had given birth to something. And that something was relevant enough for this man to want to spend three days working on it with me in his living room and pay me two thousand euros. Paolo Marchesi meant a lot to me also because he told me that it was clear from my writing that I wasn't much of a reader. So, he gave me a few books from his library to push me into reading. They were Beckett's *Waiting for Godot*, Steinbeck's *Of Mice and Men*, Conrad's *Heart of Darkness* and Dostoevsky's *Crime and Punishment*. I grabbed them, unaware that the works of this last author especially would become vital in my life.

A year after publishing my novel, four years from when I first met her, I broke up with Margherita. I didn't know why I broke up with her. We had everything—friendship, comfort, a good social life together and the promise of eternal love. It wasn't until the words came pouring out of my mouth autonomously that I realised what I was doing. The shock I read on her face when I told her I was breaking up pained me and haunted me for a while thereafter. She flushed, staring suspiciously at me with piercing eyes as though she had misheard what I just said. It hurt me so much that I was about to withdraw my words and tell her I was kidding, but no. I told her the truth. My words aligned well with my true feelings and my wishes of going on my way. I explained to her that I loved her, but that our life was too great, too fantastic, too perfect for me, I couldn't see myself keeping up such an idyllic lifestyle until the day I died. I was too young. I needed more experience before I could commit to a perfect relationship. She broke into tears. She said I should leave. I packed a few things in a backpack and left.

Since my work shift started shortly after, I went directly to work. I was working in this traditional Bolognese restaurant where I served as Chef de Partie. I worked in a strange state of mind. At the end of my night shift, I told the restaurant owners, a good-hearted couple with a son my age, that I had broken up with my girlfriend and asked if I could crash there for the night. They let me sleep in the restaurant's dining room over three tables put together to form a bed. They also lent me some blankets and a pillow from their house down the road.

I stayed there for a few days. The chef would wake me up when he'd open the restaurant at the beginning of our shift. I'd go wash my face, get a coffee and start my morning shift in the kitchen. Since we worked on a split shift basis like all restaurants in Italy at that time, I'd roam around the city in the few hours break we had in the afternoon and go back there at the start of my night shift. Then one of the waiters, a student from Calabria, offered me a place in his bedroom where I slept on a mat and sleeping bag placed on the floor by his bed. Then I slept some nights at Redeso's until I finally got a place for myself. I got it from another colleague from work, the kitchen porter, who was moving out of his place as he was returning back to Ghana. The place was a bargain—a third of my salary and was nicely located in the city outskirts, in Via Porrettana, one of my favourite areas of Bologna. The kitchen and bathroom were so small that you could only move sideways, however, the bedroom and the living room were quite comfortable. There was also a small balcony that overlooked an inner courtyard with a lone cherry tree. That was the first time I had a place all to myself. I settled in, yet not a single night passed without me thinking about Margherita. I missed her, I missed our life and I could not wrap my head around my choice of breaking up with her. Why did I need something else if I had love? Was love not enough? What did I need? One of those days I decided to give her a call. She answered the phone and said she wasn't ready to speak yet, that she felt hurt and preferred not to see me for some time. So, she left her house keys under her front doormat for me to come and collect the rest of my belongings. I drove to her house with Andrea Mancuso on his day off. He helped me load some boxes filled with a mix of books and clothes into his car and we drove back to my new home, where he stayed for a snack, then for dinner and then for a few beers, both of us filling the room with the smoke of our cigarettes. He smoked proper cigarettes, while I went with roll-ups. I was a heavy smoker during that period.

'Why did you leave her?' Andrea finally asked me.

'I don't know,' I said. 'I realised that I wasn't ok for a while in the end. Yes, I loved her a lot, but there was something in me, like a demon, that was calling for me to get out from that relationship. I have been suppressing this voice for long, until it just came out by itself.'

'And how do you feel now?'

'I think I did the right thing, for both of us. What do you think?'

'If that was the way you felt, I guess you did right. I'm sure you will get back together. I know you inside out; that's your girlfriend! Nice house though!'

'Yeah, all for myself!'

'Like a proper man!'

'Yeah, like a proper man! You? How is it going?' I turned the conversation to him.

'I think great!'

'Yeah? Work?'

'I love it. I love my work. You know, providing people with healthy drinkable water has meaning for me. Also in terms of sustainability, I mean, it's not just a paid job I'm doing, water is fucking important!'

'Cool.'

'Yeah, all good, man!'

Once Andrea Mancuso left, I set up my computer on the desk in the bedroom and immersed myself in my writing work. I was piecing together a new novel and that project was all I cared about. I would interrupt myself only to go to work at the restaurant and would pick it up again once I got back home. Sometimes my friends would call to me through the window from the street below, usually Andrea Mancuso, Gennaro, Franz and Aster. They would be sitting inside a car, honking repeatedly until I would bring myself to go to the window. 'Come down, rat, let's go for a beer!' Finding the idea of staying home alone and writing more appealing, I would often turn them down and stay writing until late in the night. Writing became my entire world. My redemption. But I also grew aware that the screen lighting my face up inside the dark room, the keyboard, my fingers resting on them as I paused looking for the right words, had also become a gateway to escape reality.

A King

A few months later, I received the news from Tantine Marielle Tawema that my dad was terminally ill. It was one of the strangest phone calls I have ever had. The first time my aunt had ever called me, bringing Benin into my life through my mobile, was to announce my Dad's impending death. I remember that day very vividly. It was the end of July 2001; summer was underway and I was walking to work. I was 25. I remember I was wearing a pair of jeans and a jumper and I was smoking. I remember I had just returned from Genoa the day before, where I went to join the protest against the G8 summit with a group of friends and the experience was still powerfully echoing in me: the train from Bologna to Genoa, full of protesters. The streets of Genoa, full of protesters. The blue sky, July heat, the view of the sea far in the distance and the clash with the police, people panicked, escaping the dense smoke of tear gas. Then, the announcement of Carlo Giuliani's death at the hands of the police.

I remember I was still in a strange state of mind; it seemed at first that my auntie's call was meant for another person, and I was about to tell her that she had the wrong number. Why would it concern me that my father was dying somewhere down in crappy Benin? I had never lived with him, and his presence in this world had never been a positive factor in my life. In every single aspect of my life, emotionally, physically, culturally, geographically, in terms of thinking, shared memories, shared intentions and priorities, my father stood so far away from me that I truly didn't give the slightest shit about his illness and the eventuality of his death. I remember thinking, *And now what? Do I have to take a few days off work just to go to his funeral in fucking Benin? Fuck no, God bless your soul, old man.* When the conversation with my aunt finished, I went back to minding my own business, 100% sure that I was going to miss his funeral.

Despite my lack of sympathy toward my dad's condition, however, the conversation I just had with my aunt was not fading as I expected but was lingering very vividly in the back of my mind. It grew louder in my head, until I realised that things were nothing like the way I believed. The picture was completely different. My father was dying, and I cared about it. No matter what bullshit I told myself, that specific death resonated with me in ways I could not yet fully grasp. But it did concern me, because of the physical, emotional, geographical, historical and cultural distance between my father and me. Because of his absence in my life. It concerned me because there has been nothing between us. Because we had never hugged, we had never talked and we had no shared history as father and son. But despite all of that, for all that we had missed out on, I wouldn't be able to ever forgive myself if missed his death too. His death was the only thing, the last thing left in our lives to share. It was immediately clear then that I had to fly to Benin. I called Redeso, who in the meantime had also received the news from Tantine Marielle. Following my same line of thought, he had reached the same conclusion. Then I called my other siblings to hear what they were planning to do. To my surprise, aside from Moon and Debra-Jo, who booked tickets to fly to Benin the day after, everyone else decided not to go. Some were too busy; others were short of money. Ocean, who had just recently come from visiting him for a few months before his illness, understandably could not deal with the hassle of going back to Benin again. For the rest of my siblings, the bottom line was that they were too resentful and wounded to respond to the old man's call.

***

Since my employer refused to give me the week off to go and assist my father during his illness in Benin, I had to fire myself. In addition, I asked for my holiday pay in advance so that I could afford my ticket. My employer complied. So, four days from the day we received the phone call from Tantine Marielle, Redeso and I took a flight from Milan to Benin. We arrived in Cotonou sometime in the evening, the usual tropical heat enveloping us as we descended from the airplane. If I had felt at home on my first journey there when I was a kid and half foreign the second time, this time I was completely estranged. As had happened the last time we went to the Congo, the border officer at the counter recognised us by name as he went through our passports, 'The sons of the *Man of the Shoes*. You guys need to come visit your old man more often!'

We took a taxi to the Tawema family home, the address given to us by Debra-Jo the night before. Not many changes had occurred since the last time we were there eight years before. The street was the same. So was the outer wall patterned with holes, the brown metal gate and the tropical tree shooting out from the Tawemas' courtyard. Maybe the only difference now was how quiet it all seemed. Attracted by the noise of the taxi, a servant came to open the gate to us. The Tawema kids no longer lived there, all had moved and successfully settled in the United States, one becoming nothing less than a millionaire after establishing a second-hand clothes empire in Chicago. In the living room, we were received by Tantine Marielle and her husband, the old colonel Tawema, both looking smaller and older, him with his eyes even wetter than usual and his body thinner and more fragile, nearly on the brink of breaking, when I hugged him. She, despite appearing robust all wrapped in a brand new pagne, gave the impression of shrinking. I realised for the first time, when she smiled at me, that she resembled my father. The house echoed as we talked, now that the old couple lived alone.

Tantine Marielle took us into my dad's bedroom. She had been taking care of him since he fell ill. Inside the room, Moon and Debra-Jo stood against one wall facing a bed covered with a mosquito net where Dad lay on his back. I first thought that we had come too late, however, judging from the smile we received from Debra-Jo I understood Dad was still alive.

I dropped my backpack on the floor and went to give him a closer look through the net. The Principal. There he was. Dad. After eight years, we were meeting again, although in such unfortunate circumstances. Dad seemed unconscious. He lay on the bed with just his pants on, so thin you could count his ribs, his cheeks sunken and his skin attached directly to the bones. The poor man seemed to be consumed by an illness that was eating him alive from within. Illness that apparently no one knew anything about. Debra-Jo told us that the medical doctor and the traditional doctor had visited him, but all were in the dark.

'He is in a state of trance, now,' Debra-Jo told us.

'What do you mean?'

'He's not with us,' Tantine Marielle added, 'He is somewhere else, if you wait a second you'll hear he is reciting a sort of verbal formula, possibly a prayer, nobody can say, reciting in a language that nobody knows.'

We waited, Redeso and I, staring at him from both sides of the bed like an archaeological relic of extreme rarity, until he started the murmurs they had mentioned. Dad started reciting what at first impression seemed like a prayer. A sort of mantra, his lips hardly moving, eyes closed, face still and his arms lying alongside his dormant body. The mantra was clearly audible, said at a fast pace, in what sounded like the natural and logical structure of a language. But what language was it? Didn't sound familiar to me at all.

Nor to Debra-Jo and Moon, nor to Tantine Marielle who, being our dad's closest relative, should have been competent enough to work out the language her brother spoke. But she had no clue, especially as Dad's language didn't match any local dialects she had ever heard. She told us, she recorded some of my father's prayers, and played it around to different tribe chiefs, to a linguist friend from a university, but the answer was that nobody had ever heard it. Moreover, she told us that Dad had been reciting it every day since he fell ill, even at night, breaking his activity only momentarily.

'He was already in this state when Moon and I arrived the other day,' Debra-Jo said. 'He woke up only yesterday.'

'So, he was conscious? Did he talk to you, did he recognise you?'

'Of course, he was happy to see us. But the whole thing lasted maybe half an hour, then he closed his eyes again and went back to sleeping and praying.'

'He said he was going to wake up tomorrow at 8 in the morning,' added Moon.

'What do you mean?'

'Yeah,' confirmed Debra-Jo, 'he told us before falling back into this state that he will wake up tomorrow morning at 8 o'clock.'

This whole thing was absurd from the very start, from when I received my aunt's dislocated phone call, to being here in Benin once again, facing my father through a mosquito net after eight years, listening to his mysterious mantras and being told the man had announced he was going to wake up from his trance at 8 a.m. sharp the next day. It was beyond my understanding.

'It's the language of the spirits,' my aunt said from the door as we stood all in silence listening to Dad murmuring his prayers. 'He's fighting his demons. Your father is a very brave man.'

She was right, if anything my father was an extraordinary man. Extraordinary in everything. Even in the way he was leaving us. A mystery kept wrapping itself around the life of this man, even on his deathbed, a mystery that would get buried with him. On looking at him, tuned into a deep meditative state that went beyond our reach, rather than grieving for the symptoms of a mysterious terminal illness I could see he was born with a unique privilege. He was gifted, up to his death, with the option to leave this world with dignity. Where did it come from? Where did my father find the inspiration to do what he was doing? How did he happen to be spiritually engaged with the process of dying? For that's what it seemed to me was happening, that my dad was busy there in the world he had sunken into, busy and focused on sorting things out in preparation for his journey to the other side. My father took himself through a resetting process. He cleansed himself, downloading both new and ancient universal codes that were keys for the passage and the existence in the afterlife. My father was realigning himself to the requirement of higher forces according to cosmological mechanics that were unfathomable to the living. But how did he happen to know how to do this? Was he taught? When? Had he spent unknown time in seclusion with some shaman deep in a remote enclave of the Sahara desert? Or was knowing how to die part of a collective heritage that only the brave had access to? Or not even the brave. No, it was not a question of being brave. Nobody gets to be rewarded for what they do. Nobody gets rewarded full stop. Things in life are there for anybody to attain. But only some of us get to grasp them because they can see the way. The right way. The only way.

Diritto. Droit. Direito. Derecho.
Right. They can see the *Direction*.
It's just a question of who you are.
René was René. He had always been able to see the way. To see what could be attained.

We spent the remainder of that day in the Tawema home looking after Dad in his bedroom, taking turns between Debra-Jo, Moon, Redeso and me. There was not much we had to do but feed him slices of pineapple while holding his head up in between his prayers. We gave him sips of water. He collaborated with no problems though he kept on sleeping. Sometimes he would say the prayer right in the middle of being fed. So we'd just wait inside the mosquito net with him, holding his hand. Redeso, who spent some time meditating next to him, told me that at some point in the day, he started gaining awareness of how a father–son relationship feels.

I remember feeling it myself when it was my turn to look after him. I held his hand and watched over him in his bed and realised that, contrary to my beliefs, I did indeed love my father. It was as if none of that distance had ever come in between us, none of that absence. Love had defied time and space. I soon opened up to him, starting a conversation we should have had a long time ago, in an ideal world maybe on a day I had just come back from school, say, where I found him home and working on one of his business projects at the kitchen table. Holding my father's hand, I bizarrely found myself talking. Yes, all the talking I had never done poured out freely and profusely, like I was another person. I told him about who I was. What I did in Italy for a living and for passion. I told him about my writing, about the book I had just published. I told him about my house in Bologna.

'It's a very small place, Dad, but it's cool. There is a single cherry tree in my garden, a beautiful sight from the balcony, you should see when it blossoms, with these beautiful pink flowers that sometimes blow inside my house from the window. I really like my house, Dad. I feel cool there, ticking all the clichés of the life of a starving writer. Yeah, I mean, sometimes it's hard, paying bills and stuff, but do you know when I come back home from work and lie on the sofa to read a book, I feel so good.'

During the time I told my father about my life in Bologna, he didn't stop a single time to murmur his mantra. However, now and then throughout his praying, I would feel his grip on my hand tightening. He would do this according to what I told him, participating in his own way in the conversation, reassuring me that he was indeed listening to whatever I was saying and loving me back.

GROUND

That night, Debra-Jo, Moon, Redeso and I had dinner with the Colonel and Tantine Marielle Tawema. It was the first time in all our visits to Africa that we had a meal in such a small number, with such silence, and the house so empty, so dark and cold. The fact that it was obsessively clean added to the coldness of it. It felt like the old couple had been forgotten by the whole world with a dying man in the room next door. But what I really struggled to come to terms with was understanding why their life turned out this way. Why this isolation? Where was everybody, now that the *Man of the Shoes* was dying? All the relatives and friends, all the witnesses to his outstanding life, the ministers, and the big businessmen, all those who had entered in the radius of the explosive life of René, and the glory, and the fame and all his women. Where was his young fiancé, all his kids, all the abundances this man had majestically been able to create? Here, in that place, in the Tawemas' house, in that very moment, there was no record of my father's life. My father was dying alone, in poverty, in a barren small bedroom accommodated by his sister. That was not the way I expected a man like René to go. However, it was interesting to note that, despite none of his women or wives being there, at least he was surrounded by a representative of each of them. Moon for Maman Chantal. Debra-Jo for Maman Natalie. Redeso and I account for a single birth for Maman Sofie. Did we come to his death by choice or did we respond to something else?

When we went to bed, our father was still lying face up reciting the mantras. Debra-Jo and Moon slept in his room on two foam mattresses they had placed on the floor next to him. Redeso and I shared a room upstairs. We woke up very early the following morning. Our father was still reciting mantras when Redeso and I got inside the room to greet our sisters and check on him. Then, I remember I went to the toilet. When I went back inside the bedroom he was awake, sitting up in bed, silhouetted by the thin clothwork of the mosquito net. Debra-Jo pointed at an invisible watch on her wrist, 'It's eight o'clock.'

Redeso checked his wristwatch and confirmed, it was eight sharp. And René, the Principal, was awake, sitting upright at the edge of the bed, his hands on the bed, feet resting on the floor, just in pants. There was something typical of old people in his expression, a dullness in his eyes and a crooked mouth, as if he had had a stroke, but he was lucid and present, throwing glances at each of us four, like he did that time he showed us the plan of the house he meant to build that summer many years ago in Brazzaville. It was an affirmative type of look, like he had acknowledged the presence of each one of us, though he did not show any sign of happiness or surprise to see us there. Something in his look was resigned. Life was just life. As he tried to lift himself from bed without a single word, Debra-Jo and Moon rushed to help him get up. It was when he was fully upright on his feet that I understood how severely ill he was. He looked more wasted away than when he was lying on bed. There was no way he could have stood up on his own. He looked at me and Redeso, then stared ahead as if to gather a degree of dignity while escorted by his two daughters to the toilet. They returned a few minutes later.

'We need to give him a wash,' Debra-Jo said. She instructed Redeso to help Moon hold him up while she went to fetch a basin with water and get some towels. Moon told me where to find some new underwear and a towel. I got them. Then Debra-Jo came back with the basin and clothes. She placed it in the middle of the room at our father's feet, and Debra-Jo took his pants off so that he remained naked. She and I began to clean him. We drenched cloths in the water, one on one side, one on the other, and we washed his upper body, his armpits, the lower body, his genitals, down the legs and his feet. It was when both Debra-Jo and I were crouched down cleaning his feet that Redeso said, 'Hey guys. I think he's gone.' Debra-Jo and I looked up to our father's face. His head was hanging down lifeless in between Redeso and Moon's heads.

'Yes, he's dead,' confirmed Debra-Jo.

GROUND

How was it possible that things went that way? It is not every day that you're there when your dad is dying. Even for people who live close to their father, in the same country, same village or maybe even in the same house. There is no guarantee that they are going to be there holding him while he dies. It could happen at any time without notice. He could die while you are journeying to the hospital where he has been admitted. Or during the night, you wake up in the morning on a couch near his bed in the hospital and discover that he is dead. You could find him dead on your way back from the toilet. The world is full of stories of people who were too late. But in our case, something that went beyond my comprehension had made it so that the four representatives of his family were present and physically engaged with him in one way or another, whether cleaning him or holding him, at the very moment he passed away. Despite being apart all our lives, separated by the Mediterranean Sea and the Sahara desert, separated by years of silence, different languages, cultural, political and individual conflicts, separated by wars and personal beliefs, we managed to be there for each other when it mattered, holding our father and cleaning him before his most important journey. I could not explain it.

It was just too absurd, so ridiculous, so displacing that my and Redeso's reaction a few seconds after realising that Dad had died was to burst out laughing. A laugh that only Redeso and I could understand, a laugh of twins, Redeso standing up, holding him, myself falling backward on my bottom, both of us laughing, with tears trickling down our cheeks, laughing to fill up the air of a room of a house in Cotonou, on a summer morning, in the event of the death of a king.

Tantine Marielle planned to set the day of my father's funeral somewhere about a week from the day he died, which was reasonable. However, as soon as she revealed her plan, Moon, Debra-Jo, Redeso and I cringed at the idea. It was only a week she was suggesting but it sounded more like a century. We were obviously not in the mood to spend an extra week in Cotonou waiting for our father's funeral to take place after all that had just happened. We all felt the need to get home as soon as possible to digest his death, like anyone would after going through a big event. We expressed our needs to Tantine Marielle to see whether it was possible to move up the day of the funeral. She understood our concerns and took the necessary steps to accommodate us. After a series of calls, she managed to set the date of our father's funeral for two days after the day of his death so that we could fly back home immediately afterwards. However, that meant she had very little time to arrange the funeral, so when the time came for her to provide a picture of our father to the mortuary so that the cards, leaflets and the plaque picture for his tombstone could be made, Tantine Marielle could not find a single photo of him. She looked everywhere around the house, she told us in disbelief and shame, in all her picture books and closets, everywhere, but could not find a single photo of her brother. What was even more surreal was that after she made a round of phone calls to the other members of the family asking for a photo, not a single one of them possessed a photo of our father either. It seemed the man never lived in Benin. Was this the Aremo's effect? The soul of the dissident prince who was meant not to exist living on through our lineage? We were incredulous. Incredulous that no one had a photo of Dad in his native country. So was Tantine Marielle as she shook her head between her calls. No one had a photo of him. Until Redeso remembered something. He opened his wallet and said, 'I have a photo.' We all turned to him, including Tantine Marielle still holding the telephone receiver, and suddenly it was there, the only visual record of our father's life that could be found in a radius of miles, held by Redeso. A guy from Italy, who had been holding the photo of his father in his wallet since he was fourteen. Since the notorious family meeting holiday, when he found the picture on a table in the living room and kept it as he moved from house to house and slept in his car while homeless. And now there he was, in the aftermath of his father's death, being the only member of the old man's family able to resolve the impasse of the missing photograph. We stood a few seconds staring at Redeso holding the photo in contemplation, at that beautiful portrait of love he personified in the moment. Then Tantine Marielle took the photo, 'This is perfect,' she said. 'Thank you.'

All the funeral materials were printed that same day displaying the ID picture of Dad in a blue tweed jacket and bowtie, his face shaved. The funeral care team came into the room the day after to prepare him. They washed him, put makeup on him, dressed him in a traditional white suit, placed him in a coffin and drove him to the funeral home. We went there in a black car hired by the Tawemas. To my surprise, there was a crowd of attendees outside the venue, although it was contained—no more than thirty people—among which were relatives and family friends. According to tradition, everybody wore white. Death was seen with a more positive attitude than in the West—the expression of celestial forces whose unknown designs people embraced with complete trust. So, you could see smiles mixed with tears in the crowd, some of the women crying, being looked after by serene and optimistic-looking people. The overall feeling was of a tranquil afternoon. The attendees chatted softly, some came to us to pay their respects to our dad with a shake of the hand, a hug and a few words, before disappearing again into the crowd. Then Tantine Ellen, Dad's closest cousin and best friend, emerged from the crowd and walked in our direction with her usual thrilling smile and sunglasses. She too wore a traditional white outfit.

'Oh, my kids!' Big kisses and heartfelt hugs. Then she felt the need to stitch together one of the things you say in situations like this. 'He must be so proud of you from above. You had come all the way down here for him. Your father will always be with you. Even when he was alive you were always in his thoughts. He wanted to do the impossible for you. All the plans he had, all the projects he worked on, the houses and lands he purchased, all his life he lived for you.'

None of us believed her, we knew that Dad was generous but also greatly a selfish man who fought all his life just for his own ego and we were at peace with that. However, we played along with Tantine Ellen, sincerely thanking her for her moving words. Then, after everyone paid their last respects to Dad's corpse in its coffin inside the venue, a quiet procession of mourners in white started from the funeral home to the cemetery. We walked in silence. We reached the cemetery, waiting at the rim of a newly dug hole in the ground was a priest with his helper. Dad's coffin, now sealed, was pulled out of the hearse by the funeral attendees and a few male relatives. It was then funnelled down the hole, all of us gathered around it. The priest went through the ceremony. At the end of his sermon, Tantine Marielle gave Debra-Jo, Moon, Redeso and me a sign with her head, the meaning of which we understood without the need for clarification. We each took a handful of soil and threw it over Dad's coffin.

GROUND

A Wedding

My mother was not aware of my father's illness and resulting death during the time she spent hiding in the bush. I roughly calculated that around the same period my father had fallen sick, my mother had fallen sick as well of a mysterious illness that no one could identify. She had wasted away like my father did. My mum was ill for eight months. It's not clear what forced her to leave her hiding place in the forest, but she claims that one day while looking for food, she, Mavie and Monique ran into a cargo train that had stopped on the railway that snaked through the bushes. It was customary for cargo trains in times of conflict to respond to the desperate conditions of food scarcity by stocking up wherever food was available—whether found in nature or trading with farmers—to supply cities and villages. In this case, the train had stopped to allow traders to collect bananas from a wild plantation in the bushes. My mother approached one of the workers to ask where the train was headed.

'To Pointe-Noire,' the man said. She knew that Pointe-Noire was relatively safe because a French military base was stationed there. Besides, given her illness and Mavie's asthma, she had no other choice but to reach Pointe-Noire. My mother begged the train driver, 'My daughter is about to die and I am severely ill, I will abandon my kids in the forest if I die. Please help us to reach Pointe-Noire.' But the only assistance the train driver could give them was to contact Pointe-Noire via radio and ask for an ambulance. My mother, knowing that it would take time before the ambulance came and that most likely it would never come, chose to go around the problem in another way. She was not going to miss the opportunity of the train going to Pointe-Noire. She walked down along the train with the girls and, making sure they were not seen, snuck with them inside the first open shipping container car and hid behind a cargo container of bananas. It was pitch-dark inside. Immediately, they understood the possible risks of a long journey with a shortage of oxygen, especially in a situation where one of them was suffering critically from asthma. The three of them went around the train shipping container car seeking air. They found some little holes on one side of the car and took turns breathing from those tiny holes.

After about an hour, the train stopped. As they heard the door of the train car being opened from outside, they rushed back to hide behind a load of bananas. They waited, hearing people loading even more goods inside their train car. Now my mother had to make a quick decision. At this rate, the wagon would be quickly full, Mavie would risk dying of a critical attack of asthma or the three of them could just suffocate during the journey. On the other hand, she didn't know where they were, and they could have run into hostile militia groups as soon as they left the wagon. She decided, however, to take the risk of the militias rather than put Mavie through another anguishing train journey gasping for air. So the three jumped out as soon as they had the opportunity.

Daylight, the noise and the people they found around the small station disoriented them. But she recognised the place as a little village close to Pointe-Noire. She walked the girls to the front of the station. There was a big truck, she said, one with an open van on the back, that was used as public transport by traders of surrounding villages to go and sell their goods in Pointe-Noire. With only enough money to buy a third of the fare for one person, my mother begged the driver to help them, until that man, moved to pity by the sight of the three bony and ill-looking girls, allowed them a free ride to Pointe-Noire.

Once they finally reached Pointe-Noire, they were three animals. My mother had no more flesh, just bones, nothing else. Mavie was pale and gasping for air. Monique's eyes were red. But at least they were home. She walked streets that were familiar to her and reached the house of one of her cousins she had grown up with. She knocked at the door. Her cousin, hardly recognising her at first, let her in, gave them food and cared for them with his small resources. Then he took them to the hospital. While Mavie was found to have developed a severe infection in the lungs and was put under medication, my mother's illnesses remained unsolved despite the many tests she was subjected to. They could not diagnose it, so there was little they could do for her.

Her last hope was now the spiritual. She left the girls under her cousin's watch while she went to a prayer venue, a sort of convent, where people in need of spiritual intervention are preyed upon by a group of spiritual healers. Apparently, my mother stayed there for a long period of time, possibly weeks. I just know that during the time of her absence, Moon and Mavie had fully recovered. My mum's cousin sent them back to school. But my mother remained there. Still very ill, she had a room and spent every day in a public area where she received prayers. She later recalled an episode where a woman, a patient herself, came close to her and told her, 'You know, you remind me of a woman I knew, she was very beautiful and rich, she was called Sofie. You really do look like her.'

Then the illness stopped. Whatever it was, it stopped. Out of the blue. There weren't any more feelings of snakes wriggling around her body and no more pain. I don't think it was a coincidence that my mother's illness seemed to have ceased around the same time my father had died. It might have been the same day. She was unable to give me a specific date, but the timing was strikingly close. It occurs to me that whatever was on them was a single force and that it had branched in two and possessed my parents and made them sick during its active stage and then resolved finally, although in two different ways. One died. The other survived.

My mother left the prayer venue. She stayed at her cousin's house for a while with Mavie and Monique as she gradually regained weight and health. She learned about René's death from her relatives. And as soon as she had managed to gather some money, she travelled to Benin to pay her respects to her ex-husband in Cotonou's main cemetery. She stayed at the Tawemas' house during her stay in Cotonou, in what she described as a positive and healing encounter with Tantine Marielle. Tantine Marielle took good care of her, giving her the best room, nice food and her friendship in a way she had never given before. Somehow, the death of the man they had both loved brought them closer.

When my mother returned to Congo, she was her old self again. Full of strength, as if the illness had never occurred. Since the girls had started school there, she decided to remain living in Pointe-Noire where she started doing business again, rented herself a house and all returned to normal, until one day, she was rashly called by her cousin at home. 'Come, there is an international call for you!' She dropped whatever she was doing, put her sandals on and ran outside with her cousin across the red dirt to his house. She picked up the phone receiver on the table and answered. On the other side of the line was Happiness. He was calling from Italy. He told her that he had fallen in love with a German girl and was getting married and he absolutely wanted her there in Bologna at his wedding. He said he was sending her a plane ticket and a visa. At that point, my mother recalled, she broke into tears.

***

I remember that Happiness stayed in bed all day, covered up to his head with the duvet, still dressed in the same trousers and jumper he had journeyed in, on the first day he arrived in Bologna. It was not cold at all, it was springtime, but the switch from the tropical temperature was so abrupt that the guy suffered a great deal from the cold during his first days in Italy. Besides, he also had to deal with the cultural shock. It was hard for him. And he was very quiet all the time. I didn't know him enough to work out by the way he responded to people if he was just very shy or if he was actually scared. Whenever I introduced him to acquaintances of mine that we came across in the street, he'd shake their hands stiffly, his big eyes filled with something I could describe as fear. He could not speak with anyone and preferred to stay home. Needless to say, I began to fear that he wouldn't settle in, but fortunately, that was not the case.

I had misjudged him. Happiness proved instead to be a force of nature. He learned Italian at a staggering speed, mainly through conversations with us, his family and some of our friends. Once he learned the basics of the language, he loosened up and gained more and more confidence. We could see him laughing and talking with people any time he had the opportunity and it was then that I realised that he was a very sociable person and very driven.

Six months from the day he first arrived, he gained some popularity in Bologna, predominantly in the hip-hop circles Klaus introduced him to on their nights out. The two of them wore oversized clothes, Happiness with a rolled-up red bandana tied around his head, like Tupac, his mythic hero. He also made many friends at the culinary school, where he trained as a waiter, and at his part-time jobs, giving out flyers and working in a supermarket. He took and successfully passed a driving lesson for high-cylinder motorbikes and bought himself a second-hand racing motorbike with his savings. Then he met Eve, an art student from Berlin. They met through Margherita, my ex-girlfriend, when we were still together, as Eve was one of her close friends. They fell in love. And two years from their first kiss, three years from when he first arrived in Italy, Happiness was getting married to Eve. Our mother came the day before the celebrations and stayed with Redeso, who now lived in a big house in the countryside with his girlfriend Daniela, for her week-long stay in Italy.

Happiness's wedding took place at Bologna's Town Hall in Piazza Mateotti. The large number of invitees reflected the extent to which Happiness was loved by the community he had built around himself. Excluding Mavie and Monique, all of our siblings were there, all in wedding attire—Ocean, Sigmund and his girlfriend, Debra-Jo with her family, Moon with her boyfriend, Klaus with his new girlfriend, Redeso and his girlfriend Daniela, and Lorenzo and me. There were our shared friends such as Andrea Mancuso, Gennaro, Franz, Ferro and my ex-girlfriend Margherita, who had long gotten over our separation and had become a good friend of mine, one of the dearest to me, practically family. She was also in charge of the wedding photography, being also the bride's best friend. Among the attendees were also various other friends Happiness had made during those three years in Bologna, plus his girlfriend's German family, consisting of an older brother with his girlfriend and mother and father. But the real surprise, the guest of honour, was Maman Sofie. Apart from Redeso, Happiness and me, nobody else knew she was coming, and, even in this way, even knowing she was coming, it was still something, something surreal, like God had edited the scene with Photoshop, to see her all dressed up for the wedding, full of being and acting all social amidst the other guests in front of the town hall after being gone for so long. She looked in perfect health, carrying no signs of the hard time of hiding in the bush she had just left behind, about which I would only learn nearly twenty years later. She seemed just fine, happy to see us all after all those years and meet our friends and girlfriends, and very much excited about her son's wedding.

Finally, the black Mercedes driving the bride and groom made its exit from the road into the town hall square, with Happiness in sunglasses and a pinstriped suit sticking out from the car sunroof and shooting with hands in all directions like a gangster holding two guns. Life never stops surprising. It felt absurd to look around and see what the boy had managed to accomplish in such a short space of time.

My mother stayed in Italy a few days more after the wedding.

GROUND

We met for a couple of serene afternoons at Redeso's with the other siblings, like in those long-gone days when she used to come and visit and stay in the hotel in the centre of Imola. It was nice, yes, warming, to be all together again, even if just momentarily. I don't know how to put it, but our mother among us had something like the ability to alter time and stretch that instant to the extent that I felt I had had no other life than the one I was living now with my family in the courtyard of my brother's house. But of course, it was only the usual comforting trick of the mind. At the end of her stay, Redeso, Daniela and I drove her to the airport, from where she took a flight back to Congo. A month from then, Happiness and Eve moved to Berlin.

Debra-Jo

There were no warning signs about the turn Debra-Jo's life was about to take. Really, nobody could have ever guessed. Everything appeared in place in her life; she seemed happy in her marriage and with her role as mother to two marvellous kids, aged ten and six, respectively. She seemed satisfied with her part-time job at a supermarket till. Now and then she met her friends from the Oasis for a quiet day out. During the rest of her time, she managed the kids and the house, went to church every Sunday morning and had a simple life.

As I mentioned earlier, Debra-Jo, now 32 years old, had discovered her devotion to Catholicism after the disappearance of her beloved nun Sister Gaudenzia many years before. Over time, it must be said, she even showed signs of fanaticism. Her house was decorated with Christian iconography everywhere: crucifixes, small statues and portraits of angels and Jesus and the Virgin Mary. Passages from the psalms punctuated her conversations and people from her local parish became part of her close community. Her quoting the priest's sermons with alacrity is the way I remember her. God was no doubt at the centre of her life.

However, despite all appearances, despite her beautiful family, her devotion to her community and God and their devotion to her, Debra-Jo was not content. She sensed that something was missing, something that she had lost on her quest for happiness, something that had to do with love. She had no doubts about the love she felt for her husband, yet she found her problem was with the nature of that particular type of love, which over time had begun to feel more like a prison, more like an obligation. A prosaic, imposed love, rather than a sincere longing for that man she had been sharing a bed every night with for the last ten years. Their relationship had come to a dead end. She did not know if she could say she was still in love with him. Too often, Debra-Jo would be crying inside the bathroom. A lump would well up in her throat when she least expected, like while playing with her kids or singing, while cooking or hugging her husband, and she would interrupt whatever she was doing and explain with a loving smile that she needed to go to the toilet a second. She would lock herself inside, sit on the loo and cry. It came then to her mind that the way she was seeing herself mirrored the way she used to see Sister Gaudenzia at the Oasis, when she could see and confirmed that the nun was not living life at her full potential. The nun seemed lost in a life that wasn't hers, lost in a forced love for a cause that was certainly noble but was meant for somebody else, not her. But then something shifted in her. And she left. If in the beginning Debra-Jo had resented Sister Gaudenzia for having left her, over time, particularly now that she herself felt miserable about her life, she understood what the nun had gone through during her time at the Oasis. Every day pretending to be ok, every day keeping up appearances, for the kids, for her husband, for her community, which had made an idea about her and will not appreciate it changing. It was too much of a burden. She imagined the nun being happy now. Maybe she had turned the barn in her native village in South Tyrol into an art gallery. And probably she was still there, managing that busy cultural space and perhaps she had married and had kids herself and was happy. But what did she mean with the analogy of the tigers she wrote in her letter? Debra-Jo never got it. '*There is this beautiful Asian saying. Two tigers cannot sit on the same mountain—so true my dearest Debra-Jo! Me and you can't stay in the same place. We are both too unhappy to be of any help to each other.*' She also wrote, '*I hope I won't see you again. If that should ever happen, hopefully not, well, that would be a very bad sign.*' What did she refer to with that analogy of the tigers? Why couldn't Debra-Jo and her occupy the same space? In what terms would it be a bad omen in the event their life should cross paths again?

Curiously, it was around this time that a man called Giulio entered the scene. None of us siblings would ever meet Giulio nor would see him in a photo. All I know about this man comes from Gabriella's description, apparently the only one to have met him in person. She described Giulio as a man who was fit and funny, dark-haired with blue eyes and tattoos on one arm and his neck. Certainly not Debra-Jo's type. Not like Gerard and Ugo. Giulio was a new kind of person for Debra-Jo, a creature of the night, more worldly, a Bohemian personality, possibly a nihilist.

Giulio and Debra-Jo met in a nightclub that Gabriella had dragged her to. Debra-Jo rarely went out at night, even less so to nightclubs, so it had taken some work to persuade her to go. I imagine her nervous, uptight and sober, as she danced primly at the edge of the dancefloor with her friends. Then one of the girls whispered about a man among a nearby group who had been staring at Debra-Jo for a while. Debra-Jo took notice of him. Although loyal to her husband down to her thoughts, she enjoyed the sensation of being liked, especially by an attractive man, but that was as far as she could take it, dismissing it with a cheeky laugh between the girls. But Giulio, the man staring at her, was determined to take it further. He left his group and approached Debra-Jo. Started talking to her. Aside from noticing that he was confident in his ways, Gabriella could hardly grasp what he said amid the noise of the disco. She saw that Debra-Jo paid little attention to him and eventually, the guy went back to his group. They came across him a few times throughout the night. He also brought them some drinks, which, of course, Debra-Jo turned down. Gabriella could not say when things shifted between the two, she just remembers that at some point she saw them standing apart engaging in a lively conversation, which seemed to take at times argumentative tones, at times amusing ones. Nevertheless, unmistakably charged with something.

GROUND

Nothing happened between the two that night; they left the venue in two separate groups. But I suppose something about Giulio must have stuck with Debra-Jo because from that night on, her attitude toward night outings changed. She became easier to persuade to go out, sometimes taking the initiative to drag the girls out to the club herself. The nightclub where she met Giulio became their first choice, and Giulio gradually became a familiar figure in her nightlife. They built up a relationship that sat somewhere between a friendship and something more. Their respective friends merged. Now Debra-Jo's life was vented by a wind of change, she had become more worldly herself, still very much religious, but with something extra, less naive, but more adult, more in touch with the reality of the world down to earth. When she looked at herself in the mirror, she didn't see just a mother anymore, but a woman, an attractive woman, sensual, possibly with more options than she originally thought. Even her look changed, her choice of clothes becoming more feminine and darker in colour, if not entirely black. She also got herself a tattoo, her first tattoo, a little quote on her wrist saying, 'Hope is Last to Die', possibly inspired by a conversation with Giulio. He was taking her into a different world, his own world, a world that she liked and she liked him. She fell in love with him.

Around the time this Giulio phase unfolded, Debra-Jo and Ugo's relationship had progressively declined. Not necessarily because of Giulio, whose existence Ugo was most likely unaware of and would not even care about, but because they had simply reached a breaking point where their marriage didn't work anymore for either of them. Ugo, for his part, had started looking away from their relationship to other women. Debra-Jo had begun to find him irritating. Arguments and fights ensued, and the kids were caught in the middle. They started sleeping in different rooms, there were threats of divorce, crying, desolation, and nothing seemed worth saving anymore.

The struggles in her marriage brought my sister even closer to Giulio, who offered her empathy, fun and understanding anytime they met. She found an ally in him, a way out of a cold, dead and damaging relationship. She found a person from whom she could receive passionate love. Giulio was indeed madly in love with her. Despite the difficulties shadowing her marriage and her growing feelings for Giulio, Debra-Jo had no intention of breaking her family apart. She would accept any sacrifice or compromise, even if it meant dying inside, if it helped to keep her family together, for the sake of the kids and her traditional Christian values. But it seemed that life had different plans for her.

Snow had fallen in that cold week of January. It snowed continuously all night until the following day. The streets of Bologna were white, and cars and buses drove cautiously. People walked unsteadily around wearing winter coats, hats and boots. Among them were Debra-Jo and Gabriella, taking a midmorning walk. Debra-Jo was doing most of the talking, lamenting her marriage problems, clearly in a state of distress. They hadn't been out for more than twenty minutes when the two women ran into a very familiar figure standing on the other side of the street. A witch, like Debra-Jo herself. The one she had made a pact with. Sister Gaudenzia. She was among a small group of nuns entering a parked van. What was more staggering was that Sister Gaudenzia was still wearing a habit under her winter coat, even though she was supposed to be a liberated woman somewhere in South Tyrol, supposedly running an art gallery. Both Debra-Jo and Gabriella felt something close to goosebumps when Sister Gaudenzia noticed them. She stood staring at them, speechless, from the other side of the street. Then she smiled at them. It was a very sad smile. A smile of defeat. She entered the van with other nuns and blew a kiss to the girls before the van drove off, the sound of snow cracking underneath the wheels.

The encounter with Sister Gaudenzia resonated powerfully with my sister. It was a coded message that was accessible only to them, the two witches. A message that carried within it a tale of both winter and summer. Of past times and buried memories, of evil genies and the black clouds of smoke from a burning house. Of red earth expanding underneath her feet and hours of flying across barren lands. Memories of friends' laughter at the Oasis, memories of duty and obligation, of social norms versus spiritual debts. Memories of a little girl riding on the back of her father's bike in the mountain countryside of South Tyrol. Her somnambular pilgrimage to a church some years after. Winds blowing through fingers. Migratory routes of nomads entering the Assante kingdom of Mali. The migratory flux of ex-British slaves from the Kingdom of Denmark across the French Empire to the Reign of Italy. The exile of the Roman Emperor Augustus's daughter Julia the Elder for walking around ancient Rome with transparent clothes. Memories of heirs to the throne fleeting cruel Nigerian traditions, seeking a new land, a new name, driven by forceful daimons that never compromise. A little girl watching vodun ceremonial drums in Benin before the departure of a villager to Ifé. *Erzule*. Like Cybele. Like Samaya. Like Ba. Like Ren. Kali. Ekate. Mary. A young girl leaves Mama and Papa's village to join the Mino warriors in Allada during the reign of Queen Hagbe. A young girl leaving home to join the Partigiani's armed resistance in the fight against the occupying Nazi Germany. A line of chained African women walking the deck in the port of Ouidah. A line of chained Italian women leaving the port of Bari to be sold as concubines in North Africa. A line of ants marching into a box of sugar in a kitchen one early morning in Brazzaville. Memories of what we are, what we have always been and forgotten, travellers. Just travellers. On coming across her old dearest carer, Debra-Jo cracked the meaning of the nun's letter to her. *Two tigers can't sit on the same mountain*: Debra-Jo and Sister Gaudenzia could not share the same place. If they could not exist in the same field of existence, but somehow ended up doing so, then their encounter would be the signal that one of the two tigresses had to go, one of them has to leave the mountain and take a journey.

Debra-Jo made a decision.

She met Giulio some days after and together they worked out a plan. They arranged things with the police, ensuring that their privacy was protected and that the location of the place they were about to go would be kept secret. According to Italian law, it was their right to not be found.

Debra-Jo put the kids to sleep, wrote a note to her husband and kids and walked out of the flat. She ran away, never to come back again. Never to see her kids again. Nor her husband. Nor us. She just disappeared, leaving no tracks, not even in the snow.

We woke up with the news of the disappearance of our sister the day after. Ugo called everyone looking for her. At first, I thought it was Ugo pulling a stunt early in the morning. Then I thought Debra-Jo must have slept at one of her friends' after she and Ugo had argued, but soon it became evident that this was a serious matter. Ugo was in despair. I imagined the poor kids, there with him holding the note she left them, while he called around to everyone looking for their mother. A crisscrossing sequence of calls occurred amongst my siblings, all of us dumbfounded by the possibility our sister could have done something like this. We simply could not believe the note she left for her husband and her kids, where she wrote that she had left with her lover, explaining her struggle lately with Ugo, her depression and that she could not cope anymore. It ended with her request for us to respect her will and to leave her be. 'Debra-Jo wouldn't do this. She would never abandon her kids,' we kept on saying.

Then, separately, both Sigmund and Ugo inquired at the police station.

'Yes, your sister has moved to another city, but we are bound by law not to reveal her location without her consent. We can only assure you she is well and safe.'

We spent a week in shock, hoping that as soon as she got herself back together, she would return home and realise the scale and implications of what she was doing. We trusted she would return.

The Aftermath

Debra-Jo's disappearance marked every member of my family permanently, sharpening the sense of disillusionment towards life that my siblings and I had inherited from our troubled history. Little was left to believe in when the person who had held us together all those years, who we looked up to as our home, had given in. We learned another harsh lesson, perhaps the harshest of all, that there is simply no end to it, that no matter where we go, what we do, what we believe in, who we try to be, how good we try to become in this exercise of living, all the houses we can find shelter in will burn down. They will crash into the soil and turn into ashes, like our family, set to go to pieces from the very beginning.

    Silence ensued. Once more, silence. Silence sneaking in and hissing in the background of our existence. Silence, when everything we know loses real meaning, becomes transient and ephemeral, and thoughts run in loops lethargically. We refrained from building anything since we could not bear watching these last efforts of ours being smashed by the waves of dire times, like yet another sandcastle we built on a shore. We distanced from each other in response to our sister's disappearance, broken and ashamed of belonging to a family like ours. Ocean lived for a while secluded in a flat on the outskirts of Imola that he had moved into after leaving St Catherina. He left home only to go to work as a crane assembler for a building firm. Sigmund moved out of St Catherina as well around the same time as Ocean. He settled in a hillside hamlet called Dozza where he opened an antique furniture shop. Redeso immersed himself in his research of Esoterism in the quiet environment of his house in the countryside with Daniela while working as a chef in a vegetarian restaurant. Klaus I had little information about, like the rest of my family I rarely saw him, but I knew that he worked in a factory and lived in a shared house behind Bologna Central Station. As for Lorenzo, I knew even less. I had no idea of where he lived and what he was doing.

I, too, created distance from my siblings. I kept a low profile for a while. Debra-Jo's disappearance was big, bigger than our father's recent death. There was nothing new about death, while whatever happened to my sister, her choice to leave us all in that way, dramatically changed my view on things and initiated me into a world that was more unpredictable than I ever imagined. I tried not to pay much attention to it and focused on my writing. I wrote even more than usual. I wrote to not think, to not talk to anyone. I would spend all day at the restaurant frying meat, cooking pasta, preparing dough for the cake and the focaccia, storing the leftovers in small containers and putting them in the fridge cellar, cleaning the work surfaces and sweeping and mopping the floor, then come back home, pour myself a glass of whisky and write. Write. And write.

I was taking a break, smoking a cigarette at the window, one of those nights, when I saw a figure walking down the street under the light of the streetlamps. It was Lorenzo. He looked somehow different than usual, dazed and lost as if he wasn't even there.

'Hey Lorenzo!' I called.

He stopped and glanced up at the window at me waving my hand at him. He looked at me vacuously as if he could not recognise me, then resumed walking without even trying to understand who I was and why I called him.

Lorenzo

Before Debra-Jo's disappearance, Lorenzo's boy-band project the 4-More, had enjoyed a few years of success. The boys had even released a single for a well-known music producer that briefly topped the summer charts in Italy and Eastern European countries. Then, something went wrong. Possibly it was the usual disputes between members, the naturally short life span of a boy band, and it ended almost overnight. Still, Lorenzo was not about to admit defeat, so he started a new project with another artist. This came to nothing, so he continued as a solo artist, writing his own songs and music and creating his own choreography. He hunted for gigs everywhere he could reach, but the harsh truth was that doors were starting to close before him, the margin of possibility to make it through as an artist shrinking the older he got, and he was grappling with the reality of competing with younger artists, many of whom were even better performers than him, more talented and fresh. Life turned bleak. Further discouraged by Debra-Jo's disappearance, Lorenzo gave up hope. Something inside him started to wither, and his appearance and quality morphed from the poster boy he once was to something increasingly scruffier. His beard grew unkept where he was once clean-shaven. He stopped caring about his clothing as he used to, and it became more common to see him going around Bologna wearing a hoodie and a pair of shabby jeans and some trainers. It was the end of him wearing braided extensions and fancy blue or green contacts. He only wore his natural hair now, and a severe blank stare that was bitter and full of spite. It was the same stare I once saw ubiquitously stared by people during that long-gone summer in Africa; the stare of people who had nothing left to lose. Lorenzo had become dark and angry as if he had growing into a disillusioned man overnight.

Contributing to his anger and disillusionment was that he was struggling a great deal with his immigration status, and therefore finding a job. His papers had expired again, the same way they had when we had returned from Africa, and he was denied entry into the country, when he had been held in custody by the border police until our social worker managed to have him released. The difference this time was that there were no more social workers to fight for us, and Lorenzo hadn't even tried to renew his papers when he was supposed to in the first place. He had trashed his expired residency permit and spat on it, turning into an illegal immigrant. I asked him, one night we were hanging around together in the streets in the centre of Bologna, why he had never applied for citizenship, why he had let his residency permit expire. Negligence, he said, and pride. He didn't consider himself an immigrant. On the contrary, he perceived himself to be an Italian through and through and felt there was something deeply wrong and humiliating to be forced to show up at an immigration office to ask for a permit in order to keep on living in his country, to apply for an allowance when he was already fully entitled to live in the country he perceived as his. Of course, all of his thinking was not entirely conscious, it had been running in the back of his mind passively over the years. He was like Klaus when he started to believe he was immune to the hatred of the racist hooligans because he had been misled into thinking of himself as a white person after growing up in a white-only reality in Italy. Or me, when I first landed at the Congolese airport during our first African holiday, when my Italian-trained mind had me fouled to the degree that I had expected to see mostly white people on African soil rather than a black majority. My siblings and I were all victims of a deep internal battle involving two colliding identities, or even more than two. Almost schizophrenic, we were. One part of our minds reflected the way we intimately viewed ourselves, as Italians. The other part reminded us that the social status we received from the Italian government from being originally from another country, and from the type of response we elicited from people around us, clearly made us immigrants. Another part chimed in that our passports showed we were Beninese, while another part reminded us that by our birthplace we were Congolese, even though we had hardly lived in either place. Indeed, we were having hard time navigating the Italian immigration laws because we were living in a sort of schizophrenic identity conundrum. Lorenzo, tired of this fractured existence, took a stand, he trashed his papers and spat on them, refusing to see himself as an immigrant, which paradoxically made him only an illegal immigrant, not more of a citizen.

Soon, with no job, no money and no papers, he was evicted. He found shelter in a squat house, the home of a group of Senegalese immigrants in one of the dodgiest districts of Bologna, and he found refuge in grass. He smoked it constantly from morning to night. Then he began selling it and smoking even more. He started smuggling it into nightclubs in some dodgy squares and around music festivals across Italy, where he spent days slinking about, having sex and smoking, sleeping and drinking, then he would journey back to Bologna to his dingy room in the squat, with no prospects nor any interest in getting out of this vicious cycle. Days, weeks and months drifted away in a nebulous torpor, leaving him oblivious to what his life was before. He eclipsed from himself to a degree that he could not tell apart one person from the other, nor recognise his own siblings. He disappeared from our lives.

Nobody knew where he was, or what he was doing, until one day, a year after he first moved to the squat, he found himself facing the umpteenth client. A black fellow who asked him for some grass. He asked him with a stutter.

'You-you-you don't recognise me?' The new client asked.

'Who the fuck are you?' Lorenzo asked, red eyes squinting from how high he was.

'I-I-I'm Klaus!'

At those words, Lorenzo woke up as if from a spell. It was like Klaus had freed him.

'W-w-where the fuck have you b-b-been? Everybody is looking for you!'

'Been away but mostly here.'

'Here? I've been c-c-c-coming here every day to buy this shit from t-t-t-that Senegalese guy there and I never came a-a-across you!'

'Fuck!'

'F-f-f-uck!'

Life in the squat and his days of drug dealing were now over. Klaus offered to have him come and stay at his house for a while, the student-shared house where he lived with his girlfriend, until he got himself sorted. Klaus said that he wanted to cook him some nice food and had some clothes for him and that he could take a bath. Lorenzo, attracted by Klaus's generous offer of being taken care of in a homey environment that wasn't the desolate environment of the squat, accepted the invitation.

It was during the walk to Klaus's house that Lorenzo noticed that something was wrong with his brother. He appeared gaunt, with strange marks on the skin of his face and hands. He looked ill. Lorenzo grew more concerned once they reached Klaus's building and started climbing the stairs to his flat and saw him panting. Klaus had to stop to gasp for air on a landing halfway to the flat. He pulled an inhaler out of his pocket and took a long breath of it.

'What happened to you?' Lorenzo became worried. 'You don't look well at all.'

'Ah, n-n-n-nothing serious. I-I-I just have asthma. And d-d-dermatitis,' Klaus reassured him, minimising as usual.

'That's no asthma!' said Lorenzo, 'Asthma doesn't make you like this, have you seen a doctor?'

'Yeah. Yeah, you mean thi-thi-this thing?' he said rubbing the mysterious dark stains over his wrist and hand with the other hand, 'It's a skin condition. You know dermatitis? The doctor ga-ga-ga-gave me a cream that I'm using every day and it's way better now. You should ha-ha-ha-have seen before.'

'But are you eating enough?' enquired Lorenzo still not entirely convinced Klaus was telling the full story.

'Not ve-ve-very hungry these days. Fu-fu-fuck food! It-it-it's not very important at the end of the d-d-day, and you and me are u-u-used to stay empty stomach, d-d-d-did you forget?'

Now, it is only in hindsight that I can say with certainty that Klaus was already aware he was severely ill. He knew. But he kept it to himself all along. He didn't want us to know. I don't think Lorenzo believed him when he justified the symptoms of his illness as being the effect of asthma and dermatitis, but we know how the mind works, it shuts down before certain facts. There are things you refuse to see even if they are right in front of you. Lorenzo didn't want to go anywhere near understanding that his brother was terminally ill. Not unless he wanted to consider the possibility that his brother was dying. No. He just left it. Some things ought not to be touched.

They went into Klaus's flat. Lorenzo took a bath, Klaus gave him some clothes and started to cook something for him. While pulling pans out of cupboards and food from the fridge, he gave him good news. There was a man who had been calling him for months asking for Lorenzo, a music producer.

'He was desperate to find you,' Klaus explained, 'because he l-l-l-liked your style and wanted you for a new project. He said he wa-wa-wa-want absolutely to sign you up. So he g-g-g-gave me his number in case I found you.'

Hesitantly, Lorenzo grabbed the piece of paper where Klaus had written the name and number of the producer, they knew this was something big since Zanetti, the producer in question, was the man behind the successes of a good number of well-placed Italian pop artists. He called him from Klaus's landline. Glad to hear from him, the producer, expressed all his appreciation for Lorenzo's work as a singer in the boy band he happened to see at a gig in Milan some time ago and was eager to make him an offer for a full LP as a single artist. He had an idea of his artistic name already, he said. Captain Ben.

'What is your schedule next week?' he asked him, 'I can meet you at the studios.'

In disbelief, Lorenzo shifted his gaze from the ceiling to Klaus, as though to ask his brother if all this was part of a stupid prank or if it was really happening.

'It's happening, you made it,' said Klaus with a reassuring smile, as he stood in the middle of the room, scratching his shoulder, his body disappearing inside his clothes.

More on Immigration

As opposed to Lorenzo, the stance I took to face the identity puzzle my siblings and I were living was to see myself as my government saw me: an immigrant. Therefore, I wanted to become Italian. I knew I had long gained entitlement to apply for citizenship, having well passed the ten years of continuous residency citizenship required. My total residence history amounted to 17 years by the time I started my application. It was time to put things in place and be done with the hassle of being treated as a second-class citizen all the time. Time to end queueing every year at the immigration office to renew my papers and end having to endure police taunts of 'watch out boy, we're going to send you back to your country.' I wanted to obtain citizenship also for a matter of dignity, for pride, for preventing once and for all myself and the others from mistaking my identity. I was raised in Italy; I sang the Italian national anthem in Italian during drunken nights with my Italian friends eh bella ciao bella ciao bella ciao ciao ciao. I longed for their same right to vote, to be entitled to apply for the same jobs, like teacher, postman, fireman, even fucking police officer, the whole lot of civil servant jobs that were denied to non-Italian nationals. I wanted to travel as freely as they did, beyond Europe's fucking Schengen Area, like to the United Kingdom, and to other countries on other continents, like Mexico and Thailand, which always demanded an insane amount of money, papers and vaccines for Beninese nationals before granting them a visa. I was tired of all these restrictions I was subjected to. I just wanted to travel, to be free, like any other of my Italian peers.

I wanted to heal once and for all from this sickening condition of owning so many conflicting identities. So I was more than ready to start the process of applying for my long-deserved citizenship.

First, I went to the immigration office, where I was given a list of documentation that I needed to provide to them. Then I walked to Bologna City Hall, the place I was supposed to obtain the documentation from. I went to the lady at the counter with my list in hand and gave her my name. After checking on the system for a little while she raised her head from the computer and said, 'It looks like there is a mistake here. Your details have been entered twice.'

Used to hitches of this type I said, 'One is me, the other one, my brother.'

Her answer was, 'Same name, same date of birth, I know my work, this is no doubt the same person.'

I went on, 'You can see there is an extra F at the end of one of the names, see, Redesof it's me. Redeso my brother. We are twins. Our father messed up with us.'

'Oh I see, you're right now that I look closely. Redeso and Redesof. It's a very similar name you have there. Anyway,' she added, thinning her lips, 'I can't give you any documents, because the system here shows that you both are not in Italy at the moment.'

'Which means?'

'That you are somewhere abroad, but not here, maybe in Congo. Are you?'

At first, I thought we were dealing with a bug in the system that had messed up all the personal data of the general public, since it was undeniable that I was there, in front of her, residing in Italy at that very moment. But as she went on explaining the findings on her computer, I could see we were facing a major problem. It turned out that Redeso and I had been erased from the public record because we had failed to declare to the police that we had moved from Imola to Bologna. We didn't know we were supposed to report to the police when we moved to a different town, especially when that town was just half an hour's drive away. But apparently, we had breached the law. After a targeted, two-year-long, immigration control-motivated search, where the police went house to house to verify the actual residency of immigrants, we were not found in Imola and the authorities assumed we had left the country permanently. They marked us as irreparably unaccounted for, our entire residency history had been wiped out of the system. Although we had both been working legally and paying taxes, the system said we were not in Italy and therefore all the benefits we had gained as immigrants with status, like the eligibility to apply for citizenship, were automatically erased. We had to reregister at the registry office as newcomers. This would start our residency history from scratch, forcing me to climb the stairs of ten years of continuous residency before being eligible again to apply for citizenship.

What an absurd day that was. I had gone into the immigration building to put things in place, to claim my Italian identity, and left it having to restore my whole existence. I felt like an alien who, in the process of being humanised, discovered that he was actually dead.

I asked the lady, 'What's the next step now?'

'Do you have your papers with you?' she asked.

'Yes.'

'Well, let me see.'

Fortunately, my residency permit had not expired yet, so she re-registered me on the spot as a newcomer. A freshly arrived immigrant with no history of any sort in this country. Even though during the two years I was taken for absent I had been working legally as a chef and paying taxes. I signed my second contract with a well-known publisher and travelled around the country for book launches and conferences. I received post and books at my home to review for a magazine I worked for. I worked as a creative writing teacher in a juvenile detention centre and got paid a salary and royalties directly to my bank account, but I was still considered officially out of the country.

The immigration lady resuscitated me, typing my credentials back into the system, and I remember thinking, how much worse the whole thing would have turned out if I had come by just a few months later when my residency permit had expired. It would have been impossible to renew it if I wasn't on the system in the first place. Would they have deported me? And where would they have repatriated me? Congo? Benin?

I let Redeso know about the whole thing. Dumbfounded, he drove from his quiet life in the countryside to meet me in Bologna to resuscitate himself at the city hall office as well and to work out a way forward. Both of us were anything but willing to wait another ten years more before applying for citizenship after we had lived in the country our entire lives.

We went to talk to a lawyer, a friend of my employer at the restaurant I had worked in. She looked pessimistic, but we tried anyway. We swamped her with all sorts of documents proving we had been in Italy in the last two years: payslips, bills, bank transactions, tenancy agreements, Redeso's qualification he achieved after three years of his Raja Yoga teaching course, his work contract at the vegetarian restaurant and his payslips and the proof of my literary. Despite her efforts in the following months, however, we lost the case on the basis that it was our responsibility to report our move to the police. *Ignorantia iuris no excusat*—'the law does not admit ignorance' as enshrined in article 5 of the Italian Penal Code. A bitter finding emerged during the legal process. We had missed a preferential right, a much easier way, to gain Italian citizenship, to which we had been oblivious. There was a legal clause that granted Italian citizenship to foreign minors whose parents had been stripped of their parental rights by an Italian tribunal. Minors in those cases were considered *apolidi*—stateless—by default and, therefore, had the right to gain citizenship of the country they lived in. However, the conversion from stateless to citizen was not automatic. It was not in the purview of the court that had terminated their parents' parental rights to grant the minors their citizenship rights. The onus was on the *apolidi* kid, who was supposed to know the law and apply at the immigration office once he turned eighteen. And he had to act quickly because such entitlement to fast-tracked citizenship lasted one year only, like a special offer. After that, he could only apply through the normal processes. In the end, Redeso and I met both requirements and failed. For ignorance, because nobody fucking told us anything about our rights. The whole social services apparatus had not thought to conduct some basic research on the matter of immigration to ensure that the stateless kids they had under their care all those years could leave their jurisdiction as citizens, or at least with a full picture of their rights.

Redeso and I left our lawyer's office. We walked down the stone staircase of the stately building typical of the historical centre of Bologna and left the building onto Via Marconi. I remember that despite having been badly beaten by the law, we were not necessarily disturbed; the results didn't come as a surprise, as we knew deep inside we would lose the appeal. We walked under the portico of Via Marconi among the usual mixed daytime crowd of well-dressed people, rough-looking students, local traders and tourists. We walked up to Piazza Maggiore, the Fountain of Neptune sieged by people and pigeons, and sat on the wide white granite staircases at the entrance to the public library entrance. The two twins. Growing more and more differentiated. Redeso, shaved, wearing short hair and neat clothes. Me, with dreadlocks, an unkept long beard and clothes that could do with a wash or some mending. I pulled my packet of tobacco out of my pocket. I rolled one cigarette. Then one more for Redeso when he asked me. He smoked only occasionally. He took a drag and said,

'Do you think we are all disappearing?'

'What do you mean?' I asked.

He looked strangely calm despite what had just happened to us—the court verdict saying that we had become newly arrived immigrants. Maybe he was just resigned.

'Dad's gone. Debra-Jo is gone, we lost track of Lorenzo, and now you and I have been wiped out from the public records. Something is trying to erase us. I'm starting to believe that story granddad told us that day in Africa is true.'

'You didn't believe it was?' I asked.

'Not really. It sounded like a fairy tale or something. But it has started making sense. The insubordination of that ancestor prince caused a mess!'

'Yes, it did.'

'Look, it makes sense right? Think about our ID. It says we were born in Congo but we are Beninese citizens. We never had a proper family house, or a traditional family setting or make-up. You and I have the same name, the same date of birth, we look the same, and we are immigrants with perfect Italian. How can this not be an attempt messing with our identity? It proves that there is something, a force that is holding us back from existing in the most conventional form. Take a random guy there, I bet if you ask him where he comes from and what his name is, he'll give you a straightforward answer. But if he asks us, "you guys, what's your name and where do you come from?" he'll be left confused and we will need to explain things to him.'

'Yeah. A mess.'

Then he said,

'I wonder what Mavie and Monique look like now. When was the last time we saw them, ten years ago? They might have grown into women now.'

'We should go visit them and Mom before we vanish entirely,' I said 'They just moved to France. At least it's part of the Schengen treaty area.'

The comment made us laugh. It was always a good laugh with Redeso. Always liberating. Then we went back talking about the legal case and wondered if there was something more we could do to overturn the results. Finding nothing, we just dropped it and accepted that we had to wait ten more years before reapplying for citizenship. We talked about other things, like his new house in the countryside, the house he had just bought with his girlfriend and how they were making it all nice by painting it together, decorating and refurbishing it with new furniture. He told me about some funny anecdotes about the restaurant staff he had been working with. I quite didn't get if Redeso liked being a chef or not. He had been working in the same restaurant for years, and whenever the argument emerged, he did not seem to be bothered at all. Was he happy? Did he not have higher aspirations? Did he not want a different life? Was it really true that some people could be fulfilled by having a simple life in the countryside with their girlfriend and working at the same place for years? Was my brother one of them? I envied my brother's peaceful life. He was a functioning member of society, even though he had just swooped down to the bottom of immigration statuses. At least he had a stable job and a stable partner, had gotten onto the property ladder and had taken a spiritual path that was transforming him into a healthier and better person. He seemed resolved. In comparison, I felt like I was missing something. I was wrong and dysfunctional. My life was a mess. There was something dark inside me that troubled me. I suffered from insomnia, kept changing jobs and I lived in a dirty, messy house. The last time there was some form of order in my life was when I was with Margherita. After that, I felt like I had been living in free fall.

Then Silvio Berlusconi came into power with Forza Italia in the summer of 2001. He teamed up with two far-right parties—Umberto Bossi's Lega Nord and Gianfranco Fini's Alleanza Nazionale, in a coalition called Il Polo della Libertá. There he was again, Umberto Bossi, the same man one of our supervisors had showed us on TV back at the foster home when Klaus was coming down the slope of his brief sympathy for the Nazis. Back then Bossi was at the head of a marginal but emerging populist party, a party that was widely ridiculed by the public but now he and his party had gained support by leveraging people's fears about the unfolding immigration crisis, to the point that he had risen to serve in Berlusconi's government as a reform minister. I remember his poison-filled public speeches when he first introduced a new immigration draft law to the public.

'We'll get the navy to fire against boats carrying illegal immigrants after the second or third warning!' He announced at a party summit. 'This new bill will save Italians from a billion foreigners who will ruin our society, destroy our history and our culture.'

The new bill he was introducing was the so-called 'Bossi–Fini' law. If passed in the senate, it would be detrimental to the two million immigrants living in Italy, since it was designed to tie their lives to the whipping post of their employer. The new bill established that immigrants were eligible to live in the country only if they had a work contract and could document that they were financially self-reliant. Residency was declined to those who earned below a certain amount or those who had been unemployed for more than six months and then the possibility of deportation hung over their heads. The meaning of unemployment changed for many foreigners at that point. No matter if you were fired or quit yourself, say due to disputes over sub-human payment terms or more serious matters like workplace abuse or safety issues, you had to find another job within six months or else you could be forced back home. Anyone trying to re-enter the country illegally was to be held accountable and would face time in jail. The Bossi–Fini law introduced the compulsory collection of fingerprints for all immigrants. It also imposed new requirements on businesses that recruited immigrant workers, like the obligation to guarantee accommodation and to cover the cost of expulsion if necessary for each immigrant they employed, making hiring immigrants less appealing to employers. The law that Bossi and Fini were pressing forward also called for the construction of detention centres for immigrants that were to be deported, which were, ironically, to be funded by the immigrant workers' taxes.

The new bill sparked widespread criticism across the country. There were protests in the streets of Italy's major cities. Lefties, intellectuals, unions, exponents of the church, charity organisations and, of course, immigrants, deemed the prospective law immoral and discriminatory for stripping immigrants of their rights. It technically criminalised the state of being an immigrant, criminalising two million people almost instantly. Some critics of the new bill also argued that it will not resolve the problem of illegal immigration but worsen it by automatically creating new illegal immigrants out of all those people who had been working under the table or who were out of work and couldn't find any within six months.

And yet, despite their best efforts, the law went through. It was approved by Parliament on July 11, 2002. It was a disaster from day one. Thousands of souls were rounded up from around several provinces by law enforcement and expelled within 24 hours, a majority of which were prostitutes and drug dealers. They were put on planes, buses and boats and driven away. Hundreds of Moroccan citizens besieged their consulate, crying for help to emerge from the underground, fearing getting deported. Many immigrants were fired by their employers right off the bat and were suddenly left struggling to put food on the table for their kids. In some cases, the employer found a way to cash in on their employees' misfortune by asking them to pay a bribe in exchange for a work contract. Others, who had been enjoying the comforts of a regular work contract all along, suddenly saw changes in the terms of their contracts, like an increase in working hours, or a slash on holiday time. Others saw their salary being halved from one day to another and then erased entirely, and they had to put up with working for free so long as their employer, their new owner, granted their signature for their residency permit to be renewed. They were told not to worry, he had all the intentions to pay them, at some point. I remember a guy, a tough-looking Romanian guy, who told me he was ashamed of himself because he allowed his employer to slap him occasionally, but he was scared to fight back or to quit without having another legal job first.

'I have been working there for two years,' he told me. 'It was all good. All good, and now people pick on me because I act like a pussy.'

The new immigration policy was based on the assumption that, if they were not for studying, visiting or seeking political asylum, all immigrants had come to Italy purely for economic purposes and so they had to prove it. Or else, why stay here? There was no allowance for grey areas, like say underpaid or unpaid creative work. An indication of how blind the government's approach to immigration was the fact that they had left out of the picture a class of migrants, like me, who didn't come to Italy to find a better life. A class of migrants who just lived in Italy, like any Italian, and were involved in any number of odd jobs, like writing, journalism and making music. There were painters and other artists, whose residency status in the country was now jeopardised just because they underperformed financially that year. When in reality, all of these people had been working twice as the amount of the average worker, doubling up their efforts to perform their creative work and sustain themselves. But now we were hearing from the government that most of our working hours were not countable, as long as we could not produce invoices for them, and that our entire lives had been condensed into a proof of income. I lost my special immigrant status, lost the eligibility to apply for citizenship, and, with the introduction of Bossi–Fini, I entered the class of immigrants at risk of deportation, judging by my poor annual performance the past tax year. With the renewal date for my status approaching, I was aware that I was heading in the direction of my application being rejected if nothing changed. Then I met Ginevra.

I met Ginevra through some work I was doing at that time casting local young people for a film in Bologna for a well-established production company from Rome. My job was simple. I had to go around Bologna with a camera in hand and interview people who I judged suitable for the roles, take their details and pass them to the production company for a second official casting. Ginevra was among the people I met. She was the least suitable for any of the roles I had on my list in that she was just too brilliant. Plus, we both knew she didn't give a damn about acting in a film. We stood there, pretending to talk business, just because we liked each other the very first time we crossed paths in the crowded Piazza Maggiore, and we started dating. Ginevra, a second-year student of communications science, was the only person I knew wearing a pair of geta in the whole of Bologna. With short jeans and a see-through t-shirt, she had something of a coquettish vibe, and she was stunningly smart, possibly one of the cleverest people I had ever met. Opinionated and academic in her thinking but punk in nature, she was into skating, urban culture, low-fi music, thick books of philosophy and shiny fashion magazines alike. With Ginevra, it was the time of bands such as Karate, Spain, Belle and Sebastian and Pavement, which we listened to in her room in her shared house. It was the time of her reading passages to me of Bret Easton Ellis, Thomas Pynchon and Tom Robbins under the covers, of her introducing me to the films of Gus Van Sant and leading me into the recesses of the semiotic world. If we were at mine I would read her my favourite bits of Dostoevsky, Robert Musil and Don De Lillo and we would watch films on my bed from my collection of Charlie Chaplin. I had moved into a shared house in the centre of Bologna by then because my landlord had sold my flat and I worked for a bill-posting agency. I was the guy in an orange work uniform sticking posters on the bill posts in the centre of Bologna with brush strokes and a bucket of liquid glue at my feet. I would go pick up Ginevra on my night shift, give her one of my uniforms to wear, and pay her to help me stick the ads on the bill posts, all illegally of course. Sometimes, we allowed ourselves some time off to stop for a pint break in a bar or to share a joint with a friend we had bumped into or stopped by a venue to watch a friend play jazz at a concert, both of us sitting at the bar in orange uniforms dirty with glue.

Ginevra was a woman of expansive views, sociable and witty, who would give you whatever she possessed, her car keys, love, sex, money, as much as she could until she shut herself down. But even then, when she shut down, when she was ill-disposed or had fallen prey to her pathological outbursts of anger, she was able to make you laugh with a hilarious comment amidst her crises, comments that were mostly pessimistic towards humanity and society in general. It was hard to say who was the more misanthropic between me and her. We were critically similar. Both of us were very chaotic and untidy. Both of us lived in messy rooms, both of us brainy but slow, lazy and into books and films and both of us equally struggled with setting up boundaries. We were two minds who took the aerial view, looking at the world as a playground, where everything was possible, every dream achievable, and we felt entitled to do whatever we wanted and to love whomever. Consequently, our relationship could be nothing but an open one. Things like, 'sex is overrated, it should be like a coffee with a stranger' or 'why seek to keep it all for one person when we are surrounded by billions of people' were part of our narrative. Despite the truth that it hurt, yes, it hurt sometimes, to lend the person you love to others, we just carried on living in an open relationship, and I think it was beautiful that we were able to talk openly and gave each other advice on our affairs, when it was required, like two good friends.

Ginevra's position on the immigration law that restricted my life was straightforward. It simply didn't make any sense. I was just as Italian as she was in her eyes. We had shared the same cultural references since the very first day we met, spoke the same language and thought alike, and she could not get her head around the fact that I was being treated differently from her, like a foreigner.

This conversation took place on a night bus, three months from when we first met. It was the first time I revealed to her my background and my condition as an immigrant after she invited me to take a trip with her to South America that I had to turn down. It was winter. We were both wearing coats and woollen hats. We were both locked out of our respective houses because we had forgotten our keys inside and her flatmates and mine were far too deep asleep to answer the door. So, we jumped on a night bus and spent the night riding across Bologna, back and forth, sitting tightly together in the backseat of an empty bus.

Everything she learned about me that night felt like science fiction to her. In particular, my travelling restrictions. She was stunned to hear the quantity of documentation—the proof of high income, the safety deposit, the vaccinations and the medical insurance—the Mexican embassy asked for in order to grant me a two-week tourist visa when for her it was nothing to get one. Like so many Italians, she had no clue about the true nature of the immigration reality in Italy. She came from an ordinary Italian family, moved within circles of white Italians predominately and had plenty of friends that she regularly visited around the world, but she rarely crossed paths with immigrants in Italy, non-EU immigrants I mean, an entirely different class from EU or North American immigrants. And even more rarely did she enter into deep relationships with them.

'And you don't care?' She asked me, to my surprise.

'What do you mean?'

'You seem so calm about all this,' she said. 'How can you take it? I would go mad!'

'I don't know. I think you just go on with your life.'

'But this shouldn't be your life. It doesn't make any sense. Nobody should tell you what to do with your time. Can you see what I'm talking about? The point here is not how you could meet the government's income requirement if you do an odd job like writing at the end of your tax year. This is not the problem. The point here is that nobody should push you into labour full stop, much less in your own country. You're Italian like me, whether the government recognises it or not! Red, you are not an immigrant. Imagine if they came and knocked at my door and told me, "You must work now." Ciao bello! You are being criminalised for having done nothing wrong, just for living your life and being a writer.'

Something about Ginevra's perspective on this matter, her dismay and her lucid observations, were a wake-up call for me, helping me to realise that I had become apathetic to the government's demands to a point where I had lost touch with the full scale of what was going on. I always knew the whole thing was perverse, saw it as bothersome to go and wait at the immigration office every year, to be forced to work or else, the fact that I could be wiped out of the system so easily and see my entitlement to citizenship evaporate, but only now with Ginevra was I able to see with clarity that the situation was more serious than I had been able to feel. The Italian government's summary approach to immigration was quick to strip me of my fundamental rights but provided no guidance or options for me to restore them as if the overall value of my life from the day I set foot in Italy to when I was riding around town in a night bus in my mid-twenties with my girlfriend amounted to nothing. Nothing at all. I was a zero. Not a person. Just nothing. Yes, there was something wrong here.

'Look, let's get married,' she said.

Again, Ginevra took me by surprise and intrigued me even more. Her child-like mind went through life as if all the odds and convoluted human vicissitudes at the end of the day could be distilled down to a lollipop.

'We get married, you get citizenship, we sort out all this immigration shit and you can spend all your life idling in a park if you want or writing and reading and watching films, and we go to Mexico. This marriage thing is the highest sacrament after all, right, and should be love-motivated, right? It would put me off to use it for any other reason other than help you to get free from all that crap if you don't mind. What do you say, would you marry me?'

It was indeed an act of pure love. We had been together for only three months. We knew each other very little still, I could turn out to be anyone, an idiot, a psychotic, whoever. She didn't have to propose. Nobody asked her to help me out. I truly believe that if there is supposed to be love behind a marriage, well, there was plenty of it behind Ginevra's youthful act of proposing to me. We had a civil marriage three months from that day, on a Sunday morning in May with no attendees other than our two witnesses—a couple of friends of ours. We stopped in a bar to celebrate, each of us with a glass of white wine. Although we had announced it to everybody, to friends and family, we chose to have a low-key celebration because it was funnier this way, intimate, something between me and her.

Thanks to Ginevra, my required wait time before gaining eligibility to apply for citizenship was slashed from ten years to zero. All that was left, once I submitted my application, was to wait from two to four years more for my application to be processed. Meanwhile, I was still required by the law to be on an annual residency permit. The only real difference was that I was no longer subject to deportation as I was now bound to an Italian citizen and my permit was linked to my marriage rather than my work. I could carry on practicing my work as a writer without fear of government retaliation.

After a one-month-long honeymoon road trip in the south of Italy, driving Ginevra's yellow Twingo, we moved in together, into a one-bedroom flat in the Andrea Costa area. I found a job as a pizzaiolo at a motorway service station right outside Bologna and finally settled. It was a nice period. Life was treating me well. There was love, work, easiness, friends and family. I had time for writing. I was working on a play and my new novel. I also enjoyed my day work, which was different from the usual chef work. As a pizzaiolo, I was doing single shifts rather than split shifts and the type of work did not require much thinking, it was straightforward. I had to dress like a McDonald's employee but for pizzas, with my coloured cap, polo shirt and a random name pinned on my chest like Alessandro, or Piero. I would produce pizzas with a press machine, filling them up with toppings and then sticking the resulting pizza in the oven. I would then slice it and put it on display. Not much fuss. At least it kept my mind empty so that I could work through my writing in my head. While making pizzas I felt less precarious, more entitled to occupy my place as a writer on Italian soil. But then the trouble started again. It seemed like the Italian immigration machine had no intention of loosening its insidious grip on me.

JADELIN GANGBO

My Boss at the Pizza Place

My boss at the pizza place was a short blonde woman in her fifties. She wore a white lab coat and spectacles that she kept on the tip of her nose while she carried out administrative work at the computer in her tiny office at the back of the kitchen. One day she called me into her office for an issue she was facing while trying to switch my contract from temporary to permanent.

'Look, I'm not managing here. See for yourself,' she said, turning the computer screen toward me. It was about my residency permit, which had expired a week ago.

'I can't renew your work contract in these conditions. Do you have your new permit?'

'Not now.'

'What do you mean not now?'

'My papers are in the process of being renewed. It's just a matter of waiting a little while.'

'What do you mean, "waiting a little while"?'

This woman didn't know? It was a mess out there. The country was facing a major immigration crisis and the implementation of the Bossi–Fini law didn't help. All immigration offices across Italy were now swamped with new administrative and reorganisational work. There were new ordinances of expulsion to issue every day, plus the new paperwork for new arrests and allocations to detention centres and the management of phone calls with social services to place kids taken from their illegal immigrant parents into care. Officers had to learn how to perform the procedure of taking fingerprints and filling out and processing new immigrant files and all of that. And yet, despite all the administrative rearrangement, against Umberto Bossi's prediction of seeing foreigner presence in the country shrink after the introduction of his new law, the number of immigrants presenting at the immigration office was surging every day, nearly doubling in some provinces. Boats crammed with desperate people were reaching the southern Italian coasts at higher rates than ever. The humanitarian sea tragedies and shipwrecks continued to make headlines in the newspapers the average Italian read while having breakfast with an espresso and custard doughnut in his local café.

However, for us down here, in our small Italian reality, the implementation of the new law meant that immigrants had to adapt to the hitches of the new renewal procedure. Unlike before, when you could just drop into the immigration office a few days before your papers were due to expire and get it renewed in a couple of weeks, you were now required to do it by appointment through a hotline number, and appointments were set one to six months from the date your paper expired. While waiting for their appointment due date, a high number of immigrants had to live temporarily without legitimate papers, facing consequences that ranged from your employer closing their eyes to it, to a more diligent employer wrinkling her nose at the idea of keeping a paperless immigrant in her workplace, even if it was just temporary.

That was my case. Since the immigration office hotline had set the date of my renewal for two months after my documents expired, I technically turned paperless during those two months. I explained the whole thing to my boss, that I was assured by the immigration office that I was eligible to keep on working even if my papers had expired, as long as I proceeded to arrange my renewal appointment.

'Well, I don't know if you are eligible to work in my place,' she said. 'Is this appointment you're talking about next week? Can you sort it all out within a week? Otherwise, I doubt I can keep you here, boy!'

'They actually set it up so that it will be in two months, as I just told you, but trust me, they told me I can work!'

'What do you mean you can work? I can't keep you here illegally. I need documents. I can't just rely on your words, this is a business! A foreigner can't just say it's legal and I trust him at his word. I need legitimate documents to prove you are entitled to work in this country. Do you have them?'

'Not now.'

She looked puzzled. This change in the renewal process had taken many employers by surprise. My boss had to put specific details in her computer in order to issue my new contract and without that information she was unable to complete the process. However, she decided to give me a hand. She took a day off to come with me to the immigration office to sort out this problem.

We met near the immigration office and walked there. She looked confident and optimistic on our way to the immigration office saying things like, 'I'll show them if this is the way things work.' But she shrunk when she caught sight of the length of one end of the queue sticking out around the street corner. She shrunk further when she saw the full length of the queue. And it was not just one queue, there were two long queues winding down in opposite directions from the immigration office. I knew from experience that in cases like this, the average wait time before you were able to get inside the office was three to four hours.

'Let's go to that policeman!' My boss said, pointing at a police officer who stood at the immigration office door. Again, from experience, I knew she wouldn't get anything out of that policeman, but I gave her room to experiment. The policeman at the door, standing like a club doorman, was in charge of regulating the inflow and outflow of immigrants to the immigration office. Legs set apart, he stood at the door like he was God on earth. He yelled to people to get back in line, or to let the cars pass to anyone who attempted to dodge the queue or just stood aside accidentally. The whole thing felt like something between a concentration camp and the entrance of an after-hours club.

There was a small crowd of desperates near him, trying to get some quick information, all speaking over each other in broken Italian. My boss crept through in between them, elbowing her way up to the policeman, while I waited behind. I noticed a woman in a burqa with a crying baby in a pushchair trying to pass through the small crowd, hitting other people's bums in the hope that they would move but it didn't work. After spending hours waiting in a queue outside, nobody gave a shit about a baby crying, especially as some people were coming for the second or third time in the space of a month, just to hear that their documents were not ready and to come back the next month.

'Now if you don't queue up like everybody else, I won't be letting any of you in!' the lone policeman yelled to the small group of dissidents stirring around him, whose ranks included my boss.

'Everyone will pay the consequences if people don't get into the queue! I want to see who's going to get in if I don't say so!' As if they were children, kids. People who had left everything behind, had seen the impossible, farmers and artisans whose lands and lives had been seized by corporations, professionals and high-skilled workers who fled genocides and famine and had to leave behind their homes and families, addressed like kids.

The insubordinate group didn't leave, however, they just kept quiet for a few seconds and then started the whole racket once again. My boss, the only well-dressed person, stood out from the group of immigrants. She threw a few glances at me in the distance while trying vainly to get her voice heard by the policeman and I saw a shadow of panic crossing her face, her fear of morphing into what she was enacting, becoming one of those desperate people. I felt sorry for her, nobody had warned her about all this. The media, her entourage, nobody said that this was happening in her country although she could swear she knew her country very well.

'Look, I just want to know if…' she was yelling to the police officer when the guy, seriously fed up with the small group's obstinance, pointed his finger at my employer and said, 'Madam, how many times do I have to say this to you, get back in your queue!'

'I don't have to renew *my* residency permit,' she found herself clarifying.

'So, get the hell out of here! Who do you think you are!'

'What do you mean who I think I am,' she stuttered here, 'I'm Italian!'

'Well, I'm Italian too!' yelled back the police officer. 'That's why I respect the Italian laws and the Italian regulations. It is written in there at that door in Italian! In the mornings we do only submission and withdrawal of the applications. For general enquiry, you need to come back at two!'

We decided to wait for two o'clock. We got a coffee and ate something in a bar. It was still our day off after all. Then we killed the remaining time by walking around the centre of Bologna doing some window shopping. It was a bit strange, I have to say, to be walking around with my employer as if it were an everyday thing. She told me about herself. She lived with her mum though she was in her fifties. She had been married once but ran away and returned to her mother. I said, 'wow.'

We managed to get to the office relatively easily this time. After half an hour of queueing, two o'clock came. We didn't get much out of our visit. The immigration officer at the counter told her exactly what I had told her the day before, that I was not to be considered an illegal immigrant as long as I arranged my renewal appointment, and that I could keep on working during the time leading up to my renewal appointment, which of course was at the discretion of my employer.

'Ok, but which documents do I use to renew his contract? What personal information shall I put in the computer, like the document reference number, the document expiry date? What do I say to a work inspector if he comes for a check?'

'I'm sorry, madam, we can't really help with the information that needs to be entered into the computer, but as for the work inspector, I can reassure you that we have made a provisional agreement where they are committed to judge each case with more flexibility if they come in for a check. That said, I need to underline, it is still illegal to allow paperless immigrants in your workplace regardless. You will still be subjected to fines in the case that the work inspectors decide to fine you, they have all the right to do so, but hopefully, they will turn a blind eye, as we have agreed, until we have sorted this transitional predicament.'

'Hopefully? What are you talking about? I can't go to my superior and tell him that maybe the work inspector might turn a blind eye. If it is illegal, it's illegal. What I want to know is, does the current Italian legislation allow this boy to work in the territory, yes or not?'

'No madam, without legitimate documents, no.'

We walked back outside. Before leaving my employer said she would speak with her superior to see a way forward but for the moment, she had to suspend me. She called me back a few days later saying she was sorry but had to let me go.

Keeping Up

I wasn't for letting the thing put me off. There was no need, if I couldn't work legally, I just couldn't. After all, it was just a question of waiting two months before I could get a new residency permit and get another job. Then there was my citizenship waiting about two years away on the horizon. All was good.

I would be relying on my last salary and redundancy pay to cover the two coming months and decided to take it easy for a little while. So I did. I spent my days slacking, feeding my obsession with Dostoyevsky's works and Japanese manga and French and Italian comic books like Jiro Taniguchi, Osamu Tezuka, Moebius and Andrea Pazienza. At home, in a park, in a café, on a bench in a square, I would be reading. Then I'd switch to the books I received in my letterbox to review for the literary magazine I worked at. Sometimes some great works came my way, like Edward Bunker's *Dog Eats Dog*, or a new edition of one of my favourite books by Thomas Bernard, *The Loser*, or Boubacar Boris Diop's *Mirambi*, a staggering novel about the genocide in Rwanda.

Every fortnight I took the train to Cesena to train with the soccer team I had joined, the Writers National Football Club. We were training in prepare for our forthcoming match with the Singers National Football Club. Our manager and coach, two girls, seemingly twins with long blond hair, handed out our team uniforms, each with our names marked on the back, and a bottle of water and sat on the bench shouting instructions to us while we went through the warm-up. Among us were some famous authors and others whose names rang no bells. We had a shower after training and ate at a restaurant, all provided by our association, while conversing about book sales, agent issues, the number of books one reads in a week and so on. Then I'd take the train back home, headphones on all the way to Bologna—I was listening to Blonde Redhead and TV On the Radio a lot during that time. Once home, I would hang out with Ginevra and we'd drive in her yellow Twingo to get films from the video shop, watch them and get carried away with our opinions. Some works—*Blueberry, Gerry, The Thin Red Line*, and *Andrei Rublev*—left a mark on me. Then we would go out, generally around the bars in Via del Pratello where we'd always meet people we knew without any need to arrange anything, except my closest friends. They rarely put their nose out before calling, 'Hey, are you outside? Yep. Meet you in five minutes.'

We had all become adults. Gennaro had become a prominent jazz player in the jazz scene of Bologna and its provinces. Ferro gave up being a waiter, went to work for his family's building company and joined Redeso's spiritual organisation. Nico, we lost track of him over the years. I knew he moved abroad, somewhere in Indonesia, where I heard he worked as a truck driver and had a daughter who rode in the truck with him from time to time. Aster, my Eritrean friend, had become a theatre actor for one of Bologna's most experimental theatre companies and carried out solo projects on the side. As for Andrea Mancuso, formerly our Kurt Cobain, was now bald, and often in a suit whenever he came down to meet us straight from the office of his family-run water filter firm.

Andrea Mancuso was the person I saw the most. We would meet two or three times a week for a beer or a walk. Or else I'd visit him at his house, or he'd visit me at mine. I would often hear the sound of him calling my name from the window, 'Hey Red!' or it would be the horn of his Volvo if he had come to collect me by car to go to the seaside, or for a ride and dinner in Firenze, or a random drive in the countryside, but mostly we hung around in the streets of Bologna. We'd get a drink standing up, chatting outside the bar among our friends and other customers, walking up and down the road, or up to Piazza Maggiore, and then down the bars in Via Zamboni. Or we joined big circles of people we knew, or didn't, in Piazza San Francesco where there was always somebody playing djembe and an assortment of spliffs going around for everyone. That was what I liked about Bologna. The ease with which people interacted with each other. The fluid social dynamics. The good disposition, and the trust that came with it. People really engaged in conversations that went beyond facts, they talked to you, they wanted to know about you and you wanted to know about them and I took for granted that it was like this everywhere, but it was not.

On one of those nights, as I was smoking cigarettes and walking around with Andrea Mancuso, he told me that he had been quite frustrated with his life lately. I had seen him be frustrated with his line of work. He couldn't take it anymore, to be serving his family company as a salesman, and wished he could change jobs and land in something more creative.

'Why don't you quit?' I asked him.

'I can't.' He said.

'What do you mean you can't?'

'Really, you don't get it?' he stayed looking at me in perplexity like he was about to reveal something I should have known already.

'They are my family; I can't quit.'

'You'll stay there even if you don't like it?'

'Of course, it's my family! The most important thing I have. I'd never dare do this to them.'

We walked in silence for a little while, and then he took a drag of his cigarette and told me, 'You know, I always envied you. You are free, you can do whatever you want. For you, life is—*Fuck this shit!* You can wake up in the morning and call work and tell them you're quitting because you want to write that morning with no need to explain to mum or dad why you're doing it. I have to.'

It was different, looking at his family condition from this

perspective. I always looked idyllically at the Mancusos; for me, they were a portrait of a perfect family, united with a beautiful and strong set of shared values. But as I grew older, I also began noticing how the same values hindered them individually. As in many other Italian families I came across, Andrea and his sister had engendered a strong sense of obligation towards their parents, to the extent that they were spontaneously willing to sacrifice their life to meet their parent's expectations. Whereas I, in contrast, owed nothing to no one. I could decide what to do with my life and who I wanted to be, what to think, how to think, and I was aware of this privilege and its potential that night while walking with Andrea. I felt that life was strange; the impact my parents' absence had on my life was not entirely a negative one. Ironically, I now felt like I had received the greatest of the inheritances.

'I can't just leave. Do you understand?' he said.

'Yes, I do.' I said.

'Do you?'

'Yes, yes, I heard you! I told you!'

'Because if you can't understand me, who the fuck can; You're my brother!'

And I felt like I was.

Now and then I met my other siblings at my sister Moon's house—she had lived her first years in Italy with Debra-Jo, after leaving Benin. She then moved into her own flat, sharing with three other girls when she became financially independent and more confident to go her own way. Since the disappearance of Debra-Jo, Moon's flat had become our new family headquarters, possibly because she was the only feminine figure left, or simply because she cared to organise dinners for us to spend some time together. We had some good times, with Sigmund at the centre and at the height of his charisma, playing along with Klaus's subtle irony, always getting us laughing. Sometimes we were quite a big group, when Moon's flatmates joined us, or our partners had come with us, Ginevra, Daniela and all the other halves. There was not a single night that passed without the conversation falling at least once on Debra-Jo. It was now five years since she went missing. Ugo was shattered by the incident and very much fed up with our family and all that it represented, so he severed his family's relationships with us all, forbidding us to get in touch with his two kids. Five years and we were still dazed by the whole thing, still looking for answers, for a motivation behind her act, imagining and speculating all sorts of things. Some of us attributed the cause of her decision to a possible psychological breakdown that we all missed. It could have been that she just had enough of everything, of her arduous relationship, of having taken on the role of a mother at such a young age and carrying the burden of the past for us, missing out on the ludicrous side of life. She was a mother to her kids, but also a mother to us, her brothers. Faced with the option to go mad or to restore her sanity, she grasped the first great opportunity that rose before her to leave behind everything, perhaps hoping that her mind would follow the same steps, erasing her memories and providing her with a blank page. Perhaps hoping that in a new environment, where nobody knew her and her story she could finally become a normal person.

Other theories, like Lorenzo's, took a more transcendental tone. He believed that Debra-Jo had moved to a higher level of existence, which implied a different set of rules and values, judging criteria, motivations and priorities, that ordinary people like us could not grasp. He advanced the possibility that perhaps only on our level of existence did people cling to their bonds and suffer a great deal when such bonds broke, while it was possible that on higher levels a drastic cut was preferable and required and accomplished in a blink of an eye when things didn't work any longer, without too much suffering resulting on either side. Debra-Jo may have reached some sort of illumination in this sense. Whatever the reasons were behind her move, however, according to Lorenzo it wasn't for us to judge her until we really knew what happened.

GROUND

Yet amid all the speculations, I could not help thinking about the kids, her kids. After all that we went through, the life in care, our abandonment, I struggled big time to understand how she could be capable of inflicting an even worse fate on her own kids, who, year after year, never saw their mother since that night she put them to bed. How could she sleep at night? How could she go on living knowing that in another city two kids, your kids, are growing with a huge void in their soul, asking themselves why their mother had left them? Asking why she had never got back in touch with them all this time. But again, as Lorenzo said, it was not for us to judge her. Sigmund was the only one in our family Ugo had forgiven and was allowed to see our nephews again, both of whom were fond of him. Through him, we learned how they were doing throughout the years, at school and socially, and we passed them our love and gave them little presents.

***

Although still quite a playful lad, Sigmund had become calmer and more sombre since Debra-Jo's departure. He dedicated his body and soul to his work as an antiques dealer and worked so hard that he started earning considerably well. I'd usually see him at Moon's dinner parties, often wearing a fine three-piece suit, expensive shoes, and top-range Ray-Ban glasses. He had become the big man, carrying Dad's same ambitious, entrepreneurial spirit. One of those evenings, he called us all out to the street to see his brand-new BMW. Another day, he took us to see the house he had just bought out in the countryside of the tiny village of Dozza; quite an impressive house, something that Dad would have bought, although it was on a smaller scale—a detached house in the middle of hilly green lawns and fields, with something like four spacious bedrooms, a large living room, a kitchen and a garage, all rooms furnished with his antiques. I wonder if this would have ever happened if Sigmund hadn't met Don Ettore, who saw his potential when he was young and nurtured it to its fulfilment.

It was also interesting to see that one of us finally managed to get a house. I remember the first day he took us there. Klaus was also with us, walking around the house with the smile he used when he was happy for other people. It was a genuine smile of celebration for other people's achievements, in the sense that he was proud to see his brother going far like he himself had made it. Yet, that smile also concealed something else—the triviality of all that Sigmund was showing us, the futility of putting so much effort into building a life as though he knew something darker about life that we didn't. To see him walking inside the lustrous and wealthy house next to Sigmund's bounty and prosperous figure, Klaus looked like a tramp in contrast. His old and worn-out clothes seemed empty, as if they were hanging on a moving bony frame rather than being worn by a person. His baseball cap was lowered more than ever to hide his eyes entirely. He had more marks on his skin and looked gaunter than when I last saw him. Klaus looked ill.

'What's this?' Sigmund asked him, nearly unnerved. 'Don't you have food at home? Look, Ocean, he's too thin! What is this?'

'It's true,' agreed Ocean, still wearing his high-top fade haircut and austere dress code with cigarette-leg jeans and a jumper. 'Have you not been to the doctor yet, Klaus?'

'Yeah yeah, I-I-I told you I went.' Responded Klaus. 'He said that I need to e-e-eat more and healthier and gave me s-s-s-some to-to-to topical creams for the skin marks.'

'Creams that are not working at all by the look of all the marks you have there. You have them all over your face. What kind of creams did he give you?' asked Sigmund.

'Since when have you stu-stu-studied dermatology, Sigmund? Tell me, you know more than my do-do-do-doctor now. He told me that it would take time to heal. It g-g-g-gets worse before getting better. Have y-y-you ever heard of the term he-he-healing crises?'

'Who cares about healing crises! I'm worried about you!'

'D-d-don't waste time worrying about me, Sigmund. W-w-worry about yourself f-f-f-for the sake of huma-ma-manity!'

GROUND

We laughed. We carried on checking out Sigmund's new house. We listened to him comment on how that chest that was made of pure oak wood and dated back to the Renaissance and that cupboard was a Louis XIV. We were served drinks and snacks, yet none of us had a clue of the kind of hardships Klaus was going through. Klaus was paperless. His last request for renewal was rejected on the basis that his annual income didn't meet the criteria of the Bossi–Fini law, an income that was in factual terms equal to zero, since Klaus had been unemployed for at least a couple of years. However, Klaus made no efforts to amend his legitimacy. He gave up, as usual, as he had on the football pitch in St Catherina, with school, with breakdancing, skateboarding and all the other disciplines he took up along the way. He just gave up and went on living his life as an illegal immigrant with all the difficulties that came with such a life. That said, none of us were aware that he was out of work and paperless. Whenever we ran into him on the street or met at Moon's he would draw a positive picture of his life, where everything worked fine, he went to work every morning in a factory in Imola by train, and nobody questioned him more than the necessary, we all just believed him, just as we believed him when he justified the visible symptoms of his declining health as a combination of dermatitis and the onset of asthma. Klaus appeared lethargic and had lost his typical spark. But we believed him. The real sad part of this story, possibly sadder than Debra-Jo's end, is that none of us had a clue about Klaus's true life. Except a girl called Tania, his girlfriend.

Tania, a young woman from southern Italy, had just moved north to Bologna to study at the University of Art. She met Klaus on February 7, 2004, in a club under the Two Towers called Soda Pops; an RnB club where Klaus used to be a regular. She was 24. He was 31. They met because of his cap, it had fallen onto the ground and she picked it up for him. They started a conversation. They clicked. When she was about to go home, he offered to walk her. 'I-I-I don't have a car,' he stuttered, 'is it ok if I walk you h-h-h-ome?'

She accepted.

They walked in the rain to her house in the Corticella Area. She let him come up to her house, a flat she shared with other students. Something about his manners, courteous and caring, convinced her to let this stranger sleep at hers. He offered to sleep on the sofa she had in her room, while she slept in her bed as usual. The morning after, they swapped numbers and he left. It took about a month before he resolved to call her, asking her out. When they met, they started dating, and they became a couple in no time, a very exclusive couple.

Her room became their house, their den. Sleeping, sex, meals, fighting, crying and watching films, all unravelled inside her room in her shared house near the central station. Watching films became their shared passion, her being a film student and him a culture geek. She was, in fact, stunned by Klaus's expansive knowledge of film, music, politics, conspiracy theories and esotericism alike. Not a single day passed without him having leafed through at least one newspaper, a current affairs magazine, and having done online research about things like the war in Iraq, the rise of Islamophobia, the booming Chinese economy, the Vatican horrors and so on. She described him to her friends as an incredible person, charming, brilliant, with an infectious sense of humour, and thirsty for knowledge, even though at first glance he seemed ignorant.

That Klaus was uncultivated was actually a shared impression of many of her friends of that time. Some nights, for example, during spontaneous debates in the kitchen of her flat with friends and flatmates, Klaus would retreat in silence rather than express his own opinions, to the point that it was usual for her to be asked, 'what's wrong with your boyfriend, he never speaks.' But then, once the two found themselves alone in their bedroom, Klaus would spontaneously open up again to lead inspiring conversations. Only with her would he let his light shine. Only she was the person allowed to meet the true Klaus. Only within that room. She felt he was a hidden gem, a person who was insecure with people, antisocial, who would rather not leave their bedroom to avoid being seen by her flatmates when she left him alone to go to university. He escaped everyone else but her, only her, day and night, developing an almost morbid attachment.

But it appears that he left Tania in the dark, too, about some key aspects of his life. For example, when it came to his past and his mother Maman Natalie, he kept things very superficial when they touched upon the subject. He'd respond with denial when she tried to encourage him to reconnect with his mother and would get very irritated if she insisted or when she tried to encourage him to talk about his father. Dad entered their conversations mostly as a recipient of Klaus's small day-to-day grievances. Let's say he lost his hashish somewhere in the bedroom, he'd swear at Dad as if the old man was in the room and was responsible for the incident. 'Where d-d-did you put it, Dad? I know you hid it from me bec-c-c-cause you don't want me to smoke! Can you see, it's always him, always him do-do-doing this kind of shit!' He couldn't find his lighter: 'What the fuck are you hi-hi-hiding it for, Dad! I will smoke anyway, I'll show you!'

With time, Tania grew suspicious about Klaus's life, about the actual state of his work and accommodation and, after he kept on finding excuses not to take her to his home, about his supposed shared house in Bologna's suburbia. He gave her hints about his flatmates, all students, and although she expressed many times the desire to meet these people, to have dinner with them, he'd postpone week after week while continuing to live in her flat, taking showers, washing his clothes, eating and sleeping there. As for the work, he told her he worked part-time as a stockkeeper in a factory in Imola following a random weekly schedule. Sometimes he went to work three times a week, other times once, then four, and his shifts would start always at 1 p.m., always after lunch. Not once early in the morning like everybody else. She'd watch him prepare himself to go to work, put his things in a backpack, and then leave, coming back later in the evening around dinnertime, 8, 8:30 p.m.

It took her a while to understand that he'd been lying to her until the day came when he was forced to let out part of the truth once she put him on the spot. He admitted he was homeless, his real home an abandoned house on the outskirts of Bologna before he met her. As for his working conditions, she didn't dare challenge him and rather played the role of partner to a working man, although she could intuit what the reality was. Coming from a very traditional culture and being younger than him, she felt that it was disrespectful to question the sincerity of her man. She was in love with him, desperately in love, ready to embrace his complexity, to be his lover and best friend, his nurse and mother, to cook for him, clean after him and wash his clothes. It was a hard job because of both his temperament and his insecurity from his problematic childhood. Klaus was a very difficult person, very stubborn and grumpy. He was specific in the way he ate and was asocial and jealous, posing restrictions to who his girlfriend shouldn't see and where she shouldn't go. The couple reached a point of a hermetic madness of jealousy where she was unable to have male friends. She was aware of being too young to take up such demanding work of caring for a person like Klaus, who required tending day and night, but she was happy that way, happy to nurture him, feeling like it was her mission to lead this lost man through the dark recesses of his troubled existence.

It was about a year from their first encounter that she started realising that something was undoubtedly wrong with her partner's health. His asthma attacks had intensified, he lost weight, and mysterious marks on his skin had spread all over his body. She thought at first that he suffered from coeliac disease and put him on a gluten-free diet, which gave no results whatsoever, so she took him to the doctor. Based on the nature of his symptoms the doctor decided to administer an HIV test. It was a day in February 2006, almost two years from when they had met, that they received the result of the test. Klaus was HIV-positive. Both were devastated.

Ground

When the day arrived to renew my residency permit, I made my way to the immigration office early in the morning. There was only a thirty-minute wait as opposed to the depressing queues I experienced with my ex-employer two months earlier. All the documentation required was in a folder in which I included as much relevant information as I could get my hands on: proof of work, P44, payslips from the past tax years, the contract with my second publisher and the contracts for the two anthologies that published my short stories. I had eight ID photos, the thirty-euro stamps, the completed application form, my tenancy agreement, a declaration from my landlord confirming I was still living in her flat and my marriage certificate. The plan was to apply for a permit based on familial circumstances rather than work-related ones, which would be easier since I was aware that my financial performance was way below the Bossi–Fini law requirement for the past tax year. Along with our wedding certificate, Ginevra wrote and gave me her own declaration confirming we were still happily married just to play it safe. She drew a little heart on the paper's corner.

Finally, it was my turn. I walked up to the counter. The officer went through all my paperwork and then I was led by another officer into a room where two more officers sat behind a desk swamped with paperwork and files. They made me write down my details on a form, then got me to place my fingertip in ink and print it in a box on the document that said 'digit'. They showed me where to go to wash the ink off my hand and set a date for the collection of my new residency permit, which was scheduled for a month afterwards. Then I was dismissed.

I felt good now that the worst was over. I just needed to hold on for an extra month then this all shit would be done. The marriage-based residency permits had a validity of four years, rather than one. By the time it expired, I would already have been awarded Italian citizenship. It was no use to go through the hassle of finding a job for a month, and I calculated that I could survive another month with the same resources I had used the last two months if I reduced expenses even further. So, life carried on in Bologna with the sunny optimism of Bologna's vibe. Ginevra graduated, I attended her graduation ceremony at the Communication Science campus with her parents from Milan and some of her friends. We stood watching her, in her black robes and graduation hat, answering eloquently and slightly nervously the questions concerning the subject of her dissertation posed to her by the four professors sitting in a line in front of her. The smarty pants got all the answers right and came out with the highest mark plus *cum laude*. We celebrated in a restaurant with her parents and close friends after the ceremony. Then we went to drink something in a bar.

I was proud of her, proud she was my partner and a friend, and glad we had bumped into each other at some point in our lives. We loved each other. We liked spending time together. We liked our life, despite the ups and downs and some drama, like when she succumbed to her blinding anger and smashed plates on the floor, kicked the wardrobe to the point of breaking it, or ran outside in the street just wearing her nightgown, furious, speeding off in her car, the wheels squealing. Sometimes, I have to say, it was difficult to trace the contour of our arguments. I guess there was jealousy upstream, unresolved jealousy flowing for both of us and frustration in our inability to land somewhere normal. We were sacrificing some deep basic needs, such as the need for exclusivity, stability, comfort, reassurance and protection for some higher cause of a boundary-free lifestyle. I had no problem sleeping at night when she was not lying next to me, clueless of where she was, but it always hurt, every night when I heard her coming into the flat, showering first. But it was alright. She'd glide back under the covers next to me, we'd hug, we'd talk. And I know it was the same the other way around that it hurt her whenever I came back home from a night out with a lover. Actually, Ginevra struggled more than me in all this open relationship business because she was more jealous than me. She could hardly bear to hear me talk about another girl. One night, she freaked out when a girl rang our doorbell as we were deep asleep. 'Who the fuck is she!' she burst out after I leaned out of the window to tell the girl, who was drunk, to go home. Ginevra and I stayed up until morning arguing about the incident and I never understood what we were arguing about in the end. What were her true wishes for our relationship? Why maintain an open relationship if this caused her suffering? Was it for fear of commitment? Was she trying to demonstrate something to herself? To me? Or was it because she was a free spirit and wanted to express that part of herself no matter the cost? I wonder how things would have turned out between us if I had never proposed for us to have an open relationship in the first place. If I had proposed the opposite, that I wanted her all for myself and I was able to make her feel safe, desired and unique.

Incidents like the one of the drunk girl were recurrent; Bologna was a small place, we could run into our lovers alone or together any time, in bars, venues or on the street. Some other times those incidents were sweeter and brought us closer together somehow, like the day she called me from her parent's house in Milan crying because of a letter she had received from one of her lovers. I asked her to read the letter, trying to help her. In short, the person writing to her was upset and called her selfish and wished they had never met. It hurt to understand how close they had gotten without me knowing as she read through the letter, sobbing. It hurt to see the impact the words of this stranger had on my wife. But I also adored her very much for this, for looking at me as the first person she sought for help, even in this type of matter. I managed to calm her down, putting the message conveyed in the letter in another perspective, like, 'he's angry because he likes you,' so that by the end of the call she was more relieved and lighter. Then we hung up.

Ginevra was a free spirit also in geographical terms. She was a nomad. She travelled alone to Latin America and North America. She had friends spread across Europe, whom she visited regularly. In Italy, it was the same. In Bologna, she was always among her friends, near or far. My life was more static. I travelled only for writing-related work; otherwise, I tended to be stationary. I stayed home and went out only at night to meet my group of friends.

One of those nights, Andrea Mancuso told me he had left his family company. Another night, he told me he was moving to Barcelona. Then a week later, he came to say bye to me outside a bar in Via del Pratello where I was having a drink. Parked at the edge of the street was his green Volvo that we had ridden in so many times, packed with his belongings from the back seats down to the trunk. I asked him if I could buy him a drink. No, he said, he had a long drive ahead. We sat on the patio smoking cigarettes, strangely with nothing to say that night. We just calmly smoked cigarettes and flicked the ashes, flinging the butts on the street. Then it was time for him to leave, he said. I accompanied him to his car. After fifteen years of friendship, it felt strange that we would not see each other with the usual frequency anymore. We hugged. I wished him good luck. He wished it back to me. Then he got inside the car and drove off, and I remember admiring him. I mean, it takes some guts to go from the place he was, where he felt obliged to stick with his family, to then cut, take, pack and go. One of the bravest acts I ever witnessed.

Then, a few nights afterwards, I came across Lorenzo in Piazza San Francesco. As it was with my other siblings, our relationship had loosened over time. I might have seen him once or twice at Moon's house since Debra-Jo's disappearance, but all I knew about him was that he had been through rough times and then managed to redeem himself with an LP he recorded for a well-placed Italian producer. And yet he looked far from content. He was run down, heavier, shadowier and bitter. More bitter than I had ever seen him. His music wasn't going anywhere, he told me. We were having a beer, sitting on the short staircase outside the entrance of the church in Piazza San Francesco. The square was partially filled with people, sitting on benches and in circles on the floor, drinking from cans and socialising. The smell of dope filled the air. The collective chat pierced the early night of that quiet corner of the piazza.

'It was perfect,' he told me. 'I had it all. Twin. All. All I wanted in my life, I had it. Zanetti gave me a flat with all the music equipment I needed to create my own music. He also gave me the keys to his Porsche. A dream. He opened his life to me, I don't know, like we became two brothers instantly. He introduced me to his circle of friends and family. Once the full album, with my picture on the cover, was completed I held it in my hands, I tell you, nothing compares to that feeling! This is my album! My album!'

He said that as if he held it in his hand, his trophy, at this very moment. But with an expression that hardly matched the one he might have had that day at Zanetti's studio, his face instead filled with frustration.

'There was just one last thing left to do before I could go public, Twin. Just one more. To shoot the video clip of the leading song.'

Zanetti's idea for the video for the song was a gangster rap scene in a swimming pool with plenty of girls in bikinis and money flying everywhere, Lorenzo told me. He arranged to shoot the video in Bulgaria with a Bulgarian crew, as that would have been cheaper than in Italy. Girls, a house with a swimming pool and the film crew, all were sorted and paid for. So were the hotel rooms for Zanetti and Lorenzo. Spirits were high, given the trip to Bulgaria. The two artist friends felt optimistic. 'We're going to rock, man. Captain Ben is going to be an absolute hit!' They said to each other. At this point, Lorenzo gave Zanetti a piece of information that changed everything drastically, when the producer, booking the plane tickets online, asked Lorenzo for his documents, intending to enter his details and go through the check-in. Only then did Lorenzo reveal to him the full picture of his immigration status. He told him he could not give him any documents because he possessed no legitimate documents and his residency permit had long expired. Without that he could not go to Bulgaria, he could not go anywhere outside Italy.

'What do you mean you don't have papers,' the producer asked him, aghast. 'You're telling me now, just a few days from the shoot after I arranged and paid everyone! Why didn't you tell me before? Why didn't you tell me before that you were not Italian? With all the people I know I would have been able to sort you out. I could have also helped you to get fucking citizenship, I know a fucking senator, who comes to my nights and wants me to work on an advertisement for him and could pull out all the papers you needed. You are an idiot. A fucking idiot!'

Zanetti went on a rampage. And of course, Lorenzo, feeling guilty and angry with himself for having blown up his greatest chance and letting down his new friend who had opened the gates of Heaven to him, responded to Zanetti by yelling and swearing back at him, until he lost it and held him by his jacket and pushed him against the wall. And from there, it was all over. The dream of Captain Ben, his personal studio, the Porsches, all over. Chased away by Zanetti, Lorenzo took a train back to Bologna to never see or hear from the producer again. Zanetti never answered the phone calls Lorenzo made in an attempt to apologise. The Captain Ben project continued without Lorenzo. The album was still released with Lorenzo's voice, and the video featured another black guy amongst a swarm of girls in bikinis, by a pool in Bulgaria. Since all the music rights for the Captain Ben project belonged to Zanetti, he was legally entitled to do whatever he wanted with it. Besides, Lorenzo was nobody, without papers he had no rights and no bargaining power. All he could do was sit and watch the video being played on MTV, the song he co-created climbing up the charts to the top ten on mainstream radio.

'But fuck it,' he carried on. 'You know, Twin, Fuck the album! What hurts me more is how I fucked up that relationship with Zanetti. His eyes, when I pushed him into the wall, still haunt me. He believed in me. We spent nights watching National Geographic on TV in his house together, drinking beers and laughing. And anger took over me. This is what weighs on me the most. It's as if everything in our life is set up to fail. To crumble all the time. Even when everything is going great, there is always that small thing that brings everything down. There is something in our family that haunts us. You heard the story of the Aremo?'

'Yes, I did'

'Well, I always thought it was bullshit, but I don't know there must be something true in it. Whatever that guy did, it cursed us. What if we are living a life we are not supposed to live, if only the Aremo had respected the royal tradition and accepted to die and be buried with his father?'

I thought it through, this idea that we were damned, cursed by the Aremo mutiny and found myself thinking the opposite, that we were blessed. But I didn't feel like telling him. I don't know why. I felt sorry hearing how things had turned sour for my brother, just over a miserable piece of paper. I justified his anger. How could you not burst at some point under this constant pressure? His illusion of being as Italian as any other Italian had the upper hand over his judgement, cracking his system, overriding his mind and driving him to believe all the way through the dealings with Zanetti that he could operate as freely as any other Italian and easily sign contracts and cross the national borders with just a national ID. No, there were some borders he could not pass. He got angry because he felt ashamed of himself for having fallen into such a stupid miscalculation. Anger at his other identity, the migrant, which seemed to have had the upper hand over his contending identity, the Italian, at last. Anger because he had lost the battle against the Italian government. My brother was still paperless when I met him. He was taking any shitty cash-in-hand job he came across and sleeping at friends'. He turned down my invitation to come and stay at mine for a while, with the excuse that he was fine there where he was. We walked together for another drink, then we went our separate ways after our usual bye, a handshake in the American way.

***

A month had passed and I was queueing at the immigration office again on the day I was set to collect my renewed residency permit. The length of the queue was the worst I had ever seen. It started in two places at both ends of the street, merging at the door. At the front, I could see from far away the next two immigrants to get in, a North African and a Middle Eastern guy. They must have been there hours before the opening time to save their places. We were not given a specific time slot, just a date, which wasn't even firm itself, in the sense that we could queue for hours to just be told to come next week because our papers were not ready yet. Or we could be refused the papers for a number of other reasons. It was an anxiety-inducing process, going through the final stage. Two long queues of refugees and economic immigrants queued for about three hours outside in the street hoping that all would go well. Hoping they will accept your request for a family reunion, so you can get your family here. Hoping that your work permit will be granted, so you can provide for your family wherever they are. Hoping that they did not reject your application because the last thing in the world you need right now and at this stage of your life is to get deported back to your country.

I was somewhere close to the middle of my queue after about an hour and behind me the queue was just getting longer with latecomers joining. A police officer stood at the immigration office door, to regulate the flux. There was order and diligence among the immigrants because no one would put up with shit that could cost time or even put themselves at risk of some crazy consequences. You never know in a time like this. You saw a lot of shit happening. You just wanted to be cool and to get it done.

Then it started raining. Just an April shower but no one wanted to lose their place by going to find shelter under the portico on the other side of the street and having to start the queue from the beginning, because there was a tacit agreement that here no one would keep your place, getting wet for you. We had no other choice than to hold on in the queue. Meanwhile, the rain flattens the hair of white people and Latinos and softens the curly hair of black people, trickles down faces, down collars and drenches clothes. Even the ones trying to alleviate the effects of the water by covering their heads with their jackets soon got soaked anyway. But we stood our ground. As every man came out of the office door, whom we all watched from afar, the queue moved one step forward, more like a conveyor belt carrying cut meat to the next stage of labour. Some mothers with kids had to move under the shelter when it became unbearable. In these cases, people made an exception and pledged to hold their places. I looked forward at the hundred people I had before me and backward at the hundred behind me. Heads sunken between shoulders to cope with the rain and the cold that came with having wet clothes, all with the same expression of humiliation and indignation at having to put up with such disrespectful treatment since each one of us, in the back of our minds, even those coming from a remote little place in the pastoral mountains of Kazakhstan, were well aware that the technological advancements of our time could provide a way for the immigration office to prevent all of this from happening, that there were ways to avoid hundreds of people queueing for hours in the rain. But no. We had to wait in the queue. The only plausible explanation for treatment of this kind was that we were not welcome. They didn't feel like investing in better technology to make it easier for a so-called 'invasion' of immigrants. If things were so tedious people would just be put off, they seemed to think.

In order to better cope with the situation, we chatted amongst ourselves. I heard lamentations of long journeys, of life savings going into the hands of traffickers, of borders and the families divided by them. I saw fierce people coming for the umpteenth time, this time with a lawyer to appeal the rejection of their permits and the subsequent deportation order, and I could see that they were not at peace while they brushed their wet hair back with their hands, telling me how they were going to fuck these fucking immigration officers up in broken Italian. Another exalted all the benefits of the progress of his life in Italy, boasting about his good salary and the boss who treated him well. The Pakistani guy next to me showed a photo of his daughter and wife somewhere in rural Pakistan to his compatriot, screening the picture from the rain with his hand. Some others hosted more people under their umbrellas. If we heard somebody start to sing a solemn song from his country, we raised our heads to see who it was.

A Nigerian guy with tribal scars on his cheeks started talking to me. It turned out he had recognised me from my literary work. He never read any of my books, he said, but remembered he had seen me in an interview on TV on RAI. He was a doctor at the S. Orsola Hospital, Bologna's main hospital. He had been in Italy for ten years, had applied for citizenship two years ago and was still waiting. I realised while he was talking that he was choosing his words very carefully. Then I realised I was doing the same. Then I realised that an Eastern European woman in front of us was also doing this, trying to sound as eloquent as possible, when she crept into our conversation and corrected the Nigerian guy by saying, 'It's not two years! The waiting time for being awarded citizenship is officially three years but realistically it takes four years.' I know she was trying to let us know she was in the same boat, a would-be-citizen applicant, a veteran like us, a special immigrant, the ones who had been there long enough to apply for citizenship, not a newcomer like most of the people in the queue, who could hardly speak Italian. We were another kind. Then she wanted to know who among us was the writer, just to take the opportunity to reveal to us that she too was an intellectual, in fact, she was a teacher, and she had also worked in a press in Rome. A pretentious conversation between pseudo-intellectuals shifted into political activism over the immigration matter. It was stupid, we said, to take the blows and not to fight back, swearing to each other to keep in touch and set up an immigration movement that would challenge shit like the Bossi–Fini law. Our motivations were high, robust, genuine and heartfelt, but it was just a game. When it was the teacher's turn to walk into the immigration office, she came with her brand new permit in her plastic folder that she put in her bag, and she just waved bye-bye. It was to be expected. As soon as we were all in possession of our new papers, after going through the humiliation of waiting three hours in the rain, our dignity returned and off we went, walking tall, as if we had never been part of this crowd of desperates.

Things didn't go as well for me when it came to my turn. The officer at the counter told me my application failed to meet the financial criteria as my annual income fell too far below the Bossi–Fini requirement. Not that they had rejected my application, just that they had to put it on hold in order for me to provide more evidence of my earnings. Fuck, I thought, queueing for nothing just to hear that I had to return with more documents another day to queue again. I told the officer that I had already given him all that I had to prove my finances. There were no hidden payslips under the bed.

'Anyway,' I told him 'This is precisely the reason why I'm applying on the basis of my marriage to an Italian citizen, rather than for work-related reasons. I gave you my marriage certificate, right?'

'I know, I know, you did,' the officer, wearing a white lab coat like in *CSI*, answered. 'Still, we need to understand how you sustain yourself, nobody can live a year with the amount you provided, unless you are involved in some criminal activity, which is part of the problem we want to solve. Is your wife working, at least? Can you prove she provides for you?'

'No, she just graduated.'

'You see. So how do you survive on such a low income then?'

That was actually one of the worst tax years of my life. I worked only six months and spent the remaining six months mainly working on a novel that was rejected by all publishers because it was too sci-fi. Plus, I hadn't gotten any royalties from my last two publications because I sold just enough to cover the upfront payment they gave me, both of which had come out in earlier tax years anyway, as the officer pointed out. As for the publishing contracts I provided him, both proved nothing, he said, because again they referred to financial activities of earlier years. One was five years old.

This didn't prove I hadn't earned sufficiently that year from the half a year of legitimate work I had done. I had earned sufficient amounts for myself to sustain myself according to *my own* standards, even though neither Bossi nor Fini would agree. I took plenty of other small jobs that fell out of the radar of the new regulation because they were undeclared jobs, like weekend jobs, substitutions and salutary jobs. I didn't have big expenses either and I never was a person who spent on new clothes, holidays or new appliances. I sold my car—a Renault 4 I bought a couple of years before—to get some liquidity, and I would get my shopping from the value range at the Lidl. I was used to eating one meal a day if that was required. Or going only on bread for a few days when I had nothing else in the pantry if that gave me more time to write. It is not as difficult as one may think; your body gets used to it quickly. You lose your appetite in general and food becomes superfluous. Plus, my rent was considerably low, and I shared it with Ginevra, although she lived there less than I did—she increasingly spent time with her parents in Milan or somewhere abroad—and our landlord didn't mind if we paid three or four months late. But how could I translate all this into a language the immigration office could comprehend?

'So, let me be clear, boy,' the officer went on. 'I notice you speak and understand Italian very well, if you have not been working, if you were not involved in any criminal activity during those six months, what have you been doing in Italy?'

'Writing.'

'Writing books, you mean?'

'Yes.'

'Books, books, books, that's not a job! You guys don't come here to play around with writing books. Look, let's say I play guitar and in my country there is no work and I move to a more developed country and I spend six months playing the guitar instead of working, is that sensible to you? Look, I certainly can't issue you a residency permit in these conditions.'

It was strange. We were both aware that we had just fallen into a loophole in the system. On the one hand, they could not permit me to stay in the country because I proved I was not self-reliant enough according to their criteria. On the other hand, they could not repatriate me because I was bound by marriage to an Italian woman. And the idea of it, the idea of a whole person's life being pinned down to a few thousand missing euros from a fucking tax year, annoyed me more than ever before. How many lives had this fucking new law affected? There were loads of people who hadn't met a Ginevra but believed in their own art and were unprepared for the new law and were now facing expulsion. Anger was boiling in me. I'd been writing on average ten hours a day. I knew who I was, I knew I had lived three times the life of that immigration officer at the counter. I knew this country inside out. I had traversed across Italy and witnessed all sorts of Italian realities, from problematic situations to more ordinary ones. I experienced the Italian music scene, I worked for Berlusconi's TV channel as a music programme presenter, I worked in the Italian literature industry, in the theatre industry, I protested in students' political upheavals, got barred by the police for hours in a tunnel near the French border during the Ventimiglia protest. I rioted and escaped the tear gas at the

G8 summit in Genoa's protest the day Carlo Giuliani was killed by the police. I saw an Italy the immigration officer would never see, all the times I'd been targeted randomly by the police and laughed at when I asked them to give me back the twenty euros they had just stolen from me, or when I got ordered to get out of my car with a gun pointed at me just because I looked suspicious. He didn't know how it felt to be on this side of Italy. What about my life with nuns and priests and broken kids, and single mothers in religious institutions, or the foster home, or the Italy of the tribunal of minors that removed me from me my parents' authority, the Italy of being stateless, paperless, of sleeping rough on benches, in parks, in a car, the Italy that told me over and over throughout the years, 'sure, we're going to give you a call in the next few days,' when I went for an interview and that never did because of my skin colour, or that told me, 'I'm sorry the room is rented already,' when I had booked to view it on that fucking same morning. What about my work experience, my time as a chef, dishwasher or nursery assistant, delivery man, retailer in a supermarket, or cleaner in a gay club where I spent mornings cleaning post-sodomisation shit from the toilet floors and picking up cigarettes butts from the courtyards, packaging nails in factories, cutting up PVC in another factory, doing telephone marketing, and glueing up ads with a brush around the streets of Bologna. I travelled Italy from north to south, east to west when I went around for book launches and conferences. I fucking played the bells of the churches for this fucking country when I was a kid. Who was this guy talking to?

'You know what?' I said. 'Fuck you man! Seriously fuck you!'

'Say it again and forget your papers!'

I looked around the room, to the officers and the few immigrants at the counters waiting for their papers, staring at me like I was the usual troublemaker. I turned to the officer and shouted, 'Fuck you!' and then to the entire room, 'Fuck you all! Fuck you!' and I walked off.

Anger banging inside my head, I carried on walking with fists clenched ready to attack the first person that came on my way. My mind advised me to keep on walking, just keep on walking. I knew that if I were to stop I would give in to some regrettable act. It was anger directed at everyone, anger against a world that kept pushing me out. I clenched my fists harder and shouted at the top of my lungs 'Fuck you all!'

I finally got home and lay down on the sofa, letting the anger subside. I thought to call Ginevra and let her know but then I changed my mind. I didn't want to spoil her time with her parents in Milan. I just turned on some music and started meditating over a way forward now that plans had changed and I had to live for longer than expected, for an indefinite amount of time, with no papers. Plus, I was in deep shit with money after I had lived three months without working. If I had been already unemployed for three months, with no prospect of legal work, my proof of income was certainly set to fail next year as well. It was maddening and tiring just to think about it. I knew I needed to get a job urgently since the last thing I wanted was to start borrowing money from people.

I began to search for cash-in-hand jobs that same day. Made some phone calls to places I knew were not fussy. A newsstand agency that I had worked for in the past, a semi-illegal temporary work agency, friends that had connections. I went around the city to give my CV to dodgy places and then Redeso found me a job in a couple of days, through a friend of his who was looking for a kitchen porter. It was practically a dishwashing job in terrible conditions, ten hours a day, split shift, and I'd get wet a lot, but at least there were no questions, no interviews and I was paid under the counter. I started scouring pots and sticking cutlery in the dishwasher all day, keeping an eye open for better opportunities meanwhile.

On the literary front, I kept receiving rejection letters from publishers saying that it was too risky to invest in sci-fi when it seemed that everything around me was sci-fi. The world was sci-fi. However,

I did receive an offer to teach once a week for a three-month creative writing course in a high school in Pavia and I went for it. I arranged with my employer at the restaurant that I would get a friend of mine to substitute for me on the days I had to go to Pavia.

'I don't mind,' he said, 'you or another, it's the same as long as this place is nice and clean.' My friend was an Egyptian guy I had been drinking with lately in Via del Pratello, paperless as well, and was therefore happy to get some shifts. I told him I would give him more with time. 'No problem, Red,' he said.

I also got a request to write an article for an online magazine for an eccentric wine producer in Piedmont, which included a helicopter tour over their vineyard, their huge property and the small town. I got paid two weeks' worth of the kitchen porter job plus a wooden box of an assortment of snobby, expensive wine. Then I had my football training days in Cesena with fellow writers to attend, and days when I had deadlines to submit book reviews to *Pulp* Magazine that I hadn't even started reading. I'd call Mohamed, give him his week rota at the restaurant, pay him at the end of the month when I received my salary in front of a pint in a bar in Via del Pratello. By that time magic Via del Pratello had become my second home, that road with cobblestone pavement, the old houses with porches all along the street, and the bars, always people standing outside, glass in hand, smoking, 'Hey Red, how're you doing?' We all knew each other. I got poured unmeasured whiskeys, no rocks, just old school where a single was half a glass or more depending on how drunk the bartender was. If he had had a bad day with his girlfriend, he was even more generous. And I would get another glass. And another. We would move from bar to bar with friends. And there would be another bar, and more chatting with the different regulars and newcomers in and outside the bar. There was always a girl I had fucked or I was fucking or I was going to fuck that would make the night more interesting. Some nights I would find myself in the company of just a male friend and the rest was a group of lovers I had been with recently, my wife included. There was always someone I had once shared a house with. Someone I worked with in this place or that place, chefs and waiters, artists and writers, performers I had collaborated with, who often would witness the worst side of me when I was very wasted, starting meaningless fights, or lying in the middle of the fucking street just for the sake of it.

'Hey Red, what's happening to you?' they would say to me.

'I'm fine, I'm fine.'

One night I got drunk sharing the last bottle of whisky with a new acquaintance who knew me by reputation, and he said, 'do you know why I love you, mate? Because you are a true outsider. No matter what you do you will always be.' It was the first time I had been addressed as an outsider. I couldn't say if it was a compliment or not, if I liked it or not, but it stuck with me.

As for Ginevra and me, three years into our marriage, the passion had decreased to such a degree that we became unsexual with each other. We looked for sexual satisfaction outside the marriage and became more like friends or perhaps even siblings. We were too similar to counter our individual unconventional drives, too young to be in such a complex open lifestyle, which required a degree of mature emotional care and management. We first needed to understand how to be in a monogamous relationship before adventuring into a polygamous one. Monogamy has its own set of rules, you need to know how to keep focused, how to keep the relationship alive, how to feed it, how to give to each other just for the sake of it and to be okay with it, while Ginevra and I went out in pure anarchic style. Except for having protected sex outside the relationship, we had no rules, and the domestic fire dwindled away.

By the time she turned 28, Ginevra was offered a place as a lecturer in Florence for a master's degree programme in fashion, which required that she settle there. She found a room in a shared house and commuted every week from Milan or Bologna to Florence. Her increasingly nomadic life meant we saw each other even less now. She came back to Bologna on some weekends, and occasionally I went to visit her in her new flat in Florence.

She started an affair with her flatmate. Then it became serious. The guy, a sweet architecture student and DJ of afrobeat and funk, was of course brainy, like all of Ginevra's lovers. We got on well, the three of us, for a while, with her introducing us to people, 'This is my husband, this is my boyfriend!' when we went out together. Sometimes we were a group of four when Ginevra's ex-boyfriend, a skater from Bologna, hung out with us too. The only girl I have ever known who could have her husband, her lover and her ex hanging happily and innocuously together in her new flat in Florence. Playing vinyl, talking about skating, music, films, books and fashion.

There wasn't a specific day Ginevra and I broke up. We never expressed it through words, never had a conversation about it. We separated over a long period of time slowly and quietly, as her relationship with her boyfriend in Florence grew stronger and stronger and ours loosened. With him, Ginevra, I guess scarred by the torment of the open relationship experience she had with me, established a monogamous relationship. As for me, I continued to only have affairs, as I was not ready to commit to anything serious.

One day I received a letter from Bologna's immigration office. I opened it and pulled the letter out. It was my renewed residency permit. I don't know why and how, perhaps they concluded that since they could not deport me due to my marriage with an Italian citizen, nor keep me in legal limbo they had no other choice but to overlook my poor earnings and rectify my status. So, there it was. A home-delivered brand-new permit, with four years of validity, which meant I never had to queue at the immigration office ever again since I would turn Italian by the time the paper expired. But to be honest, I didn't feel any true satisfaction or joy at having won against the Italian immigration machine. I didn't care anymore that I could finally reclaim my place in the social order. Things had stretched so far to the point that, as it happened with Lorenzo and Klaus, I had lost the ability to connect with life healthily. I had lost purpose; not even writing seemed like an option any longer. Everything seemed pointless and I didn't even try to change jobs now that I could and I kept the same cash-in-hand kitchen porter job I shared with Mohamed, happy to get soaked and greasy at the end of my night shift for a miserable pay. I just carried on with my life in the same nihilistic fashion, fucking around, getting wasted and getting angry. Something dark was growing within me. I'd been suffering from sleeping problems since I was a kid but there was now something new added to it. I began experiencing sleep paralysis, where my body was unresponsive but my thoughts and mind were alert throughout the night. I could hardly let a sound out, nor move a finger, but I could see the elements of my room, being consciously awake. The event was rendered terrifying by the perception of dark presences approaching me. I would see and not see them; they existed in a grey zone between my waking and sleeping mind. But there were no doubts they were there since I would perceive them coming closer, touching me, their weight hanging over me, holding me, breathing on me, but I couldn't move. I'd put all my energy trying to awaken my body and free myself from their hold, but nothing. I'd try to shout for help, but nothing.

Once on a night train on my way back from a literary event in Paris, I was sleeping on a night carriage, the one with seats that turned into two bunk beds. I was sleeping on the top bed when the sleep paralysis set in. My mind woke up, my body still as a rock, lying on one side facing the interior of the room, and this huge, horrible cat started crawling over me from the far end of my bed. It was not just the presence of the cat, its weight on me and the feeling of not being able to move it off that made it frightening, it was the whole environment I had sunk into, the fear of not knowing what was going to happen and when my body would awake. The fear could last forever. I strained like hell in an effort to call for help, producing only a muffled hiss like, 'Hhhhhelp hhhhhelp!' The people sleeping in the compartment got up anyway. I could see them coming closer to me worried and trying to understand what was going on because I was facing them with my eyes open asking for help, but I could not move. I heard them struggling to figure out what to do, to wake me up or go and call someone. Then I managed to launch myself out of paralysis, breathing heavily. 'Are you alright?' They asked. 'Yes, sorry, sorry. I was having a bad dream.'

With time the incidents of sleep paralysis worsened. It could happen several times in a single night, consecutively. Let's say I managed to extricate myself from a paralytic episode, as soon as I laid back down I'd fall back into a new one, fight to get up again, just to wake up and sink into another one and again and again any time I laid down again in a sort of diabolic loop. It was exhausting. Nighttime had become a nightmare. I dreaded going to sleep. To the point where I started to delay the onset by watching films and reading until I could not hold out any longer and I would fall asleep, falling prey to the ghosts that populated my sleep paralysis crises. I woke up in the morning exhausted and then went to work at the restaurant.

Eventually, over time, I found ways to deal with it. I understood that fear management was key to the way the phenomenon occurred. The more scared I was, the stronger the grip of the paralysis and the presence of the ghosts. I realised that the only solution was to face them, to not try to avoid them. I needed to relax, sink into the paralysis and allow the ghosts to run free. It was hard at first. Hard to control my instinctive fight or flight response. But with practice I learned how to relax and lend myself to the experience, letting the ghosts hover over me, breathe on me, grab and hold me. I learned to reach a point of relaxation that would allow my body to awaken by itself without any effort.

Once I mastered the escape technique, I moved the centre of my focus from myself to these presences. What were they in the first place? I started listening to them, training myself to stay within the paralytic state for as long as my fear allowed me in order to amass more information from the experience and get to know more about these ghosts. They never actually hurt me, yet there was always something sinister to them. They came in various forms, some more visible and tactile than others. At one point there was a wet naked woman, like she had just come out of a bath with long wet black hair, who started showing up now and then and hugging me during my sleep paralysis. I tried my best to hold on as long as I could to understand her, but fear would take over eventually forcing me out. My question then became, what was this world I had sunken into and what would really happen if I let myself go completely into it? I was fearful that I might never come back which prevented me from fully diving into the experience, as if I could fall into a deep coma or die in my sleep. But what if there was something more to it? What if there was a meaning behind it, or if the whole thing was saying something important to me? What if that world I drowned in every night was actually calling me? After all, what did I have left in waking life that was worth my staying here? What I failed to see up to that point was that I was ready to die. It was getting stronger simply because I was subconsciously calling death upon myself. In fact, it stopped being just a nighttime phenomenon, but I began feeling the presence in my house, day and night alike, asleep or awake. I heard noises and the presence of a group of people walking around my bedroom, whether I was reading in the day, or sleeping in the night, and I knew I wasn't going crazy. My brain worked perfectly. I was not alone in my house. They were there, day and night keeping the door open in their world so that I would become emboldened to leave with them and possibly never come back.

But then my mother called me. I hadn't seen her since Happiness's wedding some years earlier and we had talked only occasionally on the phone, and never about my problems. I never felt close enough to open up to my mother back then. Never told her a thing about my sleep paralysis. But then she said out of the blue, 'Your house is infested by spirits of death. Don't go with them. I'm buying a ticket to come over there right now.'

I went to collect my mother at the Bologna airport a week after that phone call. Maman Sofie was flying from Caen in the north of Normandy where she had moved with Monique and Mavie and had been settled for a few years. Mavie and Monique, women now, lived in their own houses with their French partners, all close to each other. Mavie, who had healed from asthma, worked in a charity shop, while Monique was in the middle of training to work in the mobile phone sector. As for my mother, she was now licensed to work as a nanny and was also running her own business on the side, travelling back to Congo to trade. She was approaching her fifties now and looked more like a European woman in jeans, a shirt and short straight hair when I picked her up from the airport.

I drove her home. When she walked in, she held back from commenting, although she was visibly shocked by the level of untidiness and dirtiness, the flat of someone who had long given up. We ate something. Then she spent the day tidying up and cleaning and throwing away old things that she judged were of no use while I watched TV. Then I started helping her. It was good to work with her because we could stay side by side without speaking much and we were fine.

'What do you know about a spirit, a woman, all naked and wet like she had a bath?' I asked her.

'Did she hug you?'

'Yeah'

'She is a siren, a spirit of the water. Generally, when she hugs a person, it is said that the person does not wake up anymore. They die in their sleep. But with you, it seems she didn't succeed.'

'I felt very attracted to her though, like she was a nice person, like she was loving me rather than being mean or something.'

'That's the way she manages to take people away, with love. You won't feel much like going along with someone who's threatening you, right? But if she sweetly holds you and leads you away you are more tempted to go with her without fuss. But she failed. Because your spirit is strong and wants you to live, not to die.'

'How did you know I have bad spirits in my house?'

'I'm still your mother after all,' she chuckled.

In a few hours, my house was clean and neat. At that point, my mother explained to me that she was going to call her priest in Africa who was supposed to guide us through a programme of spiritual deliverance. She spent a good half an hour nodding at the phone with the African priest talking to her on the other side of the line, possibly from Pointe-Noire, while she took notes with the man's instructions in her pocket agenda. Then she hung up the phone and explained, 'So now we're going to go on a semi-fast for three days. We will only have our meal at six in the afternoon and no more eating past midnight. We don't go out. No drinking. We just stay close in the house for three days, me and you, and pray in the morning, at noon, and in the evening. Here is what we're going to read.' She handed me a list of psalms the priest gave her according to my case. I had to wash every night before going to bed with a mixture of water, lemon, salt and cologne water. We went out shopping for all the necessary items we needed to go through the three days of the isolated prayer programme. We had dinner in the evening. Then my mother prepared the water with lemon, salt and cologne water to make it holy. She prayed over it asking for the Holy Spirit to descend on it. She then went around the house sprinkling the water onto every wall, ceiling and floor, forcefully commanding negative spirits to leave the house. Then she instructed me to carry the basin of water in the shower, to wash myself with it and let it dry on my skin without washing it off, and to sleep with salt and squeezed lemon bits on me. My mother slept on the sofa watching TV till late in the night.

There was already a huge improvement in my sleeping pattern that night. I woke only a couple of times, I kept feeling the presence of the spirits in the room, but I didn't have a single episode of sleep paralysis. They didn't dare come to bother me.

We started praying the day after, first thing in the morning. She got hold of her French bible, I took my Italian one, and we got down on our knees, facing each other. She entered a meditative state for a few seconds before improvising an opening prayer to create the appropriate spiritual environment for us to speak with God. She then spoke about me and my struggles to God and hit me to see how well she knew me. Here and there I said Amen when I felt moved. Then she made me read the set of psalms the African priest gave us. As I read out loud, I felt I was reading a poem to my mother, both on our knees, facing each other, we could have been members of a selective sect of Bible-based poetry. For the first time in my life, albeit being familiar with the Bible's texts, including the psalms through the religious education I received in the institutions, it was with my mother that I returned to it as a grown-up and I was able to grasp the voice of the real people behind each word I pronounced. David's psalms struck me; the invocations of this man, struggling a great deal to survive in a hostile environment, a man full of fears, needs and doubts, who was able to commit the most wicked actions, like killing a man to steal his girl. But he was also childish in his honesty, in displaying his weaknesses, and his desperate calls for help, and joy and chants of exultation to his God, which sounded like he was born as an orphan and was set to die as such. His words simply spoke for me. 'Amen,' my mother would say at the end of each reading.

We went on like this for three days. Three psalms in the morning, three at noon, three at six, and finally joined forces to prepare our dinner with watering mouths, set the table and eat with great satisfaction. We'd watch something on TV, then sleep and start all over again the day after. By the third day, the energy in the house had changed entirely, like the difference between day and night. No more ghosts, no more horrible nights and sleep paralysis and visits from the woman of the water. All cleared up. Just with love, care and prayers. As the final stage of the deliverance programme required, my mother called back the African priest. She stayed a little while talking in Lingala and nodding, taking down new notes in her diary, while again, I sat next to her. She then handed me the phone as the priest wanted to talk directly with me. The voice of a quiet middle-aged man said in French, 'Good evening, Redesof, how are you?' I said I was good. He stayed in silence for a while, as if listening to something only he could hear, and started praying in Lingala. 'Amen,' he said at the end. 'Well, now you are delivered, things will start going better. Take good care of yourself.'

'Thank you,' I said.

I passed him back to my mother. They went on talking in Lingala for a while, her taking new notes while nodding, 'hum, yes, yes, sure. Thank you.' She finally hung up. Stared at me directly in my eyes, then looked at her notes, and said, 'well, the priest said that you won't live in Italy. He saw something about Spain as the next stage. Do you have anyone there?'

'Yes, I have a friend there.'

'Good, so I'm going to buy you a one-way ticket for you to go there. How do you feel about the idea of permanently moving out of Italy?'

I never thought about the possibility of living anywhere outside Italy. But in that very moment, I answered my mother 'yes', because it seemed not just the most logical option, but the most natural, obvious thing I could do, to leave Italy, to cut ties with nearly thirty years of my life, leave friends and family, out of a sudden, unplanned decision. Back then I didn't have the emotional clarity to grasp the full spectrum of what my mother had done for me in those days. She rescued me and took me to the next stage of my life. I'm profoundly grateful to her for this. Grateful for the battles she carried out throughout her life. For her love, for having her as a mother.

Spain

I left Italy with my everyday backpack with some clothes and my laptop inside. All my other belongings, which mainly comprised of a purple desktop iMac, CDs, books and DVDs, I asked Ginevra to store at her parents' house. I spent the last few nights meeting people to say goodbye; to Gennaro, Aster, my siblings, Redeso, Ferro, Franz and the occasional friends in Via del Pratello, and Mohamed.

My flight landed in Barcelona early in the night. Andrea Mancuso had come to pick me up and he was happy to have me there. I was extremely happy too to see him again after a couple of years and at the prospect of again living in the same city. Happy that our friendship had lasted so long since we were kids. We hugged and grabbed each other shoulders and arms saying 'Fuck, brother! Fuck!'

He talked feverishly about his new life during the car journey and I listened to him with as much excitement. Life in Barcelona, away from home, was having a positive impact on him. He seemed to have regained the spark of the old Andrea Mancuso of our adolescence, happy, free as I hadn't seen him in a long time. His look too had changed, becoming more of a creative, carefree look than the suited office boy I had been used to seeing in the last years he had lived in Bologna. He told me about the amazing professional transformation he had undergone since he had started living in Barcelona. He taught himself video editing from scratch just by studying a handbook and watching tutorials on YouTube, and now was making a living from it, working as a video editor for an established advertising firm that had an office in the centre of Barcelona. He took me there the next day, after we spent the night awake, drinking beers and chatting on the terrace of his flat. I was happy for him. He was living proof of what could be achieved through willpower. During the following days, Andrea Mancuso also showed me the spot he carved out for himself in the nightclub scene where he worked as VJ, projecting videos he produced himself.

Now I was living in a different world, of clubbing, cerveza and running around the morphing architecture of Barcelona with my best friend. It was certainly a good start for me. I met many new people through him. I found a job as a chef and I got fired because I took too many coffee breaks. Then I got fired from my second job as a waiter because I didn't smile enough at the customers. The third time I was giving out my CV, I met Ella, the future mother of my kids, and the coolest girl in town, working behind the bar of the coolest spot in the Gothic Area. I walked into her bar and handed in my CV. She looked at it and said she would give it to her boss. I sat down at the bar for a whiskey inside the cosy environment. A crepuscular vibe with just a handful of clients sitting at the bar, her playing her own music from a broken old laptop. She told me in perfect Spanish that her name was Ella, she was 23, originally from Cambridge in England. She had been living in Spain for a few years in the north and was now settled in Barcelona. I told her about myself in bad Spanish since I could not speak Spanish or English and she didn't know Italian or French, but we managed to keep up an engaging conversation between her serving clients and pouring me more whisky for free any time I had emptied my glass and was about to go home. The Shanghai bar became my second home in no time. Every night, I would go there, sit at the bar, and go through a freefalling conversation with Ella fuelled by free whisky and a wish to improve my Spanish a bit further. Then she gave me her number. It took me some time to call her since I feared she was interested in me just in the context of the bar, like a sort of entertainment while working, but she was enthusiastic about meeting me outside the bar for a day out walking around Barcelona when I called her. We started dating. I found a stable job as a sandwich chef in a South American-staffed café in the Borneo Area. I moved out of Andrea Mancuso's flat to a shared house. My Spanish improved considerably with my Spanish-speaking workmates and the mix of European flatmates and Ella.

Then it was there, one morning, among my inbox emails, a letter from the citizenship office in Bologna. At the age of thirty, having spent twenty-six years in Italy, with just a click I became an Italian citizen. A big circle now was being closed, finally, thanks to Ginevra. I was filled with satisfaction, and a great sense of liberation, as if my sanity had been restored after a long tormented period of infirmity. I flew back to Italy where I stayed for a few days, received my citizenship award in the citizenship office of Bologna town hall and it was done. Then I applied for my Italian passport and my Italian national ID and met with some friends, including Ginevra, whom I took out for dinner to celebrate the acquisition of my new status. Then I flew back to Ella.

Ella was Cinematic Orchestra, Roots Manuva, electronica, old-school reggae and dub music. She was Nabokov, Doris Lessing, E.L Doctorow, Deleuze and Guattari, and Shane Meadows. She was riding in a hired scooter to have a meal in illegal Caribbean restaurants and whiling the day away smoking joints. Time with Ella was I'd say a hallucinogenic experience. For one reason or another, whether it was love, sex, alcohol or drugs, we were living in a permanent state of alteration. An example of our typical day would be that at the end of my night shift, at 10 p.m., I would go to her bar and drink and chat with her and the regulars. By the time she had finished, at 2 a.m., we were already drunk and high on weed. We'd then meet other people, mainly her friends, and some people I worked with, occasionally Andrea Mancuso and his girlfriend, and we would stay smoking weed in some place outside on the street, then we would continue the night at a club getting high on pills and MDMA, whatever was around.

Eventually, we would return home in the morning, and we would lie in bed smoking opium while listening to music to even out the effect of the ecstasy. We would have lunch and sleep through the afternoon until it was time for me to go to work at four, while she clocked in at six and then it started all over again. That was our lifestyle, with some variations, some different drugs, like magic mushrooms and ketamine, but yes, for a time we existed just in the night, while daylight was used mostly as a means to journey from a venue to home unless it was her or my day off. In that case, we'd use the day more constructively, like going around Barcelona for errands, getting the material she needed for her art printing work and graffiti, taking the cable car for a stroll on the hillside, lying on the beach in Barceloneta in the evening. It was a good life. However, after about nine months of this *Leaving Las Vegas* type of life I had to face the fact that we were stuck in a loop that took us nowhere but downward as time went by. With the *movida*, the secret night venues, Barcelona was turning into a dangerously small place, especially for two hedonists like us.

I had an epiphany one night while we were driving around the city in a car with two friends, all of us on LSD, going nowhere specifically, just messing around on the street, the guy driving the car over gardens and sidewalks, spinning the car around over and over until the tires smoked. That night I realised that we had to leave Barcelona for our own sanity. So, I asked Ella how she felt about going back home, I meant to England, to try a new start from there. Maybe she could enrol in a course or something while I found a decent chef job and got back to my writing. She was reluctant at first at the idea of moving back to her home country but agreed that Barcelona was too tempting for us, we were wasting our life here, and eventually grew more enthusiastic in the following days at the idea of starting a life with me in London. To be able to introduce me to her family, to her friends, to show me around and so on. So, we had a last drink with our mixed group of friends a couple of months after, and with Andrea Mancuso, who I vigorously hugged and thanked, deeply thanked for hosting me, helping me to settle in when I first arrived in Barcelona, both of us certain, even more so after that year we spent together in Barcelona, that what we had in our hands was a lifetime friendship.

Ella and I spent the first month in Whitechapel at one of her aunts' houses, which was offered to us as temporary accommodation. Then we found a room in Old Street with another couple. Then we moved into the shared house where Ella's best friend lived as a room had just opened up. It was a beautiful large double bedroom in Hackney, in the London Fields area. I can't say if it was something about London, its rigour, hectic lifestyle, shortage of slacking spots or if it was simply getting out of Barcelona, but we went through an instantaneous metamorphosis of naturally living drugs-free and staying focused, determined to make something out of our lives. Ella gradually introduced me to members of her family as we came across them, her sisters, her mother on a visit from Exeter, her granny in Camden, her father in Cambridge, plus the loads of half-siblings I would meet throughout the following months. It was hard at first to hold a conversation because I did not know English, I would just look for rescue from Ella who would translate for me in Spanish. She and I kept speaking in Spanish at home. Whatever progress I made was through conversations with our flatmates and Ella's family. At least being surrounded by only English speakers was of great help. Getting a job in a café helped me improve my English even more. When you learn a new language, there is a magical time when a new world with its details, culture and manners, opens up before you, when you jump to the next level and start understanding significantly more. It is like regaining hearing after ear surgery, and you are finally able to get a full sensorial experience of the place you are living in and understand in factual terms what is happening around you. What people on the bus are saying, what your flatmates, your workmates, the guy from the off licence you've been seeing every day are talking about. It also enables you to understand people's personalities, which in most cases surprise you. All the English-language music I had been listening to all my life suddenly spoke clearly to me, shockingly dull and containing cheesy content, such longing for love, and 'take me home' when I had grown convinced just by the intonation, the sound of the words, and the musical complexity and taste, that they were talking about radical and social issues and mind-twisting subjects. It took me just a couple of weeks to fall out of love with most of my favourite bands and reevaluate some others I always thought were flimsy. It was the same with films. I was stunned to hear for the first time the real voices of the actors I had grown used to hearing dubbed in Italy, like John Travolta and Samuel L Jackson in *Pulp Fiction*. Robert DeNiro, Al Pacino. Watching the same film dubbed in Italian and then in the original language was a different experience. As Ella pointed out, amused by my reaction, in dubbing-based countries, such as Italy and Spain, you never actually happened to see the real film.

Ella found a job as a bike repairer in a café-bike shop. Then, three months from the day we arrived, she found out she was pregnant, pregnant with our firstborn son, Bernardo.

***

It was around the time we were waiting for Bernardo to be born that I received the news from Redeso about Klaus. He called me and said that Klaus was in hospital with terminal cancer. It was hard to believe at first, receiving this kind of information out of the blue. It simply didn't add up. I would have been more surprised to hear that Klaus could fly or that he had become a millionaire. But that he had cancer? And he was in the hospital? And that it was terminal? What the fuck was Redeso talking about? Then it ceased being that absurd when I recalled the last time I bumped into him in the street in Bologna, or remembered seeing him at one of Moon's dinners, visibly in poor health , emaciated, down and skin covered in lesions, and it made perfect sense that the he was ill. He had been all along.

'He has AIDS,' Redeso went on. 'Nobody knew but his girlfriend. He didn't want anybody to know. I've just been in the hospital with him now. He has AIDS-associated cancer. The cancer has metastasised. Organs, limbs, everywhere. Doctors say he has not long left.'

Everything went dark. I was walking through a park, and I kind of felt I was bodyless, walking with no weight nor sensitivity, wobbly like a piece of jelly in a fucking dream. I used to think that this type of thing happened only to others, but there it was indeed happening to us. A brother in bed in the hospital with AIDS that had turned into metastatic cancer. And this brother was no one else but Klaus. Klaus. The most sensitive of us all. It was too painful. I told my brother that I was coming back to Italy right now. I just needed to notify my workplace and book a plane ticket. I walked back home finding no justification for his choice to keep us out of it and rather go through it alone, just with his girlfriend, renouncing the support he could have received from us or his friends. This man sitting at the dinner table at Moon's house, sharing jokes with Sigmund, a baseball cap's visor lowered over his eyes, knew he was close to dying but said nothing. I could not bear remembering how Klaus, who grew up in care longing for his family, was the only one of us to openly question why Dad neglected us, who waited for someone to come to take us to Africa, for someone to build us a home, had to die like this, from cancer at the age of 32. He withheld his pain from everybody and all this time he had been alone. I could not accept this. I believed there was a logic behind the forces that governed the universe, not a random succession of events. I trusted that things would add up at some point and something inevitably had to turn around for Klaus, to even out his history, to square all the difficulties he went through. I thought we had allies. I believed in Yin and Yang, Jesus's 'The Last Will Be the First', whatever goes in must come out, sun after the rain, but now I had to deal with the truth that it would never stop raining.

I had an epiphany at that point while walking home. That moment is where our family history finally started making sense. Of course. Dad, who did nothing for us all his life, would compensate with a spectacular act of magnanimity from the other life. He would use the inverted force of his lifetime negligence to intervene and save Klaus. Or was Debra-Jo the key figure here? Yes, why did I not see it before? This is why she left! At the origin of her disappearance, there must have been a premonition in a dream where an angel told her: 'One of you brothers will fall ill and die unless you sacrifice all you have and what is most precious in your life.' So, she made the tormented decision to give up her kids and family and disappear so that now the miracle could be fulfilled, and Klaus's illness would inevitably resolve itself and the doctor would storm into the room dazed by the new results from the tests they had made on Klaus, saying things like 'We can't explain it!' Of course. This would be the course things would take, after all, we are governed by divine justice.

Tania discovered a few months before Klaus's terminal admission to the hospital, through an HIV test, that Klaus was HIV-positive. She subsequently told us he was devastated for himself of course, but mostly for her, fearing he had infected her, and cried all the time. 'You have no place in this. You are innocent. Why, why?' he'd say. I can imagine he was shattered by guilt at the possibility of having ruined the life of his girlfriend by infecting her. But she knew she had to stay strong. For him, for their relationship. She reassured him that all was good and that they would manage to go through it together, but deep inside she dreaded any possible outcome, including the likelihood of having contracted HIV. It was twice as hard because she could tell no one about Klaus's illness. He made her swear not to reveal anything to anyone, not even his siblings. He would flip out on her every time she tried to convince him to disclose the problem to us.

Tania was HIV-negative following her first test. She would undergo regular medical check-ups during the following years, coming out clean every time. This was close to a miracle, considering they had had unprotected sex during the time they had been together. However, all of this led to Tania becoming more suspicious of Klaus because, of course, he must have contracted HIV somewhere. Was he sleeping with other people? Was her boyfriend a drug addict? And, foremost, did he really only know that he had it now or was he aware all along he was infected? Who was the man she had allowed in her house? She was tormented by fears, anger and doubts. But she wouldn't show any of this to him. She felt she was his nurse, his woman, his comforter, everything to him. She trusted him, loved him and was ready to stick with him, to care for him until death, no matter what. She held his hand while he received intensive therapy and would talk with the doctors, who looked optimistically at Klaus's prognosis. Therapies were very effective nowadays, they said, people could live a normal life and have kids. She remembered Klaus was optimistic too. Both were optimistic.

Nevertheless, Klaus's symptoms didn't improve. They worsened. He grew tired day after day, lost more weight and lost his appetite to the point he barely touched food. He underwent weekly medical checks and treatments in the hospital and received new medicine to take home. Eventually, the asthma attacks worsened to the point he had to use his inhaler all the time. Then he had a severe attack. Not even the nebuliser helped. She took him to A&E and he was hospitalised. Tania slept in his room on a chair nearly every night, until, I suppose out of exhaustion and pushed by pangs of her conscience, she decided to break the promise she had made to Klaus and reached out for us. She called Redeso. However, she omitted to mention the cancer and AIDS, she just told him that Klaus was severely ill at the hospital.

Redeso drove to the hospital the same day. The scene that opened up before him was that of a gaunt, dying brother in bed, and Tania sitting on a chair next to him. The waning afternoon sunlight cast its last stripe of light across the floor. He sat on the bed next to Klaus and held his hand.

'Hi Klaus.'

'Hi Twin.' Then he told him, 'I have AIDS.'

Something about what Klaus said, and the scene of him lying in that state prevented Redeso from grasping in full the gravity of the situation. He consciously recorded that Klaus was about to die, that he would likely die, but could not sense it on an emotional level. That allowed him to manage it with clarity of mind.

'Did you tell the others?' he asked him.

'No,' Klaus answered. 'I feel ashamed. I feel like I messed up.'

So Redeso got up and asked Tania to come out of the room with him to talk in private. She told him everything, revealing the truth about Klaus's illness and that she was forced not to tell anyone to respect his will. Redeso listened carefully and calmly put her in front of the evidence that she too had needs in this situation. It was way too big a burden to carry all alone and finally, it was important that all his siblings knew because we were his family, we could have sustained him.

He eventually convinced her to let him call everybody and let them know the truth. They all came to the hospital. Moon, Sigmund, Lorenzo and Ocean. All of them facing the unprecedented. But again, like it was for Redeso, no one caught the magnitude of what was happening, as if they didn't want to see that it was their brother who had contracted HIV and then developed cancer, that he was dying, and that he had hidden it from them all this time. They didn't want to see that they could do nothing to save their brother. It was too much to take in one single day. Their minds, however, could not avoid reorganising themselves to run down their memory timelines from recent to distant to try to figure out when he may have contracted the disease. Everything pointed toward that time in the foster home with that girl, his ex-girlfriend, Samantha, who had died of AIDS. Yet, there was no concrete evidence that he got it from her. Somebody so unpredictable as Klaus could have gotten it in many other unexpected ways, but even Lorenzo, who was cautious about coming to conclusions, didn't hesitate to suspect it was her. The problem with Klaus was that his main gift was to be senseless. People like him don't look at the consequences of their actions. Regardless of how open-minded you are, as long you are cautious and you just kiss and have protected sex why not go for it? Why not give an ill person the chance to live a normal life, was probably what Klaus believed.

My siblings visited him regularly in the following days. Even Debra-Jo came to visit him, according to Tania, when nobody else was there but Klaus and her. Tania remembers that Klaus's face lit up as if he was having a vision. This woman she had only heard about, whom he had told her a great deal about, and he hadn't seen for years, walked into the room dressed all in black and sat next to him. Klaus burst out crying as soon as Debra-Jo hugged him. Then Debra-Jo introduced herself to Tania and thanked her, thanked for the love and the care she gave to Klaus. Tania was crying too at this point. She then left the room feeling overwhelmed with colliding emotions. She went to smoke a cigarette outside the hospital. Once back upstairs she waited outside the door not to disturb the two siblings. They were talking quietly, she reported. She could not hear what they were saying. It seemed Debra-Jo was giving him some information, some instruction, judging from the way Klaus nodded his head repeatedly. Then she held both his hands tightly, walked out of the room, kissed Tania and thanked her again.

That night, persuaded by the doctors to go home so as to have a proper night of rest, Tania spent the night at home. Lorenzo swapped with her, but eventually even he, late in the night while Klaus was sleeping, was encouraged by the doctor to go home and to come back in the morning, reassured that Klaus would be okay. Tania remembers that she did something that night she had never done before in her life—she switched her phone off. She was unable to explain herself why she did so, I presume, because she needed a full night's rest after sleeping so many nights in a chair at the hospital. Besides, Klaus looked alright that day, better than usual, after Debra-Jo's visit. He actually seemed to have improved, to be feeling less pain.

GROUND

It was in the morning when she turned her phone on and saw all the missed calls from the hospital that she knew there was bad news. She made a series of calls to the siblings telling them to rush to the hospital because it was highly likely that Klaus had died. She took a taxi to the hospital and ran to Klaus's room, just to find his bed empty. Lorenzo, Moon, Ocean, Redeso and Sigmund, all came eventually, just to receive the confirmation from the doctor. He had died. Died alone during his sleep.

As for myself, I found out late in the evening on my way back from work, three days from when Redeso told me he was hospitalised, and one day before the flight I had booked to go to Italy. My phone had run out of battery throughout the day, so it was just when I reached home and saw Ella waiting for me outside the gate in tears that I understood. Understood that Redeso had called her. Understood he had given her the bad news. I put my hand over her mouth before she could speak because I didn't want to hear it and burst out crying.

I flew with Ella to Italy the day after to attend Klaus's funeral, which was scheduled five days from the day of his death. We stayed at my ex-girlfriend's house, Margherita. Maman Sofie and Maman Natalie, Klaus's biological mother, came to Imola, and Happiness with his family from Berlin. Maman Sofie stayed at Redeso's, and Maman Natalie at Ocean's. Only Monique, Mavie and Debra-Jo were missing. But an impressive number of people attended the funeral ceremony, which was held at the Piratello, the church for Imola's main cemetery, set right on the Via Emilia. Inside and outside the church were all the people Klaus had come across who had been marked in some way by his passage through this world. Among them were lots of people I had never met; like the slackers, the misfits, people from the urban scene he had frequented from Imola and Bologna, a human library that had been built throughout his lifetime. There were the guys from the 4-More he had introduced to Lorenzo, people from St Catherina, a few from St Theresa and the Oasis I hadn't seen in a while, all grown up. There were our old carers and supervisors from St Catherina. Mr P was there with his Canadian family, four kids and his wife. There were the ex-carers from the foster home, including the old director Franco. There was his skater mate Tulio with his teenage daughter from Berlin. And Yusuf with his wife. I also recognised the guy from Toscanella's petrol station that we used to chat with when we were in the foster home. Then there was Gennaro, Andrea Mancuso, Aster, Ferro, Nico, Franz, Margherita, Ginevra and Daniela. And some local random people. It was not a rock star who had died but just an ordinary man. He was a son of our community.

My siblings and I with our two mothers and Tania sat on the church's first pews. The priest went through the mass. Klaus's coffin lay open before the altar, with him dressed in a black suit lying with hands resting on his chest. The coffin was closed at the end of the mass. We all walked outside. Some guys from St Catherina—Mr P, Fulvio, the ex-goalkeeper of the St Catherina football team, Yusuf and Tulio—carried Klaus's coffin through the cemetery, followed by the rest of us. The cemetery attendees helped them to place the coffin deep in the ground. The priest said a few words and we stayed there, all of us, with all that had kept us together throughout time despite our different paths, our shared memories speaking loud in our minds. Memories of the kids we once were in those courtyards, repairing bikes, playing football and handball in the basement, those huge refectories, the fights, and laughs, the spontaneous loyalty we evinced for each other at all times. Here was who and what we had grown into, what we had gained and lost. Here we were looking at the value of life being buried. All of us trying to make our own sense of Klaus's life. A genius, dying so young, alone, with no gains, with nothing. This was a story of Via Emilia, taking place a five minutes' walk from my family's first house, the big villa that burned down.

Perhaps, each of us siblings in different ways, were seeing that there was a logic after all behind Klaus's death and that it was not as random as I ended up believing. In the end, it was Klaus who did not wake up that day of the fire. He was still sleeping in his room in the big villa, while the rest of us, in our pyjamas, stood outside the room, at the door, calling his name from a safe distance, yelling at him to wake up. But we failed. He didn't wake up. Klaus never did. He was still there sleeping, like a little prince, while everything around him in the room and beyond was burning. And everything that happened from that moment up to these very days, our individual and collective stories, were just part of the dream of a dying kid.

LONDON, PRESENT DAY
X

Dear Bernardo and April, I have written more or less all I managed to gather about our family. Now you know how I got to be here. So do I. Working through these memories has helped me to gain a broader view of my family constellation, to understand more about my siblings, my parents and myself, who we are, where we come from and what made us the people we are today. And I fervently hope that I managed to map out your own history and show you who your paternal grandparents and great-grandparents were, your uncles and all those extraordinary people we met along the way who somehow are all little parts of you.

I have no idea of what lies ahead, whether we are going to stay here or not. At the moment, I'm alright here. At the moment, I'm sitting on a bench in the courtyard of your school waiting to collect you among a heterogeneous crowd of parents. I'm sure you both remember Telma and her daughter. I miss them. I miss her terribly. I think about our days together. What a blessing it has been to have her living next door, seeing her and her daughter knocking at the window door of our terrace, her holding a box of Legos and Telma two cans of beer. Our Sundays out with you kids, at the Museum of Childhood in Bethnal Green, at the Little Angel theatre in Angel, our walks in Epping Forest, having her sitting so close to me in our house. So close, and look now what has become of me and her, flickered out from each other's life as if we were flies. This is life kids. This is how things go. It's nearly the end of July, the last day of school. Our neighbour, Telma, moved back to Portugal only a couple of weeks ago after she had been denied settled status with this anti-immigration wave sweeping through the UK. It seems like she too has paid the consequences of having directed more efforts to her artistic work rather than trying to reinforce her credit history in order to grant her entitlement to continue to living here, although she knew she could have gotten through if she tried, she could have won the appeal if she had put her head to it. It might just have been a matter of providing them more documentation as usual, but, as she said to me the last time I met her, she couldn't be bothered to go through all that paperwork again. Besides, like many others, she got tired of life in London, of the Brexit climate, and she missed home. So, she left. And that's ok, kids, totally ok. It's just strange to see how all stories eventually come to an end. All the people we meet throughout our life and that we leave behind. All these fantastic encounters. I think about Harry, my old patient, who has moved too. I think about Marco, the kid in St Theresa Redeso and I betrayed. About Livia, About Nico. Debra-Jo. Klaus. People leave. The most natural phenomenon. They leave. But they can stay with us if we make room inside us and host them and remember them, you know?

Your uncle Ocean is now 45. He still lives in Imola. His journey through the immigration ordeal went smoothly since he never broke his residency history and could provide satisfactory proof of income to the immigration office. He was awarded Italian citizenship upon request at the age of thirty. He had on his record a few months he had spent in Brazzaville trying to start up a business of trading tiles imported from Imola which he was forced to interrupt when the civil war in Brazzaville broke out once more, and his goods were seized by the Cobra's guerrilla army. He returned to Italy. He found love in the hazel eyes of a single mother from Imola called Carla and is now the father of Piero and Denise. He sent me an email recently detailing a new business project he is working on trading t-shirts, hats and sandals themed around the architectural styles of major cities worldwide. He is also asking his siblings to contribute with ideas and advice.

Sigmund, too, went through the new immigration regulations unscathed as he had never broken his residency history and had worked hard since a young age and was able to provide the immigration office with an annual turnout that was considerably above the Bossi–Fini standard. He was able to convert his annual residency permit to a five-year one. He applied for and gained citizenship in his late thirties. Sigmund, too, tried to establish some ties with Africa. He started selling second-hand Italian clothing in Benin, the same place where he would meet Benedette, marry her and bring her to Italy. Today your uncle Sigmund still works between Imola and Cotonou. The last time I spoke with him, he WhatsApp'd me photos from one of his last projects—an orphanage he is building in Cotonou. Along with the photos came some videos of his kids as he called them, a flock of street kids in shorts and tank tops playing around at the entrance of the orphanage or engaged in carpentry workshops, while the structure was being built around them. A plate on the institution's front door says Institution Don Ettore Mazzini, in memory of the priest who raised him, whom he held as dear as his own father and who had died some years ago of old age.

Similar to Sigmund, Redeso had not been affected majorly by the introduction of the new immigration law. He had had a legitimate full-time job for many years with no significant breaks in between and was always able to meet the Bossi–Fini minimum requirement to renew his papers without trouble. He eventually switched to the five-year residency permit. Ten years passed from the day he and I discovered we had been erased from the system to when he regained eligibility to apply for citizenship, which was then awarded to him at the age of thirty-five. Meanwhile, in the years in between, he carried out his life with great dignity, calm, focus and dedication. Redeso kept on composing and playing music for himself on the keyboard from the time he left our band—some very moving pieces of music, a few of which I considered pure works of genius and still catch myself singing to this day. Nevertheless, he never aimed to put his work out, despite his friends and myself pushing him. He eventually broke up with Daniela and met Giovanna a few years later, with whom he moved to Turin, in northern Italy. They had Ilaria and then Gabriele. Today, he is fully immersed in the study of theology at the University of Turin.

Moon was another one whose diligent work attendance in legit conditions shielded her from the blows of the new legislation. She currently works as a shop assistant in a renowned clothes shop in the centre of Bologna and she has not yet recovered from her sister's disappearance, she told me during the last conversation we had at her house in Bologna, where she lived with Paolo, a broker, and their new-born Erica. She often had nostalgia for the time she lived with Ugo and Debra-Jo and their kids. The good news is that she regularly sees Debra-Jo's kids, who are now nearly adults, and got in touch with her. Perhaps next time I take you two to Italy we will be able to meet them too.

Your uncle Happiness started university only a year after he moved to Berlin. He practically learned German while studying IT programming at the University of Berlin. He is still married to Eve to this day and is the father of two teenagers, Roger and Finn, and works now as a programmer for an IT company.

As for Uncle Lorenzo, it would take about a year from when he had that unfortunate incident with the producer Zanetti before he would fully sort himself out. He would restore his papers through a government-induced sanatorium—a scheme set in place to regulate a set number of illegal immigrants—and take back a legit place in society. He then found a job as a UPS courier and enjoyed very much driving his van around the streets of Bologna in his brown UPS uniform, the car stereo playing reggae music all day. He met Isabella during a delivery to her house and became Laura's father at 32. He then moved to a new house with his new family, where he found peace enough to pull out his music gear from an old, sealed box to start making music again.

GROUND

Andrea Mancuso has become a big shot in Barcelona's advertising industry. He runs his own production company and writes, directs and produces advertisements for big firms such as Nike, Philips and Whirlpool and has fallen in love with a Russian girl who is moving in with him.

Margherita has started an insect farm to promote biodiversity in the countryside of a small town near Bologna, where she moved with her partner, a prominent Bolognese theatre director. She still practises photography and called me recently for a chat and to inform me that her first book of photography was about to get published.

As for Ginevra, she is now based in Rotterdam with her partner. She teaches design at Willem de Kooning Academy. We have divorced only recently. We have been meeting once a week to meditate together via Skype for about a year now.

And then it's me. I'm here. Sitting on a bench in the courtyard of your school, dear Bernardo and April, waiting for you to come out. I don't know if I ever found the freedom Livia was talking about—'my own Freedom'. Maybe I did find it. Maybe I found it countless times. A little bit of it every day. It could be that I have been bathing in it all along, or perhaps I'll never find it, it doesn't really matter. It's nearly the end of July 2019. The last days of school. The United Kingdom is still wrestling with Brexit. I am here. I am an immigrant. On a bench of a primary school in Hackney, I'm sitting.

Finally, the line of Year One kids in green jumpers and grey trousers exit one wing of the building headed by their teachers. I wave at you, April, walking among your peers, and you smile back at me and then wait at the gate for your teacher to allow you out, while the courtyard gets swarmed with kids from different years meeting their parents or playing around with each other. You and I wait on a bench for Bernardo to come from the Year 4-5 area of the little campus. I hug you, Bernardo, and rub your head as usual. 'How was it?' I ask.

'Hum, boring!' you say.

You hate school, Bernardo. Though you are doing very well. Aside from maths where you struggle, your teachers talk enthusiastically about your intelligence as much as your personal and social conduct at the parent's assembly. Remarkable in areas such as drawing, writing and drama, they prize you. As for you, little April, there is little we can say at the moment. It may be too early to identify your skills. You are still closed in your own world and may need time to reveal yourself.

Today we decided to leave school from the other exit, the one on Chatsworth Road, to stop and eat some crisps in Midfield Park on such a beautiful grey day, instead of going straight home. We get our crisps at the nearest off-licence and sit on a park bench for a while munching, chatting here and there and watching people walking their dogs. Then we go for a walk up to the end of the park and head along the Regent's Canal to go into the Hackney Marshes. I hold your backpacks, so you're free to run around, pick up sticks, climb trees and do the things kids do. We walk on. Then we climb over a rail that marks the border between the public pathway where we've been walking and seemingly private land, probably part of the Thames Water plant. You, Bernardo, manage to climb the railing by yourself. I help April, who then jumps prudently by herself onto the other side of the railing. You both are excited to be adventuring in what looks like an off-limits area, although there are no restriction signs in sight. The place looks untouched. A combination of high weeds and thorny berry bushes have overgrown an old narrow foot trail. I grab a stick from the ground to clear the way for us along the trail, crushing down the brambles as we proceed. We reach a point where that weeds are so high that we are nearly submerged. You, April, cling to my legs. I lift you and place you on my shoulders. It is challenging to believe we're still in London in the middle of this wild green and quietness. You take the lead, Bernardo, clearing the way for us with the stick that I hand to you now that I'm carrying your sister on my shoulders. We head on, leaving stress and the usual toxicity relatively behind as we rummage further into the wildlife of Hackney Lee Valley. The silver

GROUND

sky seems even darker and lower, the grass, still high, crushes flat on the ground under your feet, Bernardo, as you stomp on it and lash your stick left and right against the brambles to create a path for us. We walk on, my lungs filling with the heavy, damp air.

Acknowledgements

Writing a novel of this scope in a foreign language was the most challenging project I have ever embarked on. There were times when I fell in despair, dropped it and doubted if I could ever finish it. Yet, some incredible people's moral and technical support made it possible. Thanks to Maura Framrose for proofreading and helping me with the English in my earliest attempt, Hannah Griffiths for giving me some great advice on proofreading. Miranda Pyne for the first big editing. Yet the hardest part, even harder than writing *Ground*, was finding an agent in the UK. After many attempts, I landed on Irene Magrelli. She saw the potential of this work and sent it to my current agent. I can't thank her enough for giving time and believing in this project. Super thanks to my literary agency, Curtis Brown, and my agent, Enrichetta Frezzato. If it weren't for her, *Ground* wouldn't be the book that is today. Many thanks to Jacaranda's editor, Kamillah Brandes, who guided me through key structural changes in this work and pushed me to bring up some challenging parts of my past that I wouldn't have otherwise faced. I also want to thank my siblings for agreeing to sit for an interview and enriching and inspiring this work with their beautiful stories—thanks to Isaac, Robert, Valentino, Jadeli, Freddy, Emerance, Jackflore and Sarah Gangbo, and especially to my mother, Liliane Mabiala, thanks for her beautiful, hard-fought and generous interview. Also, thanks to Marina Peluso for her firsthand account of her personal experience as the girlfriend of Boris Gangbo, which has inspired the character of Klaus. Thanks to Boris and Carlotta Gangbo.

JADELIN GANGBO

Extra special thanks to my kids: Orlando, Graça, Theophania, and Zacharia, for giving me time, space and being a wild bunch. Lastly, thanks to my muse and wife, Luisa Amorim, for reading and advising me on *Ground* so often, and for pushing me to keep going all the time I felt demotivated and hopeless. Also, thanks for the fun, the fights, the love.

About the Author

Photo by Ingrida Veiveryte

Jadelin Gangbo is a writer and acupuncturist based in East London. He was born in Congo-Brazzaville in 1976 and moved to Italy at the age of 4 with his parents and 6 siblings.

Jadelin has published numerous short stories and three novels in Italian, the first one, *Verso La Notte Bakonga* (1999) at the age of 23. *Rometta e GIulieo* (2001) follows, then *Due Volte*, (2007). *Rometta e Giulieo* had been adapted for the theatre and was performed at the Arena del Sole, Bologna's historic theatre. He had appeared as an actor in a short film, *Il Contratto* (2002) directed by Guido Chiesa, and taught creative writing in multicultural centres, high schools, and a juvenile detention in Bologna. His work has been studied and written about in Italian literature departments across Europe. After spending one year in Barcelona, in 2006 he moved to the UK. His latest and most personal novel is his first written in English. Taking over 14 years to complete, Jadelin started the novel when he first arrived in the country and could barely speak the language. The project was discontinued many times due to the obvious language barrier, art and musical projects, and a career in acupuncture to pursue. Jadelin eventually persisted on his main project. The result is *Ground*.